PRESUMPTIONS

"Slade Morgan, you're the most stubborn, opinionated, egotistical man I've ever met. What makes you think you know me so well?" Pamela demanded.

Her eyes flashed a message of anger, but Slade saw something else in their depths.

"Because a wolf can always recognize its own kind, Pamela. And believe it or not, you're a wolf."

"Don't you dare, Slade Morgan! Don't you dare presume we're alike!"

"I presume more than that," he said, pulling her toward him. "I presume you want me as much as I want you."

"If I wasn't so furious, I'd laugh in your face," Pamela snarled.

"Deny you're trembling because you're in my arms…"

"I'm trembling with anger."

"Or that your heart is beating wildly…"

"With rage."

"Or that your lips hunger for mine."

Before Pamela could reply, Slade's mouth came down on hers, claiming her lips in a deep, searing kiss

Scarlet Sunset, Silver Nights

Leigh Greenwood

LOVE SPELL   NEW YORK CITY

LOVE SPELL®

October 2005

Published by

Dorchester Publishing Co., Inc.
200 Madison Avenue
New York, NY 10016

ISBN 0-505-52604-2

The name "Love Spell" and its logo are trademarks of Dorchester Publishing Co., Inc.

Printed in the United States of America.

Visit us on the web at www.dorchesterpub.com.

Arizona—1888

The young man pulled up under the shade of the huge pine. He could feel his skin begin to loosen as the heat gradually left his clothes, but he could sense his nerves growing taut. I've got to look natural he thought as he stretched his limbs to ease the tension. I don't want the old man to suspect anything's up.

But it was impossible to relax completely. The tiny sounds of limbs creaking as they bent and twisted in the breeze or the rustle of dried leaves as birds looked for grubs to feed their young, sounds he wouldn't have noticed any other time, gnawed at his nerves. Sometime during the next half hour he would put into action a plan which had been taking shape in his head for several years. This wasn't a thing to be done lightly, and once more he questioned his decision.

But by the time the rider came into view, he felt no indecision. There was no going back now.

As he rode down the bank, he smiled and waved to attract the older man's attention, just like he'd ridden up with some last-minute message. He's pulling up, the old fool! Doesn't he know it's dangerous to stop on a deserted trail, even for someone you know?

The young man waited until he was quite close. He couldn't afford a mistake now. They had barely exchanged greetings when he drew his gun and shot him, once in the heart and again in the head. He didn't feel anything. Not even when the old man died looking at him in shocked surprise. More fool he was for trusting him.

He slid from the saddle and stood staring at the body. It was a nice feeling, looking down on the old bastard. But he had to move him quickly. He lifted the unresisting weight over his shoulder. The horse snorted at the smell of fresh blood and danced in a circle. He cursed. He had to get the corpse away soon. He managed to wrestle the carcass across the saddle. God, who would have thought old skin-and-bones would weigh so much!

He led the horse into a dry wash that opened out of a brush-covered ravine. The cool breeze issuing from beneath the tangle of brush and trees was invigorating, but he didn't even notice. He was relieved to be out of the sun, away from any prying eyes. Twenty yards up the wash he shot the horse and caved the sandy bank in over man and beast.

The rich, moist smell of earth filled the tunnel, but he had grown up in the city. He didn't notice it. He only noticed the bodies were completely covered.

He didn't want them found. Ever.

He rode off in the direction from which the man had come.

Chapter 1

Pamela White saw him emerge from the heat waves rising from the desert floor, and the closer he came, the madder she got. She didn't need any down-at-the-heels cowpuncher showing up on her doorstep asking for handouts, not with all the trouble she had just now. What's more, he was on foot. No cowboy worth his salt walked when he could ride. Didn't he know anything about Arizona? Being on foot was dangerous as well as stupid.

With an impatient twitch of her shoulders, she spun on her heel and headed toward the sprawling, Spanish-style ranch house. Let him come, she thought. She wouldn't turn him away, but she refused to play hostess to him. Let Belva do it. No, she would call Gaddy. He was the only human being she knew who could possibly be as useless as a pedestrian cowboy.

But she no sooner reached a low porch shaded by two thirty-foot oaks than something compelled her to turn back. Shielding her eyes against the harsh glare of the afternoon sun, she could make out the saddlebags thrown negligently over his shoulder. So he did have a horse. But where had he left it and why?

The muscles in her abdomen tightened. He was wearing guns! God, she hated guns—and the kind of men who depended on them. Guns never solved anything! She didn't want him on her ranch.

Yet on he came, each step making the silhouette of his tall body, broad shoulders, slim hips, and long legs increasingly plain. His dust-caked plaid shirt, clinging to his perspiration-wet body, did nothing to hide the bulge of his muscles. A warm flush rippled through her body. What was wrong with her? How could looking at this cowboy cause her to feel so strange?

Don't let yourself be fooled by a few bones and muscles. The most dangerous men are usually the most attractive.

Pamela's mother had drummed that lesson into her head, but her father had taught her to face every challenge squarely, to judge each man on his merits. So Pamela didn't lower her gaze or turn away—not until the man came close enough for her to make out his face under the brim of his hat.

"He has a beard!" she muttered in disgust, and her unreasoning resentment against him increased tenfold. She hated beards, especially nasty blond beards such as this one.

A man who hid behind a lot of hair hid more than his face.

With a hiss of annoyance she headed toward an intricately carved door fashioned from thick planks of polished oak, but even as she turned the gleaming brass knob and prepared to step into the reviving coolness of the interior, something about that man made her stop. In spite of a tattered appearance that rendered him almost indistinguishable from a dozen other cowboys riding the grub line, it seemed unlikely anybody would forget this man.

Again she turned to watch him.

The closer he got, the more intrigued she became. The barely perceptible sway of his hips, the swing of his muscled arms hanging loosely at his sides, his long easy stride, the slight rise and fall of his silhouetted hat as he approached nearly hypnotized her. Men didn't impress her easily—she'd been surrounded by them for most of her life—but she had never seen one walk off the desert so calmly, as though he were stepping in off the street. He didn't seem the least bit concerned by the fact he could have died out there.

Suddenly she knew what bothered her. He didn't limp. Any man who walked more than fifteen minutes in those toe-pinching boots would have terrible blisters. From the looks of his clothes, he must have crawled. But he moved toward her with a relaxed, easy, swinging stride. He couldn't have been afoot for more than a quarter of a mile. But where had he come from?

With sudden decision, Pamela sat down on the porch to wait. She had too many unanswered questions about this stranger to leave him to anyone else.

But instead of coming directly toward her, he crossed the hard-packed dirt yard and headed right for the rough-hewed water trough. He stripped off his shirt and plunged his head and shoulders into the sun-heated water. When he stood up again, showering droplets about him like a desert Neptune, he looked more unkempt than ever. But Pamela hardly noticed that.

A wave of warmth enveloped her body and she felt a strange tingling sensation unlike anything she had ever experienced before. What was wrong with her? She gave herself a mental shake and deliberately tried to think about how much she hated beards, but the thought wouldn't stay. The sight of his half-naked body, glistening in the sun, filled her mind until it left no room for anything else.

She ought to go inside. She was hot and uncomfortable. Besides, intuition warned her against meeting anyone when her mind and body were in such turmoil. She certainly had no business coming face to face with the cause of her uneasiness, particularly when she doubted she could control either her words or her response to him.

But he had seen her, and she couldn't leave without being

9

rude. Whatever else she might be, Pamela White was never intentionally rude.

Slade Morgan was used to danger, but he felt a prickle of uneasiness skitter down his spine. From the moment he reached the dry streambed issuing from the mouth of the canyon and read the handcarved sign welcoming him to the Bar Double-B Ranch, his instincts had warned him he'd be safer in the desert. This cool, green valley was a place most likely coveted by many men and the more dangerous because of it. When he saw the woman sit down to wait for him, he knew he should turn back.

But he couldn't. He had no horse and only one more day's provisions.

Slade avoided rattlesnakes, grizzly bears, and trigger-happy drunks because he liked his skin without holes in it. He avoided women for much the same reason. The mere sight of a beautiful woman had been known to make him turn tail and run. Such a woman had destroyed his father; a second had destroyed his own youthful dream of happiness; a third had put a price on his head. Now it looked like a fourth would decide whether he reached California.

Slade twisted his ankle on a loose stone, and a shaft of pain shot up his leg. His boots felt like they were filled with boiling water. He had walked the better part of sixty miles, most of it at night to avoid the killing heat of the desert. He didn't have to take off his boots to know what his feet looked like. He could tell by the dampness in his socks, a dampness caused by blood, *his* blood. Slade consciously forced his body to relax even more. He'd crawl on his belly before he would let anyone see him limp, especially this woman.

Slade's walk became a virtual swagger.

The faded sign had informed him that Josh White owned the Bar Double-B. The enormous, white-washed ranch house sprawling in the shade of at least a dozen trees said he was a rich man. The poised, aloof manner of the woman on the porch said she must be his wife. Mighty tender meat for a man salty enough to have wrestled this land from the Indians and held it against rustlers and land grabbers. But then this woman didn't look the type to lose her head over some penniless cowboy. If she set her sights on any man, it would be the boss.

Oh well, he wouldn't stay here for more than one night. He had money in his pocket for the horse he needed. His saddle was still out in the desert, if he decided it was worth the trouble to retrieve it. It might be easier to buy a new one. He had money for that, too.

The almost unbearable pain in his feet pierced the barrier his mind had erected against it, and Slade felt his face tighten into a momentary grimace of pain. His dousing at the trough had made him feel better, but it had done nothing to ease the agony in his feet. He wanted to sit in the shade of those trees. He'd never seen such trees in Arizona. In a few years their spreading limbs would completely cover the house. White must have planted them. Watered them, too, to judge from their size. But he resisted the temptation to show any weakness before this woman, and when he came to a stop a half-dozen yards from the porch, he knew his face showed no trace of suffering.

"What can I do for you?" the woman asked without moving out of the shadows.

Nice voice, Slade thought. Slightly clipped with a hint of an eastern accent, but low, throaty, and with just enough of a whisper to the consonants to make it sound damned sexy. Old Josh never had a chance.

"Speak up," she said, not so sexy this time. "The desert can't have withered your vocal cords regardless of what it may have done to the rest of you."

Compassionate and sensitive, too, Slade thought cynically.

Obviously the kind who would take infinite patience to make a man comfortable and content *as long as he was useful to her*. He wondered if old Josh was still useful.

He appraised her. She possessed a body that caused his tired blood to throb with excitement, but Slade doubted she could be melted by anything less than an inferno. Everything about her bristled with challenge: the tension in her stance, her squared shoulders thrown back as though already mocking any attempt he might make to breech her defenses, the firm line of her jaw, her unwavering gaze, her complete lack of movement. She might as well have been carved from a piece of the black, volcanic stone which littered the desert.

Yet all this stood in direct contrast to a voice that beckoned him onward and a body which almost begged him to lose himself in its softness.

Slade refused to be tempted, even for a moment. He knew all about women who used their voices and bodies to lure a man to his destruction. He had already had two narrow escapes. He doubted his luck would stretch to a third.

"If you can't bother to speak, you can turn around and head back to where you came from," she informed him. She still hadn't stepped out of the shadows. "I don't have time to waste on drifters who come looking for handouts but haven't the courtesy to speak when they're spoken to."

At least this iceberg put her cards squarely on the table. She clearly didn't take to wandering cowpokes. She would probably remain a mite snappish until she had seen his backside fade into the distance. He wanted to move on, too, but it wouldn't do to let her know she bothered him. She might think that she, and not the sun, was responsible for the rivulets of sweat running between his shoulder blades and down the small of his back. No, letting them know what effect they had on you usually turned out to be the worst possible way to deal with females.

It wouldn't do to get too friendly either. As long as she

kept thinking he was an illiterate drifter, she'd keep her distance. He wanted to get out of here with his hide in one piece, and he didn't relish the thought of having her husband's shotgun providing him with an incentive to move faster.

Slade moved a few steps closer and raised his gaze to the shadowed porch.

"Good afternoon to you, too, ma'am. If you're done trying to make me skedaddle out of here with my tail betwixt my legs, I'd appreciate you telling me where I could find Mr. White. I got to be moving on, but I need to speak with him first." He paused and stared hard into the shadow, shifting his weight on his hips, tilting his pelvis forward just enough to make it impossible for Pamela to ignore. "Besides, it won't do for you to be standing here talking to the likes of me. A lady's got to watch out for her reputation, especially when any rag-tag stranger can just drift on in here."

Pamela gasped. "Are you talking about me?" He was insolent as well as a saddle bum.

"Yes'um. Womenfolk do love to gossip. If I stand here too long, it could turn into a touchy situation." He shifted his weight to the other hip to make her even more aware of him. "I'm sure your husband does his best to look after you, but he can't be expected to hang about all the time just for the pleasure of running his eyes over your curves." Slade's grey eyes became more intense. "I sure could understand it if he did though. Mighty tempting you are, ma'am. A man could be excused for doing all sorts of things if he owned a wife like you."

Pamela's brain was too overwhelmed by his physical presence, as well as his incredible nerve, to do more than utter a few strangled protests. "Husband! . . . Curves! . . . Owned me!" They went unheeded by this leering vagabond.

"I sure have enjoyed our little chat, ma'am, but I'm not a man of leisure. Do you think you could work yourself up to telling me where I could find your husband?"

"There are a lot of things I could *work myself up to,*" Pamela burst out, her anger at last able to punch through her astonishment, "but none of them have anything to do with the whereabouts of my husband."

Slade was suddenly tired of his game. He was nearly dead from thirst and about to pass out from exhaustion. Not that either of those compared to the pain in his feet. And this "lady" seemed determined to keep him standing in the sun. It was a hot day, too. Spring had come late this year, but when it finally arrived, it turned into summer almost overnight. He could feel the welcoming pull of the bunkhouse, a structure nearly as large as the ranch house though shaded by fewer trees, and just as blindingly white. He fought down a desire to charge forward and choke the information out of her. Calling on the last of his reserves, he squared his sagging shoulders.

"I don't know why not, ma'am. I promise I won't hurt him none."

"Hurt him . . . ! You . . . !" Once again she was virtually speechless.

"Ma'am, no doubt your husband understands all these little gasps and spurts, but I haven't had the pleasure of your company for more than a few minutes, and I don't know what the hell you're talking about."

"How dare you curse around me?"

"Surely you can't mean to get worked up over a piddly little word like *hell!*"

"I'm not accustomed to profanity."

"Poor thing," Slade said sympathetically. "Don't your husband ever take you anywhere?"

"What my husband does and does not do—I mean would and would not do," Pamela corrected herself in some confusion, "is none of your concern."

Pamela had taken enough from this low-down tramp, but

14

before she could open her mouth to disabuse him of the notion he belonged to the human race, her cousin came ambling around the corner.

"Thank goodness you got company," he said in a lilting Southern inflection. "I was afraid you'd started talking to yourself. I told Uncle Josh this place was making you queer in the head, but he wouldn't listen to me." He cast a glance about him at a landscape which couldn't have had anything in common with the state which gave birth to his accent. "All these rocks and cactus are enough to drive a body crazy." He directed his glance at Slade. "What do you want?"

"That's what I've been trying to get him to tell me," Pamela said, "but he seems curiously reluctant to come to the point."

"You should be used to that by now," her cousin said with a smile. "I can't remember when I saw a man who didn't lose his tongue after just one look at you."

Slade grinned at a teenage boy as tall as a gate post and about as skinny. With his shirttail half out, his pants miraculously clinging to invisible hips, and his flat-brimmed hat squashed well back on his head, he was the antithesis this imperious female.

Slade opened his mouth to make it plain they were both under a grievous misapprehension when Pamela took a step forward. The sunlight fell full on her face, and the sight took Slade's breath away.

He hadn't seen a woman in weeks, but that didn't keep him from realizing that the best looking woman he had ever seen stood right in front of him. Blessed with a body endowed with lush, womanly curves, she turned a practical, dark blue-ankle-length skirt and a simple, lace-trimmed blouse into the most elegant ensemble Slade had seen this side of New Orleans. But she had a tough quality which belied any feeling of frailty.

Honey-brown hair cascaded down her shoulders. The

streaks of gold that ran all through it gleamed brilliantly in the sun. Ordinary brown eyes seemed liquid and luminous. She kept her mouth tightly compressed, but Slade could imagine it full and relaxed and the thought stung him. Her skin looked so soft his hand ached to touch it.

Damn, she sure was good-looking. She stood there waiting, almost as though she dared him to come a step closer. No, this particular brand of self-confidence had nothing to do with challenges. It came from a lifelong experience of being one of the most beautiful creatures around.

Just like Trish.

He didn't know Josh White, but a woman like this one could cause a man to do all manner of things. If anybody knew that, Slade did. And the bitterness still remained. Not that she showed any inclination to try her wiles on him. From the look of her compressed mouth and tensed muscles, he'd be lucky if she didn't sic the dogs on him.

"She's a fine looking woman," Slade said to the slender youth, "but I'm more interested in a horse."

Shocked looks on two faces caused Slade to curse his tongue and try to hide his grin. If he didn't get himself in trouble by saying things he shouldn't, he made it worse by saying things he didn't mean. "I mean to say I came here looking for a horse," he explained, his irritation with himself making him forget his assumed drawl. "Mine broke a leg, and I had to put it down." Neither spoke. "I'm not particular about how it looks, but I need a sure-footed animal long on stamina. I'm heading for California. Maybe I'll drift on to Wyoming or Montana from there."

"And you expect us to just give you a horse?" Pamela asked, recovering her powers of speech at last.

"I didn't . . ."

"And not just any horse, but one of the best."

Slade uttered a grunt of exasperation. "Ma'am, a man just naturally wants the best of everything."

16

"And how long do you think it'll take you to earn the money to pay for that horse?"

"Ma'am . . ."

"We could use an extra hand," the boy said. "Always need more hands during roundup." He looked Slade over quickly. "From the looks of your boots, I take it you're more used to riding than walking."

"Been around horses since I was knee-high to a fresh-dropped calf."

"Any good?" the boy asked.

"Okay, I guess. I ain't never fallen off."

"How about the one that broke its leg?" Pamela inquired.

Slade allowed a ghost of a wry smile to tease his lips as he turned to look at her. "I guess you got me there, ma'am. I hadn't figured on counting that one."

Now Pamela felt self-conscious. She hadn't said it to embarrass him. It just popped out. Everything about this man irritated her. She suspected him of laughing at her, but she couldn't tell since he was hiding behind that preposterous beard. Why did he wear it? He didn't even trim it properly.

The young man spoke up. "Take your pick. There's half a dozen horses in the corral."

"Aren't you getting ahead of yourself?" Slade asked, the wry smile curving across his lips once again. "I don't have a job, and the lady has already made it clear she doesn't cotton to drifters."

"Of course you got a job." He glanced from Slade to Pamela, then unaccountably, he laughed. "Aw, Pamela don't mean nothing. We're so short-handed right now we'd hire just about anybody."

"Take him around to the kitchen and have Belva give him something to eat," Pamela said to the young man. "And try to remember you're neither the owner *nor* the foreman around here."

17

The boy didn't look the least bit abashed.

"Good day, Mr. . . ." Pamela said as she turned back to Slade. "I don't believe I know your name. You do have one, don't you?"

"I've had several," Slade replied, a mocking sparkle in his eyes. "Which one would you like?"

"The *real* one," Pamela shot back, her composure apparently only slightly shaken.

"In that case you'd better call me Slade, ma'am. Slade Morgan."

"My foreman's out on the range with the crew," Pamela told him. "I'll tell him about you when he comes in. You can stay in the bunkhouse tonight. Do you have a change of clothes?"

"Yes, ma'am. A saddle, too, somewhere out in the desert, but it's probably too far to go back for. I guess I'll need one of them too."

"That's only the beginning of what you need," Pamela said turning toward the house.

"Ma'am . . ."

Pamela was tempted not to answer. She didn't want to waste any more time on Slade Morgan, but his voice was hard to ignore. Against her will she found herself turning to face him.

"I don't know your name either."

Pamela flushed. "I'm Pamela White, and this young rascal is my cousin, Gaddy Pemberton." She started to tell him she wasn't married but changed her mind.

"Whew!" Slade said as the door closed rather too loudly behind Pamela, "I've never been made to feel so much like a desert rat. That's some high-stepping woman."

Gaddy laughed easily. "She's okay, but you'd better wash up and get around to the kitchen before Belva starts fixing dinner. She don't let anyboJy in the kitchen when she's cooking. You look like you could use some fattening up."

18

"No more than you," Slade replied, but his thoughts were elsewhere. He found himself wishing Pamela White was unmarried, and that made him wary of staying a minute more than absolutely necessary to get a horse, saddle, and something to eat. The undeniable feeling of excitement he felt building inside unsettled him. It was the same kind of reckless excitement he felt before his most difficult stunts, the same kind of exhilaration that filled him when he faced a challenge.

Don't let your good sense fail you now, he told himself. Your luck's run out. There's no place for you in a setup like this.

"Looks like you're not in very good standing with your cousin," Slade said somewhat absently as he and Gaddy walked toward the bunkhouse. "Maybe she'll turn us both out on our ears. You got a hankering to see California?"

Gaddy laughed again. "I'm kin, so Pamela's stuck with me whether she likes it or not. She used to be a great gal before her Ma sent her back East to school. Ain't never been the same since. She'd light a shuck to Baltimore right now if she could. Has to if she wants to find a husband."

"Isn't she married to Josh White?"

Gaddy laughed merrily. "Not likely. Josh is her father. He's my uncle."

"Then what's stopping her from going to Baltimore?" Slade asked, partly out of curiosity and partly to cover his confusion. They had reached the trough behind the barn. He bent down to get a slow drink from the pump.

"No cash. Uncle Josh has a fortune in cattle, but he's got to round them up before he can sell them. That's why we need hands. Oh, I almost forgot. You'll need to wash up and change your clothes before you go up to the house. You can borrow some from one of the boys if you don't have any. You look to be about Cade's size."

"What's all this worry about clothes?"

19

"Cousin Pamela sets a lot of store by a man's appearance. She don't like people to be dirty. She won't let you in that house if you don't clean up. Her ma did that, her and that school back East. Never did see why females should be so particular about things that don't mean nothing, especially out here."

"Most women are like that. Seems they can't rightly help themselves."

"You don't know the half of it."

"Don't tell me the rest until after I get something to eat. I'm so weak from hunger I don't know if I'll make it to the house."

But Gaddy noticed that in spite of his devitalized condition, Slade Morgan had no difficulty making it to the kitchen.

Chapter 2

Pamela let the leather-bound copy of Jane Austen's *Emma* fall to her lap. She couldn't concentrate with all that laughter coming from the kitchen. This had never happened before. It had to be because of Slade Morgan.

She told herself she ought to be thankful the arrival of this wandering vagabond had taken her mind off her father, even if only for a few minutes. She couldn't help him by worrying. The best thing she could do was make sure the ranch ran smoothly until he got back from Santa Fe.

But she worried anyway. She hadn't felt comfortable since the other ranchers started running cattle on Bar Double-B range. Her father had made it clear he wouldn't tolerate any encroachment on his grazing land, but Pamela hadn't expected the trouble to go away that easily. When her father told her he intended to go to Santa Fe to buy barbed wire and hire extra hands, she knew it hadn't.

"You've got nothing to worry about while I'm gone," Josh White had assured his daughter. "There hasn't been any real trouble. Some barbed wire and a few extra hands ought to nip things in the bud."

"But won't they take that to mean you'll fight?" Pamela had asked. Her mother had told her terrifying stories of her first years in Arizona.

21

"They already know that," Josh had replied. "This is just to convince them they can't run me out."

Pamela couldn't make up her mind what she thought her father should do. On the one hand, she didn't see why he should give up a ranch he'd worked so hard to build because of somebody else's greed. She might not want to live in Arizona, but it went against the grain to allow anything to be taken from him. This ranch was a measure of the man who created it, and she couldn't look out over the valley without taking pride in her father's accomplishment.

Yet she couldn't forget her mother's warnings. She had never seen a range war, but she knew they could be brutal, horribly cruel to everyone involved. No ranch was worth her father's life. Even if she loved every foot of ground, she wouldn't want the Bar Double-B at that price.

"I ought to be back in a couple of weeks," her father had said, " but don't worry if I'm late. It may take a little while to find the kind of hands I want. I thought I'd look for one or two married men. I never realized until Belva came out here how badly you must want for female company."

Pamela hadn't bothered to tell him the only kind of company she wanted, male or female, was back East. It had been three years since she returned home after graduating from Garrison Normal, an exclusive boarding school in Baltimore, yet she still felt like an outsider. She couldn't wait to get back to Maryland. Now that her mother was dead, nothing tied her to Arizona except the father she loved so dearly.

But now she had a stranger in her kitchen, and although she doubted he would hold her interest for very long, she had to admit his presence had cut into her peace. After a shout of laughter shattered another attempt to become interested in her book, she laid it aside and got to her feet. She *had* to know what they were doing.

But when she reached the kitchen, everyone had fallen silent. Gaddy had disappeared, and Slade had almost finished a small slice of pie and a cup of coffee. Belva Bagshot, six months pregnant and barely able to reach the back of the stove, was beginning her preparations for dinner.

"That's not enough food for a child," Pamela said to Belva. "I thought he was hungry."

"You can't make a man eat what he don't want," Belva said without taking her eyes off the bowl of beans she had simmering on the heavy iron stove. "That's what he asked for, and that's what I gave him."

Pamela pretended not to notice when Slade looked up and blinked. She had changed into a white gown with a high neck, full sleeves, a tight waist, and a full skirt that reached the floor. She had also pinned her hair up under a frivolous lace cap. It pleased her to know her appearance had momentarily silenced him, but it angered her that she even noticed. She didn't care what this disgraceful cowboy thought about her or anything else.

"I haven't had much to eat in three days, ma'am," Slade said with his infuriatingly slow, mocking drawl. "If I was to eat more than a few bites right now, my stomach wouldn't know what to do. I plan to make amends at dinner." The twinkle was back in his eye.

Pamela was uncertain of what to do next, and that irritated her. She had never felt ill-at-ease in her own house, but this stranger seemed more at home than she did, and that irritated her too. In fact, nearly everything about him irritated her.

"Do you have any experience as a cowhand?"

"Some."

"Are you any good at it?"

"Enough."

"What kind of job do you expect?"

"I don't."

"I beg your pardon?"

"I don't expect a job."

"But you need one."

23

Slade shrugged.

"What do you do best?"

"Whatever you want done."

She wondered what he had been saying to make Belva and Gaddy laugh so. He was about as talkative as a hermit and as funny as a saddle sore now.

"You can sit down, ma'am. I don't bite."

"I never supposed you did." Pamela had been about to sit, but perversely she decided to remain standing.

"Just thought you might not want to give me a crick in my neck."

"A *gentleman* would have risen when I entered the room." But no gentleman she'd ever known filled out a shirt the way Slade did.

"A *woman* would know not to interrupt a man when he's eating."

Pamela bit back a stinging retort. She refused to argue with a saddle tramp.

"You better sit down, Miss White," Belva said, an unmistakable chuckle in her voice. She placed a second cup of coffee on the well-scrubbed table. "You know your father doesn't like to be talked to while he's eating."

Pamela didn't want to sit down, but she couldn't think of anything else to do without looking foolish, so she settled into a ladder-backed chair opposite Slade. She sipped her coffee and studied him more closely.

"You don't seem like the type to come in here begging for a horse and a job."

"I didn't . . ." Slade started to say then changed his mind. "I'm just a man like anybody else."

You sure are a man, but you're not like anybody I ever met, Pamela thought to herself. But aloud she said, "I'm waiting, Mr. Morgan. If you want me to give you a job, the least you can do is tell me something of your background."

"It's not where a man comes from that counts, ma'am. It's what he does."

24

"A person's roots are important, too."

"Ma'am, I'm from Texas. Folks there don't have many roots, leastways not in Texas. I shouldn't suppose folks in Arizona have half as many. Now if you will excuse me, I got to go pick me out a horse."

Pamela's presence distracted Slade so badly he stood up without thinking. The agonizing pain in his feet made him falter.

Pamela didn't miss that, or the grimace of suffering that flitted across his face.

"What's wrong?" she asked, starting to her feet.

Slade recovered quickly, but the smile on his lips wasn't reflected in his eyes. "Nothing, ma'am. Just took a misstep. Comes from sitting in a chair too long. Not much like setting a horse. Makes a man careless."

But Pamela knew something wasn't right.

"There's something wrong with your foot."

"It's nothing much. Must have a cramp in my leg. I walked a mighty long way."

"You *may* have taken a misstep when you got up and you *may* have a cramp in your leg, but there is something wrong with your foot," Pamela insisted. "Sit down and take off your boot."

"Now, ma'am, there's no need to . . ."

"Sit down."

"And what if I don't?"

"You walked in here. You can walk out again."

"Ma'am, you sure do drive a hard bargain. It just ain't ladylike to put a man over a barrel and then order him to take off his boots."

Much to her surprise, Pamela felt the urge to smile. Why this man should make her feel like that when he hid his thoughts behind a beard she didn't know. She forced herself to keep a somber expression on her face. "I have a strange feeling no one has even been able to get you over a barrel. . . ."

25

"Boy are you ever wrong," Slade mumbled.

". . . but I'm ordering you to take your boots off."

"You won't like it."

"Take them off!"

Slade sighed. "Some people just can't help taking advantage of folks when they're helpless. I come in here half starved, dying of thirst, and plumb worn to a nub and what do you do? Order me to take off my boots." Slade looked up at her like a sudden thought had come to him. "You ain't going to take my boots away and then make me walk out of here, are you, ma'am? Cause if that's what you got in mind, I can tell you I'd take that as downright unfriendly."

"Sit down and take them off," Pamela ordered. The devilish twinkle in his eye robbed her of any feeling of amusement. She suspected him of making fun of her. She could *feel* Belva's silent laughter without looking around.

Slade sat down and tugged ineffectively at his boot. "I can't seem to budge it, ma'am. I guess I'll just have to keep them on for a spell."

"Try again."

"I can't. I'm plumb wore out."

"The only thing that's *plumb wore out* is my patience," she snapped. "Pull."

God, how she hated beards. She couldn't tell what he was thinking with hair all over his face. She began to feel uneasy, but she wouldn't back down. This had turned into a battle of wills. If she couldn't handle a wandering cowboy when she had him in her own kitchen, how could she handle the ranch? Abruptly a vision popped into her mind of him standing in the yard stripped to the waist—his chest and shoulders dripping with water, sunlight turning each drop into a sparkling crystal—and she almost lost control. In desperation she concentrated her thoughts on his beard until she could steady herself again.

"I'm waiting," she said quickly, before her mind could conjure up any more dangerous images.

All the laconic mockery had gone from his voice when Slade spoke. "I expect you'll wish you hadn't." He pulled the boot off with a single tug.

Belva gasped.

Pamela felt sick to her stomach.

Blood and dirt discolored Slade's sock, some of it dried and black, some of it moist and red. The recollection of his swaggering walk as he strode up to the ranch house rose before her eyes. How could he stand on those feet, much less walk like they didn't hurt? What kind of man could walk miles across the desert with his feet in that condition and then sit at the table eating a piece of pie and light-heartedly mocking her? The pain must have been excruciating.

She forced herself to speak despite the gorge rising in her throat. "Now the other boot." The second foot looked just as bad. "Belva, pour some warm water into a pan. I'm going to have to soak his socks off."

She knew he hadn't wanted her to see his feet, but now that she had, his expression dared her to offer him sympathy. But there was no danger of that. Any man crazy enough to cross the desert without food and water and pretend nothing was wrong didn't deserve any sympathy. His entire nervous system had to be dead.

Belva placed a basin on the floor at Slade's feet. He didn't utter a sound when he lowered his right foot into the warm water. But Pamela saw the skin tighten around his eyes and his fingers grip involuntarily as the pain wrenched his body. She seemed to feel his pain, too, and that confused her. Why did she care about this saddle tramp's feet?

"Now the other one."

She waited until he put the second foot in the water. Then, after assuring herself he wouldn't take his feet out of the basin, she left the room. She returned a few minutes later with salve, cotton, bandages, a bottle of whiskey, and a pair of worn moccasins.

She knelt at his feet. She wasn't aware of what she had

27

done until Slade attempted to protest.

"Save your heroics. You'll need every bit of your stubborn pride when I take off your socks."

Slade focused his gaze on Pamela hoping to forget the pain tearing at his body like pincers. There was no expanse of milk-white shoulder or bare arch of neck to tantalize him, but he was fascinated nonetheless. Inside, away from the brilliance of the sun, the streaks of gold in her hair turned to burnished copper giving her hair a wondrously warm, soft appearance. Several individual strands had escaped from her pins, clustering about the softness of her neck like champagne-colored gauze.

Slade felt a tightening in his groin and immediately refocused his mind on his feet. He didn't want to have to explain to Pamela why his body was stiffening with desire. If he didn't think of something else quickly, it would be impossible for her not to notice.

For a moment Slade wondered if all his pride would be enough to keep him from crying out. The pain cut deeper than anything he had ever experienced, even worse than the walk in from the desert. But he forced himself to sit still, forced himself to watch Pamela as she cut off first one sock and then the other to reveal his ravaged feet. He forced himself to remain silent because he could see Pamela struggling just as hard to prove the appalling sight didn't affect her.

He couldn't understand why this girl should worry about his feet. Why should she care if he insisted upon wandering about the world on bloody stumps? She could barely contain her revulsion. When she left the kitchen, he was sure she wouldn't come back. He felt like a cynical fool when she returned with an armload of supplies. Shocked and revolted she might be, but Pamela White had courage.

With incredible gentleness she dabbed his feet with cotton, soaked off the dried blood, and cleansed the broken blisters.

"Hold still," she said, her fingers gently but firmly

grasping his foot. Then, with quick, decisive movements, she cut away the dead skin.

A stab of pain caused Slade to flinch.

"I'm sorry," Pamela said. "I'm almost finished."

He didn't flinch again.

Pamela had never looked at a man's foot. Not *really* looked at it. Slade's feet did nothing to cause her to regret the omission, but there was something strangely appealing about the ravaged member. She remembered Frederick once saying something about a nicely turned ankle. Of course he was talking about a girl, but why couldn't men have ankles fashioned just as attractively? He made her think of the picture of a statue they once studied in school, one by Michelangelo she thought.

She felt like she blushed. She fixed her mind on her task. What would her mother think of her daydreaming about statues of naked men and blushing because she held the foot of a very live one in her hands?

When Slade's feet had been carefully patted dry, Pamela paused and looked up. He couldn't say exactly what he saw in her eyes, in the expression on her face, but it affected him so powerfully he almost forgot the pain. He didn't think it was her beauty, though God knew she had enough of that to startle any man. It appeared to be something more subtle, something he had never encountered.

But how could he guess what lay at the heart of a woman like Pamela White? He had never gotten along well with women, not the decent ones anyway. His mother and Trish had pretty well convinced him no lady could find anything of interest in him. And except for the occasional visit to a small room up a narrow stairway, he'd given up on females.

Now this woman threatened his resolve. Not that her eyes contained any kind of invitation. He might be rusty when it came to reading female signs, but it wasn't invitation he read in her face.

It was something even more rare. It was interest, maybe

29

even a kind of admiration. Hell, he couldn't remember when his presence had elicited anything except momentary curiosity. He had more than enough manly attributes to draw a woman's attention, but it never endured. If they were "nice" women, it didn't go beyond learning of his reputation. If they weren't nice, their interest lasted exactly as long as the money he spent on them.

But he could sense something more this time. Her eyes seem to ask, what kind of man are you? They held no condemnation, no calculation, just a searching for the things that made him Slade Morgan.

Involuntarily, his eyes drew a veil between them. He resisted the impulse to share even the smallest part of himself. His safety depended upon divulging as little as possible.

A frown of understanding clouded Pamela's eyes. Her gaze said she recognized his withdrawal and accepted it.

"I'm afraid this is going to hurt even worse," Pamela said as she reached for the bottle of whiskey, "but if I don't clean the wounds, they'll become infected. Then I can't give you that job. You'll be no use to me laid up."

Slade stared at Pamela. She understood. She knew he could accept almost anything in the world except sympathy.

"Do what you have to," he said.

Belva set down a basin of clean water, and Pamela poured the whole bottle of whiskey into it. "Put both your feet in at the same time."

Nothing in his whole life had prepared Slade for the pain that racked his body when he put his feet in the whiskey water. It felt like the fangs of a thousand snakes were buried in his flesh. Every muscle in his body jumped in an involuntary spasm and then clamped down, hard. For a moment he couldn't breath. It took all his strength to keep his feet in the water. Gradually the shock receded and his muscles relaxed sufficiently for his mind to be able to think of something besides the pain. Gathering his wits he looked up. Pamela's eyes were on him, her face purposely expressionless.

"On the whole, I think I prefer to drink my whiskey," he managed to say.

A slow smile relieved the rigidity of Pamela's features. "Dad always said the same thing, only this isn't the good whiskey." Her smile grew. "It would be even harder on your insides than your feet. Is the stinging all gone?"

"Good Lord, Miss White," exclaimed Belva, "the stinging has just started. It's that awful pain that's finally let go of the poor man."

"I've got to dry your feet and put some salve on the blisters," Pamela said, ignoring Belva's outburst. "If they don't swell too much, you'll be able to wear your boots in a couple of days."

"And what am I supposed to do until then?" Slade asked. "You can't be in the habit of hiring cowhands and then having them lie up in the bunk."

"Miss White won't let anybody work who isn't fit," Belva stated. "She's very firm about that."

Slade gave her an inquiring look which virtually demanded a response.

"It's really quite practical," Pamela explained as she carefully patted his feet. "Men work better when they're healthy. Besides, there's always something they can do to keep busy while they recuperate."

She gently rubbed an herbal salve into the raw flesh of his blisters. She was careful to keep her mind off Italian statues and her eyes away from Slade's ankles.

"That stings right smart, too," he said. "You got something against a man feeling better?" Slade made sure the twinkle in his eyes took the sting out of the words. The burning faded quickly and left a cooling, soothing sensation. After the misery of the last two days, it was a blessed relief.

Pamela relaxed at his words. She hadn't realized how tense her fear of hurting him had made her. "I won't pay you

31

until you can work," she continued as she wrapped his feet in strips of thin gauze. "Tomorrow or the next day you can start on the bunkhouse and tack room. They need to be cleaned before Dad brings the new hands from Santa Fe. By then you ought to be back in the saddle." Pamela finished the bandages and stood up. "I want you to stay off your feet until supper. Don't get up!" Pamela exclaimed when Slade started to stand.

"I have to, ma'am. I can't float over to that bunkhouse."

"You can use one of the bedrooms here. You'll have those blisters caked with dust if you set foot outside."

"But the moccasins . . ."

"They're for later. You wait right here. I'll get Gaddy to give me a hand. We'll carry you to the bedroom."

Slade immediately got to his feet, despite the arrows of pain which nearly blinded him.

"No one has ever done anything like this for me, ma'am. I'm mighty grateful, but I'll have to be dead before anybody carries me to a bed. Now you just show me where you want me to go."

"Are you always this stubborn?"

"No, ma'am. I'm being awfully polite just now."

"You probably are," Pamela said. A reluctant smile banished the seriousness of her expression. "Well, if you must walk, follow me, but if you get blood on the floor, you'll have to clean it up yourself."

"Yes, ma'am. That seems only fair."

She was kidding. It was the kind of thing she would have said to Gaddy—men never seemed to be aware of the mess they made—but he sounded sincere. Or was he making fun of her again? Pamela whipped around and directed a challenging glare at him, but with that beard covering his face, she couldn't tell what his thoughts might be. His eyes looked so blandly innocent she decided it would be wiser to ignore his remark. Regardless of how much this man acted like a dumb cowboy, she now knew he was no such thing. She didn't know what he was, but she was becoming curious about him. Nothing in her experience had prepared her to understand him, and she felt excited at the prospect of the challenge.

"At least lean on me."

"Ma'am . . ."

"Don't say it," Pamela warned. "If you're rude, I'll throw you out. If you refuse, I'll have Gaddy knock you out. Either way you'll do what I want."

"I don't know what they taught you in Baltimore, ma'am, but it certainly wasn't how to play fair."

Pamela laughed, easily now, naturally, as with a friend. "Stop complaining and put your hand on my shoulder. After being in the desert for so long, I would have thought you'd jump at the chance to exchange your horse and saddle for a nice soft bed."

Slade didn't respond. His fingertips could feel the softness of her body underneath the fabric of her dress, and all desire for conversation left him. Memory flooded back reminding him of all the women he had known, of the ones he had turned his back on, of the ones who had turned their backs on him, but none of them had ever affected him like this. Pamela might think his body trembled from pain, but he knew he trembled from a yearning to forget the ingrained feeling of unworthiness, of inferiority which came from being rejected by the two most important women in his life, and start anew.

He could feel it through his fingertips. Hope. And the certainty that if he could make a new beginning, the results would be different. Don't be a fool he cursed himself. Nothing's changed. She only cleaned up your feet because she pities you. No sensible man builds a dream on such as that.

But his heart wouldn't listen, and he had to make himself concentrate on the rooms he was passing through to keep from dreaming dreams which could easily turn into nightmares. He knew it was a large house, but because of the pain in his body and the shock of meeting such a woman, it had made little more than a vague impression on him until now.

However, after he had passed through a dining room large enough to seat twenty people and a parlor which looked like it belonged in a San Francisco hotel, he realized this was not just a large ranch house. Nor was there anything ordinary about it.

The walls were plastered or paneled in carved oak, the ceilings decorated, and the polished stone floors covered with oriental rugs. But it was the furnishings that made the biggest impression. Slade had never seen anything like it.

Velvet curtains hung at the windows. Pictures in massive gold and silver frames graced the wall. Chairs, sofas, and tables filled every room, all made of carved mahogany and rare marble and upholstered in silk damask or heavy brocade. There were several lace-covered tables bearing small figures in rare stone, crystal, or gold and silver gilt. Josh White had to be a very wealthy man. It must have cost a fortune to fill his home with such beautiful things.

It was a long way from the kitchen to the bedrooms. Slade wasn't sure he would have made it without Pamela. The effort to keep from giving in to the pain, or the lure of her tempting body, he wasn't sure which, completely exhausted him.

"If I'd known I'd have to walk through a dining room large enough to seat the entire population of Arizona," he said pausing to catch his breath, "or an even larger commons room," he continued, leaning heavily on her now, "I'd have let you and that boy carry me." They reached a long hallway with four doors on each side. "Good God! How much farther do I have to go?"

"You can use this bedroom," Pamela said. She opened the first door and stepped into a room such as Slade had only dreamed of. Only a tiny fraction of sunlight penetrated the heavy curtains at the window, but enough entered for Slade to see the room was dominated by a large, four-poster bed piled high with thick mattresses and pillows and covered by a thick comforter heavily embroidered with silk thread. The filmy, crocheted canopy looked unutterably feminine. The furniture, unlike the pieces he had already seen, was solidly built and covered in plain, sturdy, cheerful fabrics. A large mirror over a marble-top chest dominated one wall; a huge antique chifforobe covered most of the second. A pitcher and basin stood on the chest. A cedar chest at the foot of the bed gave promise of thick blankets for cold winter nights, but on this hot spring day, the room felt deliciously cool and comfortable.

Slade thought of the distance they had traveled from the kitchen. "If I had gone to the bunkhouse, I could have been asleep by now." Much to his surprise, Pamela seemed embarrassed by his comment.

"It is a rather big house, but mother had hoped to have a lot of guests. It's rather lonely out here for a woman."

Slade felt reproached even though she obviously intended no reproof. Besides, it was none of his business if old man White wanted to spend every cent he made on his house. What had possessed him to suddenly start asking questions anyway? This kind of curiosity could be dangerous. He ought to turn around and ride out of here now.

"I'll bring your dinner in here," Pamela said, breaking in on his thoughts. "We can talk about your job then."

"I'll eat at the table," Slade said.

Their gazes met in open challenge, and Pamela could tell Slade didn't mean to give in this time.

"I'll see that Gaddy calls you in plenty of time."

Slade was momentarily thrown off stride by her unexpected acceptance. He got the impression she usually had things her way. "Speaking of that job, I've been giving it some thought. . . ."

"You shouldn't worry about anything until you've had some rest. You'll think much better tomorrow."

35

"Yes, ma'am, I'm sure I will."

He would leave tomorrow as planned, but right now that bed looked mighty inviting. He didn't mind sleeping in the open, he preferred it most of the time, but there were times when a man wanted a bit of cossetting, and this bed looked like just the thing to do it. The cool and quiet of the room beckoned, and the pain in his feet urged Slade to spread out on the bed.

"You sure you don't mind me sleeping here? Everything looks awful nice."

"There's nothing you can do to this room which can't be fixed with a little soap and water," Pamela said. "Besides, a room is no good until somebody uses it." Then, with a smile, she left and closed the door behind her.

Slade suddenly felt too weak to stand. He had no idea how much the tension of being around Pamela had bolstered his flagging energy. Now that she was gone, he felt almost sick with exhaustion.

He didn't know just what to think about the mess he found himself in, but he figured he could think just as well stretched out as on his feet. He was mistaken. No sooner did his body relax into the welcoming softness of the mattress than sleep began to clog his mind. Two weeks on the run with little sleep, less food, and no chance to relax his guard had worn him down. Walking sixty miles across the desert had left him utterly exhausted. He had a lot of thinking to do, but it wouldn't do any harm to wait a few more hours to do it.

He fell asleep inside a minute.

On the other side of the door, Pamela reached the conclusion that she needed to do some thinking, too. Only she didn't know what to think.

What had made her clean and bandage his feet herself? Belva had looked stunned. Even Slade had tried to protest. She always saw to the health of the men, but she had never personally tended their cuts and scrapes. Yet the minute she saw Slade's feet, she thought only of doing what she could to make them better. Why? What made this cowboy so different?

His down-at-the-heels-cowhand bit had to be an act. He might be what he seemed, but there was more to Slade Morgan than he wanted anyone to see.

Even as her fear receded that Slade was nothing but an ignorant cowboy she would do well to be rid of as soon as possible, she started to worry he might have done something unlawful. He could be a fugitive. Her father had often told her that while many cowboys carried a rifle in a scabbard, few of them wore two guns, especially tied down. That equipment belonged to a fighting man, a man who was used to guns and knew how to use them.

Pamela hated violence, and guns stood for killing, the thing she hated most about the West. Nothing could excuse the unnecessary death of a man, and she didn't want anything to do with a gunslinger. Most particularly, she wouldn't have one living on the Bar Double-B. If Slade Morgan was a gunfighter, he would have to go.

Now?

Well, no, not right away, but as soon as he could stand on his feet.

Chapter 3

Slade opened his eyes. For a moment, he didn't recognize the room, then he allowed a crooked smile to soften the lines of his face. You're in a pickle now, he thought. Your every footstep is being hounded by a blood-thirsty Texas sheriff, you have to keep an eye out for green kids itching to make a reputation by killing the infamous Billy Wilson, and you're laid up in a fancy bed with blisters all over your feet.

He considered it highly unlikely anyone would come looking for him here. Not the Billy Wilson they knew in Texas. No self-respecting female would be seen with him, much less invite him into her house. Hadn't Trish McDevitt broken their engagement when he got into a brawl with the Whittaker crowd over a stolen horse? Well, she hadn't broken it then. She had waited until after he had shot up two Whittakers and well-nigh beat a third to death before she told him not to come back.

Funny thing about that. Nobody in Brazos ever bothered to ask those Whittakers why they stole Billy's horse or what they did to make him so mad. No, he was nothing but the trouble-making son of a no-good drunk. The most widely accepted opinion held that if a pillar of the church like Sarah Wilson couldn't do anything with Sam or his son, it was pointless for anybody else to waste time trying.

As for the Whittakers, well, they shouldn't have stolen Billy's horse. Everybody knew he set great store by that animal. He had raised it from a colt and taught it to do all manner of tricks. But Billy still shouldn't have acted the way he did.

Of course that wasn't the worst of the things Billy Wilson did. It was merely the first.

With a growl of disgust, Slade threw his legs over the side of the bed and stood up. He regretted it immediately. Blinding pain reminded him why he was in bed in the first place. He lay back down and let the pain gradually subside.

It looked like he would have to stay here for a few days. It would be foolish to get back on the trail before he could put his boots on. Besides, he'd never had such a good place to hole up. Not only did he have food to eat and a place to sleep. Unless that sheriff came to the door asking after him, no one would suspect he wasn't who he claimed to be.

He could even take off his guns.

Slade couldn't remember when he had been without a gun. Certainly not in the ten years since he had fought the Whittakers. That fight earned him a name as a gunman. After that someone always lurked around the next corner waiting to challenge him in hopes of making a reputation of their own. That's why he finally changed his name, gave up appearing in the carnival, and became a cowhand. It was also his reason for heading to California. There had to be somewhere he could go where his past wouldn't follow.

He thought of Pamela's questions about his roots. A man's past wasn't always his doing. Things happened he had no control over, things he had to do if he was to keep on calling himself a man. Strange though how these same things could prevent you from living like a man.

Slade used to think if he could find where he had taken that wrong step he would know what to do about it. He thought people were basically fair. But he was younger then. He had learned differently since, and he had stopped asking himself questions about his past. Lately he had begun to wonder if there was any point in asking them about his future either. If anyone ever figured out he was Billy Wilson, he wouldn't have one here.

Hell, he never had a future here anyway. As far as he was concerned, it was just a place along the way. As far as they were concerned, he was just a passerby.

Slade prayed the meal would soon come to an end. He had eaten his dinner sitting in flea-infested sand, on rocks that cut into his flesh, kneeling until the muscles at the back of his legs ached, or in the saddle on the run. But he'd never been as uncomfortable as he was now, seated in a silk-covered intricately carved mahogany chair.

His mother used to make them dine formally every evening, but he had never sat down to a twelve-foot long, linen-covered, mahogany table, or served himself from bone china, drunk wine from crystal goblets, and eaten with sterling silverware. And all in the kind of room he had seen only once, and that in New Orleans. He felt so miserably uncomfortable he could hardly swallow his food. But the brocade curtains and candle-filled chandelier didn't seem to bother anybody else. It certainly didn't stop Gaddy from enjoying his dinner. That boy had enough appetite for two.

And to top it off, Pamela had *dressed* for dinner. He had dressed too—he hadn't come to the table naked after all—but Pamela wore an evening gown of primrose silk. If she had looked stunning on the porch this afternoon or unbelievable as she knelt at his feet, she looked absolutely breathtaking now.

Slade couldn't figure out why someone hadn't started a war over her. Hell, how could anybody think of cows or grazing land with a woman in their midst who looked like something out of a dream?

Slade put another piece of steak into his mouth and forced

himself to turn back to Gaddy. If he kept looking at Pamela he would soon lose all sense of reality. Her kind of woman caused men to do desperate things, but Slade had already had two turns with such a woman. He didn't feel anxious to step up to the line again.

"I'll think about it. That's the best I can do," he said when Gaddy pressed him for the half-dozenth time to sign on for the roundup. Dave Bagshot had failed to show up for dinner, but Gaddy was making a gallant attempt to convince Slade to stay on.

"You got to hang around because of your feet," the boy pointed out. "Besides, Pamela says you blew in without a cent. Uncle Josh doesn't keep just any kind of horses. It'll take a couple of months to earn enough money to buy one."

"I expect it will," Slade said glancing at Pamela. "Miss White has already warned me not to expect charity."

Pamela's expression didn't change one iota. "You know what I meant," she said as she looked directly at Slade. "But there's another consideration Gaddy hasn't mentioned. It's not fair to offer you a job without telling you of the risks."

"There's no risk. . . ." Gaddy began, but Pamela interrupted him.

"My father has gone to Santa Fe to hire extra hands and buy barbed wire. He *said* he wanted to look for family men because women help settle the country, but married men can't afford to work as ranch hands. I think he's looking for gunfighters."

"He's doing no such thing," Gaddy protested, but Pamela ignored him.

"I do know something about ranches, even though I've spent a lot of my life in Baltimore. We always hired hands as they drifted in. I don't think Dad ever sent out for them. He certainly never had to pick them out personally."

"There's pressure on the range from some new herds," Gaddy explained, "but it's nothing we can't handle."

"I've been in trouble most of my life," Slade said carelessly. "I doubt I'd even notice this little fracas."

"That's something else I want to mention," Pamela said.

Something in her voice caught his attention, and Slade looked at her, straight into her eyes. He could see wariness there but no flagging in her sense of purpose. However reluctant Pamela might be to broach this issue, it concerned something about which she wouldn't compromise.

"I couldn't help but notice your guns. My father insists that men need to be armed when they're on the range, but I won't allow anyone to wear guns here at the ranch."

"Pamela's still skittish about western doings," Gaddy explained.

"That's not true. I don't expect anyone to allow himself to be shot without defense," she said, turning back to Slade, "but I dislike violence. I particularly disapprove of guns being used on other human beings. My father is responsible for the welfare of the men who work for us, and we wouldn't be setting a good example if we encouraged the use of guns to settle disagreements. Don't you agree, Mr. Morgan?"

Slade couldn't tell her he had left his home to avoid having to use guns or that he had given up the only work he knew to be free of the necessity of having to wear them for the rest of his life. Neither could he tell her that even though he disliked the way most people used guns, he didn't disapprove of them. After the way she looked as she knelt to bathe his feet, he wouldn't willingly do anything that would make her look on him with disfavor. No one had ever done anything like that for him. Hell, Trish wouldn't even have let him in the house looking like that, much less have allowed him to lie down on one of her beds.

But worst of all, this afternoon, while he slept, he had dreamed of having just such a place as this. No, worst of all would be trying to explain to her that for a ranch such as this, half the men in the world would use a gun. Himself included.

Now, sitting at this table, looking at her in the candle-light, listening to the soothing sound of her voice, feeling the excitement of her presence, he couldn't believe such a dream was impossible. As long as he could sit at the same table with her, anything was possible.

"I agree in principle," Slade said, pulling himself out of his thoughts, "but it's been my experience that people don't always live up to the good in them. I don't know how it is in Baltimore, but out here it seems the badness is the first thing to show. Guns are just about the only way an honest man has to protect himself."

Pamela's expression relaxed into a smile. "My mother always said if you showed people what you expected of them, they would try to live up to it. I've found that to be true."

It wouldn't do any good to tell her about his experiences. Besides, he couldn't imagine how any man living could look into Pamela's eyes and not try his dead level best to do anything she asked. He had to get out of here before he started making promises he couldn't keep.

"I suppose I could do without my guns for a day or two, but I won't turn them over to anybody. Now if you'll excuse me, I think I ought to see about settling into the bunkhouse." He did his best to ignore the pain that radiated up from his feet. "If you'll just tell me where you put my boots."

"Gaddy took them over while you were asleep. I don't want you wearing anything but moccasins until those blisters heal."

"Ma'am, you're going to ruin me with all this cossetting. A couple more days and I won't be fit to hit the trail."

"By then maybe you won't want to."

It just slipped out. Pamela didn't mean anything in particular by it, but it sounded like she did, and that made her blush.

Slade knew she didn't mean anything by it either, but the blush meant she might possibly mean something someday. His heart seemed to skip a beat at the thought.

If he just didn't have a beard, Pamela thought, I might be

able to tell what he's thinking.

Thank goodness I've got a beard, thought Slade. Now if I could just keep my eyes from giving me away.

"Everything tasted mighty good, Mrs. Bagshot," Slade said as he slipped his feet into the moccasins, "especially after eating my own cooking."

Belva acknowledged his compliment with a nod.

"Thanks for taking care of my blisters, ma'am," Slade said, turning to Pamela. "However, there were a few moments when I wondered whether the cure might not be worse than the disease."

"Just make sure you wear your moccasins." She paused, clearly struggling with herself. "I guess you'd better call me Pamela. It makes me feel strange when you call me Ma'am. I keep thinking you must be referring to my mother."

"As long as you don't think it's disrespectful."

"Everybody does it."

"Okay then, Pamela, I guess I'll say good night."

"He seems like a nice man," Belva said after the men had gone. "I can't imagine why he should want to go wandering around the desert by himself."

"His horse broke a leg."

"I heard him, but you and I both know the trail to California ain't no sixty miles away. And it doesn't go across the desert neither. He must have come in through Mexico. Now why would he be doing that?"

"He could have gotten lost. He did say he was from Texas."

"If he can find his way around a place as big as Texas, he can find his way across Arizona," Belva stated. "I like him, but he's not telling you everything."

"If I give him a job and a place to stay, he'd better tell me everything."

"You don't ask a man out here about his past. He'll leave if you do, and I have the feeling you don't want him to go just yet."

44

"I don't care what he does. You've just tried to convince me he's a liar. Maybe I should tell him to leave in the morning."

"I didn't say he was a liar," Belva corrected her. "Do you think that man would lie?"

"Yes, if he thought it was important." She paused for a long moment before adding, "But I don't think he would lie to me."

Pamela's words surprised her more greatly than the shock that showed on Belva's face. She didn't know what made her say that, but even as the words passed her lips, she knew it was true. He might try to evade telling her what she wanted to know—he had already done that several times—but his eyes told her he wouldn't lie to her.

But why? He didn't know any more about her than she knew about him, yet a vein of understanding existed between them, something she felt almost from the first. Though how this could be, when he represented just about everything she disapproved of, she didn't know.

But even as these thoughts crossed her mind, she reminded herself she didn't really know anything about him. He didn't *look* like the kind of man she would approve of. He didn't act like it either, but she had no proof he'd actually done anything wrong. She had to keep an open mind.

But why should she bother? He would ride out in a day or two. She'd probably never think about him again.

Yet even before she completed that thought, she knew it wasn't true. If he were to ride out this very evening, she would never forget the way he had walked up to the house, the way a man walked who knew he was a man, the way a man walked when he was afraid of nothing and asked for nothing. That he should have done so with his feet covered with bleeding blisters was an act of courage, or stupidity—at this point she didn't know which. But she could be sure of one thing. She had never in her life seen the equal of his nerve.

"He's probably laboring under the illusion that pride is a substitute for character."

"If it's Mr. Morgan you're talking to yourself about," Belva said, turning her attention from the pot she was scrubbing, "I doubt he has illusions of any kind."

"But he does have pride."

"I imagine it'd be more exact if you called it a sense of honor. I bet he's chock full of that. Men like him usually are."

"What do you mean *men like him?*"

"I don't know. To tell the truth, I've never seen anyone like him, not really like him. Your Pa is the closest one I can think of."

The thought that Slade could resemble her father in any way shocked Pamela. She loved her father deeply and considered him perfect. But no sooner did she reject the notion than she realized her father would have behaved exactly as Slade did.

Pamela didn't know what to make of that.

"Well, for all his sense of honor, he doesn't have much ambition." That wasn't like her father. He had more ambition than any man in Arizona. "You'd think he would want to do something with his life besides wander about the desert taking any job he can find just to stay alive."

"I don't know what he's doing, but he's not just wandering about. As much as you may dislike to admit it, that man is going somewhere. What's more, I'll bet a lot of people know where he's been."

Pamela *didn't* like to admit it, but she thought Belva was probably right. She couldn't imagine anybody ignoring Slade, not even for a few hours.

"You got to make allowances for Pamela," Gaddy was saying to Slade as they walked to the bunkhouse. "She used to be a great go until her Ma sent her to school back East.

46

She could ride better than a boy, but now she insists upon riding sideways. She learned that back East, too. I never saw such a crazy thing in my life. I can't figure out why she doesn't fall off."

"It's no concern of mine how she rides," Slade said, wondering why Gaddy felt it necessary to explain Pamela to him.

"Thought it might explain some of her feeling about guns and fighting. Her mother felt the same way. Wonderful woman, Aunt Mary, in some ways, but you never saw a more closed-minded female. You couldn't tell her anything. She flat refused to listen. Don't know how Uncle Josh put up with it."

"I doubt Pamela would appreciate your telling me any of this," Slade said, hoping to stem the flow of confidences. "She doesn't look like the kind of girl to make excuses for what she does."

"She'd sooner run you off the place than explain," Gaddy said with his ready chuckle, "but she's got a lot of common sense. She won't like it when you disagree with her, but if you can show her your way's best, she'll let you do it."

They were approaching a thick-walled, adobe bunkhouse, in its own way as big as the ranch house. "Looks like you carry a right big crew," Slade remarked.

Inside it looked much like any other bunkhouse. Big, plain, and offering few comforts. The rough, narrow beds were double bunks made of thin mattresses on frames nailed directly to walls covered with layers of pages taken from catalogs. Wish books to pass the empty hours. An oil lantern hung from a rafter, and several chairs sat gathered loosely around a large pot-bellied stove in the center of the room. Pegs on the wall provided a resting place for winter coats and rain slickers, but everything else had to be kept in the cowboy's bedroll under his bunk.

"We used to, but not now. Uncle Josh had a time holding on to this land when he first got here. In fact, if he hadn't found this canyon, he might have been wiped out a couple of times. But things have been pretty easy the last ten years, and he just let the numbers drop off. But now we got trouble again."

"I didn't see any signs on the way in," Slade remarked. "Things seem pretty quiet around here."

"That's the only reason Uncle Josh went off and left Pamela alone. Mind you, Dave tried to talk him out of it, but Uncle Josh is sure nothing is going to happen until the fall roundup. There's men trying to muscle in on his land," Gaddy explained. "This valley carries no more than half our herds. The rest are on the desert this side of the river. Uncle Josh ain't greedy, and he never tried to run too many cattle on the land. It's stayed good all these years."

"So what's the trouble now?"

"Several new ranchers have brought herds in the last couple of years. They've overgrazed until they've just about ruined the rest of the range. Now they're pressing Uncle Josh from all sides, the old ones and the newcomers. Our boys spend all their time just keeping strays on the other side of the river. But we can't do it much longer without more men."

"The ones Pamela's father plans to hire in Santa Fe?"

"Yeah, but he'd better get back soon."

"What about this place?" Slade asked.

"There's no threat to the valley. A single rider could get in over the mountains, but the only way to bring a herd in is the way you came in. Uncle Josh says it won't come to a fight, not after he has the extra hands. Things aren't like they were twenty years ago. People can't just come in and take a man's land."

"What's the point in telling me about your troubles?" Slade asked. "I'll be gone in a few days."

"How? You can't buy a horse."

"I have money."

"But Pamela said . . ."

"Your cousin has a tendency to jump to conclusions. I can

48

pay for what I want. Now unless there's something else I need to know, I'll turn in. I'm bushed."

"I've half a mind to ride out and see what happened to Dave."

"Don't you think you ought to stay here?" Slade asked casually. He didn't want anybody to know where he was, and if Gaddy went to find Dave, he was bound to tell him about their guest. If anybody came to the ranch to check on him, they might recognize him.

"Why?"

"To protect your cousin. You don't know anything about me. I could be meaning to rob the place. Pamela had enough silver on the table for me to live on for years."

"It'd take a wagon to carry away all the silver in that house," Gaddy said. "Besides, Pamela would shoot you if she caught you stealing anything of hers."

"Without a gun?"

"Cousin Pamela may try to be like her Ma, but there's a lot of her Pa in her too. She can shoot better then any woman in Arizona. Until she went off to Baltimore, you never saw her outside the house without her rifle."

That disclosure surprised Slade so much he almost forgot the real problem. A contradiction always intrigued him, and Pamela White seemed to be bristling with them.

"It would be the gentlemanly thing for you to stay. Besides, if your cousin is all that good with a rifle, you might have to protect me."

Gaddy laughed. "Oh, all right. Dave probably wouldn't want me around anyway."

Slade thought the boy looked disappointed at not going to the camp. At the same time, he seemed a little relieved. Slade wondered why. He seemed like a nice enough kid. Maybe he had a secret. Why not? Everybody else seemed to have one.

"You really riding out in a day or two?" Gaddy asked after the lights were out.

"Sure. Why not?"

49

"I don't know. I sorta thought you might want to stay, at least for a while."

"Why?"

"This is a good place. A man might as well work here as in California."

"I'm not looking to settle down just yet."

Then why did he leave Texas? True, he hadn't met Pamela then and maybe his dreams hadn't crystallized with their present painful clarity, but didn't he want to find some place he could settle, whether it be here, California, or Montana?

"You'll have to stop someday," Gaddy said. "Why not here?"

"I don't think your cousin approves of me," Slade answered.

"Maybe not, but there's big trouble brewing," Gaddy said with unexpected seriousness. "You wouldn't cut out in the middle of a fight, would you?"

"Don't make me into somebody I'm not," Slade said. "I'm not a man to run, but I don't see trouble here. And even if there were, it's not my fight. Nobody's asked me to jump in."

"I'm asking you."

Slade smiled. Surprising how the dark could change a teenager busting his britches to become a man into a kid looking for something to hold on to. He wondered if he had ever been like that.

"I don't imagine Mr. White is going to allow a fifteen-year-old boy to do his hiring."

"I'm sixteen," Gaddy said indignantly, "and Pamela's already offered to let you work to pay for your horse. I'm just asking you to stay on, that's all."

"You'd better talk it over with your cousin before you start inviting desert bums to take up permanent residence in her bunkhouse. I get the feeling she might object."

"Not in your case. She likes you."

"She just feels sorry for me."

"No, she doesn't," Gaddy insisted. "I don't mean to talk

50

against Pamela, she's a good one for all her persnickety ways, but I never saw her give the time of day to a stranger, particularly one who looks as down on his luck as you. Her Ma taught her to have some pretty fancy notions about the kind of people she takes up with."

He was tempted to stay. Even without the trouble, they could use an extra hand. But there were other reasons. Lines of tension seemed to run between him and Pamela. Lord, how that woman could get his blood boiling with just a look.

If he did stay, it wouldn't be because he expected anything to come of it; this might be a better place to hide than California. From here he could always take the outlaw trail north to Montana. It would make it even harder for the sheriff to find him.

But Slade didn't want to do that. He had never been an outlaw, he had never had anything to do with them, and he didn't see any reason to let the law push him into doing something he didn't want to do. Not if every marshall in Texas was on his trail.

Maybe he should talk to Gaddy about buying one of the horses. It would be better if he left without seeing Pamela again. He hadn't expected to ever again be so vulnerable to a woman, especially not one so far above him. He could just imagine what Josh White would think if he came back from Santa Fe to find a dust-covered cowboy making eyes at his daughter. He might find an immediate use for those gunslingers Pamela was afraid he had hired.

Slade decided it would be a good idea if he left while he could still choose the time and manner.

51

Chapter 4

Slade woke with a start. A sixth sense warned him of danger. Gaddy's slow breathing fell heavily into the silence, but through the open window he could make out the whisper of clothes against rough leaves. Somebody was outside. People frequently moved around at all hours on a ranch this size, but Slade had never been one to turn his back on unexplained noises. Not when something didn't feel right.

It took him less than a minute to pull on his clothes and slip his feet into Pamela's moccasins. Instinctively he buckled on his guns before tiptoeing to the door. A full moon flooded the canyon with a silvery light. Anybody out there wouldn't find it easy to hide.

The bunkhouse and a barn with an adjoining corral had been built about a hundred yards from the house in the shadow of a ridge which rose more than two hundred feet into the air. The sandy stream bed, littered with stones and overgrown on both sides by mesquite and an occasional cottonwood, twisted its way through the jumble of brush and boulders between the barn and the ridge.

Pausing at the door, Slade closed his eyes and listened again. He hoped he would hear the regular plop-plop of a horse's hooves on the hard-packed yard or the steady shuffle of a man walking openly toward the bunkhouse. Instead he heard the stealthy whisper of a man's clothes as they rubbed against the brush and the occasional clink of shod hoof on stone.

Someone didn't want his presence known.

Slade reminded himself that checking on night visitors was none of his business, that he was a stranger here, but his instincts told him anyone coming up the creek was an enemy. But he had to be careful. He didn't know any of the men who worked for Josh White, and he doubted Pamela would forgive him for shooting one of her hands, even by mistake.

Being careful to keep in the shadows, Slade slipped out the door and around the corner of the bunkhouse. No sound of heels on stone or cloth against wood betrayed his presence. The whispers were loud enough for him to hear them now. There were two of them, and they were coming toward him. He felt an unexpected sigh of relief. Whoever they were, they weren't headed for the house. At least Pamela was safe.

Slade absentmindedly let his hand rest on the handle of his gun.

You said you wanted to get away from guns, he told himself, yet you reach for one at the first sign of trouble. Slade felt beads of perspiration break out on his forehead. In order to be free of guns, he had to learn to take care of trouble without them. And he wouldn't learn by reaching for his gun before he even knew who, or what, was out there.

Slade shivered. He wore no shirt, and without the warmth of the sun, the night was cold. He dropped to a crouch and moved toward the sounds. He could hear them clearly now. They were bringing their horses through the brush toward the barn. He couldn't understand their words, but he knew they weren't Bar Double-B hands coming in from the night camp. They were here to cause trouble, and they needed their horses to make a quick getaway.

Once again Slade's hand found the handle of his gun. He had promised Pamela not to wear them at the ranch. What would she do if he broke his promise the first night?

He cursed silently. Did he intend to subordinate principle, the ambitions of a lifetime, to an insane hope Pamela White would think kindly of him? If he did, he was an utter fool who deserved to be shot to ribbons. Every instinct told him those men were dangerous, that they would kill him if they got the chance, that only a madman would leave himself defenseless because of a woman.

But he did it anyway.

Consciously he forced himself to remove his hand from his gun. Having decided to depend on his brain, Slade knew he couldn't wait for the intruders to make the first move. He had to surprise them before they were ready; he had to draw them out of the brush.

"You boys coming in,"—Slade spoke as casually as he could—"or you going to play in the creek all night?"

The moment Slade opened his mouth, two things happened. First, a point of fire pierced the night and one of the men threw a lighted torch at the hay-filled barn. It fell short. In the same instant, a gun flashed, an explosion shattered the silence, and a searing pain burned Slade's left arm.

He had been shot.

In the split second that followed, Slade drew his own gun and fired three shots, the first directly on center and the others a little to either side of the flash. He heard the soft thud of a bullet encountering flesh followed by a startled whiny and a furious curse. He had hit his target. But before he could congratulate himself on his success, a second torch was lighted and sent arching through the air toward the barn.

Slade's next two shots shattered the torch in mid air and showered sparks in all directions. Three bullets crashed into the log wall of the bunkhouse right behind him. Seconds later he heard the sound of pounding hooves as the arsonists galloped away.

"There's water in the trough between the barn and the

corral," Gaddy called out as he raced across the yard to the barn. "I hope to God it's full." His skinny body clothed only in his long underwear, Gaddy resembled a strange, gangly ghostly figure, but the hungry flames left no time for dressing. Slade's shots had prevented the torch from reaching the barn, but the shower of sparks had ignited the dry hay. If the flames took hold, they'd lose the barn.

His injured feet and shoulder forgotten, Slade ran after Gaddy. Behind them, lights came on in the ranch house. Soon they would have help.

The flames raced over the loose hay and straw scattered about the barn, but they hadn't reached the baled hay stacked in the loft yet. The fire would have to eat through the timbers before it could climb that high.

"Wet down the hay," Slade called to Gaddy. "I'll go after the flames." Almost unbearable pain shot through Slade's shoulder when he picked up the bucket, but he gritted his teeth, filled the bucket with water, and threw it on the burning straw. The injury cut his strength and spoiled his aim, but he went back for a second bucket.

He and Gaddy worked as rapidly as they could, but they would have lost the battle if Pamela hadn't arrived quickly.

"Get on the pump!" he shouted. "The water's low in the trough." Could she pump water as fast as they used it up?

They worked without talking, concentrating on their tasks, conserving their energy, each aware of what they faced. Slade was sure no one thought of the screaming horses that threatened to break down the corral fence or the escaped arsonists. Nothing mattered except the fire.

When the last tongue of flame had been doused, Slade stole a look at Pamela. She wore a lace-trimmed bathrobe over her nightgown and a pair of pink slippers on her feet. Her hair fell over her shoulders almost concealing a face flushed from excitement and exertion. She looked as perfectly turned out as she had at dinner that evening. My God, he thought to himself. She doesn't even get mussed when she puts out fires!

She was incredibly beautiful, but something about her perfection chilled the desire even as Slade felt it surge through his loins. It was almost as though she wasn't entirely human. In the pale white glow of the moonlight she looked unreal, like a huge beautiful doll.

Slade shivered.

"What happened?" Belva asked, hurrying up. The Bagshots' cabin lay further up the valley along the stream bed. Because her size slowed her down, she had arrived too late to be of any help. "I heard enough gunshots to cripple half of Arizona. Then I saw the barn on fire."

"Somebody was coming up the creek," Slade explained. "It woke me up."

"You're wearing guns," Pamela said. She didn't know why she noticed them when Slade was standing before her naked to the waist, his abdomen heaving from his exertions. She was mesmerized by the cords of powerful muscles that played across his stomach. A strange feeling akin to nausea spiraled out from her middle making her feel weak and light-headed. "Were those your shots?" she asked in a breathy voice.

"For Christssake, Pamela!" Gaddy exclaimed. "The man's just saved your barn from being burned to the ground."

"She has a right to know, especially after I promised to hang them up," Slade said. "I picked them up without thinking, a matter of habit, but I wouldn't have left the bunkhouse without them. With all this talk of trouble, I couldn't know what I might be getting myself into."

"But I told you it was perfectly safe here." But that didn't make sense now, did it?

Slade glanced expressively at the still-smoldering barn. "I called out, just in case it was some of your boys. You'll find their answer embedded in the walls of the bunkhouse. I shot at the torches, but the sparks started the fire."

56

"He hit them while they were in the air," Gaddy exclaimed. "I wouldn't have believed it if I hadn't seen it myself."

"Did you shoot anybody?" Belva asked.

"They both rode away."

"How do you know there were two?" Pamela asked.

"I heard them whispering."

"I don't know about you, but I could use a cup of coffee," Belva said, interrupting the tense exchange. "I'll have some ready in a jiffy."

They both turned toward Belva when she spoke, and the moonlight fell on Slade's shoulder.

"You've been hurt!" Pamela exclaimed. She automatically reached out to touch him, but he jumped back as though the fire in her fingertips burned hotter than the pain from the bullet.

"It's nothing much," he protested. "Just a flesh wound."

But Pamela didn't see it like that. The streaks of blood and torn flesh were an accusation against her. He might not have been hurt if he hadn't promised not to use his guns.

"Come up to the house so I can take care of it. This is precisely why I don't approve of guns." Caught between her disapproval of guns and her concern over his wound, her indecision amused Slade.

"I don't like them either, especially when they're being used on me. Unfortunately your visitors seem to believe in them rather strongly."

Pamela refused to be drawn into an argument she couldn't win. Nothing could change her feeling about guns, but what would have happened if Slade had been unarmed? What could have happened to all of them? At the very least they would have lost the barn.

But that didn't concern her at the moment. She felt only relief that Slade was safe. Why? Certainly a man's life was more important than a barn full of hay, but wasn't the hay more valuable to her than this man? He could disappear tomorrow just as though he never existed. She had known from the moment she sat down on the porch to wait for him he wouldn't stay, but he hadn't been out of her thoughts for as much as five minutes since he arrived.

The way he dominated her thoughts scared her. She felt this overwhelming compulsion to know everything about him. She had never felt this way before, and she didn't like it.

All the more reason to go back to Baltimore, Pamela thought to herself. Then she wouldn't have to worry about Slade Morgan. Besides, people there understood how to live peacefully with each other. They didn't go around stealing land or burning barns. They most certainly didn't go around shooting each other.

"Sit down and let me look at your shoulder," Pamela said as soon as they reached the kitchen.

"Are you the official nurse of the Bar Double-B?" Slade asked, his eyes unsettling in their intensity.

"I see the men's wounds are taken care of if that's what you mean," Pamela said rather stiffly. "That's more than a flesh wound."

"It went right through the muscle," Belva added. "You're lucky it missed the bone."

"And to think he hit one of the men anyway," Gaddy said.

"What?" Pamela demanded, whirling to face her cousin.

Slade did his best to warn Gaddy not to say anything, but the boy was so awed by Slade's shooting he couldn't wait to tell Pamela what he had found.

"After you left, I went over to where those guys must have been."

"I hope you didn't destroy the hoof prints," Slade said, hoping to forestall Gaddy. "Maybe we can identify their horses if we see them again."

"I didn't," Gaddy assured him, impatient to get on with his story. "I found traces of blood in the sand. They rode out, but I'll bet you one of them didn't do it under his own power."

When Pamela returned her gaze to Slade, he saw an expression in her eyes that made his heart grow heavy in his chest. It wasn't hate. It wasn't even anger. He saw abhorrence, as though he were some kind of monster. On the whole, Slade would have preferred hate or anger. He had seen revulsion, disgust, even loathing in his mother's face. It had flashed from Trish's eyes as well.

But he didn't deserve it now any more than he had deserved it then. Sure, he had put on his guns after he had promised not to, but he had tried not to use them. Like a fool, he had spoken up and betrayed his position. He might as well have stepped out in the moonlight to give them a better target.

When you looked at it in a certain way, Pamela was responsible for his being shot. If he'd done things his way, he would have circled around behind and fired the second he saw them light that torch. Then the barn wouldn't be a smoldering mess, he wouldn't be sitting here with a hole in his shoulder, and the foolish woman wouldn't be glaring at him like he had arranged the whole thing on purpose.

It wasn't his fault no one had thought to place a guard at night. It wasn't his fault that someone had a grudge against her father. And it certainly wasn't his fault they had tried to burn her barn. But you couldn't tell that from looking at her now. She looked mad enough to use a shotgun herself.

And there she stood, still looking like a fashion plate out of a ladies' magazine and holding him responsible for the outcome of a situation not of his making. She hadn't even thanked him for saving her barn.

And that made Slade mad.

"What's really going on around here?" he demanded, the ragged edge of his temper showing in his voice. "It didn't matter before, but when anybody shoots at me, I want to know why."

"I told you," Pamela said. "Too many cows on the range."

"This wasn't about too many cows. There's a lot more to it

than that, and I mean to find out what it is."

"I have no idea why they wanted to burn the barn," Pamela said, too shaken by her reaction to Slade and the shooting to be able to relax the rigidity of her expression. The attempt to burn the barn didn't help either. Until now, all this talk about cattle and barbed wire and extra hands had been just that, talk. But now it was much too real.

"Someone ought to tell Mr. Bagshot what's happened," Slade suggested.

"I'll go," Gaddy offered. Now that he had news to tell, Slade noticed none of his previous reluctance.

"You'll need some breakfast," Belva said.

"That'll take too long," Gaddy protested, his excitement apparent to everyone. "I can eat with the boys, but you could wrap up one of your sausages. Angus can't cook anything like you do."

"We don't keep you just so you can eat, you young wastrel," Belva admonished. "Now get going. If Dave finds out we had a barn burning and you didn't come tell him straight away, he'll skin you alive."

"Daybreak will be soon enough," Pamela decided. "I don't want you riding about at night," she explained when Gaddy looked ready to argue. "Besides, someone has to watch the barn to make sure the fire's completely out. Mr. Morgan has had a very eventful day. I think he ought to go to bed."

It wasn't a severe speech, but it had so much the feel of a boss speaking to her employees that it made everyone feel uncomfortable. Gaddy slipped out the back door and Belva busied herself at the stove.

"There, it's all cleaned up now," Pamela said as she handed Belva the pan of bloody water. "Come with me to Dad's office. That's where I keep my medicines."

Slade fell in love with Josh White's office. For the first time since he'd stepped into the house he didn't feel out of place. A huge stone fireplace dominated one wall. The weather was too warm for a fire now, but the soot of age and use indicated that Arizona winters often made a fire desirable. A bookcase spilling over with books almost entirely covered a second wall. A third wall contained an enormous window that during the day afforded a view from the ranch house of the valley to where it opened onto the desert floor. The last wall held another window that provided an equally unobstructed view of the moonlit valley floor as it inclined and disappeared into the mountains that rose behind the house.

The room itself was quite large, and in its center stood an enormous table which served as Josh White's desk. Other furnishings included several deep, leather-covered chairs, hand-carved wooden tables, and rag rugs spread two and three deep over the flagstone floor. Several paintings and countless mementoes, presumably of Josh White's years in Arizona, hung on the whitewashed walls.

"This is a beautiful house," Slade told Pamela as she directed him to sit in the light of an oil lantern so she could begin to bandage his wound. "No wonder your father is so determined to protect it. This is a place worth fighting for."

"Then you'll stay on." It sounded like an assumption rather than a question, and it angered Slade.

"No."

"What?" Her gaze riveted on him, disbelief and consternation just two of her conflicting emotions.

"I said no."

"What's wrong with working for us?"

"I don't want a permanent job. And I don't want to work for anybody."

Odd how feeling vulnerable moments ago could make her feel betrayed now. She had no real reason to take Slade's refusal as a personal affront, but she did. She had no reason to care whether he stayed or left, but she did. Nor did courtesy require that she clean a wound he got from using guns after he had promised he would hang them up, but she did. In fact, she could conceive of no reason for her to concern herself with him in the least.

But she did.

"I'm grateful to you for keeping those men from burning our barn. That alone is of sufficient worth for me to give you the horse you need."

Slade stiffened. She didn't need to talk to him like he was some lower form of life. She didn't sound exactly condescending, but he didn't know what else to call it. It certainly seemed close enough. His anger boiled over.

"I didn't ask you to give me a horse. I have more than enough money to pay for it. Money I *earned,*" he added when he saw surprise fill her eyes. "I don't ask you to thank me for saving your barn. Those men could have set fire to the bunkhouse just as easily. However, I do thank you for taking care of my feet and my shoulder. It's not something I could have done myself, at least, not half so well. I'll leave as soon as we can settle on a horse."

"I didn't ask you to leave," Pamela said, angrily pulling a bandage around Slade's wound so tightly it caused him to wince and stare at her questioningly. "I'm sorry," she said quickly. "I didn't mean to hurt you, but you made me mad. Why won't you work for us? My father has the best reputation in the territory and the finest ranch. There hasn't been any trouble here in more than five years."

"My leaving has nothing to do with your trouble, Miss White."

"My name is Pamela."

"Okay, Pamela. I'm just passing through. I'm going to California, and I can't do that if I stay here."

"Where are you from, Mr. Morgan?"

Damn! The way she called him *Mr. Morgan* made him feel like curdled milk. It was a form of rejection, an impersonal way of referring to him. People had called him worse and it hadn't bothered him, but from Pamela it hurt. "If I'm going to call you Pamela, you've got to call me Slade."

"Okay, Slade, where are you from?"

"I told you. Texas."

"You didn't get here from the Texas trail, not if you walked those sixty miles." She stared at him. Her words laid down a challenge.

Now how did she know that? Either she had been asking questions about him, or somebody else had. He felt the old uneasiness begin to stir within him. "I am from Texas. I just didn't take the usual route."

"Did you come up from Mexico?"

"Why does it matter where I came from?"

"You came to this ranch asking for help. We gave it. If you're running from something, we have a right to know. I won't do anything to endanger my men."

Here we go again, Slade thought. Why do people always assume if you didn't do a thing the way they do it, you must have something to hide? He could say one thing about the carnival. As long as he kept the customers coming, nobody cared what he did. Maybe he had made a mistake by leaving. No, he didn't want to go back.

"You won't have to worry about *your men* any longer." He started to rise, but Pamela pushed him back down in his seat. After walking through the desert and taking a bullet in his shoulder, he felt too weak to resist.

"If you want to leave now, that's your decision, but you won't set one foot out of here before I've finished with your arm. *Nobody* is going to say I turned you out with a bleeding wound."

That's it, Slade thought cynically. You don't give a damn about me, just what other people will think of you. You ought to fit well in Baltimore.

"Why should you care what anybody says about you?"

"What people think of me is my reputation, the value I have in the eyes of the world. It's what a person sees when they look at me."

"But suppose everything else they see is false? Does that

63

make you the kind of person they say you are?"

"Of course not."

"Then why worry about what they say? You and I both know you've had to fix me up twice. Nobody else needs to know. They're more likely to take advantage of your kindness than praise you for it."

"I'm not looking for praise," Pamela said haughtily, "and I can't agree with you. I've always been taught that a person's reputation, what other people think of you, is extremely important."

"Only if the people doing the thinking are important to you. And sometimes not even then. No person knows all there is to know about another person."

"You're a strange man. Where did you learn to think like that?"

"Don't you mean how did a saddle bum like me ever manage to have a thought that didn't have to do with his basic urges?"

"I didn't say that."

"You might as well have. The way you've treated me since I got here has underscored how little you think of people like me. You're one helluva snob, lady. But don't let it worry you," Slade added caustically when he saw the look of shock on Pamela's face. "You hurry on back to Baltimore, and you won't have to be concerned with me any more than I have to be concerned with you."

But he did care what she thought of him. For the first time in years, somebody else's opinion mattered. He didn't know why it should but, in spite of Pamela's surface coldness and disapproval, she had reached out and touched him. He had felt it. It had been ten years since anyone had wanted to know anything about him. He had to reach back.

A great need had risen up within him; no, it had literally burst forth from some deep chamber where he thought it had been safely contained. His need stemmed from loneliness which had grown into a painful ache over the years. Now,

64

like a parched desert plant in a rainstorm, it thrust out its tentacles toward the promise of nourishment.

"I did come through Mexico, but there's nothing wrong in that," Slade told her. "It just so happens a lot of people like you aren't too anxious to have me around."

"That's not at all what I meant," Pamela hastened to assure him. His calling her a snob had shocked her, but that was nothing compared to the horror she experienced when she realized he was right. Against that, the chance that he hadn't told her the whole truth about himself didn't matter. "I don't dislike having you here, but I'm responsible for the ranch while Dad's gone. I have to be careful whom I hire."

"And that doesn't include saddle bums with no future and a questionable past," Slade finished for her.

Pamela tried to speak, but she was so stunned—the course of the conversation so unexpected—she couldn't think of anything to say.

"Don't feel you have to apologize. I don't think you're even aware of your attitude. You probably can't help it." He stopped, a little ashamed of the harshness of his accusation. It was true, but if he could judge from her reaction, she hadn't done it consciously. Now, seeing her crushed, he experienced a strange kinship with her. "I had the feeling you were almost afraid to touch me," he said with a question in his voice, "as though I would somehow contaminate the perfect little world you have here."

"I . . . You . . ."

"But you did touch me," Slade continued in a softer voice. "Why? You didn't act like a great lady lowering herself to help someone beneath her."

"No."

"Then why? You don't want me here. You don't like me. You don't approve of me."

Pamela struggled to keep her hands steady; she clenched her jaw to keep it from trembling. She had never felt so much like crying and screaming at the same time. She finished her bandaging and straightened up, her face flushed with anger and humiliation. She hadn't actually thought any of the things he accused her of, but she had felt them.

"Don't put words in my mouth," she told him.

"Then don't give me cause," Slade said, rising to his feet, too. Her flash of anger vanquished his momentary tenderness. You're all too anxious to think up excuses for this girl, he told himself. "I'll go as soon as I can saddle a horse. What'll you take for that hammerhead dun I saw in the corral. And a saddle to go with him?"

"You want the dun?" The unexpected request jolted her out of her misery. "That's the meanest horse on the place."

"I'll lay you a bet he's also the best."

"Possibly, but no one will ride him."

"How much?"

Faced with the reality of his departure and the suspicion that her snobbery was driving him away, she was overcome with shame, so overwhelmed she didn't realize at least a small part of her reluctance to see him go had nothing to do with guilt.

"You really shouldn't leave yet," Pamela said abruptly. "Your feet aren't well, and I doubt you'll get very far with that arm. Even a slight jar could start it bleeding again."

"I've taken care of myself for a long time. I'll survive a few blisters and a flesh wound."

Pamela changed her tact. "Are you going to let those men who shot you get away without finding out who they are?" Why did she stand here arguing with him, trying to get him to stay? It would be better if he left. She hadn't had a moment's peace since he arrived. He would only cause more trouble if he stayed.

But she didn't want him to leave. She had never met anyone like him. She felt a tug of attraction despite his lack of polish. Immediately she thought of Frederick and their years together in Baltimore. He had always been her idea of the perfect man. Taller than this cowboy, better looking, richer, and brimming with ambition to make his father's bank the biggest of its kind south of Philadelphia, he had remained her ideal. But despite finishing way behind Frederick in virtually every way, something about Slade wouldn't let her ignore him. He had a kind of presence, an aura, Pamela didn't understand, but she had experienced its powerful effects from the moment she set eyes on him.

Let him leave before you make a fool of yourself, the voice of caution whispered. Whatever it is about him that fascinates you, it's not worth it.

"Thirty dollars," she said. "Ten for the horse and twenty for the saddle."

"He's worth more than that."

"The saddle's used and nobody will ride the horse. I ought to give him to you just to save the cost of feeding him."

"I'll pay," Slade said. He took off his hat and dug two gold coins out of their hiding place in the hat band.

"That's forty dollars," Pamela pointed out.

"The other ten's for food, lodging, and medical care."

"I won't take money for that," Pamela replied, furious over his implied slight of her hospitality. She handed Slade a ten dollar silver piece from her father's drawer, but he refused it.

"Take it or walk out of here without a horse."

"You're one tough lady," Slade said, a reluctant smile lighting his eyes. "Looks like your father knew what he was doing when he left you in charge." He took the proffered ten dollars. "Sorry I can't stay to find out who tried to burn your barn, but your father is bound to return soon."

"I'll manage until he gets back."

"I'm sure you will. And I don't imagine you'll need any help. You'll make some rancher one hell of a wife, if you can find one strong enough to handle you."

"I won't be *handled* by anyone." She hadn't meant to shout at him, but his words were insulting. For a moment longer her anger had the upper hand, then she took a deep breath to calm her racing heart. "Besides, I don't intend to marry a rancher. I'm returning to Baltimore after the round-up."

She hadn't intended to tell him that—it didn't concern him at all—but the startled look of surprise and disapproval made it even worse. She didn't need or want his approval. She admitted she had no right to prejudge him, but by the same token, he had no right to presume to know her motives. He also had no right to look disappointed. Whether she stayed or left wouldn't mean anything to him, not with him in California.

"I'm sure your friends will be sorry to see you go," Slade said after a pause.

"They'll be glad to see me return," Pamela corrected him.

"Oh, it's like that, is it?"

Pamela didn't know why her tongue should suddenly turn into a malevolent force. She hadn't meant it that way, but she couldn't take her words back now. Why couldn't she control her temper around Slade? Why did he make her motives seem suddenly shameful? He had no right to make her wish to go back to Baltimore sound like something distasteful. What was so wonderful about Arizona and its suffocating heat, terrible cold, and constant shortage of water? Nothing here could compare to life in Baltimore or any other eastern city.

It was none of his business what she did or why she did it, and she wouldn't dignify his curiosity by recognizing it.

"I'll have Belva put together some food for you. Come by the kitchen on your way out. You're welcome to stop by if you're back this way. I'm sure my father would like to thank you for saving the barn."

She was dismissing him now, just like a queen dismisses a subject. Well, he would go. There was no reason to stay.

Chapter 5

After Slade left her, Pamela tussled long and hard with her conscience. His accusation hurt her deeply, and she closed the door behind him determined never to let a single thought of him cross her mind again. But no sooner had he gone than her anger began to evaporate. Then her own innate sense of honesty made her examine her actions since he arrived. She had to know if his words were true.

She decided they weren't. She hadn't wanted him here, she admitted that, but once he arrived, she had done her best to make him welcome. Hadn't she taken care of his feet and his shoulder? And with her own hands, too. She hadn't done that for anyone else.

But why had she done it? Her mother had always been careful to preserve a distance between herself and those she considered to be the hired help. And Pamela had always tried to follow her mother's example.

So why did there seem to be no distance between her and Slade? Why had she been determined to see to him herself, even before he set foot on the place? Why did everything he said and did affect her so? Why had she cared for his wounds with her own hands? More importantly, why was she still thinking about him? He had no intention of coming back for the food she offered him.

With sudden decision, Pamela hurried to the kitchen. "Put some supplies together for Mr. Morgan," she said to Belva. "He'll be leaving at daybreak."

Usually she would have stayed to help. She felt a little guilty now that she hadn't, but she wanted to be by herself. She wanted to think, but she was almost afraid to. She was unlikely to appreciate any answer she came up with. And the one she was going to dislike most was the knowledge that Slade Morgan had made a much stronger impression on her than anybody since Frederick.

Of course nobody was like Frederick. He was unique, but there was something rare about Slade, too. There wasn't much about his looks to attract her. True, his grey eyes were wonderfully expressive, especially when they sparkled with amusement, but he wore a beard and she hated beards with a passion. True, he was tall, slim, and well-muscled, but he still looked like a dusty saddle tramp. He seemed to be intelligent, but he had no ambition to be anything more than an ordinary cowhand. Worst of all, he wore guns, and if Pamela knew anything about his kind of man, he had used them many times. He had used them just last night, and she was certain he would use them again.

Was it possible to separate the essence of a man from the things he did? Wasn't his life largely a series of actions which he made by choice and thus the result of what he wanted to do?

Maybe not.

She thought of her mother. She'd never been able to control the course of her life. Pamela felt the same way sometimes, but she couldn't imagine Slade being helpless. There was something about him which conveyed the feeling that he would always be in control of his destiny.

Pamela got to her feet. There was no point in devoting any more time to this fruitless exercise. Slade Morgan was going to ride out of her life about fifteen minutes after sunrise, and she knew it was the best possible thing that could happen. If he had some mysterious attraction that wouldn't let her stop thinking about him, especially when she didn't want to, then she wasn't safe. The sooner he left the better.

But she knew she would never forget the fire that flamed between them.

"You couldn't talk him into working for you?" Belva asked when Pamela returned to the kitchen. "We sure could use a man like him around here."

"We'll get along," Pamela said, slightly irritated that Belva should be so anxious to have Slade stay, especially after she had pointed out he couldn't have come from where he said he did. "Dad will be back soon with the extra men."

"I always say a bird in the hand is worth two in the bush," Belva continued obstinately.

"I don't think we ever had him in hand," Pamela replied, half to herself. "I don't think anybody ever did."

"I thought he liked it here." Pamela was sure Belva meant more than she was saying.

"Maybe he did, but not enough to stay. Now go on back to bed. I'll see he gets this before he leaves."

"You need your rest, too."

"I'll catch a nap later. I ought to be here when he leaves. Anyway, I'm not sleepy now."

Belva regarded her young mistress skeptically, but she didn't say any more. There really wasn't anything to say that Pamela didn't already know.

Belva still made no comment when she returned to the kitchen hours later to find Pamela sitting by the window, a cup of coffee at her elbow, her abstracted gaze directed somewhere between the bunkhouse and the corral. Their day proceeded much as it always did, but by the time Slade emerged from the bunkhouse and headed for the corral, Belva had been wishing him gone hours earlier. Pamela never said a word, but Belva could see the strain in her eyes and hear it in her voice. She knew it wouldn't ease until he was gone.

Belva barely suppressed a sigh. Pamela wouldn't be in very good spirits for the next few days, but if she must be disappointed—and it had to happen—then the sooner the better.

By the time Slade got back to bed, it was nearly four o'clock. His wound made him feel weak and extremely tired. He had intended to get up at dawn, but he didn't wake until mid-morning. Two more hours passed before he completed his preparations for leaving.

The hammerhead dun put up a good fight, far too much of one for a man with a wounded shoulder, but Slade didn't feel any triumph as he prepared to climb into the saddle. On the contrary, he experienced a great sense of loss. Leaving Texas had been easier. What could have gotten such a hold on him in less than twenty-four hours?

He looked past the house to the lush, green land rising to meet the mountains in the distance and the towering ridges that protected the valley from the drying winds and sand storms. He felt the cool quiet of the spring morning settle all around him, and he had all the reason he needed to want to remain. But he knew his reluctance to leave had its real roots inside the ranch house. He didn't want to leave Pamela White.

Slade gave vent to an audible snort of frustration. He couldn't change the way he felt, but he hadn't expected his brain to let him down just because his heart chose to act like it belonged to an impetuous adolescent instead of a man of twenty-eight. He would ride out immediately, and in a few days everything would be back to normal. The passing of a dream never came easy, but it hurt less if you never had any hope to begin with.

He didn't intend to take advantage of Pamela's offer of food. He would go back and pick up his own saddle and abandoned supplies. If they were gone, he would kill an antelope or stop at the next ranch, anything to get him off the Bar Double-B as quickly as possible.

He knew if he gave himself half a chance, he could fall in love with Pamela. About the only thing more stupid would have been to stay in Texas and try to convince a jury he had been set up.

Yet he couldn't help but think about what might have been if things had been different? *If!* His life had been a series of sharp turns, any one of which could have changed everything else. *If* his father hadn't taken to drink, *if* his mother hadn't deserted them, *if* Trish hadn't broken their engagement, *if* the Whittakers hadn't stolen his horse, *if* . . . well, after that it didn't much matter what happened. It looked like Fate didn't intend for the Bar Double-B to lay at the end of his trail.

With a smothered curse, Slade started to swing up into the saddle. He paused, then he heard a door at the ranch house slam; Pamela had come out of the house and was heading toward him with a package under her arm. He relaxed against the side of his horse but stepped aside just in time to keep the dun from taking a bite out of his good shoulder. He smiled. That girl knew he hadn't meant to come up to the house, so she decided to bring the food out to him. He wondered how long she'd been watching at the window.

You had to give it to her. She could out-think just about any man he ever knew, and so far she had done a right fair job outmaneuvering him. He had already started to move in her direction when the sound of an approaching horse halted him in his tracks. He didn't know why he pulled the hammerhead back around the corner of the barn, but a sixth sense warned him it might be a good idea if he didn't advertise his presence just yet.

Pamela had just stepped outside when she saw the approaching rider. It took only a second to recognize Mongo Shepherd, the biggest of the new ranchers to have moved into the area. Pamela groaned. At this moment she would rather see almost anybody else.

Mongo had arrived in Arizona a year earlier with a fat bankroll, a crew ramrodded by a pugnacious foreman, and enough cattle to overgraze the whole area. Everybody told him to keep going, that he could find plenty of open land farther west or north, but Mongo had taken one look at Pamela White and decided he would stop here. He got a look at Josh White's valley and decided he had found exactly what he had been looking for.

Mongo was a big man in every way, and he won acceptance from the other ranchers almost immediately. Eastern born and reared with polished manners and elegant dress, Mongo's good looks and his tendency to see himself as a white knight in a savage land had all the women panting after him in no time at all. All except Pamela. But Mongo had set his sights on Pamela, and he immediately began a campaign to win her hand. At first he found an ally in Pamela's father. Josh White knew several men he liked better than Mongo, but he wanted to keep Pamela in Arizona, and he thought the best way to do that would be to marry her to a rancher.

By the time he decided he didn't want Mongo for a son-in-law, Pamela knew she didn't want him for a husband. In fact, Mongo seemed to be the only person who hadn't figured that out. He treated her polite refusals as a coy invitation to continue his visits and increase his flattery. From the gossip in town, Pamela knew the other ladies had decided Mongo persisted in this hopeless pursuit because he was too arrogant to believe anybody would turn down the chance to become his wife. The men had decided he was just plain dense.

Pamela didn't want to see Mongo on this particular morning and would have slipped out of sight if she could. Even less did she want to explain her reasons for giving food to a drifting cowboy.

Mongo waved to her the minute she stepped out of the house. She waved back and started toward the bunkhouse with quickened steps. If she didn't invite him in, maybe he wouldn't stay long.

She had nearly reached the bunkhouse when he came abreast of her. But even before he opened his mouth, she wished she had waited at the house. It was virtually impossible to miss seeing the charred barn timbers from where they stood.

"Good morning," Pamela said before her visitor could speak. "What brings you over this way?" She positioned herself to face the barn forcing Mongo to stand with his back to it.

"You," the big man said to her in his deep, rumbling voice. He spoke with a careful deliberation that always irritated Pamela but never more so than this morning. "I've been inspecting my herds, and I couldn't go back to town without coming by to see you and your father."

"Dad's not here. I'm afraid you've wasted a trip."

"It's never wasted when I can see you."

Pamela had never been able to decide why nearly every word this man spoke annoyed her. When she dreamed of a lover, she dreamed of a man who spoke just such words. When she visualized him riding across the desert to rescue her from the wilds of Arizona, he rode just such a flashy chestnut and wore the same kind of dark suit trimmed in white. But even though Mongo Shepherd came from Boston, rode a horse with Morgan blood, dressed like an Eastern tenderfoot, and courted her with flowery phrases, Pamela didn't love him.

"It's nice of you to drop by, but everybody is away from

the house right now. I'm rather busy."

"You're always busy. What is it today? You can't be holding one of your soul-saving meetings if there's nobody here."

"My mother instituted those gatherings to help instill in our men a sense of right and wrong, of justice, of the importance of what they do in this life," Pamela said, her words clipped. "And I'd appreciate it if you didn't mock her work."

"But you misunderstood me," Mongo protested quickly. "I admire what you're doing. In fact, I wanted to ask if my men might come as well. It would do them good to listen to some well-chosen words from someone as lovely as you. I will guarantee their close attention."

"I would love to include your men," Pamela said hoping God wouldn't punish her for lying, "but there's not enough room."

"But your crew is small."

"Dad has hired more men, but I'll tell him you're interested."

Pamela had been so busy being irritated with herself for telling Mongo about her father's new hands, she barely caught the momentary flash of surprise and then anger that blazed in his eyes. But a moment later his face was again composed into a look of deep concern.

"I'll make it a point to speak to Dave. Will he lead your crew on roundup?"

"If Dad doesn't do it himself. Now if you'll excuse me, I've got to deliver this food."

"Would I be too bold if I asked who it's for?"

Yes, you would, Pamela thought to herself, but aloud she said, "It's just something for a drifter riding the grub line."

"Do you provision every idle cowhand who wanders through?"

"No," Pamela said, irritated at having to tell Mongo about

76

the fire after all, "but he saved our barn from being burned last night. It's the least I can do for him."

"Your barn was burned!" Mongo exclaimed. While he stared in shock at the charred side of the barn, Pamela hurried inside the bunkhouse. But she found no one inside, and all of Slade's things had disappeared.

He was gone.

She didn't understand why she should feel so disappointed.

"Don't be a silly little fool," she told herself, too angry to realize, or care, that she spoke aloud. You knew he meant to slip away without coming up to the house again. He just managed to get away before you caught him.

"Is he gone?" Mongo asked when she came out still carrying the package.

"Yes. I thought he would be. He was rather self-effacing, not the kind to draw attention to himself. I'm afraid the size of the house and my rather formal way of treating people made him feel uncomfortable."

"How did the fire start?" Mongo asked. "We didn't see any lightning over at the camp." He had no interest in anonymous cowboys.

"It wasn't lightning," Pamela told him, resignation sounding in her voice. "Two men stole up the canyon last night and set the fire. If Slade hadn't heard them, we wouldn't have awakened in time to put it out."

"How much damage did it do?" Mongo asked as he walked toward the barn. Pamela had to follow.

"Not much. We lost some hay, but the fire only scorched the barn."

"This wouldn't have happened if you were married to me," Mongo said, rounding on Pamela. "I would surround the place with men. An army wouldn't be able to get through. When are you going to let me announce our engagement?"

"Mongo, I've told you several times. I don't want to marry

77

a rancher, and I don't want to live in Arizona. I'm still planning to go back to Baltimore as soon as Dad sells the herd."

"I know how you feel," Mongo said, changing his position to one he thought Pamela would favor. "There are times when I can hardly wait to get back to Boston. I especially miss the libraries and the concerts. But Arizona isn't so bad, at least it won't be in a few years when more people move out here. Give them a little time, and they'll be as genteel as anybody you can find in Boston."

"It's not that . . ."

"I know. It's the coarseness of their manner you don't like. And that's as it should be. I wouldn't expect any woman I'd ask to be my wife to concern herself with the hands, but I promise you will live in more luxury, be more pampered than you could be in Baltimore," Mongo said as he removed the package of food from Pamela's hands. "You know I'm rich, and I don't mind spending my money. Nothing is too good for you. You'll have all the servants you want, the biggest ranch house this side of Texas, and we can go to San Francisco or New Orleans as often as you like."

"Please, Mongo. . . ."

"There's nothing I wouldn't give you, Pamela."

"I'm sure you would. And I just might stay in Arizona if I loved you, even without the big house and servants, but I don't love you. I never have, and I don't think I ever will."

Slade knew he shouldn't be listening to Pamela, he especially shouldn't be listening to Mango's impassioned attempts to convince Pamela of his devotion, but he couldn't move without being seen.

At least he no longer suffered from the harsh pangs of jealousy which had attacked him when Pamela greeted Mongo with easy familiarity. He had never felt anything like that in his life, not a jealousy that made his stomach turn somersaults. Mongo represented everything he could never be. You only had to look at him to know he enjoyed the advantages of wealth, education, and being comfortable in the most exclusive social circles. He was also taller than Slade, expensively dressed, and quite handsome. Slade felt certain this was exactly the kind of man Pamela wanted to marry.

He could hardly believe his ears when Pamela said she didn't love him. He found it even harder to accept her statement that she might stay in Arizona for the man she loved.

Did that mean she might be able to love him?

Slade shook his head *hard* to rid it of the insanity which seemed to be invading his brain. He had first set eyes on this woman less than twenty-four hours ago. She hadn't said or done anything to suggest she had any interest in him other than ordinary curiosity, possibly combined with loneliness and boredom.

You're as dumb as your father, Slade told himself angrily. That hapless man had been so overcome by the loveliness and cultivated manners of Miss Sara Anne Billingsworth he couldn't see past her luminous eyes and slender curves to the hide-bound intellect and ingrained prejudice that pervaded every sinew in her body. He never even suspected his pleasures in life would be redefined as sins or that, as his wife, she would disapprove of virtually everything he did.

You have no excuse this time Slade said to himself. This woman has told you how she feels about you.

But lecturing himself didn't seem to have any effect on his heart. It kept right on beating a little faster. His breathing became shallow, and he almost forgot the pain in his shoulder.

"But you shouldn't be left to run this place by yourself," Mongo was saying. "You should never be left alone." By now he had set Pamela's package on the ground and taken both her hands in his.

"Mongo, I've already told you. . . ."

"I know you say you don't love me, but you do like me.

How do you know that isn't enough, at least at first? And you will come to love me, Pamela. I swear I will do everything in my power to make you love me."

Pamela attempted to evade his embrace, but Mongo would not be denied.

"You know I can't be around you without being overcome with your loveliness. I want to hold you in my arms and kiss you until you forget all about Baltimore."

"Mongo, please. . . ."

"Don't push me away. Just give me a chance."

"Stop it, Mongo. Let me go." Pamela struggled to avoid his lips. He seemed determined to kiss her despite her objections. In desperation, she pushed his face away.

Before Mongo could mount a second attack, Slade stepped around the corner of the barn.

"The lady has asked you to leave. Get on your horse and ride."

Mongo spun around to face this unknown man. "Who the hell are you?" he demanded.

"Slade," Pamela said, almost under her breath. For a moment it didn't matter that Mongo still held her in his arms. Slade hadn't left her.

"It doesn't matter. You're annoying Miss White, and that does matter."

"This is Slade Morgan," Pamela said, trying hard to keep a foolish grin off her face as she slipped from Mongo's slackened embrace. "He saved my barn. He even managed to shoot one of the intruders. In the dark, too," she added nervously.

The two men faced each other like snarling, battle-ready beasts.

"A gunslinger, eh?" Mongo growled. "This is peaceful country, mister. We don't want the likes of you around. Take those provisions and get on your horse."

"That's what I had in mind," Slade replied, his eyes hard

and cold. "What say we ride out together?"

"I've got business with Miss White."

"Sounds to me like your business is finished."

"Who do you think you are to be telling me what to do? Do you know who I am?"

"I don't need your name to know you're a loud-mouthed braggart who's not worth five minutes of her time. Get on your horse and ride out *now.*"

Mongo eyed the tied-down guns cautiously. "I know your type. Give them a pair of guns and they bark like real bad men. Take the guns away and they whine like the mongrels they are."

"You got an itch to test that theory?"

"You taking off those guns?"

In answer, Slade undid his gun belt and let it drop to the ground. "I'm still telling you to get out," he said.

"You'll be lucky if I don't beat you to death," Mongo snapped, his hard hands gathered into tight fists.

Pamela stood speechless, unable to believe that Slade had come to her rescue in such a dramatic fashion, horrified to realize they were about to fight because of her. Abruptly what had seemed somewhat thrilling had turned into something ugly and vicious.

"No," she suddenly shouted. "Stop."

"He asked for it," Mongo said, so furious he didn't see the shock and revulsion in Pamela's eyes. "No saddle bum tries to order me around and gets away with it."

"But you can't fight him," Pamela insisted. "He's hurt."

"He should have thought of that before he stepped from behind that barn."

Pamela's expression of shocked horror finally registered on Mongo's rage-clouded brain, and he realized she was shocked and horrified *at him,* not this unkept cowpuncher. With superhuman effort, he reined in his anger.

"Of course, I'll let him go if he apologizes. I could forgive a man almost anything as long as he thought he was defending you."

For the first time in her life Pamela thought a flowery compliment was going to make her sick.

"I'd have stepped from behind that barn if it took my last breath," Slade told him, scorn evident in the cadence of his voice. "Your kind is worse than a rabid dog. You go about hiding behind your fancy clothes and smooth talk, but you're rotten all the way through. You destroy everything you get your hands on."

"I'll kill you!" Mongo roared and charged Slade.

"Stop, both of you!" Pamela cried, but apparently neither man heard her.

Stunned and helpless, she watched the two men lunge at each other. She wasn't surprised at Slade. He had already shown himself ready to fight. But Mongo was from Boston. He knew she didn't approve of violence, yet he completely ignored her.

But if the fight upset her image of Mongo, it also shook her faith in her own ability to influence the actions of the men around her. She had never controlled her father, and she obviously had no power over Slade; apparently she had none over Mongo when he got angry.

As Pamela watched in growing horror, Slade sidestepped Mongo's rush and drove his right fist deep into the big man's stomach. Mongo staggered, the breath nearly knocked out of him, but he was tough for all his fancy clothes. He was also smart.

He couldn't move as quickly as Slade and received several punishing blows in his attempts to bulldoze his opponent, but in less than a minute he seemed to realize all Slade's punches were delivered with his right fist. He immediately went after Slade's left shoulder. But try as he might, he couldn't get his hands on Slade.

His feet might be covered in blisters, but Pamela couldn't

tell it to see him move. He danced around like a trained professional, landing punches with skill and precision, always keeping Mongo off balance. Once Mongo moved for an opening, but he had no sooner rushed in than Slade's suspect left fist smashed Mongo in the face and broke his nose.

Mongo went crazy.

Slade was moving awkwardly now; his feet obviously hurt him. Mongo aimed a blow at Slade's head. Slade ducked and rammed his own head into Mongo's midriff, lifting the bigger man off the ground.

But that proved to be a tactical error. As Mongo fell to his knees, he got a grip on Slade's shirt. Holding with the iron grip of a desperate man, he drove his fist hard into Slade's left shoulder. Even though the expression in Slade's eyes never changed, he turned white and staggered. That was all the time Mongo needed. Rushing his smaller opponent, he rained blows at his head and shoulder.

Slade fought back with incredible tenacity, but the blows to his wounded shoulder had almost exhausted his strength. If that happened, nothing could stop Mongo from beating him to death as he threatened.

"Stop it," Pamela cried. "He's bleeding."

"All of him will be bleeding when I get through," Mongo grunted.

But even with his strength draining away, Mongo couldn't overpower his opponent. Using both fists, Slade gradually turned Mongo's aristocratic face into a mass of bruises.

Pamela tried to pull Mongo away from Slade, but he shook her off, throwing her to the ground. She saw Slade stumble and Mongo pounce on him. Slade managed to twist away, but Mongo followed after him immediately. Pamela knew Slade wouldn't be able to keep away from Mongo for much longer.

Without thinking, she jumped to her feet, pulled Slade's

rifle from its scabbard, and fired it into the air.

Both men froze in their tracks, but as soon as Mongo realized that Pamela, rather than some man, held the rifle and that she had fired into the air, he turned back toward Slade.

"Stop it!" Pamela shouted furiously. "If either of you tries to keep fighting, I'll shoot."

Slade got slowly to his feet, all the while staring at Pamela in surprise.

Mongo's temper got the better of his judgment. "You won't use that rifle on me. No woman would," he said, and started for Slade once more.

Pamela shot the heel off his right boot.

Both men stared in undisguised amazement.

"Get on your horse and leave this moment," she said to Mongo. "And if you know what's good for you, you won't come back until you've apologized."

"You're protecting him instead of me?" Mongo asked, gawking at his boot in disbelief. "He's nothing but a trail bum."

"He defended me, so right now I'm not very particular about what he is or where he came from. You, of all people, should know better than to try to force yourself on a woman."

"I lost my head," Mongo said. His anger had cooled enough for reason to tell him he must recover his ground as quickly as possible or risk losing Pamela altogether. "I can't think straight when I'm around you. You're like an obsession."

"You'd better go," Pamela said. "I don't want anybody to know what happened."

"I'll be back."

"Not unless her father or Mr. Bagshot is around," Slade added.

"As for you," Mongo snarled, whipping around to face Slade, "you'd better ride out of this country as fast as you can. If I ever see you again, I'm going to kill you."

"That's been tried before," Slade replied.

The coldness in Slade's eyes made Mongo decide that killing Slade Morgan might not be an easy thing to do.

"Just make sure I never see you again."

"You don't have to see anything you don't want to," Slade replied.

Mongo wasn't quite sure how to take that, but he reminded himself that Slade was unimportant to his plans. Gaining Pamela's regard lay at the center of his strategy. Even though she was obviously impressed by this cowpoke playing the hero, ten to one she'd forget him quickly. There was nothing like opposition to make an underdog look good. Give her a little time to see through his valiant front and she would send him on his way herself, if Bagshot didn't do it for her.

"I'll be back after the roundup," Mongo said. "I love you, Pamela. I'm not going to let you marry anyone but me."

Chapter 6

Slade took a minute to dust himself off and watch Mongo ride out before he turned to Pamela. He needed time to think. In less than ten minutes things had changed considerably. Pamela had admitted she might be willing to stay in Arizona for the man she loved, and she had used a rifle, quite effectively too. What else might this surprising woman do if given some time? Could she change her opinion about him?

"I thought you didn't approve of guns," Slade said. He allowed himself to smile in hopes it would aggravate Pamela.

It did. "Would you rather I let him kill you?"

"No, but if I had known you were good enough to shoot the horns off a steer, I wouldn't have given up my guns."

"Is that why you called out to those men last night instead of shooting them?"

He was supposed to be asking the questions. Besides, he didn't want her getting this close. "I'm new here," Slade said, trying to make his words sound off-hand. "I thought maybe some of your boys were coming back and trying not to wake you."

Pamela had never used artifice on Slade. She considered it now, but decided against it. Nothing worked with his kind like a direct attack. Somehow they never expected it from a woman, especially a lady. "I don't know who you are," she said fixing him with an accusing gaze, "where you came from, or why you're here, but I do know you're not stupid. You knew none of my men would creep along the creek carrying torches."

"They didn't light the torches until after I called out. I guess you could say that was a tactical error." Now that Pamela was after him tooth-and-tong, Slade felt like he was in control again. If she had looked even the slightest bit helpless—God only knows what would have happened if she had shed a tear—it would have been all over with him.

"What happened?" Belva cried. She had covered most of the distance from the house under cover of the cottonwoods along the bank of the stream, a shotgun under her arm, but the minute she saw Pamela and Slade standing in front of the bunkhouse talking, she waddled out of the trees.

"Slade was just helping out again," Pamela explained. Clearly annoyed at having her interrogation interrupted, her baleful gaze said she wasn't through with him yet. "Come on up to the house. That wound's got to be cleaned up."

"What happened?" Belva repeated impatiently as they started toward the house. "Why were you firing a rifle in the middle of the day?"

Slade saw the apprehension that lurked in Belva's eyes, and winked. She was startled at first, but some of the tension seemed to drain away.

"It wasn't me this time," Slade said.

"I did it," Pamela called over her shoulder as she turned and strode swiftly back to the ranch house. She had noticed the wink, and it only served to irritate her more.

"But what on earth for?" Belva asked as she hurried after her.

"Mongo came by."

"That never caused you to go shooting off rifles before. What happened?"

"He pressed me to marry him and used the burned barn as an excuse."

"What did you tell him?" Belva's anxiety was plain to see.

"I told him I didn't love him and was planning to go back East."

"Thank God for that. Well, for the first part of it at least," Belva added. "I don't think I could stay here if you married that man."

"Did you ever mean to marry him?" Slade asked, aware the minute the words were out of his mouth that this was none of his business.

Pamela seemed annoyed that he would ask such a personal question, but she didn't hesitate to answer him. "I did at first, when I thought I might have to spend the rest of my life here," Pamela admitted a trifle self-consciously. "He can be quite charming when he wants to."

"He's overbearing and hard-hearted as a stone," declared Belva.

"And dangerous," added Slade.

"Mongo's not the least bit dangerous," Pamela replied, rather impatiently Slade thought. "He's just used to having his own way. I guess he has something of a temper, most rich men do, but he's really quite nice."

"Then why did you shoot him?"

"I didn't shoot him," Pamela snapped. She stopped in her tracks and spun around to face them. "I shot the heel off his boot."

Slade said nothing, but Pamela got the definite feeling he wasn't satisfied with her answer.

"You got shot at because of me," she added speaking a little less stridently. "The fight was my fault, too. I couldn't let him keep hitting you."

Slade had been probing, trying to find a weak spot, but now that he had found it, he hesitated to probe deeper. Hearing the undertone of warmth in Pamela's voice gave him the same feeling of euphoria as unearthing an unexpected vein of gold. Only he valued this far more.

"Where's your horse?" Belva asked in the uncomfortable

88

silence that followed.

"In the corral, saddled and ready to go," Slade said without taking his gaze off Pamela.

"You go on in and let Miss White fix you up," Belva said quickly. "I'll go take care of him."

Slade started to object, but Pamela stopped him.

"You can't leave now."

She turned back toward the house before he could see the expression in her eyes, but Slade could tell she had herself under control again. She had closed the window to her emotions. Shrugging off a feeling of disappointment, Slade followed her inside and sat down in his usual chair while she collected all the things she needed.

"I don't know why I bother putting anything away as long as you're here," she commented. "This is the third time in less than twenty-four hours I've had to patch you up."

"I guess I'll have to learn to be more careful."

"What made you fight Mongo?" Pamela looked him full in the eyes. There was uncertainty and bewilderment in her expression. "Common sense should have told you not to drop your guns. It should have also told you not to get into a fight, especially not with two sore feet and a useless shoulder."

Slade didn't feel up to any deep discussion, especially with Pamela asking the questions. Weariness racked his whole body, his shoulder throbbed so badly he could hardly keep his mind on what she was saying, and he cursed himself for a meddling fool. Now she wanted to know why he had done it. Hell, he didn't know himself.

"Chalk it up to a misplaced sense of chivalry if you want to. Maybe I listened too much to what they said in church. My dad told me a man would always defend a woman, at least the kind of person he called a man."

He was getting in too deep. If he didn't stop now, the dam would break and then all the stuff he'd been storing in the basement of his soul would come pouring out.

"If I'd known you were that good with a rifle, I'd have just sat back and watched you take care of him."

"I don't think you would," Pamela said as she carefully removed the bandage she had put on his shoulder only a few hours earlier. "I think there's more to it than that."

"Well you're wrong," Slade lied, "about the first part," he added when he saw disbelief flare in Pamela's eyes. "I never could stand to see a woman mistreated. Can't see it done to animals either. That's what got me in trouble the first time. But you're right. There is another reason."

Why explain all this? What would it do but cause more trouble? He should just stick with his first story and light a shuck to California the first chance he got. But he looked into Pamela's eyes and lost all chance to move an inch until he had to. He didn't know what he saw there, but it was the closest thing to liking he had seen in anybody's eyes since Trish. To a man starving for friendship, it was a chance he couldn't waste. It might last only for a short time, but it promised more than he had when he walked in here.

"I never had anybody do anything for me, not since I was a boy," Slade began haltingly. "From the moment I stepped up to your porch, you made it clear you wanted my hide on the other side of that ridge. Still you invited me to eat at your table, sleep in your bed, and share your company. You also fixed up my feet and shoulder. Ma'am, nobody ever did anything like that for me before, not even those that had cause to be grateful to me. I don't forget things like that."

"My name is Pamela." She kept her head down as she cleaned away the blood that had drained down his arm when she removed the last of the bandages. "I don't forget my debts either. You're going to stay here until this shoulder is better."

"Only if that job is still open."

"But you said you wouldn't work for anyone else."

"I can't stay here doing nothing. Kindness only goes so far. Besides, people might talk."

Pamela wondered if he might be laughing at her again. Why does he have to have a beard she asked herself for the hundredth time. His eyes can be totally empty when he wants them to be.

"This may change your mind about my kindness," Pamela said as she poured whiskey directly into his open wound. A hiss of pain escaped Slade's clenched teeth, but nothing more.

"Why do you do that?"

"Do what?"

"Refuse to show that anything can hurt you. I've seen you endure pain that would have caused half the men I know to faint. All you do is sit there, staring back at me."

"I don't know."

"Are you afraid to let anybody know you can be vulnerable?"

Hell, where did this woman get off digging into him like an ice pick, and without any warning either. If he wanted to go around pretending to be a hard case and tough as buffalo leather, nobody had the right to ask him why. Besides, why should he let people know they could hurt him? They'd only take advantage of it.

"Can't see any sense in it. Only gives people the idea they can take something from you. Sometimes it can be a real bother to convince them otherwise."

"I can't imagine anybody trying to take advantage of you."

"I haven't always been what I am now."

"What's that supposed to mean?"

"It means I was brought up to live by the Golden Rule. Only I found out people don't respect you for it. They're just interested in what they can get out of you."

"I can't believe everybody's like that."

"Why not? You're a hard case yourself."

"Me?" Pamela could hardly have been more shocked if he had struck her.

91

"Sure. There's not a particle of give in you. You know exactly what you think of everybody and everything, and nobody can tell you different. And once you make up your mind to do something, there's nothing can change it."

"I've changed my mind about you."

"Not really. Maybe you don't object to me quite as much as you did yesterday, but you're still opposed to everything I am. And that won't change. You can't make it change."

"That's not true," Pamela protested. "Of course I have my own ideas about things, and I stick with them—everybody does—but they're not written in stone."

"Would you agree to stay here in Arizona if I could show you it's just as beautiful as Baltimore, that most people out here can be as fine and honest as anybody in a city?"

"I don't like the desert, even if it is beautiful," Pamela stated emphatically.

"Would you marry a cowpoke if you fell in love with him? I mean go live in a cabin with him, bear his children, cook his meals?"

Pamela looked at him, speechless. "How could I fall in love with a cowboy?" she managed to say at last. "We'd have absolutely nothing in common."

"See, you're just as prejudiced as I am. We're just prejudiced about different things."

"I didn't say I *wouldn't* fall in love with a cowboy," Pamela replied angrily. "I merely asked how?"

"What would you do if you did? Would you take him back to Baltimore with you?"

A hiss of exasperation escaped Pamela. "I don't know what I'd do. I never considered it before, but I suppose it would depend on what the cowboy wanted."

"Would you give up living in this house?"

"Would you give up looking like a vagabond and move to Baltimore?"

"You saying you've fallen in love with me and want to make a gentleman out of me?"

"No more than you're saying you've fallen in love with *me* and want to run off and live in some line cabin in the hills."

"Would you go if I asked?"

"Certainly not, but then you wouldn't ask, not if you thought I might go."

Slade felt like he had been hit with a fence post. He should have known better than to try to get around her. Pamela had shown too much cleverness for that, but something about her wouldn't let him quit. She saw too much, felt too much. "What makes you think that?" he asked.

"Your misplaced sense of chivalry. You're rather sour on the world. I might even say bitter. You don't think much of other people, but you expect an enormous amount from yourself. You're exactly the kind of man who would tell himself he couldn't marry a woman unless she would give up everything in the world for him. But the moment she decided she *wanted* to give it up, you wouldn't let her because you'd feel you didn't have enough to give her in return. You'd end up making both of you miserable because your sense of what is right is just as inflexible as my idea of what I want."

Slade felt himself becoming angry again. He disliked it when people tried to probe inside his mind. "When did you start being able to see into people's souls?"

"I never could. I usually make the most awful mistakes about people. It's different with you, though I don't understand why. I didn't even like you at first."

"And now?" Hadn't he learned with Trish not to ask for trouble? Besides what difference would it make if she did like him? He would still have to ride out of here soon, and he would have to ride out alone.

"A woman can't help but think more kindly of a man who's willing to fight for her."

"Even if she disapproves of violence."

Pamela laughed in spite of herself. "Maybe especially because she disapproves of violence."

"And you accused me of having twisted motives."

"I'm not sure I can explain."

"Don't try," Slade said, inspecting Pamela's work before getting to his feet. "The last time I tried to understand a female, I ended up in jail."

"I promise I won't call the sheriff, at least not until that shoulder is well. Now let me see your feet."

"They're doing just fine."

"They didn't look too fine when you were hopping around trying to get away from Mongo."

"I was not *trying to get away from him.*"

Being careful not to let Slade see the amused smile on her lips, Pamela bent her head as she poured some hot water into a basin and then diluted it with cold water. "Okay, trying to stay out of his reach," she corrected herself.

"I was doing that," Slade admitted, and the smile returned to his eyes.

Once again Pamela cursed his beard. It kept her from getting to know the man behind. She was sure it was cheating her out of something wonderful. She wondered if she would ever find the courage to ask him to shave it off?

Slade's socks showed red when he took off his boots.

"Just as I thought," Pamela said and poured some more whiskey into the water. She tried to keep the sympathy out of her voice, but the pitiful condition of his feet brought a lump to her throat.

"Ma'am, your father is going to be mighty unhappy when he comes home and finds out you've poured all his whiskey over my feet."

"I'm going to pour it over your head if you ever call me Ma'am again," Pamela said, smiling threateningly at him.

"It's right hard to call you Pamela when you're ordering me about like a schoolmarm."

"How can I do otherwise when you act like a little boy?"

"Does that mean you're expecting me to yelp when I put my feet into that water? I warn you, I've got a pretty loud holler. It's liable to bring people running, and then you'll

94

have to explain what you're doing. Might be better if I just sat here quiet like."

Pamela stifled an urge to empty the kettle over his feet. That would give him something to yell about. It might also make him forget to use his drawl to get under her skin.

"I want you to stay off your feet. And I want you here in the house where I can watch you. Judging from your present rate, I've got about twelve hours before you get hurt again."

"I don't ordinarily make such a habit of it."

"What will it be next time? Maybe I should plan ahead."

"How am I supposed to know? I've never been in such a place for shooting and burning and fighting. If you were to pour a little of that whiskey down my throat, I could imagine it was Saturday night and I was in a St. Louis saloon. Who do you think will come after me next?"

"I don't know. I mean, we didn't have any of this trouble until you got here."

"Doesn't sound like we're very good for each other. Maybe you'd better tell Belva to bring that hammerhead up to the door. I can still hobble that far."

"Stop talking foolishness. You're not going anywhere."

She patted his feet dry and put more salve on them. "Now go lie down, in the bedroom. You've lost a lot of blood. If you don't get some rest, you're going to come down with a fever."

Pamela started toward the door before him. "I can find my way," Slade said, "but I'd appreciate it if you would warn me when you see your father coming up the canyon. I have a feeling I might not recover from that wound."

"Do you always joke about everything?"

"Not always, but I find it saves a lot of trouble if I don't take things too seriously."

But Slade didn't feel the least bit like joking when he lay down on the bed. He didn't need to have drowned to know he was going under for the third time. And it looked like nothing could pull him out this time.

He had lived rough all his life. When he was growing up, his mother had always been careful to turn him out neat and clean, but his life had been cold and harsh. There never seemed to be a good reason to do things, only the threat of bad things that would happen if he didn't.

In the years since, he had traveled over much of the West, at times with little more than his horse and saddle. He spent his nights in the open despite rain, snow, and marauding Indians. Food was what he could shoot or carry in his saddlebags and fix over a camp fire. There never really had been anyone to make his life a pleasure.

Then he stumbled into Pamela's valley.

Staying at the Bar Double-B ranch was like living a dream. Set in a lush valley surrounded by hogback ridges to protect it from weather and intrusion, it provided a man with a quiet oasis separated from the rest of the world, a place where he could set aside everything harsh and cunning and replenish his soul. A man could get in touch with himself here, find out whether he could grow into something more than a fast gun and a tough reputation. He could find out whether he was worthy enough to earn the love of a woman like Pamela.

On a more practical level, a man could fight for a place like this. This solid and spacious house would comfort a man without seducing his senses or sapping his strength. The scent of cedar, pine, and some herb he couldn't identify gave it the smell of a more natural cleanliness he had never experienced before. The thick walls guaranteed cool, dark comfort in summer and warm, dry security in winter, a life-giving refuge from the brutal Arizona climate.

But it was Pamela herself who made the difference. Her softness excited his every sense. Even though his wound throbbed painfully, he could feel his body responding to his thoughts about her. Lord, he hadn't been this randy since he first discovered girls!

Slade realized now that he had never understood softness

96

or femininity before. He had thought of his mother and Trish in that way, but their elegant clothes and polished manners merely camouflaged natures harder and more unbending than dry leather. With them softness was only an illusion; with Pamela it was a life-giving force.

It wasn't just her beauty; it was the *way* she was beautiful. Something about her manner warned him to keep his distance, but an underlying, intimate layer of femininity lured him on. It was rather like a fence around a fire to keep him from being burned. But he could leap over that fence.

If only he could find the courage.

Her contradictions intrigued him. Even though she groomed her hair meticulously, she allowed her long, brown tresses to fall freely over her shoulders, glinting with the sparkle of gold strands of hair bleached by the sun until they gleamed like something alive. Many would consider her complexion flawless, but sun and wind had given her skin a touch of golden brown. Slade even thought he might be able to make out a freckle or two. But her lips were perfect, smooth, moist, and incredibly inviting, and Slade felt his body tense at the thought.

Her clothes were modest enough for a young woman with a rich father, but with Pamela it wasn't quite the same. He couldn't explain it, but a man could tell when a woman's clothes said *hands off* or *take it off*. Pamela's way of dressing said neither of these, but Slade couldn't quite put his finger on what they did say.

The straight and simple lines of her clothing accentuated the rise of her full breasts and the slimness of her waist as she moved about with an unconscious grace. She seemed as relaxed and at ease when kneeling at his feet as when sitting across from him at dinner or telling him he shouldn't be afraid to admit his vulnerability.

And she wondered why he was tense all the time! It was almost easier to stand the pain in his feet and shoulder than to continually be in her presence and keep his hands, thoughts, and desires to himself.

Slade wondered if it was wise to remain here, even with his wounds. Instinct warned him to leave at the first opportunity, but he knew he wouldn't go now. And it had nothing to do with chivalry, misplaced or otherwise. There was something going on. And he had an idea it was more than either her father or Dave Bagshot suspected.

Even though Slade made up his mind to stay and look after Pamela until her father returned, he knew the real reason he didn't leave. He didn't leave because he didn't want to. But if he was going to hang around, he'd better learn to control his body's response to Pamela. Otherwise he'd be a dead man about one minute after Josh White walked in the door.

Pamela's thoughts were equally unsettling, but she didn't have the opportunity to ponder them in solitude. Slade had hardly left the kitchen before Belva returned.

"That horse can wear his saddle until the end of his days before I'll touch it again," she declared as she waddled in the door. "I don't know what Mr. Morgan had in mind when he picked that beast, but it must have been a death wish."

"I'll unsaddle it later," Pamela said, her mind elsewhere.

"You'll do no such thing," Belva declared. "If anybody's to do it, it might as well be your worthless cousin. We won't be losing much if that animal grinds him into the dust."

"Slade didn't seem to have any trouble with it."

"Mr. Morgan's not your average kind of man. I don't imagine there's too many as can stand in his way. And that includes a worthless horse too ungrateful to know when it's well off. If he was back in those hills with a half dozen mountain lions on his trail, he might see things a little different."

"I don't know," Pamela said, thinking of a man who didn't seem to care any more for comfort or convention than that

98

hammerhead dun, "some creatures don't seem to care about being safe and comfortable."

"I know," Belva said with disgust, "and nearabout every one of them is male. You won't see no female hankering after living wild. No siree. We're not that foolish."

"Why are they like that, Belva? What made Dad come out here and fight Indians and rustlers and I don't know what else to build a ranch in this terrible place? Mother always hated it, even from the first. That's why she insisted I go to school in Baltimore. She wanted me to know there was another way to live."

"What are you asking me for. I've only known your Pa a few months."

"I don't know," Pamela admitted. "I guess he came out here because he was determined to be his own master. He couldn't do that in Virginia, not with a ruined plantation, and taxes, *and* reconstruction. He was too proud to bend his head before that rabble."

Belva looked up from where she had begun her preparations for lunch and surprised a faraway look in Pamela's eyes. "You're not asking after your Pa," she said. "You're asking about that Mr. Morgan, and I can't tell you about him. That man is altogether different from anybody I ever saw."

"Is that so awful?"

"Why do you want to know? When did you start getting all worked up over drifters? Besides, I thought you hated beards."

"I do. My hands are itching to shave it off. I feel like I'm talking to somebody I can't see, but that's not it. I don't think he is a drifter. I don't know what he's done, and don't think I want to find out, but he's no saddle bum. He's in trouble of some kind, or he's had trouble and he's running away. It wouldn't matter if he didn't go to California. Oregon or Mexico would be the same thing. He just wants to get away."

"When did you start paying so much attention to cowboys? I didn't think you were interested in anybody who didn't grow up in the East, live in a city, and change for dinner."

Pamela detected a note of censure in Belva's voice. "Just because I don't like Arizona and enjoy being comfortable and wearing beautiful clothes doesn't mean I'm heartless," she replied, stung by the same accusation twice in one morning. "But Slade isn't like anybody else. I think it's his ambition to be a nobody, to virtually disappear. I have the feeling he had a chance to be somebody and turned it down."

"Doesn't seem to me like he's the type to be content with what other people are willing to give him."

"He'd be more likely to take everything they had," Pamela said with a chuckle, but then stopped abruptly. "You know, I think he would take what he wanted, but he'd be just as likely to give it away again. I don't know. I don't understand that man."

"Is it so important that you do?"

"Yes," Pamela said, realization suddenly dawning. "Yes, it is."

Chapter 7

Slade entered the kitchen a little after three o'clock. He didn't see Belva, but Pamela was making dough for the dinner rolls.

"Why didn't you wake me?" He was a little crotchety as he sat down at the table. His feet hurt worse than his shoulder, and he was irritated with himself for having slept so long.

"You needed the rest. Or have you forgotten you have a bullet hole in your shoulder? Add to that being up half the night and being exhausted when you went to bed." She rolled the dough into a big ball and dropped it into a heavy bowl.

"I can't afford to get in the habit of sleeping so heavy. It can be dangerous on the trail." He twisted in his chair. It felt hard, and the ladder-back cut into his shoulder blades.

"Are you planning to spend the rest of your life on the move?" Pamela asked. She draped a damp towel over the bowl and set it in a warm corner of the stove. "Don't you want to settle down?"

If Slade hadn't been so cantankerous, he wouldn't have answered the way he did. "Never met a woman I thought was worth it."

Pamela's expression didn't change one iota, but she couldn't fool Slade. He hadn't meant to be insensitive and regretted his words, but she had no business asking questions like that if she wasn't prepared to accept some pretty raw answers. Still, he looked for a way to soften the effect of his words.

"Never had much success with ladies. They don't seem to go for my type. Something about me just naturally sets their teeth on edge."

Pamela's expression changed to one of curiosity.

"Even my mother didn't find much to like about me."

Now it changed to sympathy and Slade couldn't stand that.

"I guess I gave her plenty of reason."

"Why?" Pamela asked. She set a cup of coffee in front of him and then followed it with a bowl of hot beef stew and a slice of peach pie.

"You don't want to hear about her."

"Yes, I do."

No one had ever asked Slade about Sara Billingsworth Wilson's effect on his life, and now all the years of accumulated bitterness came tumbling out.

"She was a whirlwind of destruction for all everybody thought her a pillar of the church," he said, the years of pent-up anger still under tight control. "My father never amounted to much, not the way most people measure a man, but he could have if he'd married the right kind of woman. You never saw such a tall, handsome, fun-loving man. He couldn't believe God had put him on this earth for nothing but sorrow and suffering. He drank a little too much when he married my mother, but it was mostly high spirits and poor company. He would have grown out of it if he'd been given a chance."

"But my mother believed carnival people were dyed-in-the-wool sinners and drink was Satan's brew. She badgered him to quit both of them. Her people had been bankers back East, and she wanted my father to work some place respectable. She didn't think being a carnival showman was a suitable job for a man fortunate enough to marry a Billings-worth. Actually he made a lot more money with the carnival than he could have in a bank, but the more successful he became, the more she nagged him to quit. And the more time she spent in church praying God would change him."

"Then one night—I'd just turned fourteen—Dad and I both came home drunk. I'd been working with him for some time by then. Anyway, mother took one look and locked us both out. Next day she packed up everything she owned, including my sister, and left town. I haven't heard from her since."

Slade leaned back in his chair, drained but feeling better. Until now he had never told anyone about his parents. He had never guessed the kind of pressure that secret had created inside him.

"What happened to your father?"

Slade stared at his coffee. What *had* happened? He hadn't noticed the change at first—he was too young and confused to know what was going on—but it must have started even before his mother left. The kernel of ambition, that germi-nator of dreams in every man that can make him more than he is, dried up, and his father just started to die.

"He started drinking more. He caught pneumonia after sleeping out one night and died."

Pamela didn't know what to say. She wanted him to tell her something about himself, but she hadn't been prepared for such a heartbreaking tale. Her own mother had been hard and cold, but she had used her strength to protect her daughter, not to destroy her.

"I know words won't do any good, but I am sorry," she said finally.

"Don't be. She was right. I *am* just like my father."

"It doesn't sound that bad."

"It wouldn't, not unless you were married to him. Women change. They're attracted to a man for the very things which, in a few years, they come to dislike. Mother knew what my father was like, but she thought she could make him over into what she wanted. When she found out she couldn't, she began to hate him."

Pamela would have given anything to be able to see his face. His grey eyes were cold and hard, but she still wanted to see his features. She wanted to see *him,* not a lot of hair.

"I didn't mean to start on my mother," Slade apologized. "I suppose I can't blame her. She was brought up expecting a husband to act a certain way. She didn't know what to do about my father and me, and after a while she just gave up trying."

"Not all women are like that."

"So I thought when I became engaged to Trish."

"Are you married?" Pamela couldn't describe the feeling of shock his words produced.

"No. Trish realized her mistake in time."

Thank God he was too absorbed in his thoughts to see her body actually sag with relief.

"What happened?"

Why stop now, Slade asked himself angrily? You might as well tell her everything.

"I paid some boys back for something they had done to one of my horses, only the sheriff and the rest of the community said I'd been too harsh. They put me in jail. After all it was just a dumb animal. Trish agreed with them. She said she could put up with being married to a carnival showman as long as I was making plenty of money, but she wanted nothing to do with a gunslinging jailbird."

Pamela's own words pierced her conscience like the point of a knife. Did he lump her with this Trish whoever-she-was just because they both disliked guns and violence? Did he lump her with his mother because she disapproved of what he had done with his life and his lack of desire to change it? Never before had she wanted so desperately to explain how she felt to anyone, but she didn't know how to begin. From the harshness of his voice and the coldness of his eyes, she knew he still harbored deep resentment against those two women. Other people had probably influenced his life, but clearly no one else had affected it so profoundly.

"Not everybody places such rigid demands on other people."

"Don't you?"

"I don't know," Pamela replied honestly. "I would hate to think I was so lacking in understanding, but I don't know if I can compromise with what I want."

"I know I can't," Slade said getting to his feet. "And I know from experience trying doesn't count. I've got to go see about my horse."

You goddamned fool, Slade cursed himself as he strode toward the corral, the pain in his feet completely unnoticed. Why did you have to tell her about Trish and your mother? Talking isn't going to make any difference. She's rich, been to a fancy school, and lives in the kind of house people like you get thrown out of. Why should she fall for a guy like you?

He cursed the day he stumbled into the Bar Double-B ranch, cursed the Texas sheriff who had driven him there, and cursed the whole Briarcliff clan. He hoped they'd all burn in Hell. If he ever did go back to Texas, he swore he would send as many of them as possible on their way ahead of schedule.

Gaddy was inspecting the damage to the barn when Slade reached the corral. It was a large structure containing seven stalls and a tack room and a loft for hay. The support beams and rafters were massive hand-hewn pine logs, probably cut from the hills behind the ranch house.

"It's a good thing you have trouble sleeping," he said as Slade came up. "If the fire had ever gotten going, nothing could have stopped it."

"I don't have trouble sleeping," Slade barked. "I woke up because I heard someone moving around outside." He had spoken more sharply than he intended. A muttered apology didn't improve his mood. He entered the corral and walked over to the hammerhead. The horse was still tied to the post where Slade had left him. He pawed the ground impatiently. When Slade reached up to remove the saddle bags, the dun tried to bite him. Slade cuffed him across the muzzle.

"I always sleep sound," Gaddy remarked.

"Sleeping too sound can get you killed," Slade told him. He walked around the hammerhead; the horse kicked at him as he passed. Slade gave him such a resounding slap on the rump his hindquarters bunched in protest. "Where's Bagshot?"

"At the night camp."

"Why aren't you with him?"

"He sent me back to stay with Pamela so she wouldn't get worried."

That boy's sixteen, old enough to be doing the work of a man, Slade thought. He shouldn't be lying around the bunkhouse with nothing to do. He'd never grow up if they keep treating him like a kid.

Slade looked at him over the back of the dun. "Trouble?"

"The boys think so."

"What kind?"

"Don't know. Nothing's happened yet, but everybody's wound tight as barbed wire. Something'll bust soon. Maybe at roundup time."

"I think it's already started."

"What do you mean?"

"The barn. That was no accident. Somebody got paid for that job."

"I suppose you're right, but who'd do a thing like that?"

"You're the one who lives here. Who do you know who might want to make trouble for your uncle?"

"Every rancher within a hundred miles would give their trigger finger to have this valley," Gaddy said. "It's got a natural fence all around, and it can support three or four times as many cows as the rest of the range."

"But who'd use force? Mongo Shepherd?"

106

"He's pretty sly, but he's an Easterner. He's too soft to go in for anything like that."

"In my experience, if you can find the motive, you'll find the man."

Slade backed the dun against the corral fence. Holding on to the pommel with his good hand, he stepped up on the bottom rail of the fence and swung himself into the saddle. The hammerhead dun gave a few half-hearted bucks then settled down.

Slade's injured arm never moved.

Gaddy stared at him with surprise and a good deal of admiration.

"Lower the bars, will you. I'm going for a ride. I want to see some of this valley everybody talks about so much."

Gaddy watched Slade ride off. He took off his hat and shook his head as he ran his fingers through his damp hair. "I don't know who that dude is," he said as he turned and headed for the ranch house, "but as long as he's around, anybody planning to come after the Bar Double-B had better watch out. He ain't no pilgrim."

Pamela met Gaddy at the kitchen door. "Where's Slade going?"

"Said he wanted a look around. He seems to think Mongo's behind those men last night."

"That's absurd," Pamela objected. "Mongo wants to marry me, not burn me out."

"Don't jump at me. It's Slade's idea."

"He's trying to hang a guilty verdict around the neck of the first person he comes to." But she couldn't totally dismiss the possibility that Mongo might be guilty. Slade was no fool, neither was he the kind to make ill-founded accusations. It wouldn't do to discount what he said no matter how absurd it might sound to her right now.

"By the way, did you talk him into staying?" Gaddy asked.

"I don't know."

"You mean you didn't bat your eyes and watch him come

107

begging for a chance to work for free?"

"Gaddy Pemberton, you know I wouldn't do a shameful thing like that."

"Only because you never had to before," Gaddy said, not the least bit apologetic. "Men just naturally fall all over themselves trying to please you. This one's different though. He might stay a year or ride out tomorrow, and there's nothing you can do about it."

"Well he's not going anywhere now," Pamela snapped, "not with that bullet hole in his shoulder." But she knew Gaddy was right, and the fact that he knew *she* knew riled her. "He shouldn't even be riding a horse," she added with a touch of acerbity, "especially not that dun."

"Goes like a charm for him. That man's got a way with animals." He glanced at his cousin's puckered brow. And that ain't all he's got a way with he thought. But Gaddy took care not to voice that thought out loud.

Slade made up his mind.

He had been born and bred in Texas, and he shared the usual Texan's belief that no better place existed on this earth, but his ride over the Bar Double-B range had convinced him this valley was as close to paradise as any man was likely to find. No place in California or Montana or Canada could suit him better. A longing to stay, to settle down rose inside him. Pamela had offered him a job, a permanent position if he chose. Well, he did choose. If the Texas sheriff didn't find him, he would stay here for the rest of his life. If he did find him, well, he would face that when the time came.

He returned to the corral and unsaddled the hammerhead dun. He cuffed him when he tried to bite him.

"Instead of biting and kicking every time I come around, you ought be grateful I'm willing to put up with you," Slade chided as he rubbed him down. "This freedom of yours is no great thing. I walked through your precious desert, and there's not enough food and water out there to keep a burro alive. You'd be down to skin and bones inside a week."

"You always talk to horses?" Gaddy asked. Slade looked up to see him leaning against the corner of the barn, a wide grin on his face.

"Sure. Most times it's the only company I have. Besides, they don't argue with you."

"Just bite and kick."

"He's not a bad fella. Just showing me he's got a mind of his own."

"Well you can talk to him all you want. Don't guess anybody else around here will be anxious to horn in on you."

"I've been wondering why that stream was dry," Slade said, changing the subject. "Being late spring, I figured it ought to still have a pretty good flow of water."

"I guess you found Uncle Josh's dams."

"Four of them."

"There's two more higher up. They keep the whole valley green right through till fall. Something about subterranean irrigation."

"Now I understand why Mongo's so anxious to marry your cousin. This valley's like finding a gold mine."

But Gaddy had no interest in irrigation. "Got something over in the bunkhouse to show you. One of the boys found it in the desert and brought it in. Thought it might be yours."

It was Slade's saddle and bed roll.

"You tell whoever brought this in he saved me a trip. Can't say I wanted to go after it."

"You planning to stay?"

Slade thought Gaddy tried not to sound too optimistic, but he could see the hope in his eyes.

"Yeah," Slade said slowly, "I think I just might."

Gaddy whooped and grinned from ear to ear. "What changed your mind?"

"Several things, but mostly I don't feel right about leaving just now. Not with Pamela's father gone and things a mite unsettled."

"I knew it," Gaddy said. He slapped his leg in happiness, convinced his hunch about a budding romance had proved right. But he sobered quickly. "If what you suspect is true, though, things could be in a hell of a mess soon. What do you plan to do?" His expression was serious enough, but his eyes gleamed with the eagerness of a boy bored with day-to-day routine and anxious for excitement.

Slade decided right now was the time to start stripping gunfights and range wars of their glamour. Many a kid just like Gaddy had died before learning that lesson.

"Now that I've got my gear, I think I'll get cleaned up. Thought I'd take a bath and change my clothes. Might be a good idea to impress the boss lady."

Gaddy looked disappointed. "Nothing will impress Pamela half as much as getting rid of that beard," he told Slade with a candor verging on rudeness. "Boy, does she hate seeing hair on a man's face. She says a man with a beard is hiding something."

"Did she tell you that?"

"Not all at once, mind you, but off and on. My parents died when I was four and Uncle Josh sort of adopted me. I grew up with Pamela. She's sorta like a big sister. There's not much about her I don't know."

"I'll keep that in mind," Slade said.

"I ought to tell you we eat promptly at six. Pamela hates for anybody to be late. Says it's rude to the cook."

"I'll remember that, too."

"If you change your mind about the beard, you can use my gear," Gaddy offered as he started to wander off. "It's in the house."

"Why do you sleep in the bunkhouse?" Slade had been wondering that ever since he got here.

Gaddy turned back, but he kept his gaze lowered. "It

110

wouldn't do to look like Uncle Josh was making a pet of me, not if I wanted to get along with the boys."

"Hadn't thought of that," Slade said as Gaddy went off. It would be even worse if they thought Pamela was making a pet of him. The boy was obviously trying to fit into the crew, and it was just as obvious no one was letting him. He'd have to see what he could do about that. That kid had the makings of a good man.

He made a mental note to mention it to Pamela.

Slade stowed his saddle in the barn and sorted through his gear. He separated what should go in the barn with the saddle, what provisions he would offer to Belva, and what he would take up to the house with him, but his mind was on Gaddy's remarks. The thought of shaving off his beard, a thought Slade had never even considered until just now, seemed strange. He felt like he had been born with a beard. He had started growing it at thirteen.

He rejected the idea quickly, but the thought bedeviled him as he walked up to the house, lurked in the back of his mind as he talked to Belva, and was only temporarily banished while Pamela explained how the bath worked. The remark needled him as he watched, fascinated, as the large bathtub filled up with sun-heated water. It sprang into the center of his thoughts again as he soaked his body clean of the dust and sweat of the last several days.

Luxuriating in more hot water than he had ever enjoyed in his life, the idea of shaving wouldn't leave him alone. If he intended to stay here, he ought to make a clean break with the past. Shaving off his beard would be a solid step in that direction.

He had been twelve years old and headed home from choir practice the day he decided to grow it. A couple of neighborhood boys followed him, always at a safe distance, teasing him, calling him, "Pretty boy," "Angel face," "Choir boy." Slade liked singing in the choir, but he hated being told he had the face of a cherub. He was a tall boy for his age, blessed with a sturdy frame, and he had more interest in being a man than an angel. In the west Texas of 1872, angels weren't much in demand.

He gave both boys bloody noses and then got a beating with the razor strap when he arrived home with torn clothes and a dirty face. But along the way he noticed a man with a full beard covering his face, and he decided right then he would never *ever* shave. Now, fifteen years later, he was thinking of doing it for the first time.

Because Pamela was right. He was hiding from himself, and if he ever hoped to live in this valley with any degree of contentment, he would have to stop. This might only be a small step, and it might prove to be the easiest one, but it would be a step in the right direction.

But as he dried himself off, being careful to move his injured shoulder as little as possible, he grew less certain of his decision. Could shaving off his beard really mean a new beginning all by itself? No, not unless he admitted he wanted to do it because of Pamela.

Pamela. Yes, he'd shave for Pamela.

And for himself.

Slade vigorously whipped up the shaving cream and worked it into this thick beard. Gaddy didn't have enough beard to shave, but he had enough shaving equipment for two men. Gaddy wanted to shave because he felt it would make him a man; Slade had grown a beard for the same reason.

And now he was about to shave it off for a woman who barely liked him.

There was no doubt now; he was falling in love with Pamela White. The shock of full realization was so great he lowered the razor he had poised to make the first swipe at his beard. After years of carefully avoiding any entanglement, he had fallen into the net *even though he was staring right at it all the time.*

His razor bit deep into the stiff matt on his face, but it was so thick it took several passes before he had cleared a patch of skin.

Suppose he still looked like a cherub. It had been bad enough at twelve, but it could be fatal at twenty-eight. No point thinking about changing his mind now, even if he did end up looking younger than Gaddy. He moaned. Whatever his reason, whatever the consequences, he had committed himself to removing his beard, to pursuing Pamela, and to being in danger of discovery because he hadn't moved out of reach of that Texas sheriff. He saw all of this and still ruthlessly shaved off the barrier that had protected him from the world for fifteen years.

Moments later he stared back at a man whose face had no meaning to him. He might as well be looking at a stranger. No, there was still a little of the youthful Billy Wilson about his face. He recognized Slade Morgan's eyes, too, but nothing else was familiar. Hell, now he'd probably need another name. Before long, even he might forget who he really was.

They stared in bewilderment when he came to the table.

"Who the hell are you?" Gaddy demanded, coming out of his chair with a jump.

Slade laughed. It was worth every minute of the painful indecision to see the look on Pamela's face. *She* knew who he was even if Gaddy and Belva didn't.

Slade's hair turned several shades lighter whenever he washed it; tonight it was neatly combed, freshly trimmed, and a golden blond. He knew he didn't look like an ordinary cowhand any more. Age had matured his features into those of a man of distinction. Nothing of the boy remained. His clothes were different too. Instead of his usual faded jeans and checkered shirt, he had put on a black shirt with a string tie, black pants, and a wide black leather belt. Only the moccasins Pamela had given him for his feet were familiar.

His feet still hurt and he wasn't about to force them into boots until he had to.

He wasn't wearing his guns.

The expression of disbelief on Pamela's face lasted only a few moments before she managed to collect her wits. "You're just in time, Slade," she said, finding her voice at last.

"I'll be damned if it's not," Gaddy exclaimed, his threatening look turning to one of delighted surprise. "I would never have recognized you."

"Me neither," Belva agreed.

"The moccasins gave him away," Pamela said aloud. But it was the eyes. *His* eyes. With or without a beard there could be no mistaking their intensity.

"I sure never expected this when I told you Pamela hated beards," Gaddy disclosed ingenuously. "People don't generally pay much attention to what I say."

"I had a reason for growing this beard," Slade told him. "You just made me realize it wasn't there any longer."

"And what might that have been?" Belva asked. Pamela shot her a reproachful glance, but Belva lifted her chin in defiance.

"Nothing more than a young boy's desire to look like a man," Slade said with a disarming smile. "The ladies in the church used to call me a cherub. You might think that's a compliment, but it's a terrible cross for a twelve-year-old."

"I'm surprised you didn't take to wearing guns then," Pamela said, and Slade was glad to see some of the tension leave the corners of her mouth.

"My mother didn't approve of guns any more than you do. She was furious with my Dad for teaching me so young."

"When did you learn?"

"I was shooting rocks out of the air by the time I was six."

"Six?" Pamela's voice virtually squeaked.

"You can't start too young in the carnival business. Folks will pay to see almost any kind of gun trick, but they'll pay even more when a kid's doing the shooting. Especially if that kid is a blond cherub."

"You were a trick shot in a carnival?" Gaddy asked fascinated.

"Sure was. My Daddy and I went all over Texas, Louisiana, and Missouri, even up to Chicago on occasion. There wasn't an act to compare to us."

"Will you show me some of your tricks?"

Slade looked at Pamela. It was hard to tell what thoughts were going through her mind. It looked like she was doing her best to school her features into impassivity.

"I haven't done them in quite some time now. I don't know that I still can."

"Why did you quit?"

Slade looked at Pamela. "Because of a woman."

He wanted to tell her that Trish meant nothing to him, but he knew this wasn't the time or the place. Considering how she felt about guns, there might never be a good time.

"Damnation," Gaddy exclaimed, "I wouldn't have quit a carnival for a female. Just think of going to all those big cities. What's it like?"

"Noisy and crowded," Slade told him. "And full of people who'd sooner cheat you than say good morning. There's not a single place I've ever been I wouldn't trade for this valley."

He was still looking at Pamela. He could feel the tension of wanting her approval spread down into his groin and made his pants downright uncomfortable. He wondered if she believed him. She might not be wearing a beard, but her face was just as much a barrier to his being able to know what she was thinking as his beard had ever been. Maybe she hadn't gotten over the shock of seeing his face. It doesn't matter, Slade told himself. She's bound to tell you what she thinks. She's never hesitated before.

A continuous stream of questions from Gaddy and Belva about his life in the carnival followed throughout the meal, what the cities were like, and some of the famous people he had met. Slade answered them all, making everything seem

115

almost ordinary. Pamela asked a few questions too, but Slade got the impression she asked more to keep him from thinking her rude than from any desire to have them answered.

"I'd better be going," Gaddy said rising abruptly the minute he had swallowed the last of his dessert. "Dave told me to be back early, but he might not come in after I tell him you're going to be working for us."

"Make sure he knows I'll have his dinner waiting," Belva said.

"Maybe you could spare a few minutes to tell me what I'm supposed to do around here," Slade said to Pamela as they all rose from the table.

"The usual stuff," Gaddy assured him, answering for Pamela, as he settled his hat on his head. "We don't do nothing different from anybody else."

"Maybe not, but I need some special orders. There isn't much *usual stuff* I can do in my present condition."

"You two talk it over," Belva said to Pamela. "I can clean up here. And you'd better get going if you're going," she said practically shoving Gaddy out the door. "Dave doesn't like to be kept from his supper too long."

Pamela rose from the table. "We can talk in Dad's office."

"Why don't you use the front porch," Belva suggested. "It's a nice evening."

Pamela looked daggers at Belva.

"I would like that," Slade said. "I'm more used to being outside," he added when Pamela turned her frosty gaze on him.

Actually Pamela didn't want to sit with Slade on the porch or anywhere else right at the moment. She could have cheerfully choked Belva for leaving her no graceful way out. She desperately wanted to be alone to try and sort out her thoughts. Everything inside her was in confusion. She doubted she could think clearly enough to tell Slade what his duties would be.

116

God, what a hold he had over her.

As much as she had wished he would shave his beard, she had never suspected the attractiveness of the face it concealed. Her fingers burned to stroke his face, to touch that fresh, soft skin. Just looking at him had made her nipples hard. No other man had ever caused such a reaction before. She hoped he couldn't tell from looking at her, but from the glint in his roving eyes, she guessed he had.

Her heart pounded in her temples as she led the way through the house to the porch. She tried to keep her mind on business, but she couldn't think of anything except Slade as he entered the dining room. She had known him instantly—he didn't look a thing like she had imagined he would—he was almost too handsome to believe. There was nothing of the innocent little boy about him now.

The small lines about his eyes hinted at the cost of his lost idealism. Slate-grey eyes, frosty like her memories of a cold, bitter Chesapeake bay, drew her now. His firm mouth, chiseled from skin never touched by the sun, invited her kiss. It was a bold, magnetic face, but without a smile there was no softness in it, no give.

Whenever he smiled, it was as though he changed character completely. He smiled just like everyone else. When his lips curved upward and a light danced in his eyes, Pamela felt sure it was genuine. But then it would quickly fade away, and she would wonder if she hadn't been mistaken.

She couldn't understand him at all. But she didn't need to understand him to appreciate him, to enjoy the excitement generated between them.

But she couldn't understand her own feelings either. What she had labeled mere curiosity, a tepid liking at the very most, had exploded into a full-blown fascination underlain by a hot, restless current of desire.

Desire? That was almost more of a shock to Pamela than the notion of her being captivated by a drifting cowboy. The

117

tingles he set off in her own body confused her. She had never had this terrible awareness of a man's body before. It got more intense each time she looked into his deep grey eyes.

None of this was right, none of it was in accordance with what she had been taught, and none of it fitted into the plans she had made for herself. Yet if she had been given the chance to leave for Baltimore at that very moment, she would have asked for a later ticket. Whatever drew her to Slade Morgan was more powerful than anything she had left behind in Maryland.

Chapter 8

It wasn't yet dark when they stepped out onto the porch. Looking down the canyon to the entrance of the valley, Slade watched the fiery desert sunset streak the horizon orange and purple and rose. In contrast, the shadows of the valley deepened until the evening air turned a dusky blue. Cool air, channeled by the high ridges, flowed down from the mountains to rustle the leaves of the oaks which surrounded the house. Slade breathed deeply of the sweet air.

Higher up on the ridges juniper and ponderosa pine whispered to one another and box elder rustled noisily. Spring had blessed the valley and consecrated it with lush flowers and new grass nourished by the bountiful winter rains. Great masses of golden poppies cloaked the hillside, their brilliant mantle of color polka-dotted by the many hues of the tulip-like mariposa lilies.

There was softness in the air, a touch of gentle warmth in the midst of the cool draft. It reminded Slade of summer evenings in Texas. He could almost believe he was standing under the spreading arms of a hundred-year-old pecan with the breeze stirring the leaves of the wild grape thicket down by the gate, soft light streaming from the windows of neighboring houses illuminating shadows without being bright enough to intrude. It gave the night a friendly feeling.

The door closed behind him, and he turned to face Pamela.

"Why did you do it?" she asked.

"Do what?"

"Any of it. The barn, Mongo, your beard. Why didn't you just get on your horse and ride out?"

Slade was sure he would be making a fool of himself if he answered with the only word which would be the absolute truth—"You." Instead he responded with a question of his own.

"Didn't you ply me with enough questions this afternoon?" He waited for her to decide where to sit. "I think we ought to stick to business."

Realizing he didn't intend to give her an answer right away, Pamela walked over to the large sofa-like chair which had been supplied with several plump, enticingly thick cushions. She sat down. Slade sat down next to her without waiting for an invitation.

She stifled a gasp. She couldn't think with him that close. Forcing her mind to block out his nearness, she said, "When a man like you shaves off his beard for the first time, it could mean any number of things, all of them important to the woman who hired him yesterday."

She was telling him the truth. He *was* still a stranger, but it was almost impossible to keep her mind on her questions or his answers. She had been aware of his tremendous magnetism from the very first but never more so than when he sat down next to her. She didn't lean back against the cushions. She couldn't. Her body was stiff with tension.

Her nipples were so hard they almost hurt and the slight touch of material brushing against the peaks sent rivers of fire coursing down her body. Her secret female parts were hot and embarrassingly wet. It was hard to sit still and just talk. She wanted to touch him.

His physical attraction was almost overwhelming. Even now she could recall the feel of his corded muscles under her fingertips as she cleaned his wounds. She could picture every detail of his broad chest, muscled shoulders and powerful arms. Even with his left arm virtually useless, he radiated the sense of a powerful and dangerous animal.

She found her eyes straying toward the full bulge behind the zipper of his jeans. She fought to keep the warm blush from staining her cheeks. A lady simply didn't have these carnal thoughts. Her mother would be horrified.

Before she had felt like she was being drawn to a faceless man, someone she couldn't quite reach, but that was gone now. She could see the man behind the mask, and she liked him more than she ever thought possible. His eyes could be cold, his lips compressed, his jaw rigid, but there was an element of humanity about his face which could not be erased. He was the most appealing man she had ever met.

And that included Frederick.

"You haven't answered my question," she said, forcing herself to look into the gathering dusk rather than at Slade. She wondered if he would. He might consider it none of her business. To her surprise, she realized she considered everything about him her business.

"I did it because of you."

Pamela whipped around to stare at him. As soon as the words were out, she knew that was the answer she had been hoping for. But having gotten it, she was thrown into confusion. What did he mean by *I did it because of you?* Those words could mean so much. They could also mean so little.

"Gaddy told me you didn't like beards. He said you were sure a man with a beard had something to hide."

He did it for the job. He didn't really care what she thought of him just as long as she gave him the job. Well, she shouldn't have expected a declaration of eternal devotion. He'd given her no reason to expect it would be forthcoming, and she'd give him every reason to think she would reject it if it were.

"I also did it for me. It's a way of coming face to face with myself. Whether or not I like it, this is my face."

She wasn't sure she could believe that. How could any man not be happy to look like he did? She had never met anyone who could compare to him, not in Baltimore, New York, or Newport. Frederick would probably have given half his fortune to look like that.

"I also hoped it would make you look a little more favorably on me."

Her heart beat faster.

"I found I had an unaccountable hankering to sit beside you in the moonlight. I was afraid the beard would keep you away."

Pamela's heart started to race. There was no doubt about what he meant by that. The only question now was what did she *want* him to mean. She wasn't sure. Something about this man defied explanation, but then she wasn't looking for explanations.

At least not right now.

"You could have asked." Pamela was shocked by her own words, even more so by what they implied. Quickly she added, "Of course, asking doesn't guarantee you'll get the answer you want."

"That's what I was afraid of. I told you before, I'm not very good with ladies. They don't usually cotton to me. Besides, I started out on the wrong foot with you."

"Not all ladies like the same things." And not all ladies know what they like. Until yesterday, she would have sworn she would never *ever* be interested in anyone like Slade Morgan, yet here she was, sitting with him in the moonlight. And, God help her, she was hoping he would kiss her.

"What do you like?"

"Yesterday I thought I knew. I was so sure I had everything figured out, that it would go just the way I planned. But that was before you wandered in here. Now I don't know."

"How could I have confused you? I haven't said much of anything."

She looked up at him and a slow smile spread across his

122

face. His stomach fluttered uncomfortably.

"You had me confused before you reached the porch," Pamela admitted. "By the time I finished patching you up for the third time, I didn't know what I wanted. I still don't."

"You want to sit out here with me?"

"If I didn't, I wouldn't be here."

"Then at least you do know a few things."

"Tell me why *you* wanted to sit with *me.*"

"Only if you promise not to laugh."

"Why should I laugh?"

"Trish did, only I don't think she felt too much like it at the time."

"I'm not Trish."

"No, you're much prettier." Pamela felt a blush steal over her cheeks. "Much nicer, too." She turned to face him. "And your dad's a lot richer."

"Slade Morgan!" Pamela exclaimed before she heard his soft chuckle. "You're teasing me," she said, pretending offense. "You meant to upset me."

"No, I just didn't want you to think I had gone all soft in the head."

"And what makes you think I would take nice compliments as a symptom of a soft head?"

"Everybody's after something."

"Well I'm not. No, I am too, but it's not something you can buy or keep or control or make do what you want it to. It just *is* all on its own."

"You mean like the hankering I have to touch your cheek? Should I tell you how velvety soft your skin is?" Slade's fingers brushed the softness of her skin and Pamela felt herself go all weak. No one, not even Frederick, had had this effect on her. Why should Slade?

"Yes, something like that," she replied in a breathless whisper.

Slade slipped his arm around her shoulders. "Does the desire to hold you in my arms count?"

Pamela was almost unable to move, she felt like a lump of melting butter, but she managed to mold herself into a comfortable armful as she settled against him.

"Everything counts," she murmured.

"I must be dreaming," Slade murmured as he took her hands in his. Please, God, don't let it stop, he added silently.

"You don't look like the kind of man to spend a lot of time dreaming."

Slade sat up to look deep into her eyes. "Don't you think I've dreamed of sitting on a porch like this, holding a woman like you, and busting a gut wanting to kiss her? I have, many times. I just never thought I'd be doing it." His warm intimate voice sent shivers down her spine. It seemed to caress her just like his hands would.

"You aren't doing it. Kissing me, I mean."

"If I was to do that, would you laugh at me?"

"Why should I?"

"I haven't kissed a girl in ten years. Not *really* kissed her."

"Next you'll be telling me you forgot how."

"I'd remember a lot better if you helped."

Pamela smiled. She leaned forward and took his face in her hands. Gently she leaned it to one side. Then leaning her head in the opposite direction, she kissed him. Gently, tentatively.

"Is it coming back?" she asked, her lips not entirely separated from his.

"Yes, but I could do with a mite more reminding." Pamela kissed him again, only not so tentatively this time.

"That help?" she murmured. Her hand reached into his hair to draw him even closer.

"I think I can take it from here," Slade said huskily. He closed his arms around Pamela and took her in a powerful embrace, an embrace as devastating as his kisses were gentle.

"I think I'd better rest up a bit now," Slade said after a kiss that was not really gentle at all. "I didn't remember that kissing could wear at a man's heart so. Mine's beating fit to bust my chest wide open."

"Mine is too," Pamela said and placed his hand over her heart.

Slade thought he would explode. His manhood was hard and swollen behind his jeans. This gentle teasing was almost more than he could stand. If they kept this up he was going to embarrass himself. Only by employing the greatest self-restraint did he manage to keep his fingers from the mound of her breast. He longed to take it greedily in his grasp.

"If you want me to be fit for any kind of work, you'd better give me back my hand," Slade said in a constricted voice. "Much more and I'm liable to keel over dead right here."

"You'll do nothing of the kind," Pamela said, smiling in the dark, "but it was a sweet thing to say."

"You won't think so when you're trying to explain to Belva why I'm lying dead with my arms locked around you. Your father wouldn't appreciate it much either."

"You don't look that feeble to me."

"I never was till now. My Daddy always told me some women could have a mighty unaccountable effect on a man, but I never knew what he meant until this moment."

"You're teasing me. I can't believe a man like you has never been excited by a woman."

"Hell, I've been excited hundreds of times, but this is not the same."

Pamela suddenly grew rigid in his arms. "I should hope not hundreds of times."

"Every time a nice looking female looked at me. When I was with the carnival, that happened nearly every night. But I didn't get a craving to sit with them in the moonlight."

Pamela relaxed against Slade.

"Is it okay to talk at a time like this? I got a powerful lot of things inside just bursting to get out."

"It's not necessary, but I guess it's okay," she said, hoping his words would drown out the pounding of her heart.

"Did you ever think much about the moonlight? It's not

125

anything like the sun. The sun throws everything into bright color. Into conflict. There's so much going on, a person can get so caught up in it he forgets himself. He just acts like he thinks he's supposed to act. But everything is different in the moonlight."

"I never thought about it like that."

"The same world is still out there. You can see it and you can hear it, but it's not pulling at you, making you go places and do things you don't want. Everything fades into the shadows and you're left alone in a quiet so deep that sometimes you think you're the only one alive. But you can finally see what it is you really want."

"And what do you want, Slade?"

"I want to be sitting like this fifty years from now, looking at the moon and holding the woman I love in my arms. I want her to love me as much as I love her. I want to have children and grandchildren and great-grandchildren who will do a lot more than I have done. And I want a place like this, somewhere I can stay and be content until it's time to move on for the last time."

"You want a lot."

"Wishes are free. It's just getting them that costs so much."

"You're a strange man. I never knew cowboys thought about things like that."

"There's nothing like sitting with a cup of coffee over a campfire on the backside of a mountain to get a man thinking. There's all that quiet and nothing to disturb his thoughts. Most of us don't have much money, nor any hopes of getting any, but it costs nothing to dream."

"What do you want to do with your life, Slade?" she asked dreamily.

"I don't know that I want to do much of anything with it. It's just fine like it is."

He obviously didn't understand what she meant. "I mean what do you want to become?"

126

"I don't reckon I want to become anything except what I am."

His words struck a discordant note, and she became quite unromantically alert. "But you can't want to remain a cowhand all your life, working for somebody else, never having much of anything to call your own."

"A man doesn't need much to make him happy. I'd like a small cabin somewhere, preferably in some hills like those behind the house. I'd like a view so I could look out over the cows."

"You want to be a rancher?"

"Not a rancher exactly. About thirty or forty good cows and a couple of well-bred bulls would be all I'd need. I don't know that anybody would exactly call that a ranch. More like a spread."

"Don't you want anything else?" Pamela asked, unable to keep the disappointment out of her voice.

"Like I told you, I want a wife and a bunch of kids. I always wanted children. I think I could cotton to them."

"No doubt, with just a small spread, you'd have plenty of time to spend with them." She couldn't conceal the impatience in her voice. She didn't try. "Your thirty or forty cows wouldn't take up much of your time. What do you plan to do for money, Slade? How are you going to buy your wife and children clothes? How will you send them to school or get them started in life?"

Pamela had become so exasperated with Slade's total lack of drive and ambition she failed to notice his drawl became more pronounced as her disapproval increased. It was positively glaring now.

"My wife could weave homespun cloth, at least for a while. A kid doesn't need much until he goes a-courting. They don't need much learning except reading and writing. I can teach them that. As for setting them up in life, they can set themselves up. Nobody set me up, and I got along fine."

"No you didn't, Slade Morgan," Pamela said jumping to her feet. "You're a grown man and all you can do is gun tricks and chase cows. That's not getting along fine at all."

"I know it's not much by some people's standards. But houses in town and fancy dresses and traveling about in trains aren't for me. I don't need any of that. A few years up on one of those hills and I bet you wouldn't even remember there are such things."

"Oh yes I would, even if I did spend a few years up in those hills, which I will *never* do, not even if you held a gun to my head. A woman needs to have nice things, Slade Morgan. She doesn't expect love to turn her into a broodmare, or to sew clothes out of homespun, or cook and clean until she's too old and too tired to care about new clothes or dancing or traveling on trains. You can have your old cabin in the hills, and you can absolutely drown it with moonlight, but you'll sit up there alone."

Pamela stalked into the house more angry than she'd been in a long time, but if she could have seen Slade's face, she would have fallen into a rage. He was grinning from ear to ear.

"Barring the bit about the moonlight, old son," Slade said to himself, "she hasn't liked a thing you've said tonight. But it's upset her. For a while there I thought she was going to slap your face. No female gets that upset unless she cares about a fella."

Yep, Slade was sure of one thing. Pamela White cared about him. And she cared a lot.

Pamela flipped the pages of her school photo album with sharp, rapid movements, but the images of the young ladies and men she had known in Baltimore hardly registered. She was too upset to do anything as humdrum as look at photographs, but she was too irritated to do anything else. She wasn't sure who made her more angry, Slade or herself.

After a moment she decided it didn't matter. She was furious enough at both of them.

Of course she had no real right to be mad at Slade. He had never pretended to be anything but himself. Except for hiding a terribly handsome face behind a scruffy beard, he was still the same aimless, shuffling, shiftless, ambitionless drifting cowboy who walked through the pass yesterday. He'd proved to be good with a gun, proficient with his fists, and as stuffed with courage as a scarecrow with straw, but she had expected that. Cowboys always seemed to combine some of the best qualities with some of the worst. And Slade Morgan was no exception.

Realizing she had become infatuated with this good-for-nothing lump of lethargy demoralized her. She couldn't explain why she would sit mooning on the front porch with Slade Morgan. Not only did he kiss her, she encouraged him! Good God, didn't she have any pride at all?

A loose picture tumbled from the album. Absentmindedly, Pamela picked it up intending to slip it back into the album when her eyes focused on a picture of herself at age ten, astride her favorite pony and dressed up as a cowgirl. At that time her sole ambition in life had been to marry a cowboy and live on an Arizona ranch for the rest of her life.

Pamela smiled wistfully, but her mood was bittersweet. She couldn't return to the simplicity of those years, to a time of innocence at the cost of knowledge. She had been so certain she could never love any place as much as she loved Arizona. But she found a new dream when she went to Baltimore. Could it be that some of that love for the land still lurked inside her?

No, her plans hadn't changed. She just felt strongly attracted to a man who seemed to be the exact opposite of her in nearly everything. What could she do about it? She put the photograph into the back of the album.

For a moment she thought of sending Slade away. Then she reconsidered. Maybe it would be better if she never allowed herself to be alone with him again. No. That would be cowardly and she refused to act like a coward. Anyway, she didn't want to be separated from Slade. He certainly wasn't the kind of man she wanted to spend the rest of her life with, but she had never met anyone as exciting. It didn't make sense to send him away just because he wasn't husband material. After all, she had never considered marrying him in the first place.

But how could she account for his hold over her?

She had told Mongo she would consider staying in Arizona for the man she loved. Up until yesterday she had never considered staying in Arizona under any circumstances. She had found Slade interesting when he was wearing a beard, yet until yesterday she had had an absolute aversion to men with beards. She hated the thought of using a gun against another human being, but this very morning she had used a gun on Mongo. She didn't like hiring strangers, but she offered Slade a job without knowing a thing about him. She generally kept her distance from the men, but three times she had personally taken care of Slade's wounds. Worst of all, she had never sat necking with a virtual stranger, but she had allowed Slade Morgan to take her out to the porch and kiss her silly.

What enabled this man to turn everything she believed upside down? And she couldn't blame it on his looks. She had already started acting like a fool before she knew he was more handsome than Frederick. He even laughed at her; she suspected he talked the way he did intentionally, and she still let him get away with it. Was she crazy or was he?

She couldn't say what made her feel totally unlike herself around Slade. Something about the way he held himself made him different. He walked like a man who was content with himself. He asked nothing of anyone but willingly risked his life to save her barn and honor her wishes about guns. There she thought, embedded in those actions, you will find the key to what makes him different.

She had known many men with more polished manners—she had to admit she didn't know any who were more handsome or whose bodies were more wonderfully masculine—but he embodied a generosity of spirit they couldn't match. Still he could be as hard as flint. Amusement danced easily in his eyes, but his gaze could turn to ice just as quickly. She would never forget the way he looked at Mongo or the cold, calculating way he fought. She didn't always feel totally comfortable around him, yet she liked knowing that he liked her. There was an excitement about it that had been lacking in all the other men she had known.

She flipped back through the album until she came to a picture of a handsome young woman. Amanda. Pamela smiled down at the black-and-white photo as her memory provided all the vibrant color the photograph lacked. Amanda was a vivacious redhead with brilliant green eyes. Best friend, confidant, and her entree into Baltimore's upper social circles, Amanda had taught Pamela a whole new way to see life. She had also given her a new way to look at men.

Pamela used to worry about herself because she didn't feel the same way Amanda and all the other girls said they did, not even about Frederick. Well there was obviously nothing wrong with her now, but why did she have to go and feel this way about a cowboy?

Too disgusted with herself to think about it any more, Pamela put away the photo album and made her way to the kitchen. Maybe helping Belva would get her mind off Slade. Later she would find a good book. Somehow reading Jane Austen always helped her forget the outside world. Maybe it would work on Slade Morgan too.

Chapter 9

"You got his job all settled?" Belva asked over her shoulder as Pamela entered the kitchen. Her pregnancy made it difficult for her to keep on with her work. Even though Pamela offered to relieve her of some of her duties, Belva insisted upon doing as much as possible until the baby came. No one had really thought about what would happen after that.

Pamela didn't tell her they hadn't gotten around to talking about his job.

"He's not up to riding yet, but I'm sure I can find enough around here to keep him busy."

"He can start by clearing away the burned part of the barn and replacing some of those boards," Belva said. "You *might* ask Gaddy to do it, but not if you want it done before the first snow."

"The bunkhouse needs a good cleaning, too, but I thought I'd get him to help me in Dad's study first. I need to dust the books and clean the shelves. It wouldn't hurt to shake out the rugs either. I'd better get everything done before Dad gets back. He won't let me touch anything in that room while he's here."

"Do you think he'll do it?" Belva asked, pausing in her work. "Most men consider that woman's work."

132

Pamela started to speak and then stopped. What would Slade say about it? He didn't impress her as being particularly sensitive to what others thought of him, but he probably saw himself as a tough man. He might refuse to help her dust and clean.

"Of course, since you'll be helping him, he might not object so much." Belva eyed Pamela expectantly.

Pamela looked her straight in the eye. "I don't know much about Slade Morgan, but if I'm any judge, my presence won't cause him to do anything he doesn't want to do. I haven't the slightest idea what he considers right and proper for a man of his stripe, but I have no doubt he'll tell me. That man doesn't talk much, but when he does, he manages to say a lot."

Belva returned Pamela's stare. "I think he's right nice. I don't know many strangers who'd get themselves shot at by barn burners and beat up by a loud-mouthed bully for some gal they don't hardly know. He's just like one of them long-ago knights you read about."

"Those *long-ago* knights were, in reality, terribly bloodthirsty and forever starting wars. I'd rather Mr. Morgan not start fights on my account."

"You'd better hope he's plenty bloodthirsty. From the looks of things, you're going to need someone around here who is," Belva declared somewhat cryptically. She padded off to bed leaving Pamela to wonder at her meaning.

Slade could smell the coffee long before he reached the kitchen. There was no aroma of bacon and he was conscious of a feeling of disappointment. His grandmother had been born in North Carolina, and she always loved bacon better than beef. It was a smell worth getting out of bed for on a cold Texas morning.

It surprised Slade to find Pamela at the stove. She always seemed to be in the kitchen, but he had never actually seen

133

her cook. This morning she appeared to be fixing breakfast by herself. The huge, iron stove loomed over her like a condor over its chick, but Pamela seemed to have no trouble handling the pot and two frying pans on the black burners. As usual her appearance was perfect. Not even the heat from a cooking stove could cause this woman to wilt.

"Don't stare at me like you're afraid I'll burn the eggs," Pamela said. "I can cook."

"I'm sure you can," Slade said recovering quickly.

"The coffee's ready. Help yourself."

Slade poured himself a cup and settled into his now accustomed place. The wooden table was spread with a white cloth this morning, and that made him uneasy. He wondered what it meant. He smothered a grimace of distaste before he even tasted his coffee. Like all western men, he liked it strong enough to float a horseshoe. Women tended to like it thin. Gingerly, he raised a half-filled cup, inhaled the aroma, and sipped. Much to his surprise, it tasted even better than Belva's.

"Good coffee," he said, reversing one more of his opinions about Pamela. "You ought to start making it every morning."

"I may. Belva's not feeling very well these days."

"Is all this food for me?" Slade asked seeing only one plate.

"Belva's not hungry, Gaddy ate earlier, and I never eat breakfast."

"A holdover from your school days?" he asked. She only smiled, but he had already decided she needed a little fattening up. He'd have to see what he could do about teaching her to eat breakfast.

"Sleep well?" she asked.

"Sure. Why shouldn't I?"

"Your shoulder didn't bother you?"

"Not so's you'd notice. After sleeping on the ground, that bed feels softer than a cloud."

"Do you sleep on the ground very often?"

"They don't have beds out in the desert, or in the mountains and on the plains for that matter. I bet I've slept on half the rocks in Texas."

"Don't you have a home?"

"There you go asking questions again."

"What do you expect when you make comments like that?"

"You could tell me something about yourself. I told you about me yesterday."

"Precious little." She faced him with disarming frankness. "I wasn't really pumping for information, though I would like to know more about you." She had a sudden thought, one that seemed to amuse her. "You should be glad you're not facing my mother. She wouldn't stop until she knew everything about your family for at least five generations back."

"Wouldn't do her any good. I don't know anybody older than my grandparents, and not much about them."

"Mother didn't trust people without a past."

"Tell me about her," Slade asked. He didn't have a bit of interest in Mrs. White. He was much more absorbed in contemplating a wisp of hair that had escaped Pamela's bun and wafted seductively about the nape of her neck. Pamela was such a neat woman, always perfectly turned out in clothes much too elegant for her setting. To find a flaw, even one as minor as an escaped tendril of hair, pleased Slade tremendously. Now if he could just get her talking about her mother, maybe he could carry out his study unhindered.

Pamela hesitated. What could she say about a woman she understood so little but who had done so much to shape her life? What could a man like Slade know about a woman who felt dispossessed, cut off from her past, and forced to live in a world she couldn't understand.

"She was born into an old Virginia family. They weren't rich by the time mother was born, but they had a beautiful home, several thousand acres of land, and were related to

135

just about everybody of importance. They lost it all in the War. They even fought a battle in the middle of Granddaddy DeLand's best pasture."

Slade found his attention shifting from the stray lock of hair to the graceful arch of Pamela's neck. He'd never actually studied a woman's neck before, somehow it just never came up, but he realized now that had been a terrible oversight. Her slightly tanned and perfectly smooth skin held out an almost irresistible attraction. He longed to touch it with his fingertips, caress it with his lips, nibble it with his teeth until she squirmed wildly and lost some of her interminable control.

"Mama had to live with relatives in Baltimore during the war. They were kind to her, but she couldn't be happy there. She desperately wanted a home of her own," Pamela continued. "That's when she met Daddy. He had his own plantation, so when he asked her to marry him, she accepted. She never forgave him for not telling her he had sold everything he owned and planned to go to Arizona and start a ranch. She refused to leave Baltimore until he had built a house for her to come to."

Slade would rather have kept scrutinizing the nape of her neck, but Pamela had finished at the stove and began setting food on the table. "I don't know much about houses in Virginia, but this is just about the biggest house I've ever seen. Your mother must have been real proud of it."

"She didn't come to this house, but it wouldn't have made any difference. She hated Arizona and everything about the West. She wouldn't leave Daddy alone until he agreed to send me back East to school."

"And you wanted to go?"

"Not at first, but I soon grew to love Baltimore. Of course I missed my parents, but I've never been as happy anywhere else."

"Why did you come back?"

"Mother was killed in an accident. I came home to take

care of Daddy. He's finally agreed to let me go back. He might even come with me."

"When?"

"This winter, after he sells his herd. That's why he wanted to hire extra hands. He needs them for the fall roundup."

"And to make sure outside herds stay off his range so his cows will be in good condition to sell?"

"That too," Pamela admitted.

"Why do you want to go back to Baltimore?" Slade asked abruptly. Pamela gave him such a resentful look he thought she intended to ignore his question, but after she finished filling his plate with eggs, steak, and some fried potatoes, she poured herself a cup of coffee and sat down at the other end of the table.

"I'm not happy here," she confessed.

"Why not?"

"That's really not your business." It wasn't stated resentfully, just as a matter of fact. She was silent a few moments and Slade settled down to the serious business of eating his breakfast. "This is my home. I guess I'll always feel that way about it, but everything I like to do is somewhere else. The people I like to be with are somewhere else. Just about everything I like about being alive is *not* in Arizona."

"What's that?" Slade asked with a mouthful of food.

"Oh, lots of things," she temporized, not wanting to have to explain herself.

"Name one."

"Okay," she replied, goaded, "I've never come across anyone who's read Jane Austen."

"She wrote books about English girls falling in love," Slade said without pausing in his eating. "They're a little too full of starch for me, but they're not bad."

"She's my favorite author," Pamela exclaimed, but her astonishment was not at Slade's opinion but that he should know of her at all.

"I'm not surprised," Slade said, still eating steadily. "Now

137

that I think about it, she's just the sort of woman you would like."

"What do you mean by that?" Good Lord, she was already taking it for granted he knew what he was talking about. And he couldn't, could he?

"She goes on and on about the right thing to do, and feel, and think. Hell, it took Elizabeth nearly three years to catch her Mr. Darcy. I guess that's okay in England, but it wouldn't do for Arizona. A woman could blossom and fade in that length of time."

"Which is precisely the reason why *I* won't do for Arizona," Pamela snapped. But her curiosity got the better of her thoughtfulness. "How do you know so much about Jane Austen?" she asked, not meaning the question to sound condescending.

"My mother was a lot starchier than yours. She made me read all kinds of books that didn't do me a bit of good. But you didn't hire me to sit around discussing books, at least not while there's work to be done," Slade said as he finished the last of his breakfast. "Not much use to you like this." He indicated to his arm in the sling.

"You can help me with Dad's office. I always wait until he's away to clean it."

Slade watched her for a moment, no particular expression on his face but the faint suggestion of a smile. The longer he watched in silence, the more uncomfortable Pamela became.

"You don't have to help if it offends your masculine pride or something. All that debris at the barn needs clearing away. And there's also the bunkhouse."

"You afraid I'll consider this woman's work?"

"Belva said you might."

"And you?"

"I don't know. You're odd enough to do it just to prove me wrong."

"I promise to try to behave properly. It's the least I can do for your patching me up so often."

138

"I'd rather you promised to stay out of trouble."

"I try, but it seems to follow me wherever I go." He stood up. "At the risk of confirming your worst suspicions, I think I ought to start on the barn. Your dad can use his study no matter how dusty it might be, but no horse is going to set foot inside that barn with it reeking of burned hay."

"Okay, but lunch is promptly at noon," Pamela said as she got to her feet. Then, not knowing quite how to tell him she had forgiven him for last night, she added, "Be careful with that shoulder. I don't want the wound to break open again."

Slade wondered how long it would take his feet and shoulder to get well. For once he wished he could be one of those slow healers who languishes for weeks at a time. Would Pamela banish him to the bunkhouse when he got well? He'd sure as hell be sent there double quick when her father got back. Staying in the house didn't give him a whole lot of an advantage, but he intended to make as much use of it as possible. All kinds of wonderful things had come from just such humble beginnings. How else would he have spent the morning in intimate study of the nape of her neck and not gotten shot for it?

"Letter for you," Slade said coming into the kitchen. "One of the boys brought it in from town." He held it at some distance from himself. He had seen expensive stationary, his mother had always insisted on it, but he was unused to letters that smelled of damask roses.

"It's from Amanda," Pamela exclaimed, excitement shining in her eyes. "I haven't heard from her in months."

"Amanda?"

"Amanda duPont," Pamela said tearing open the letter. "She's my best friend. We went to school together."

Slade poured himself a cup of coffee and sat down at the table—it was covered with a fresh cloth—but something about that letter, or rather about Pamela's reaction to it,

139

bothered him. He knew she liked this Amanda duPont and wanted to go back to Baltimore, but the way she acted now, well, you'd think she'd been given the one thing she most wanted in the world. And that disturbed him.

"She's coming for a visit," Pamela exclaimed excitedly, "and she's bringing Frederick."

Slade's hackles rose instinctively at the mention of a man. "Who's Frederick?"

"Shhh. I'll tell you when I finish reading," Pamela said.

Ever since he arrived at the ranch, he had felt like Pamela was constantly comparing him to people in Baltimore. He didn't like the feeling. Now it looked like things were going to get a whole lot more specific.

Hell, now he was starting to feel mediocre all over again, and that made him angry. He knew in his mind he wasn't inferior, but no man can be rejected by his mother and the first woman he falls in love with and not suffer doubts. Even if he won't admit them, they're there all the same. And Slade knew it. He couldn't help feeling there was something about this Frederick that made him better than he was. It looked like the same thing all over again. First his mother walked out on him. Then Trish. Would Pamela be next?

She can't exactly walk out on you he told himself. You just work here. But he knew better. Something already existed between them. Preferring this Frederick to him would be the same as walking out on him.

Slade drank his coffee, but it tasted bitter now.

"They're coming for a visit this summer," Pamela said when she finished the letter.

"You already said that." The coldness in Slade's voice was unmistakable, and it stung Pamela.

"They're on their way to California and they want to see me. They even changed their route."

"I wondered why they weren't traveling by boat. A stage-coach seems a little rough for their kind."

"And just what do you mean by that remark?" Pamela

demanded. "You know nothing about them."

Slade cursed himself for a fool. Here he had been thinking that maybe Pamela had changed, that she might consider staying in Arizona, even consider falling in love with him. It surprised him to discover that all this time she had never wavered in her determination to return to Baltimore. It made him angry, too, but he knew he had no one to blame but himself.

Obviously her kisses hadn't been any more than a friendly gesture. Well, maybe it had been more than that, but obviously not much more. Certainly not what he had hoped they meant.

He swore he wouldn't let himself hope again.

"I know their type. They come West to gape at the land and the people, just like we're animals in a carnival. They complain about the heat and the dirt and marvel that human beings could live like we do. Some of them tolerate us pretty well, even pretend to like us, but they can't wait to get back to their comfortable cities so they can entertain their friends with tales of the savages they've seen."

"How dare you speak of my friends like that."

"I doubt they're any different from the rest of their society." Slade knew he shouldn't be saying anything, that it would only make things worse, but he couldn't help himself. He could see her slipping away from him, but the knowledge he had said exactly the wrong thing didn't stop him.

"Amanda belongs to one of the most prestigious families in the United States," Pamela told him with an indignant toss of her head. "They own this terribly big company. They've been important forever."

"And that makes her special?"

"Of course it does. She knows everybody and can go any-where. She's beautiful, knows just what to say to every kind of person in any situation, and is still the most wonderful friend. I don't know how I've stood it so long without seeing her.

"We used to have the most wonderful times," Pamela continued, dropping into a reminiscing mood. "We went everywhere together. She didn't have to take me along—I didn't know anybody—but she refused to allow us to be parted. We went to balls, weekend parties, trips to the mountains or the seaside, the theatre and museums, all kinds of things I'd never done before. I know you can't understand any of this, but . . ."

"And this Frederick," Slade interrupted, unwilling to hear any more about the experiences which separated them, "is he a paragon as well?"

"Frederick is the most perfect man I've ever met. He's wonderfully handsome, tall, and rides a horse with the most unbelievable style. You ought to see him play polo. There was a time when I was madly in love with him—maybe I still am—but I knew he would never marry me. I couldn't have been happier when he and Amanda announced their engagement."

Knowing that Frederick was married ought to have made things better, but for some reason it made them worse. An unreasoning anger rose up inside Slade. He could see the brush-off starting all over again, anticipate the humiliation of being rebuffed in favor of someone else, predict the hurt he would feel when everything he had to offer got rejected in favor of the emptiness of money and social position.

"I wish we could have a party," Pamela thought aloud. "They'll be bored with so little to do."

"Why don't you meet them in Santa Fe?" Slade said, barely able to keep the anger out of his voice. "You could be with your father and they would be spared the discomfort of putting up on a ranch."

"I can't do that. It's the ranch they're coming to see. Besides, Dad needs me here." But Slade's bitterness penetrated Pamela's happiness, and she lost some of her enthusiasm. "You act like you don't want them to come."

"That's none of my business," Slade said. "They're not my

friends. This isn't my ranch."

"True."

"Then it doesn't matter what I think. I'll stay out of sight while they're here. You can have Belva send my breakfast out to the bunkhouse. Or maybe you'd prefer I stayed out on the range until they leave."

The rage in his voice shocked Pamela. Anger that had obviously been bottled up for a long time boiled over. She wondered why he should object so much to people he had never met? Why should he care whether they came to the ranch? And what had she said to make him think she wanted him to hide until they left? It wasn't like she was going to show him off or anything. He was just another one of the men who worked for the Bar Double-B. Amanda and Frederick would expect to see lots of men around the ranch.

"Don't be ridiculous. There's no reason for anyone to hide. They won't dress the way they do in Baltimore or expect you to be interested in the things they enjoy."

Slade rose abruptly to his feet. "You don't expect your guests to hobnob with the rest of the hired hands, so there's no reason for anybody to bother with me. You'll have lots of things to talk about. I don't belong to that world. I never have and I never will."

"I never expected you to." Pamela realized she had put her foot in it again. Could she be such a terrible snob that she didn't even know she *was* a snob? "I mean I don't expect you to be anything but yourself."

"Who're we kidding? It may be exciting to have a wild man around the house for a little bit, to try to tame him, keep him as something of a pet,"—Pamela tried to interrupt him with an indignant denial but he barrelled ahead—"but we both know it can't go on. You have your world and I have mine, and they have nothing in common. Pretending otherwise will just give me unsuitable notions."

"Slade, that's not what I meant, and you know it."

Slade did know it, but he wasn't going to stand around

143

waiting for her friends to look down their noses at him.

"It would be better for everyone if I just made myself scarce," he said, angry at himself now for upsetting Pamela. "Who knows, I might be in California by then."

It never failed to give Pamela a sick feeling when Slade mentioned leaving. "You don't have to go anywhere, and you don't have to be nervous about my friends. They'll enjoy talking to you. I'm sure they've never met anybody like you." That was the wrong thing to say and Pamela knew it the minute the words were out of her mouth, but it was too late then.

"Let them talk to Gaddy. He's related to all those Virginia folks. All he has to do is clean himself up and he'll be acceptable. I have no family. Nothing will make me acceptable."

Then he walked out of the kitchen. Just left her standing like she was nobody, without even giving her a chance to explain she hadn't meant any of the things the way he took them.

But he was gone, and she knew he wouldn't come back. Well, she wouldn't go after him. Pamela White didn't have to explain her actions to anybody.

But that didn't make her feel any happier or the day seem any less empty as hour after hour went by and Slade stayed away. She quickly discovered that pride could be a comfortless companion.

Chapter 10

Pamela heard the sound of running feet only moments before the kitchen door burst open. "Dave's been shot!" Gaddy said between gasps for breath.

Pamela could hardly believe it. They had talked about it, but she never thought it would happen. "Is he . . . ?" No, he couldn't be dead. "How badly is he hurt?"

"He looks pretty awful to me, but Belva says it's a clean wound."

Pamela jumped to her feet and ran to her father's office to gather her medical supplies.

"How did it happen?" Slade asked.

"Dry-gulched," Gaddy announced dramatically, his face an almost comic display of adolescent excitement.

He's dancing with eagerness, Slade thought, as though he has suddenly found himself set down in one of those penny westerns. "Anybody else hurt?"

"Naw. Dave always rides alone."

Pamela hurried back into the kitchen. "Come on. We can find out what happened from him," Pamela said heading toward the door, her arms full. Slade held the door. "You're sure he's all right?" she asked Gaddy.

"Yeah. You don't need all that stuff. Belva had him all bandaged up before I got there. He was trying to sit up when I left."

The Bagshots lived in a small cottage which had been built with the same care and quality of materials as the ranch house. The furnishings, however, were a careless mixture of Mexican, western, and Indian. Gaddy led them to a small room dimly lighted by a single oil lamp. Dave lay on a cotton-filled mattress in a rope bed.

He was completely bandaged from hip to knee. Bloody clothes lay in a corner, but Dave wouldn't let Pamela inspect the wound.

"Belva's already fixed it up."

"You know I'd have taken care of you," Pamela said.

"I didn't want to bother you. It was clean. The bullet went right on through."

Slade tried to see Belva's face—she stayed so far back in the shadows he couldn't see her features clearly—but he could tell she didn't look right. She didn't act like the Belva he knew. She was nervous and jumpy. He would have sworn she had been badly frightened by something. It was natural to assume it was because someone had tried to kill her husband, but that didn't feel right to Slade. He was certain she was afraid of something else.

"Make sure he stays in bed," Pamela told Belva. "I don't want him up until he's completely well."

"What are we going to do about the roundup?" Dave asked. "It's supposed to start tomorrow. They can't change it now."

"I can lead it," Pamela said.

"No!" All three men spoke at once, but Pamela turned on Slade.

"Why not?" she demanded. "I *am* the daughter of the owner of the Bar Double-B. And if it comes down to it, I can shoot."

"Have you ever ramrodded a crew?" Slade demanded.

"No."

"Have you ever worked cattle?"

"No, but . . ." She wanted to explain that she could learn

146

while she supervised, but Slade wouldn't let her.

"Do you know anything about a roundup?"

"No." The admission was forced from her.

"It wouldn't matter if you did," Dave said, trying to soften her disappointment. "The men would be shamed if anybody saw them taking orders from a woman. Besides, there's going to be trouble."

Pamela forgot her irritation. "What kind of trouble?"

"I don't know. If I did, I'd do something about it. Right now it's just a feeling, but I think there's something big brewing. The boys feel it too. They're working themselves silly throwing stray cows off our side of the river. You expect some mixing during the year, but they're driving back whole herds. If they don't, our cows won't have any grass."

"Whose cows are they?"

"Can't say for sure. The brand is new to the area, but I figure they belong to Mongo Shepherd. He's the last one to come here."

"It can't be Mongo," Pamela said, her gaze clouded by thought. "He wouldn't do anything like that." Belva glanced uneasily at her husband, but he shook his head ever so slightly. "You'll have to ramrod the crew," Pamela said. "I can go along and you can give your instructions to me."

"I'll do the best I can, but I wish . . ."

"And I'll ask Mongo to lend us some of his men. Even if Dad were here, we'd still be short-handed."

"I'd rather you didn't ask Mr. Shepherd for any of his riders," Dave said. "I know you like him and he might help us to please you, but some of our boys have had trouble with his crew."

"What kind of trouble?" Pamela asked anxiously.

"Shooting trouble," Dave explained. "And none of our boys are up to handling that kind of affair."

Some of the color drained from Pamela's face. "What makes you think there'll be any more shooting?"

"Somebody shot Jody Flint from behind the other day.

He's not hurt too bad, but the boys are all upset over it. Jody's right popular, and he's the youngest kid on the crew. No one but a low-down skunk would shoot him in the back. We don't know who did it, but Bob Sprevitt found some tracks near where the gunman laid up. He swears it's the same tracks he's seen from one of Shepherd's horses. Of course, since they all use the same horses, there's no way to know who fired that shot, but the boys are certain someone on Mongo's crew is responsible."

"That's all the more reason to talk to him," Pamela insisted. "I know he would put a stop to that."

"Belva tells me he came here today, and that Slade had to fight him to keep him from forcing himself on you. That so?" Pamela flushed from embarrassment.

"He just got carried away. He doesn't like to be refused, but he wouldn't allow his men to shoot at our men," she added quickly. "People aren't brought up that way in Massachusetts."

"You're talking about thousands of cows that'll starve this winter if he doesn't find range," Slade interrupted impatiently. "That could add up to a hundred thousand dollars. They shoot people in Massachusetts and anywhere else for that kind of money."

"I still don't believe Mongo had anything to do with it," Pamela insisted, pointedly speaking to Dave rather than Slade. "Tell the boys to keep moving strays but not to start any fights. I'd rather have hungry cows than get anybody hurt."

"You don't understand," Dave said wearily. "Almost all the land we graze outside this valley is owned by the government. Once cows become established on a range, they have a right to it. If that happens, their owner won't let you drive them off without a fight."

"Two of your men have been shot already," Slade broke in again. "And setting fire to the barn was no accident. Somebody is trying to run you off this range."

Pamela wouldn't listen to Slade. She wouldn't let him panic her into believing there was a plot against her. There had to be a rational explanation for these shootings. She would find it. She would show him. "Why are you so worried about the roundup?" she asked Dave.

"What better time to cause trouble?" Dave asked.

"I would have thought almost any time would be better," Slade volunteered, clearly surprised at Dave's remark. "Too many witnesses."

A spasm of pain caused Dave's expression to grow rigid, but it relaxed almost immediately. "Maybe you're right. Still, what I said is true. None of the boys want the job."

"Dad will be back soon."

"We can't wait on him. I think you ought to let Slade lead the roundup," suggested Dave.

"What?" demanded Pamela, her voice rising an octave.

Gaddy looked from Slade to Dave, his expression of excitement growing. "Sure. He can shoot the wings off a bat."

Slade's expression didn't change. "Why choose me?"

Dave looked Slade straight in the eye. "Because I know who you are."

The tension in the room closed in on Slade. Pamela stared at him, an element of fear in her expression. He watched her body stiffen as though preparing to withstand a blow. Slowly all expression drained from her face until nothing remained but a beautiful mask. "Who is he, Dave?"

I should have left last night Slade thought to himself. All I wanted was a horse. I should have paid her and gotten out of here. Instead I had to hang around and get involved with a shooting and a fight. Well, Slade old man, you can put paid to this account. If Dave tells her half of what you've done, she won't be able to sit still until the trail dust has settled behind you.

"He's a famous sharp-shooter," Dave said. "I saw him in a carnival once. He obviously doesn't remember me, I was

149

only twenty at the time, but we worked a drive together about a year before I came here."

The tension didn't evaporate entirely, but Slade relaxed considerably.

"What do I want with a sharp-shooter?" Pamela demanded. "I need someone who can handle a crew."

"You ought to see him, Pamela," Gaddy said excitedly. "He can draw faster than you can see."

All three adults ignored the boy.

"From what Gaddy tells me, he tackled Mongo with that busted arm. Any man who will do that can handle our boys. They're nothing but a bunch of cowhands. As for the rest, his reputation with a gun should scare off trouble."

"Or cause it."

"No, it won't," Gaddy contradicted. "You let him show what he can do, and there won't be a man within a hundred miles that would draw a gun on him."

"I wish Daddy would get back," Pamela said half to herself. "How can I trust my crew to a man I hardly know?"

Don't you know enough about him already, a voice inside her asked. Aren't you about ready to trust your heart to him? The shock of that realization nearly caused Pamela to stop breathing. She had told herself that her interest was primarily curiosity, that their kisses were nothing more than innocent stolen fruit, that his nearness comforted her rather than filled a need. Now, in one brief flash of understanding, she knew she had been more than curious about Slade before he reached the water trough. By the time he reached the porch, he had become essential.

"All you have to know is he's the best man in Arizona with a gun."

And that's about the last thing she wants to know, Slade thought.

"You know the way I feel about guns, Dave. I can't hire a gunslinger. I'd look like a hypocrite."

"I'm not a gunslinger," Slade corrected. "I'm a trick shot. I

150

shoot just about anything *except* people."

"I don't see how that makes any difference. I'd be hiring you to at least threaten to shoot people. We'll just have to find some other way."

"There *is* no other way," Dave said, "at least not one you can find by tomorrow morning."

"Do you know anything about working a roundup?" she demanded turning abruptly on Slade.

"Yes. I've been on several."

"I'm sure you would do your best," Pamela said, clearly undecided, "but I still don't know enough about you to feel comfortable handing over my crew."

"Your father hired me knowing a hell of a lot less," Dave said.

"But you didn't walk in off the desert. For all we know, he's a wanted man."

"Really?" Gaddy asked, his wide-eyed eagerness more than enough indication he hoped Slade would turn out to be a notorious gunman wanted in at least five states and three territories.

"You apparently believe you know him well enough to let him settle in here," Dave remarked.

Pamela hadn't sorted out her feelings for Slade, but she wasn't about to explain that to Dave. From the very first something felt wrong about Slade. No sooner had he set foot on the ranch than trouble started. No sooner had she set eyes on him than the foundations of everything she had believed her whole life began to crumble. And no matter how much she wanted to see him in a different light, Pamela knew he could be hard and ruthless. She knew he would use his guns. He'd already done so.

"Well, what *do* you think of him?" Dave asked.

"I think he would kill any man who gets in his way," Pamela said harshly, the truth pulled out of her. "I think he would use that gun on a man just as readily as he would use it for a trick shot." She exhaled a deep breath and seemed to relax just a little, like someone who had gotten past the difficult part of an assignment. "I also think he would go to any length to do what he thinks is right, to keep his word."

"Good. Then he's your man," Dave said.

"You want me to hire the kind of man I just described?"

"If Slade is the man you described, he's perfect for the job. I can go along and see that the boys know they're supposed to take orders from him," he explained when Pamela started to protest.

"What about your leg?" Pamela asked, clutching at straws. "You won't be fit to ride for days."

"I'll go in a wagon."

Pamela could put forth no further objections. It would be churlish as well as silly to argue any longer. "Will you take the job?" she asked.

Slade hesitated.

"If you don't, she'll try to do it herself," Dave added.

Slade knew Dave was trying to goad him into accepting, but he continued to stare at Pamela. He almost refused, but then he gave in with a fatalistic shrug. He could think of a hundred good reasons why he should leave, but he wanted to be near Pamela as long as possible.

"I'll do it on conditions."

Pamela stiffened. "Conditions?" She tried to see Slade's face, but it was shadowed in the dim light.

"You don't want to give me the job, and I don't particularly want to take it, so we'd better understand each other from the start. When I take on this kind of responsibility, I have to know where I stand."

"That seems fair. What are your conditions?"

"I'm the boss. Period. You'll back me in everything I say."

"I'm used to giving orders to people I pay," Pamela told him as calmly as she could, but every fiber of her body screamed in revolt.

"That's my second condition. I won't take any pay."

"Don't be crazy," Dave said. "This job pays a hundred

152

dollars a month."

"Also, I can't be fired until the roundup is over."

"No," Pamela said. It was almost a shout. "Why should you insist on such a condition? Are you afraid we'll find out you can't do this job and get rid of you the second day?"

"No. Your temper is up one minute and down the next. You're just as likely to fire me today as beg me to come back tomorrow."

"I don't beg! If I had cause to fire you, I'd never rehire you."

"It's still a condition."

Pamela chewed her lip in frustration, but she couldn't see a way out. She looked hopefully at Dave, but he shook his head.

"You really can't lead them yourself, Pamela. It's a matter of pride with the men. Believe me, being led by a woman would cause more trouble than Slade ever could."

"Okay," Pamela said. She had to choke the word out.

Slade didn't misunderstand. Her words might say she had capitulated, but her eyes signalled open rebellion. He didn't know what she might do, but he knew she hadn't resigned herself to his control.

"If I agree to your conditions, you have to agree to mine," Pamela announced. "I'll go on the drive."

"No." Dave voiced the protest. "A woman has no business on a roundup. It's too dangerous, and it's bound to cause trouble. Besides, where would you sleep or change clothes?"

"I think her presence will be a real morale booster for the men," Slade said. "We can take a wagon for her, too. I'll personally guarantee her safety." Slade's ready acceptance of her presence at the roundup startled Pamela, but Dave didn't give up so easily.

"I don't like it," he protested. "You aren't the one who promised her father you'd take care of her."

"Nevertheless, I'll do it."

"I can take care of myself," Pamela stated, furiously. "I

153

don't need to depend on a cowboy."

"My first order to the crew, Pamela, will be that your safety must be our first responsibility. If you wish to come along, you·will have to do exactly as I say."

Pamela would have given anything to be able to say she wouldn't go, but she couldn't, not after she had made it a condition of giving Slade the job. To stay home would be admitting defeat, and she refused to be defeated by anyone, especially Slade Morgan. He was going to have to *prove* he could do the job better than she could before she would be willing to take orders from him. She shrugged and turned on her heel.

"You and Dave settle between you when we leave."

Pamela left the men to make their arrangements. She had to get away before she threw something. She had been brought up to behave decorously at all times, but nobody had prepared her for Slade. No matter what happened, he always seemed to be able to maneuver her to exactly where he wanted her. She *knew* he had laid down his filthy conditions merely to make her so mad she would insist upon going with them. Now, in a silly spurt of temper, she had committed herself to a roundup. She hated roundups. Even more, she loathed cows. Actually they frightened her, but she'd die before she let Slade Morgan guess.

She had to admit that most of the time Slade was easy to be around. She could anticipate his good moods because his eyes softened and turned a blue-grey. When that happened, she could imagine he might be falling in love with her. Those were the moments which confused her, the moments when she felt helpless to resist the powerful attraction which existed between them. Most of all she felt powerless to resist the pull of his long, lean body. The way he walked, the way his bulging muscles rippled under his shirt, the tight fit of his jeans that seemed to showcase his manhood.

Those moments shook her.

Other times she felt utterly helpless to have any affect on

154

him. He seemed like another person, distant, unfeeling, almost cruel in the harshness with which he made decisions. His eyes turned the color of old snow, and his whole face seemed like it had been fashioned from dry leather. He treated them like so many chess pieces to move about. And she had the feeling he would be a ruthless player, one who would do almost anything necessary to win.

No, at least not with her. She didn't know what kind of limits he imposed on himself, but she knew he lived by a set of standards he believed to be as honorable as her own.

But why was she agonizing over this? Because you *want* to go on that roundup her inside voice whispered.

The thought startled her, but no sooner did it come than she admitted it to be true. She wanted to be with Slade so much she didn't care about the discomfort of the roundup or her dislike of cows. Good God! Had she already fallen that much in love with him?

No, surely not. But the thought of not seeing him for two weeks or more terrified her. He had only been here a short while, but already she couldn't imagine his not being there forever.

Good Lord, what would Amanda say? What would your mother say? What about her father? He wouldn't be thrilled with the idea of some saddle bum waltzing in and taking over the ranch it had taken him twenty years to build. It's going to hurt, but it's time to get this man out of your mind, and probably the best way is to go on the roundup. If you're around him all the time, you'll soon get tired of him. Then you'll know it's over.

But deep within her something hoped it wouldn't be over, that being around him all the time would merely cause the feeling between them to grow stronger.

Slade picked up a shirt and slammed it down on the pile of things he meant to take with him. He wasn't happy about the way things had turned out. He felt himself sinking deeper and deeper into this morass. In fact, he had probably already lost his last chance to escape. So why hang around here inviting that scalp-hunting sheriff from Maravillas to find him? His leading a roundup, especially if it turned into a fight, would attract attention from as far away as the California border.

Nothing would start people talking faster than a drifter starting a range war. What better invitation for some young fool to want to measure his skill against a man of his reputation?

And just what else did Bagshot know about him? He couldn't believe Dave would remember him after all this time without also remembering some of the gossip floating about these last five years. People in the West loved to gossip.

"What're you going to do?" Gaddy asked. He had been following Slade about like a puppy ever since he had agreed to take the job.

"About what?"

"Mongo Shepherd. Dave says he's got to be the one behind this."

"I don't know."

"You mean to let him get away with shooting Dave and Jody?" Gaddy looked so disappointed Slade had to work hard to suppress a smile.

"No, but we don't have any proof he did it, at least not yet."

"Oh, I see," said Gaddy, his enthusiasm immediately revived. "You plan to catch him in the act and then blast him."

He still thinks it's all a game, Slade thought. He doesn't realize bullets play for keeps. "I hate to disappoint you, but I'm going to do my best not to blast anybody, especially Mongo Shepherd."

"Why not? He's got to be guilty."

156

"Maybe, maybe not. Anyway, your cousin is mighty soft on Mr. Shepherd. Maybe she wouldn't like it if I *blasted* him."

"Pam don't like Mongo worth a damn, not since you got here."

Slade felt his heart swell with hope, but he forced himself to be realistic. Love might have blossomed if there hadn't been any gun trouble, but there seemed little chance for them now. Now he had a job to do, and the sooner he did it, the sooner he could get started down the trail to California.

"What about this Frederick fella who's coming." Hell, what did he mean asking a gawky teenager for advice? His wits *were* addled.

"Pamela can't seem to stop talking about him even though he's married to someone else. It makes you wonder about her, don't it? Hey," he said brightening, "you could show that fella up. I bet he couldn't shoot the head off a quail."

"Nor ride the hammerhead dun, put out a fire, or ramrod a roundup crew. But I got the feeling your cousin doesn't admire that sort of thing in a man."

"I told you that fancy school ruined her, that and her ma always telling her Arizona wasn't worth a hill of beans. She could have been a right good girl given half a chance."

"She can ride and shoot," Slade reminded him.

"Yeah, but she don't like it much."

And that seemed to just about sum up Slade's position as well. She didn't like him much either, so why put his neck on the line again? Because he'd suffer blisters, bullet wounds, and another fight with Mongo if he could just kiss her again, hold her in his arms, close, until he knew she would never leave. He could feel his body start to grow stiff just thinking about a deep, wet kiss. God, that woman had the sexiest, sweetest lips! A man could die happy with her in his arms. He had never experienced anything like the fire Pamela kindled in his veins. He'd never endured the ache which kept him awake at night or the constant, nagging sense of longing which kept at him until he couldn't think of anything else.

He felt like one of those rockets they shoot off on opening night at the carnival, one of the real big ones which soar high into the air before they explode into a shower of sparks. He had been primed when he walked into that valley. Pamela had lighted the fuse. The only question remaining was how high he would skyrocket before the explosion.

Slade refused to look over his shoulder. He knew Pamela rode behind him and the temptation for just one glance was almost too much, but he steeled himself to look ahead. She had kept her distance since he laid down his conditions. That she didn't like them was obvious; his determination to hold her to them had to be just as obvious.

"I'll do all the talking," he had informed her when they gathered that morning. "I'll consult both of you when I think it's necessary, but I want every rancher there to know from the start that no one except me speaks for the Bar Double-B."

Pamela had had to bite her tongue to keep from virtually shouting her objection. Only Dave's sympathetic glances enabled her to remain silent. She couldn't understand why Dave had so much faith in Slade. But she had faith in Dave, and if he thought she should give Slade complete control, then she would do it. After all, she kept reminding herself, Slade hadn't threatened to take over the ranch, just boss her around for a couple of weeks. If he tried to throw his weight around after that, she would settle his hash pronto.

"We'll be arriving at the roundup site before the other out-fits," Slade called back over his shoulder. "I want to talk to the whole crew."

"I want to hold a short service, too," Pamela told Dave. "We haven't had one in weeks."

"What kind of service?" Slade asked. That word gave him an uneasy feeling.

158

"It's a lot like a church service," Gaddy answered.

"My mother used to hold them several times during the year," Pamela explained. "My father always led them, but since you're foreman, it's your job."

"I won't have anything to do with it," Slade stated. His voice trembled so with rage they stared at him in surprise. "If I'd known anything about it, I wouldn't have taken this job."

"Does that mean you're quitting?" Pamela asked. Her eyes issued a direct challenge.

"I never quit what I begin, but you'll have your service without me."

"The foreman should be part in everything the crew does."

"I'll bring them through without your prayer meeting."

"It's not a *prayer meeting,*" Pamela said. "It's just to help the men be clear about their values, to help them make their choices carefully."

"I find men always know what's right."

"But they don't always have the resolution to stick to it," Pamela replied, not backing down an inch. "This just gives them a little moral support."

"Just as long as they don't start praying when they're supposed to be working," Slade threw at her over his shoulder and galloped off.

"What set him off?" Gaddy asked.

"I don't know," Pamela said, trying to feign indifference. "He's been angry and withdrawn all day."

"You two didn't have a fight, did you?"

"I do not fight!" Pamela stated indignantly. "It's merely that we haven't agreed on anything since he got here."

"Did you try to find out what got under his skin?"

"Several times, but his response has been quite similar to what you just saw."

"Something's sure biting him hard. Wish I knew what."

"Don't waste your time on him. He's not worth it."

"You can fool yourself if you want to, but you can't fool me. That man has gotten to you like nobody I ever saw, not

159

even your precious Frederick. Don't tell me you don't care."

"Okay, I won't tell you, but I don't," Pamela snapped and then galloped off.

"Looks like we got a whole lot more to do than brand calves," Gaddy said to his horse. "We got some mighty unhappy folks along with us this time."

The panorama of the desert lay before him, but it was a different desert from the one he had walked through. This land was also harsh and arid, but it bristled with life. Prickly pear cactus, pinion juniper, and mesquite only served to distract the eye from the numerous plants and grasses which enabled it to support a large number of cattle. On one side lay the Blue River, the narrow ribbon of life which made the desert habitable. On the other, mountain ridges covered in oak, pine, juniper, cedar, and spruce rose abruptly from the desert floor only to run back to the mountains in the distance. Traces of snow, the life-giving force of this land, still lay on its peaks.

Slade tried to block the sound of the badly sung hymn from his ears, but he couldn't. One part of him struggled to hear just as much as the other part struggled to block it out. He walked through the scrub growth kicking the light grey soil with his feet, snapping twigs off greasewood, all the while trying to calm his anger. All that was over and done with. Pamela's harmless service didn't give him a reason to dredge it up again.

But try as he might he couldn't forget the years of going to church with his mother. He didn't mind church. Actually, he liked some of it quite a bit. For years his mother and the preacher had lectured him about his duty, about the punishment God would visit on those wicked enough to depart from his ways. More than once they had scared him into doing things he didn't want to. Later, they coerced him with threats. Through it all, they drummed into his head the necessity of doing one's duty, honoring one's promises, no matter what.

Then his mother up and left them, and he swore he'd never set foot in church again.

What about her duty to her son? What about her vows to her husband? What about her responsibility to the family? He couldn't understand why everybody praised her for having the courage to leave his father. And what about the preacher? He kept telling everybody about their duty to save lost souls—actually used it as an excuse to butt into people's lives—kept telling them how Christ left the ninety-and-nine to save the one lost sheep. But this same man refused to come to his father when he was dying. Said he wasn't worth praying over.

Pamela could have her services if she wanted, but he'd be damned if he'd have anything to do with them.

But even though he kept so far away he was unable to hear what she said, he drew close enough to know the moment the service ended. He came striding into the center of the group before they could disperse.

"You don't know me," he began brusquely, "but I've been hired to take you through this roundup. If you've got any questions about my right to be here, take them up with Miss White. If you've got any questions about my ability to do the job, you can take those up with me." He glanced around the group. There were a few sidelong glances, but no one seemed disposed to argue.

"I've got a few rules I want you to remember. They may not seem very important to you now, but they could be the difference between coming through with a whole skin or getting shot to pieces. First, nobody goes anywhere alone. I don't care if it's just behind a bush. I want two of you together at all times. Any questions?" There was an undercurrent of curiosity but no objections.

"Second, don't let anybody with a gun get behind you. You may end up eating a lot of dust, but nobody can shoot you in the back if they're in front of you."

"You know my objections to firearms," Pamela stated as she jumped to her feet. Her eyes swept over the crew then came to rest defiantly on Slade. "They never solve anything. Besides, you could be the one to get shot."

"That was a fine speech, Miss White," Slade said, his voice thick with sarcasm. "And you delivered it with all the fire and passion of a true believer while still keeping to the decorous behavior expected of a lady. We truly thank you for your concern for our safety."

"How *dare* you mock me, Slade Morgan," Pamela hissed in an undervoice. "You knew all along I didn't want my crew to carry guns. You did this intentionally."

The crew looked from Slade to Pamela, and Pamela was dismayed to notice that her objection had made them uneasy rather than give them a feeling of relief.

"I respect Miss White's feeling," Slade responded, "but she has given me complete authority for the duration of this roundup. Additionally, she has agreed to support every decision I make. Isn't that true, Miss White?"

Despite her distaste for guns, Pamela would have cheerfully shot him with the first gun she got her hands on. He had used her own words to support his decision to have the men wear guns. She was too furious, too boiling angry at his duplicity to speak. She could only nod.

"She also agreed that I could not be fired until after the roundup was over. Isn't that true as well, Miss White?"

"Yes, damn you," Pamela hissed too softly for anyone to hear. They only saw her lips move and her head nod.

"I regret to say that I see the necessity for every man to be armed and alert at *all* times. Is that understood?"

Pamela could have cursed at the alacrity with which the men agreed with Slade.

"I want you to keep your eyes open. I want you to know everything everybody does. Don't start any fights, and don't get drawn into any arguments. You see a problem, come to me. That's what I'm here for."

"I just have one more rule, but it's the most important of all. Keep your eyes on Miss White. I don't care how you work it out, but I want one of you detailed to stay with her at all times. If anything happens to her, the creeks will flow with blood."

"There's no need to employ bad theatrics," Pamela said, unable to restrain herself any longer. "I can't think of a single reason why anyone would want to harm me."

"I hope you're right," Slade said, "but maybe you've forgotten that as long as your father is away, you're the owner of the Bar Double-B. If anything were to happen to you, your range would be up for grabs."

Pamela started to protest that she'd never heard anything so foolish in her life, but the expressions on the faces of her men stopped her. She didn't know if Slade's arguments had convinced them of the danger to her or whether they already agreed with him, but they clearly intended to keep her under surveillance for the duration of the roundup whether she liked it or not.

"You're just alarming everyone unnecessarily," she said, "trying to get the men to do something they don't want to do."

"Are you willing to fight for Miss White?" Slade asked the crew.

"I'll fight 'til there ain't nobody left to fight," one young man promised. "Ain't nobody hurting her and getting away with it."

"We already got a score to settle for Dave and Jody," a second man added.

"Yeah," assented a third, "somebody's gonna eat lead."

The enthusiasm with which they vowed to back her alarmed Pamela, but she refused to change her position.

"I swear I wouldn't have ordered the men to go armed if I didn't believe you were in danger," Slade said apologetically, hoping to calm Pamela's anger. "In fact, I only agreed to your coming along because I couldn't protect you at the ranch."

"You didn't *agree,*" Pamela snapped, too angry to care what she said. "You made me furious knowing I would insist upon coming which is *exactly what you wanted me to do!*"

Slade grinned unabashedly. "You're right. This is no place for a woman, especially one who knows nothing about cows."

"I promise to stay out of your way," she said furiously. "And I *do* know something about cows." With that, she turned and marched off to her wagon. After the coolness of the ranch house, the midday sun felt uncomfortably hot.

"Keep an eye on her," Slade said to Gaddy. "I'm going to take a look around."

Pamela watched him go, a tall man sitting tall in the saddle, and she felt bereft. Something about that man made her feel more alive, more secure, more vibrant than ever before. Dear God, why did it have to be *him?*

Chapter 11

The half dozen cooking fires appeared as circles of wavering light. Spangled with intermittent sparks from popping wood, they illuminated the night, throwing into relief the dark humps of chuck wagons and the smaller shadows of men and horses. The soft murmur of voices, an occasional shout of greeting, the clank of pots, the scraping of forks against tin plates, the jingle of spurs, the creak of saddle leather, the muffled thud of horses stamping their feet to drive away the flies or blowing through their nostrils blended into a soothing backdrop of friendly sound. The enticing aromas of baked beans, fried ham, brewing coffee, and the sharp tang of tobacco filled the air. Even the faint taste of dust added a bit of necessary color.

It was roundup time.

The crews of the six ranches participating in the roundup drifted among the chuck wagons. Because the dry, clean, cloudless air couldn't hold heat and the temperature had plummeted fifty degrees from the daytime high, they clustered around the camp fires as they renewed old acquaintances, swapped stories, and generally tried to be sociable. Most of them knew each other—they had worked together at one time or another—but they now remained fiercely loyal to their own brand. They all knew trouble could explode at any minute. Subtly, even though they may not have been aware of it, they were also taking each other's measure.

Pamela sat near the center of the encampment eating her dinner, uncomfortably placed between Dave Bagshot and Mongo Shepherd. She struggled to maintain an appearance of polite interest in the conversation between the two men, but thoughts of Slade occupied her mind. He had gone off shortly after they arrived. Night had fallen and he hadn't returned. Pamela couldn't help but worry about him. Besides, his shoulder still troubled him a good deal. He shouldn't try to stay in the saddle for so long.

"I know there's no excuse for the way I acted the other day," Mongo was saying to her, "but I worry about you. I know you feel safe in that valley of yours, but I'd feel a lot better if you'd let me protect you."

"I'll be fine until Dad returns," Pamela told him, only half listening to him.

"I still don't understand why you didn't stay back at the ranch," Mongo continued. "This is a hot, dirty job. I wouldn't let *my* wife come along. A roundup is no place for a lady."

"Then it's a good thing I'm not your wife," Pamela replied sharply as she got up. Her leg muscles were starting to cramp, she didn't think she could stand another minute of Mongo's suffocating attention, and she couldn't sit around making polite conversation while Slade's absence had her so worried. "Dad agrees with you," she said, trying to make her departure seem less rude. "I decided if I didn't come now, I might never get another chance to see what goes on. Now if you'll excuse me, I think I'll turn in. I understand things start very early in the morning."

"You don't have to get up," Mongo said. "There's not much to see until the boys start drifting the cows in."

Pamela repressed a shudder at the thought of so many cows in one place. "I want to see everything," she said and turned toward her wagon. She had just placed her foot on the steps when Slade stepped out of the shadows.

"Did you and Mongo make up? Won't that be a little awkward when Frederick arrives?"

Pamela gasped and jumped. "You scared me nearly half to death," she said, once her heart slowed down enough for her to speak. "What do you mean sneaking up on me out of the dark! You could have been shot by one of these men you've armed."

"I don't want Mongo to know I'm here."

"You can't hide for long," Pamela said. She wondered if Slade could be afraid of Mongo. No, that couldn't be it. He would have won the fight if he hadn't been injured.

"Tomorrow morning is soon enough. I don't want to give him time to change his plans."

"I don't know why you're so determined to make me believe Mongo wants to steal our range. You're wrong, you know. He spent half of dinner apologizing for the way he behaved the other day. He even invited Dad and me to town for a visit after the roundup."

"Let's not waste our time together talking about Mongo," Slade said. He took Pamela by the elbow and guided her around the end of the wagon. "He'll show his colors soon enough. There's something else I want you to see."

"What?" Pamela demanded warily. "You're not going to surprise me with something terrible are you? I'm not particularly comfortable in the dark."

"A man soon learns the dark can be his friend."

"You already told me about your love of moonlight, but the dark can work two ways. Besides, I don't know that I want to talk with you, not after the underhanded things you've done to me."

"I promise I won't do a single thing without asking you first."

Pamela couldn't be entirely sure she believed him, but even if she did, she wasn't sure she could trust herself alone with him. Slade had an unaccountable way of making her unsure of her own mind.

"It's not proper for a lady to run off in the dark."

"We've got more than fifty chaperons," Slade pointed out.

"And every one of them is studiously looking the other way."

"Everybody expects the boss and her foreman to have to talk sometimes, private like, so they can make plans."

"Okay, but the moment you start talking about anything else, I'm heading straight back to camp."

"Don't you trust me?"

"No," she replied emphatically. She didn't tell him she didn't trust herself either.

The main camp was situated on a creek which provided water for cooking and washing. They walked in silence through a grove of cottonwoods along the small stream as it bubbled merrily with water from the spring run-off—it would be a dry stream bed by late summer—until they came to a rise. Slade helped her climb over the rocks until they came to the top.

"Look out there. What do you see?"

In the distance Pamela could see ridges of mountains rising out of the desert, low ridges running back into mightier ridges that ran back to the spine of the Mazatzal mountains. Two of those ridges enclosed her valley. Before it, bathed in the pale light of the moon, lay the open range. Some people called it desert, but in reality it encompassed a rich strip of land lying between the mountain valleys and the open desert, land watered by infrequent rains and mountain run-off, land rich with food on which cattle grew fat.

"Your range reaches as far as you can see," Slade told her. "It's the best there is in this part of the country. Will you fight to keep it?"

"If I must. But I won't have to. Nobody's trying to take it away."

"I didn't ask you that. Will you fight with guns or knives or whatever you have? Or will you let it go to the first person who threatens you or your men?"

Pamela had always thought she was against violence of any kind, so she was thunderstruck by the feeling of fiercely possessive pride that rose up in her when she looked at the land stretching before her. She wouldn't allow anybody to take what was hers. "I'll fight," she muttered unwillingly. "I might not want to live in this country, but I refuse to allow anybody to take it from me."

"Good. Remember that when you want to disagree with what I'm doing."

"Why should you risk your neck for land that isn't yours?" she asked, suddenly more interested in Slade than in her land. "Why don't you get on your horse and head for California?"

"I don't know myself," Slade admitted and his eyes twinkled in the moonlight. "I guess I never could resist a challenge. Or a damsel in distress," he added.

"Just any damsel?"

"You know the answer to that," he said. His voice lost some of its clarity.

"What I told Dave yesterday is true. I don't know very much about you. You might give this 'line' to every woman you meet."

"My past is depressingly free of damsels," Slade observed dryly. "Besides, what 'line' am I giving you?"

"You know, the poor wandering cowboy without a horse or a place to lay his head." Pamela's lips twitched.

"I suppose I made up the fight and the gunshot wound?"

"No, they're real, and that's what has me confused. Why would anybody risk his life for someone he didn't know?"

"Any self-respecting man would protect a woman."

"Any man might, but not the way you did it." Pamela longed to have him say he wanted to protect *her*, not some

169

nameless representative of the female gender. His habit of referring to her as a member of a large, formless group piqued her.

Slade cast her a questioning glance. She found it hard to think when he was so close. God, but he was handsome. She felt like a silly school girl for harping on his looks, but she couldn't help it. Every time she saw him, they just reached out and grabbed her.

Just like she wanted *him* to grab her.

"You acted like you cared about me, not just the fact that I'm a woman," Pamela said, trying to pull her thoughts back to their conversation. If she let herself think of Slade's face, she would never make any sense.

"You're easy to care about," Slade replied. "Besides, how often does a man find a beautiful woman kneeling at his feet?"

"Is that what you want, a good looking woman who'll worship you?"

They faced each other, barely inches apart, but Slade felt like they were surrounded by an aura which bound them together as it cut them off from everyone else. How could he tell her she was wrong about what she felt just now, that she would realize it the moment her precious Frederick arrived? How could he tell her she was mistaken about him, that he was no Sir Galahad looking for a damsel to rescue?

Nothing but a drifter running from the law.

But he couldn't deny the invitation in her eyes, turn away from her upturned face, or ignore her parted lips. Hell, why should he try? He had never thought it would last. He had no reason to think Pamela wanted it to. But they were together now, just the two of them, alone in the night. No matter who owned tomorrow, this moment belonged to them.

Slade lifted his hand and caressed Pamela's cheek with the back of his fingers.

"I never wanted just any woman," he said softly. "I want one who wants me as much as I want her, who *needs* me as

170

much as I need her." He feathered a fingertip over the high ridge of her ivory cheekbone. "It wouldn't hurt if she looked like you and had a penchant for kneeling at my feet, but that's not necessary. Oh Hell," Slade said when he felt Pamela start to draw away, "I forgot I wasn't supposed to talk about anything but cows. You running away?"

"I ought to," Pamela said hesitantly, "but I confess I'm intrigued by what you want in a woman. Tell me, what *is* necessary?"

"Well, I don't suppose necessary is the right word exactly, but I'd be mighty pleased if she fitted in my arms as nicely as you do," Slade said. To demonstrate he slipped his arms around her waist and tugged.

Pamela allowed her body to lean against him, her head to settle into the hollow of his shoulder.

"It wouldn't hurt if she could put her arms around me. It can be a might chilly out here sometimes."

"And after she does all that?" Pamela asked, looking up at him in a way that made him want to crush her to his chest.

"She ought to want to kiss me. Some winter evenings there's an awful lot of time to fill up."

Pamela's expression didn't change, but her eyes glittered with amusement. "And if you could find a woman compliant enough to bend herself to your demands, what then?"

"I sure wouldn't tell her to go start supper."

"Will you be serious?" Pamela said as she tried to find enough spare flesh on his lean frame to pinch.

"I'm trying not to be," Slade said, all amusement gone from his eyes. "If I was to get serious, what with you here in my arms and nothing but that old moon to keep us company, there's no telling what I might do."

"Then let's *suppose* you were to be serious."

"This is all playacting now? You won't go thinking it's the real thing?"

"It's all playacting," Pamela assured him, settling back against his shoulder. "Now tell me, what would you do?"

171

"I can tell you one thing. I wouldn't waste a lot of time talking. I'd just grab her and kiss the daylights out of her."

"Are you always so rough?"

"Only when I'm serious."

But Slade wasn't rough. His arms tightened about Pamela, drew her closer to him, pressed her against his suddenly tense body. She could feel the rigid length of him pressed against her stomach, sending waves of heat pulsing through her body.

Slade lowered his head until he could feel Pamela's luxuriant hair against his cheek, until he could smell the fragrance of her expensive French perfume. He nuzzled her hair, reveled in the feel of the silky strands against his rough cheek; he nibbled her ear until she squirmed in protest; he kissed her neck until she was limp; he whispered in her ear until she was stiff with desire.

Then he kissed her.

His gentle lips captured her waiting mouth. Those lips sought to meld with hers as his arms involuntarily pulled her into his embrace. Gradually the pressure increased as he slowly forced her lips apart until her mouth opened to his seeking. The shock of his tongue in her mouth caused Pamela to pull in hard for breath, but she released it in a rush of compliance.

Never had she experienced anything even close to this. The crushing strength of his embrace, the lean hardness of his body, the sudden tenderness in her breasts, the slowly building warmth in her abdomen, all of it intoxicated her. It tempted her to abandon herself completely to this celebration of her senses. Her mouth opened wider, inviting him farther into its depths; her body pressed harder against him, heedless of the growing hardness pressing against her abdomen; her arms held him tighter hoping he would never let her go.

Slade broke the kiss, but his hold on her body never slackened.

"You're a very good actor," Pamela said when she could finally catch her breath. "I could almost believe you meant that."

Slade removed one hand to run his fingers across her cheek, then through her hair. "I worked in the carnival, remember. A man learns all kinds of tricks in a place like that."

"Show me another."

"My repertory isn't very big. Can I show you the same one again?"

"I guess so," Pamela whispered before she lost herself in Slade's embrace.

Slade hesitated almost too briefly to notice, but when he kissed her, Pamela forgot all about that split second of doubt. His mouth crushed hers in a desperate kiss, his lips demanding, seeking, plunging as though this kiss would have to last him a lifetime. The steel band of his arms tightened about her until she thought her ribs would break, and still he could not seem to hold her close enough. Pamela felt herself being swept away on an undertow, a current too strong to resist, a feeling too wonderful to want to.

Then Slade abruptly broke off the kiss and put her an arm's length from him.

"That's enough playacting for tonight." He sounded winded, like a man who'd been in a fight.

"But you weren't acting," Pamela said. She wasn't any more calm than Slade, but surprise steadied her.

"No," Slade agreed. "It would have been better if I had been."

"But you like me, don't you?" It was almost a plea.

"You know I do."

"Then why have you avoided me ever since I got Amanda's letter?"

"You know the answer to that, too. We're different people, Pamela, and we're headed in different directions. We can't do anything about it. We can't *be* anything but who we

173

are. There's something deep within us that makes us that way. We'd be fools not to recognize it."

"But that doesn't mean we have to stay away from each other."

"In a couple of weeks, maybe even a few days, we'll go our separate ways and never see each other again. No sense starting something we can't finish."

Pamela started to tell him she didn't want to start anything, but hadn't she done just that? She told him she would leave if he didn't stick to business, but she had been the one to sidetrack the conversation. And she didn't want it to end.

She did want something, but she didn't know what. She had always known what she wanted from Frederick, but Slade didn't resemble Frederick at all. Something about him drew her irresistibly, gave a whole new meaning to her concept of the relationship between a man and a woman. She needed more time to figure out what it was.

"We can still be friends," she offered.

"Maybe. Come on, it's time to go back."

"It sure is," someone said from behind a nearby boulder. "I'm so tired I can hardly keep my eyes open."

In a movement so quick it left Pamela breathless, Slade had dropped to his knees, both guns drawn.

"Come out slowly with your hands away from your guns," Slade ordered. "I get mighty jumpy when people follow me around."

"But you said one of us had to always keep the boss in sight," the aggrieved cowboy muttered as he emerged from his hiding place. "You didn't say we had to hold back when you went courting her."

Slade slid his guns back into their holsters. He started to say something but burst out laughing instead.

"How can you stand there guffawing?" demanded Pamela, caught between embarrassment and the realization that Slade had drawn his guns as a reflex action. "Someone

174

could have gotten hurt."

Slade only laughed harder.

Pamela's irritation with Slade had not disappeared by the next morning. Somehow she felt he had betrayed her, that he had played with her emotions, had not taken her feelings seriously. And that made her angry. She had enough difficulty justifying her interest in this cowboy. She doubted Amanda would approve of it, even as a lark, and she knew her mother would have been horrified.

What would your father think she suddenly wondered. It came as something of a shock to realize he might possibly approve of Slade. He wouldn't be pleased about his lack of background, he was too much a product of his Virginia heritage for that, but he would respect the man and like him for what he was.

Or was he too much of a rootless vagabond?

Yet oddly enough, Pamela found that wonderfully exciting and liberating. Slade made her feel totally free of any worries. Sometimes she felt that if things could go on like this forever, she would ask no more of life.

But it wouldn't last. It couldn't. She might be happy for a few weeks or months, possibly a year, but she would never be satisfied to remain at the ends of the earth, cut off from the kind of life she had grown to love. Neither did she wish to stay cut off from female companionship. She didn't want her children to grow up on a ranch. She didn't want her sons to grow up like Gaddy, and the thought of her daughters never setting foot off the Bar Double-B until they married some cowboy made her shudder.

Slade had been right. They had no future together.

But did he have to refuse her offer of friendship or to push her away? At least he could treat her with a little more consideration.

175

But Pamela was inexperienced, not stupid; she knew she wanted a lot more from Slade than *consideration*. It didn't need to be much. She would settle for a few sweet words and several kisses stolen in the moonlight.

No. It was better that Slade had seen they were about to go too far, that it was time to pull back. Their relationship had no future.

But what about now?

Beyond the intoxicating excitement of being held in his arms or the electric sensation of his kisses, she enjoyed the enervating warmth as heat from his body flowed into hers. Could he expect her to ignore the feeling of pleasure she experienced when she caught him watching her? When she could see desire in his eyes, sense the tension in every line of his body? Did he think she could rid her dreams of a face so handsome it banished her ordinary thoughts, or a body so disturbing it gave rise to a crop of new ones? Did he think she could ignore the tingling of her breasts or the hot, heavy wetness she felt in her private female parts?

She wouldn't willingly give up any of this, at least not without a struggle.

Or was it all simple pride? No man ever put Pamela White at arm's length. And she wouldn't make an exception for Slade Morgan. As of this moment he was a marked man.

Pamela climbed down from her wagon a half an hour before sunrise. The cold air made her gasp and pull her coat more tightly about her, but most of the men had already eaten their breakfast and rolled up their beds. The various camps gathered around fires according to the outfit they worked for, but they would soon saddle up and ride out together. Pamela had hardly set both feet on the ground before Mongo materialized out of nowhere.

"Would you do me the honor of riding with me today?" he asked in his most practiced, charming manner.

Pamela had not intended to ride with anyone, and Mongo's invitation only strengthened her resolution. If one of the men followed her—and one of them would—it could cause trouble. She planned to stay in camp, but Slade had unwittingly guaranteed she would have no choice. Or had it been unwitting? Had anything that man had done from the very first been accidental?

"This is my first roundup," she told Mongo, "so I thought I would watch from here today. If nothing else, I won't get in anybody's way."

"You'd never be in the way," Mongo assured her.

"Yes, she would," Slade said coming up and handing Pamela a cup of steaming coffee. "You can bank on a tenderfoot always being in the worst possible place."

Pamela didn't like being called a tenderfoot, even though she knew she was one. She liked even less being fenced in by Slade Morgan.

"I won't stay in camp every day," she said to Mongo giving him an encouraging smile just to spite Slade.

"Then I'll ask you again tomorrow."

"Save your breath. She can't ride out unless someone on the crew rides with her."

Mongo looked at Slade like he couldn't decide whether to get angry again or be flabbergasted at his presumption. "What's a two-bit cowpoke got to say about what Miss White does?" he demanded.

"I'm ramrodding this outfit," Slade said, his grey eyes hard and cold. "No one in the Bar Double-B outfit does anything without my permission."

"Is he telling the truth?" Mongo demanded of Pamela. The shock of his disbelief made him look comical.

How *dare* he say it like that, Pamela raged to herself. She wouldn't let him treat her like a child who needed permission before she could leave the house. She ached to deny his control of her actions, to fling Slade's arrogance in his face— she had *never* meant this when she agreed to follow his orders—but she had agreed to all his conditions. She couldn't deny his authority now without going back on her word. Besides, she refused to give Mongo Shepherd the pleasure of knowing Slade had forced her into a corner. As far as anyone on this roundup knew, she had made Slade Morgan her foreman because she thought he could handle the job better than anyone else.

"Of course it's true," Pamela said forcing a smile to her lips that belied her inward urge to hit Slade over the head with something made out of stone. "You didn't think he would be willing to fight over me for no reason, did you?"

"Do you mean you were *paying* him then?"

Pamela longed to say yes. Slade had hurt her pride. He had flat rejected her, and he had done so in front of one of her hands, but one look at his stiff-necked stance killed the strength of her anger. He expected her to deny his honor; he expected to be rejected by another woman he cared for; perhaps he even believed he wasn't good enough for her. For those very reasons she wouldn't salvage her pride at the cost of his.

"He did that on his own. But since yesterday, he's been working for me." She couldn't look him in the eye even though she wanted to, badly. She didn't deserve any thanks. Chivalry had been his motivating impulse, hers pure spite. "If you want to talk business, talk to Slade. I'll back any decision he makes."

Then without looking at either man, she walked over to where Dave sat and knelt down to talk with him.

Slade wished he still had his beard. He hoped his face didn't reveal his astonishment, but after the way Pamela had backed him, he couldn't help but feel a little smug. Mongo's face was a study in chagrin.

But only Pamela's face interested him. He knew she was still angry at him for last night. It had been on the tip of her tongue to repudiate his reason for fighting Mongo. He had hurt her vanity, and whether she knew it or not, she was a woman of many vanities. So why had she stood behind him without reservation? The answer came with the impact of

178

a rifle stock slammed into his stomach. Because of the roundup, you fool. She wants the money to go back to Baltimore and her precious Frederick. You're the only way she's going to get it.

But Slade couldn't believe that was the only reason. She had refused to meet his eyes. There *had* to be another reason.

But he didn't have time to figure it out. He had to deal with Mongo and the rest of the ranchers.

"I mean to know what's going on at all times," Slade told Mongo. "You don't round up from Bar Double-B range without talking to me, and you don't brand mavericks without one of our men present."

"I'll be damned if that's so," Mongo blustered. "I'm not taking orders from any two-bit drifter. I almost beat you once. I'll finish the job."

"I'm still a little sore," Slade said. He pointed to his shoulder, and his lips curved into a cold smile. "You'll have to forgive me if I don't offer to take off my guns this time."

His lips curled with scorn, but his eyes flickered uneasily between Slade's face and his guns. "A foreman shot in the shoulder and an ex-foreman shot in the leg," Mongo blustered. "Looks like Pamela's got herself one helluva crew."

He turned on his heel and walked back in the direction of his own camp. Slade knew it wouldn't end there. Mongo wouldn't back down or give up. He just hadn't decided what to do next.

The day turned into a long, hard struggle. The men went out in pairs to systematically cover the more than two million acres of grazing land. It took from forty to fifty acres to support a single cow in this kind of country. With something like forty thousand cows to be sorted through so the new calves could be branded, the men had their work cut out for them.

The branding fires of each camp blazed high long before noon as each crew busied itself branding its own cattle. The bawling of cows and calves separated for just a few moments—calves roped and branded and cows just irritated at being driven from their familiar territory—filled the air with a mild roar. Branding irons clinked; dozens of horses' hooves echoed on the hard-packed ground; men shouted back and forth to each other as they cut, roped, and branded; the rank smell of dung, sweat and burning hair and hide fouled the air; sweat poured down men's faces, touching their lips with salt and tightly molding their clothes to muscled bodies; spiraling heat made it hard to breath, and a thick, choking dust rose everywhere.

The chilling sound of a single gunshot from the direction of the Slash Seven fires brought the whole panorama of action to an abrupt halt. Pamela raced toward Mongo's camp as fast as she could run, her heart pounding in her throat. She had seen Slade ride over there just minutes earlier. The sight that met her eyes caused the hairs on the back of her neck to stand up in fear.

Slade stood in the center of Mongo's crew, his gun drawn on Peak Bolin who, moments before, had been holding a branding iron. No one drew a gun when Mongo and Pamela shoved their way inside the circle, but Pamela could tell the men were tense, on the verge of a gun battle.

"What the hell is going on here?" Mongo demanded, his face a mask of rage. "What do you mean busting into my camp like this?"

"He shot at me," the stupefied Peak told Mongo, the hand which had held the branding iron still shaking. "He tried to kill me."

"Slade . . ." Pamela began.

"That's a maverick," Slade said pointing to the calf still lying on its side. He spoke to Mongo, but his glance included everyone who had joined the circle. "We agreed there would be no branding of mavericks without every owner being represented."

"You tried to kill me," the cowhand repeated somewhat hysterically.

"I shot the branding iron out of your hands."

"No man can shoot like that," Mongo contradicted. He approached Slade menacingly, his hand on his own gun. "You *were* trying to kill him."

"Get your hand off that gun, Shepherd. I'd take you before you could clear leather."

"I'm not afraid of you, cowboy. I have boys who can shoot you out of a running saddle without opening their eyes wide."

"But you'd already be dead." Slade's gun pointed directly at Mongo. "Now I don't aim to start a fight," Slade said addressing the assembled men, "but there'll be no branding of mavericks by individual crews."

"That's no maverick," Mongo said.

"Then show me it's ma," Slade challenged. "Let him up," he shouted to the cowboy who, so startled by the unsuspected turn of events, still held the calf down. The man loosed the ropes and the calf leapt to its feet. But no cow emerged from the herd to claim it as its own. The calf ran off by itself, away from the herd.

"It was an accident. I didn't know," Peak sputtered. "I just brand what they throw."

"So he made a mistake," Mongo shouted. "That's no reason to kill a man."

"I've already told you I shot the branding iron out of his hand."

"And I already told *you* nobody can shoot that good. You're lying. I think we ought to hang him." The rumble of agreement was stilled when Pamela stepped inside the circle.

"I can prove he's telling the truth," she announced. She didn't know what to do, the idea was only half formed in her mind, but she couldn't afford to wait. If the mob mentality ever got hold of these men, there'd be no way to stop them.

"Pamela, honey, you don't have any business being here," Mongo said solicitously, coming immediately to her side. "Hanging is a messy business. You don't want to see it."

"Nobody is going to hang anybody," Pamela said, her voice quivering slightly. "Slade can prove what he said." Think, she told herself. What can he do to prove to everybody, once and for all, that he's not only telling the truth but that he's too dangerous to mess with?

"That's impossible," Mongo said, confident of himself, determined to get Pamela out of the way and back to the business of hanging Slade. But Pamela knew what to do now, and she didn't move an inch.

"Do you have any coins in your pocket?"

"Sure, but . . ."

"Give them to me." Mongo grumbled, unsure of what she intended to do, but he handed her three twenty-dollar gold pieces. "I need three more. Anybody else got any?" She just hoped Slade turned out to be as good as Dave thought he was.

The other ranchers, who had all joined the circle by now, managed to come up with three coins among them. Gold was not all that common, even among wealthy ranchers, and they weren't too pleased to part with them.

"I'm going to give them to Gaddy." The boy pushed his way through the crowd, anxious to take his part in the show. "When I give the nod, Gaddy will toss them as high as he can. Are you ready, Slade?"

Slade hadn't moved. He had known the danger when he shot the branding iron out of Peak Bolin's hand, but he had laid his plans well. He still didn't know but what he may have made a mistake, but he would be the one to pay if something went wrong.

He never expected Pamela to step into the circle in his defense. The trick she proposed nearly bowled him over. Did she have any idea how difficult it was to hit anything that small? The idea that he could hit six coins *in the air* made him

182

feel weak in the knees.

But he had to bring it off. He risked ruining Pamela's credibility as well as his own. Everybody expected her to back her own man, but they clearly hadn't expected her to make a public stand out of it. They had all heard of Dave's injury, and they could all guess that Slade must have given her some proof that he could handle the job. But they hadn't expected to be faced down by a woman. It had taken tremendous courage for her to step out of that crowd. He couldn't let her down.

No woman, no matter what she said or what she thought she felt about ranches, cowboys, Baltimore, or anything else, *no woman* would put herself on the line for a man, like Pamela had just done for him, unless that man meant one helluva lot to her.

For the first time Slade believed he had a chance against this Frederick. In the same moment he realized he wasn't just in love with Pamela. He wanted her to be his wife.

The realization almost rattled his nerve. Whether he knew it or not, that's what he'd been wanting from the moment he saw her standing on the porch, maybe even from the moment he left Texas. It was the reason he left the carnival, the reason he changed his name, the reason he'd never been able to stay in one place very long. All the time he'd been looking for some place he could call home.

Now he'd found it.

It wouldn't be easy to convince Pamela she had misunderstood her feelings. It would be even harder to convince her she liked what she thought she hated, but he would worry about all that in good time. Right now he had to bring off this trick.

If he failed, Mongo would do his best to hang him.

Slade ejected the empty shell, dropped a new cartridge into the chamber, settled the gun back in its holster, and backed a little way from the group. Tense, his concentration on Gaddy's handful of coins, his own hands suspended above his guns, he forced himself to empty his mind of everything except the challenge before him. Slowly his body relaxed and his mind stopped teasing itself over the consequences of failure. His vision narrowed until he saw nothing but Gaddy's hand. He waited until the sounds around him dimmed from his ears, until his mind emptied itself of everything except his gun and those six coins.

Only then did Slade nod his head.

"Toss them," Pamela called out.

Pamela watched the coins sail into the air more than twenty feet above the heads of an audience that strained its necks to follow them. The coins turned and spun in the sunlight, sending streaks of gold light flashing in all directions. They shot upward quickly, slowed, and seemed to hang in the air for a slender moment before plummeting to earth.

During that brief pause, Slade fired six rapid shots.

The circle of cowboys surged forward the moment the coins hit the ground. No one made a sound as Gaddy laid them before Mongo. All six had holes in them, four of them dead center.

Chapter 12

Pamela didn't dare look at Slade. She felt such a wave of relief that for a moment she feared her legs would go out from under her in front of all these goggling men. But that really didn't matter. Nothing mattered now that danger no longer threatened Slade. Nobody would even think of hanging him now.

"In the future, I think it's safe to assume Mr. Morgan hits what he aims at," she said. Ostensibly she spoke to Mongo, but she allowed her gaze to wander over the crowd, to make eye contact with as many men as possible. She wouldn't let them easily forget what they had almost tried to do.

"That's no excuse for him shooting at Peak," Mongo said when he could pull his gaze away from the incredible sight of the six coins. But the steam had gone out of his anger. Even he believed Slade had fired at the branding iron.

"Then you'd better see that your men are more careful about what they brand," Pamela said, this time looking directly at Mongo. "All of us have a stake in those mavericks." The other ranchers nodded their agreement, and she finally relaxed. Slade no longer held their complete attention. Their thoughts had returned where they belonged, on the cows.

Only Slade didn't let it stop there.

"All the land north of Blue River is Bar Double-B range," he said after everyone had satisfied himself that Slade really had been able to hit all six coins. "After the branding is done, everybody make sure your beef is off our range. Anything there in the fall will be sold."

Everybody forgot the coins. Slade had just challenged every man in the group.

"You can't do that," Pamela squeaked, too startled to keep her voice down. "Cows wander all over."

"Not across the river," Slade said loud enough for everyone to hear him. "They have to be driven."

Pamela's gaze focused on Slade's face, but his gaze was locked on the hard, pioneering men around them. Pamela looked from Slade to the circle of severe faces that surrounded them, and for the first time she saw these men as enemies—grim, hard-fighting men. They didn't think of her as Josh White's little girl any more, and they weren't here to put themselves out to please her Ma or to make her laugh. She stood for the Bar Double-B, the boss of the man who threatened their ability to survive in this harsh environment. Each one of them deliberately measured the man who opposed them.

Only one man stands in their way, Pamela thought. And it's so easy to get rid of one man when he stands alone.

What could have possessed Slade to make such a threat? Not even her father had dared to go that far. But she knew Slade wouldn't back down now. One brief glance told her he had lost every bit of support his shooting might have won from the ranchers. For years, they had looked at her father's land with envious eyes. For years they had been in the practice of swimming part of their herds across the river to graze on the more bountiful grass.

They were hard men who had taken their range from the Indians and held it against long odds. They had all killed men in their time. Maybe that had been a long time ago, but she doubted they would be overly worried about killing one

186

more. Now a stranger, a common cowboy, a nameless drifter had told them there was something they couldn't do any more. They might take that from Josh White, but they sure as hell wouldn't take it from Slade Morgan.

She had to talk to him, warn him of the danger, or he might not be alive come fall.

"You can't make that stick," Mongo said, arrogance in his voice and facial expression. "Look around. There's not a man who'll support you. If Pamela hadn't thought of that coin trick, you'd be dangling from a rope by now."

Slade smiled, and Pamela shuddered; she had never seen such a menacing smile.

"*You* look around," Slade said. "Do you see any Bar Double-B men?"

Mongo scanned the crowd and then broke out laughing. "Hell, you're all alone except for a woman and a boy. I could still hang you if I wanted."

Slade gave an ear-piercing whistle. All along the perimeter of the group, men stood up from where they had crouched or stepped forward from where they had hidden themselves. All were Bar Double-B men, and each carried a rifle and a gun. Mongo's color became a little less ruddy; the laugh froze on his lips.

"I never make a stand unless my back is protected," Slade said.

"You wait," Mongo threatened as he stalked off. "You'll open your mouth one time too many one of these days. Not even Pamela will be able to save you then."

"I've got to talk to you!" Pamela whispered imperatively as people began to drift back to their jobs.

"Just a minute," Slade said as he turned to speak to Gaddy. "I want you to go back to the ranch. Don't make your departure too obvious, but I want you there by nightfall."

"What for?" Gaddy protested. "I ain't never been on a roundup before. Uncle Josh wouldn't let me."

"I want you to keep a careful watch on the ranch," Slade said. Pamela could find no gleam of amusement in his eyes. This was no attempt to make Gaddy feel good by giving him a mock important job. Slade was serious.

"You think they might try to burn the barn again?" Despite his growing disenchantment with the reality of a range war, the excitement of the struggle had a firm grip on Gaddy.

"There's more to the ranch than a barn."

"You don't mean the ranch house!" Pamela exclaimed.

"We can't take that chance. Gaddy, I'm depending on you to see that nothing happens while we're away."

"You mean to use a gun?"

"Do what you have to," Slade answered.

Gaddy swallowed, once, twice, then he stiffened up ramrod straight before Slade. "You can depend on me," he said, just as if he were a cadet facing his commanding officer. "Anybody trying to get in that canyon will have to shoot my liver out first."

"Pamela wouldn't want you to do that. She can replace stone and timber, but she can't replace a loyal cousin."

Speechless with pleasure, Gaddy blushed.

Pamela stared at Slade. She still saw Gaddy as a useless boy, but she wouldn't say a single word that would take away from Gaddy's developing vision of himself as a man.

"Slade's right. Don't take any chances," she added. "I'd be very upset if anything happened to you."

Pamela guessed if she was ever going to see a human being walk on air, she was seeing it now. Gaddy had never been so happy in his life, and he hurried to get his things together.

"It's about time somebody gave that boy something to do instead of telling him how worthless he is," Slade said. "Out here boys are men long before they reach his age."

"Do you really think somebody will try to burn the ranch

while we're away?"

"I don't know. I might if I could only figure out what's going on."

"I thought you knew."

"So did I, but I'm not so sure any more."

"Why?"

"I don't know that either."

Pamela looked at him in considerable surprise. "I've never known you to be unsure of yourself."

Slade smiled. "It's playacting," he said, and Pamela blushed at the memories that word brought back. "There haven't been many times in my life when I *have* known what I was doing."

"You sure gave a good imitation just a minute ago."

"Oh, that."

"That just might have gotten you killed. Whatever possessed you to tell those men you'd sell their cows?"

"It seemed like as good a time as any."

"Even Dad didn't dare go that far."

"He should have. Then he wouldn't have to be going to Santa Fe for barbed wire and gunfighters."

"Slade, be careful. These aren't mean men, but Dad says they'll stop at very little. They've each killed several men. That's how they got where they are now, and they're not going to give it up because of you."

"Are you backing down?"

"Of course not," she replied angrily, "but you don't have to hurl a challenge in their faces. You certainly didn't have to do it to everybody at once."

"It saves time."

Didn't this man understand the seriousness of her warning? She had grown up mostly in Baltimore, yet it looked like she had a better understanding of western men than he did. "It could also get you killed," she snapped.

Slade's eyes twinkled in amusement, and Pamela had to banish the thought of how handsome he looked so she could

189

remember she wanted to hit him. Couldn't he understand? This was no joking matter.

"I would never have made such a statement except for two things," Slade explained. "First, the river gives us a perfectly good fence everybody can see. It's also pretty deep. Everybody knows those cows don't come over on their own. Anybody who pushes his cows over now does it knowing he risks a fight. Second," he added before Pamela could argue, "pressure's been building up on this range for months. If something isn't done to let everybody know where you stand, one of those greedy fools is going to keep on pushing until all hell breaks loose."

"For God's sake, Slade, are you determined to start a fight?"

"I don't need to. There's one headed your way right now. This is just a last attempt to stave it off. I hope it's not too late."

"You should never have shot the branding iron out of that boy's hands. You don't know these men. You could get hurt. Will you never learn that guns don't solve anything?"

"Is this lecture just for me, or does it go for the other ranchers too? If you're going to reform them, do it right away. I'd feel a little foolish if I kept my hands behind my back while they filled me full of lead."

"Don't make fun of me, Slade Morgan," she hissed. "Not after I helped save your neck."

"Why?"

"What do you mean?" she asked, so startled by his question she forgot what she intended to say.

"Why did you save me? You didn't even know if I could do that trick."

"I had to think of something that would convince them you were good enough to shoot that branding iron intentionally instead of by mistake. Those coins were all I could think of."

"I've never done a trick like that," Slade said.

Pamela saw amusement literally do somersaults in his eyes.

"What?" Her brain felt like cotton. She couldn't think when he smiled at her like that. His smile sent delicious shivers down through her body which all seemed to center in the hidden area between her thighs.

"Those coins are too small for the audience to see. Besides, the glare inside a tent makes it impossible to see them."

"You mean you've never shot the center out of a coin?"

"Not before today. Besides, it's too expensive. At a hundred and twenty dollars a pop, I'd be ruined before the end of the night."

Pamela swayed. She had no idea why she didn't go ahead and faint. Thinking about what would have happened if Slade had missed all those coins certainly made her feel weak enough. Fainting seemed like a small price to pay for the chance she had taken.

"But I take it as a great compliment you had that much faith in me."

"Get away from me, Slade Morgan," Pamela said. She didn't feel at all steady on her feet, but she firmly removed his arm from around her waist. "Before you came ambling into my front yard, I was a normal, sane, responsible, *happy and contented* adult. Knowing you has reduced me to a ball of nerves. I never know what's going to happen next. Disaster follows you like sunshine follows rain. Get yourself filled full of lead over a few cows if you insist—they aren't even your cows, for God's sake—but don't expect me to bandage you up this time."

She stalked off toward camp, but a broad smile of satisfaction settled on Slade's lips. For the moment he forgot about Mongo and the coming struggle. Right now he didn't want to think about anything except Pamela. If he knew only one thing, he knew *nothing* would keep her from his

191

side if he were wounded.

For such a reward as that, he just might get himself shot at again.

Gaddy stood in the mouth of the canyon and pondered the situation. It was all right for Slade to tell him to guard the ranch, but he couldn't stay up all night. Not even thunder and lightning had the power to wake him up. He hadn't waked up the night they tried to burn the barn until Slade's gun had gone off right under his window.

What would it matter if he fell asleep? Pamela wouldn't blame him. Neither would her father. After all, he was only sixteen. Hell, Dave didn't believe he could protect a henhouse from a three-legged coyote. Of course he'd never be able to keep awake all night, so why should he worry so much about it? He'd just stay up as long as he could. Probably nothing would happen anyway. Nothing ever had before.

But even though Gaddy had fallen into the habit of taking refuge behind any handy excuse, he knew enough about Slade to know that no excuse would work this time. Slade had told him to watch the ranch, and he expected it to be done. Period.

What would Slade do to him if he failed?

Nothing.

But Gaddy realized Slade didn't expect him to fail. Slade didn't make excuses for himself, and he probably wouldn't accept them from anyone else. *It only mattered that you failed.* For the first time in his life, Gaddy decided he would not fail. He couldn't. He'd rather be sent to his Ma's relatives in Alabama than confess to Slade he'd fallen asleep and let someone burn the ranch.

But how could he stay awake? Even if a confirmed killer held a gun at his head, he doubted he could keep his eyes open all night. He'd probably fall asleep and miss his own murder.

He thought of and discarded idea after idea as being too fraught with possibilities for disaster. He could strip down to his underwear. The frigid night air would keep him awake, but just the thought of being surprised in his long johns, especially by Pamela or Belva, caused him to turn crimson. He would have to stay on his feet. He couldn't go to sleep standing up. Or could he?

Gaddy decided to take no chances. He would booby-trap the canyon.

Working with feverish haste to get the job finished before nightfall, he stretched a roll of wire across the opening and prayed no one would try to come in during the night. Just in case some intruders should see the wire and try to climb over it, he laid tin roofing across the trail. It would be impossible for anyone to cross that, even on tiptoe, without waking him up. For added insurance, he raided Pamela's box of Christmas tree ornaments for the dozen small crystal bells she had brought back from Baltimore. He tied them to the limbs of the bushes near the canyon walls. Now it would be impossible for as much as a coyote to slip through unnoticed.

Then he laid out his bedroll behind a rock off the trail just in case he wanted to get off his feet for a while. If trouble did come, he'd be right on top of it. He laid his shotgun on one side and his rifle on the other. He kept his hands on the pair of tied-down six guns at his waist. He used to wear just one until he noticed Slade wore two. If he had to protect the ranch all by himself, he needed as many guns as possible.

When he had finished, Gaddy stood back and surveyed his handiwork. He had to admit to a feeling of pride. Wouldn't anybody get across this barrier without him knowing it, not unless they had wings.

Next morning when Belva came up to milk the cow, she saw Gaddy staggering back and forth across the mouth of the canyon like a soldier on a picket line. At first she thought he had been drinking, but after a moment she realized he was merely very sleepy. Intrigued, she started toward him only to be flabbergasted by the barricade he had erected. "What in the name of thunder have you been doing?" she commanded. "You better clear that right away. Mr. White will skin you alive if he comes back and sees this mess in his front yard."

"Got to leave it," Gaddy mumbled almost incoherently. "Slade said to watch the ranch."

"Maybe, but you can bet he didn't mean for you to wrap it up in bailing wire and tie it up with Miss Pamela's Christmas bells."

"Leave it alone," Gaddy repeated and started toward the bunkhouse at a stumbling walk.

"Well I never," Belva said to herself as she examined the barricade a second time. "I didn't think a branding iron could keep that boy on his feet all night. Looks like Mr. Morgan knows something the rest of us don't."

"How did your first day go?"

Pamela jumped. Slade had come up on her unexpectedly as she stared into the fire. She didn't realize it had gotten so dark. A person could stand just outside of the ring of light, no more than a dozen feet away, and not be seen. It was black as ink.

"A little boring, if you want the truth," Pamela confessed. "After watching them brand half a dozen calves, I lost all interest. Besides, I always did hate cows."

"You hate cows!"

"What's to like about them?" Pamela asked. "They're noisy, dangerous, and smelly. The filthy-tempered beasts won't even let you milk them."

"They're wild," Slade said, his eyes dancing in the firelight.

God, if he keeps looking at me like that, I'll go crazy Pamela thought. Doesn't he know what he does to me?

"I know that," she replied, pulling her mind back on the conversation. "I don't like them anyway."

194

"I'm afraid you're in for a long week."

"It won't be so bad once I start riding three or four hours a day. I'm actually looking forward to it. At last I'll get a chance to see some of the range that's causing so much trouble."

"I don't want you to leave the camp."

"Why?"

"It's too dangerous."

"Don't start that again. You can't make me believe anyone is going to try to kill me. Western men practically worship a good woman."

"Let's go for a walk," Slade said holding out his hands to help her up. Pamela quickly grasped his fingers and pulled herself up close to him. She didn't want to go walking, but she never refused the chance to be with Slade. The touch of his hands on hers felt like a burning brand. It marked her.

"It's too dark out there. I can't see a thing."

"It's easier to see once you're away from the fire," Slade explained. "Firelight actually blinds you rather than helps you see."

Pamela felt a little doubtful, but she wanted to be alone with Slade too much to care. As long as he walked at her side, she would enter the blackest cave in the world.

But he was right. Five minutes away from the fire and she realized she could see the entire panorama of the roundup, the herd in the distance, the cowboys riding the night watch, the glow of the campfires of the other crews, and the dark shapes of the extra horses in the ramuda.

"It's the moon," Slade explained.

"You seem to have a most extraordinary affinity for the moon."

"Moonlight never lies."

Do you, she wondered, then quieted her doubts before she spoke. "What does it say about me?" Pamela felt brazen, but rather than feel ashamed of it, she felt exhilarated.

"It says you're an extremely beautiful woman. A mere

smile from those lips, or a single glance from your eyes, can drive an ordinary man crazy. Just your presence can make him lose his control."

"What about the extraordinary man?"

"All men are equally susceptible when it comes to women."

"Then when did you succumb to my wiles?"

"Long ago."

Pamela gave him a look of patent disbelief.

"I just haven't lost control."

Pamela laughed. She wasn't sure whether she laughed at his words or herself. She guessed it was more important that she still could laugh.

"Okay, what did you bring me out here to tell me? It obviously isn't that you love my hair or that my eyes are your favorite color of brown."

"No, but I do like to feel your hair against my cheek. It feels just like silk. And I adore brown eyes. They're so much warmer than blue."

"Get on with it, you shameless flatterer," Pamela said. "I don't like to mix business with pleasure."

"Which do you prefer?" he asked.

Pleasure, she answered silently. "Business," she said aloud. "It doesn't confuse my senses."

"I'll bet you've never been confused."

"I didn't used to be, but lately I feel that way all the time. Now you've destroyed the mood, so you might as well tell me what's bothering you."

"I'm not sure," Slade said, allowing himself a few minutes before he tried to explain. "Right now it's just a feeling, but there's something very wrong here."

"You can't expect me to take action based on feelings."

"I've been a performer all my life. One thing all successful entertainers have in common is a feel for the audience. Sometimes the lights are so bright you can't even see them. Sometimes there are so many faces you'd swear they represented every emotion in the world. But work the crowd a few minutes and you begin to feel their mood. It's nothing you can put your finger on, but it's just as real as you or I are."

Pamela listened, suspended somewhere between total disbelief and wonder at the continually unexpected facets of this man. One minute he shot branding irons out of people's hands and challenged every gun-hardened rancher in the area. In virtually the next, he rhapsodized about moonlight and the mood of a carnival crowd. Sometimes he moved completely beyond her experience. For all she understood of him she might just as well have never met a man in her life.

"There is something wrong here. And it's more than Mongo trying to set fire to one of your barns so you'll marry him. There are too many questions about that. If all he wants is the ranch, marrying you won't necessarily get it for him. Your father is still alive. You could leave it to your children or even divorce him. Besides Mongo is already rich. He might be greedy enough to fight for your land, but he doesn't have to have it. He could just as easily go somewhere else. Who told him about this place?"

"I don't think anybody did. He just stopped when he got here."

"That sounds right. He's too impatient to lay out a careful plan and stick to it. He'd blow up and cause some kind of confrontation, like he did today, like he did at the ranch."

In spite of herself, Pamela felt a shiver of fear. "What are you trying to tell me?"

"I feel like we're all being manipulated. I think there's somebody somewhere pulling strings and making us dance to his tune."

"That's preposterous." How could she keep from laughing at such an absurd suggestion?

"Then why didn't that gunman kill Dave? Why did he just shoot him in the leg?"

"He missed."

"Has Dave ever been shot at before I came to the ranch?"

197

"No."

"Then it's possible they shot him so I would have to take over his job."

"But they couldn't be sure of that. I could have chosen someone else." Slade might be jealous of Mongo—Pamela rather liked that idea—but it wasn't like him to talk so irrationally.

"Not if no one else would take it."

"This is all crazy," Pamela said, openly skeptical. "What makes you think there's someone behind all this?"

"A lot of little things, but I didn't start to put them all together until after we got here. Remember, I spent most of that afternoon looking about? Well, I saw six cowboys sitting together under a tree some distance from here. I didn't think anything of it at the time because I didn't know any of them. But I saw them again after we arrived in camp. They each belong to a different crew."

"You think . . ."

"I think somebody is out to cause trouble, and he's got a man planted at each ranch to keep him up-to-date with what's going on."

"Is that why you sent Gaddy back to the ranch?" Slade nodded. "You should have sent one of the men."

"Gaddy doesn't know what to do around cows, but he's more than capable of watching the ranch house. By the way, if you really want to turn that boy into a man, give him something to do. Keep him sitting around while everybody belittles him, and he'll become as worthless as you expect."

"Okay," Pamela agreed, too preoccupied with what Slade had just said to give Gaddy's situation much thought just now. "I still don't understand what you think is going to happen."

"I don't know, but somehow I think Mongo is the key."

"Really, Slade, I can't believe he would do any of this. I know he's greedy, but to shoot Dave? I can't believe that of him."

198

"Okay, have it your way," Slade said, tired of trying to warn her against Mongo, "just don't leave camp."

A wave of anger swept over Pamela. She didn't know whether he wanted to keep her in camp because he really believed this nonsense or whether he just didn't want her going off with Mongo. Either way she had had enough.

"I'll go where I please and with whom I please. I promised to support you," she continued before he could respond, "but I thought you were referring to the roundup. It never occurred to me it would extend to a jealous attempt to keep Mongo and me apart."

Slade saw red.

"You think all this is just jealousy of Mongo?" By God, not even Trish had been that conceited.

"What else can it be? You start a fight with a man you've never seen before the first morning you're here. Two days later you have a confrontation over my riding with him. You shoot at one of his men, and you accuse him of I don't know what kind of crimes. I've known Mongo for six months. He's always been a perfect gentleman. I've only known you for a few days, and you've been in trouble the entire time. What am I supposed to think?"

"Think what you damned well please," Slade said in a strangled croak. "I quit."

"Oh, no you don't." Pamela grabbed his sleeve as he started to stride past her. "If I can't fire you, you can't quit."

Slade was too mad to consider his words. They just tumbled out. "Look, lady, I can do anything I damned well please. And you can take it from me that hanging around you is high on my list of things I *don't* want to do."

Pamela's gaze didn't waver. "So is quitting a job you've started."

Slade didn't move. She had him there.

"Look, I don't mind your being jealous over me. In fact, if the circumstances were different, I think I'd probably like it." Slade looked absolutely furious. Pamela wondered if she could finish everything she wanted to say before he exploded. "But you can't run a ranch or be foreman of a crew if you can't make objective judgments. It's too dangerous."

"Now you listen to me, Pamela White, and you listen good. I haven't been in my right mind since I got here. I couldn't be, not and do all the crazy things you talked me into doing, but I'm not a lovesick fool. You're right. I *am* jealous of Mongo Shepherd. I'm jealous of Frederick too, whoever the hell he is. I'm jealous of every man you've ever smiled at, talked with, dreamed about. I wish they'd all been me. If I walk out of here tomorrow, I'll never stop wishing I'd stayed."

"But," he added before she could interrupt, "no woman—do you hear me?—*no woman* has ever got me so crazy mixed up I couldn't think. You're right. I won't quit. I'm going to stay and prove I'm right. I'm also going to prove that all those notions you learned in Baltimore aren't worth a hill of beans." He grabbed her and pulled her so close she could feel the heat of his skin through her clothes.

"I'm also going to prove that one drifting cowboy is worth a dozen of your Fredericks and Mongos. I'm going to prove you made one hell of a mistake when you looked down your beautiful nose at me."

Pamela woke up with a start. She had been dozing fitfully. Her argument with Slade still upset her, but the way he left her disturbed her even more. He had marched her back to her wagon, told her to get inside and *stay* there and then walked away. Just like she was a tenderfoot being disciplined for misbehaving. She had simmered with rage before finally talking herself into getting some sleep.

At first she couldn't figure out what had waked her. The night seemed perfectly silent. Even the cows had stopped their incessant complaining about their confinement. Then she heard it, softly at first, but gradually growing louder. It was a man, and he was singing with the most beautiful baritone voice Pamela had ever heard.

Pamela sat up in her bed mesmerized by the sound. She had heard many singers in Baltimore, but never had she heard such a voice. And to think it belonged to a common ordinary cowboy. Why, with some training, that man might be able to sing in New York.

She listened for a while, unable to distinguish most of the words because the tent muffled the consonants, but he seemed to be singing a religious song. That surprised her even more. Even the hands on her ranch couldn't sing without the help of words and somebody to lead them. But this man kept on singing, going from one song to another with hardly a pause, the quiet power of his voice floating over the desert unhindered.

Finally Pamela's curiosity got the better of her. She had no business getting up at night, not in a camp full of men, but she just had to know where those songs were coming from. She had figured out that the cowboy on watch duty was singing to the cows as he circled the herd. Perhaps if she crept softly to the edge of the camp, she could recognize him when he came by.

But just as Pamela started to climb down from her wagon, one of the men nearby stirred and sat up in his bed. Pamela scrambled back inside.

"What the hell is going on?" the man demanded. He prodded the sleeper nearest him until he woke up. "What's all that infernal racket?"

"Just some fella on guard duty."

"I know that, but what's he doing?"

"Singing, you fool."

"I know he's singing. I mean *what* is he singing?"

"Something I doubt you ever heard before. Them is hymns. Baptist hymns at that. And he's singing every last verse, too. Apparently our man has had himself inside a church a powerful lot if I'm any judge."

"Who the hell is it? Can you make out?"

"Look's like that Morgan fella to me, though it don't seem too likely."

"Morgan? He don't strike me as any church-going fella. Why he'd as soon shoot you as be bothered with you."

"No doubt you read your Bible every night."

"I do not," the man declared indignantly. "I ain't even got one."

"Then you ain't likely to know. The Bible's full of salty characters. Old Mongo wouldn't stand a chance against the likes of Nebuchadnezzar or that Sennacherib."

"You sure you ain't cussin' me?" the cowboy said, sitting up so he could reach his gun.

"Them's heathen kings, you fool."

"How'd you know all that stuff?"

"I may be a hell-bound cowhand, but at least my ma brought me up right."

Slade! Pamela practically fell back into her bed, too shocked to care if she stubbed her toe or got a splinter. Slade, singing like an opera singer, and singing hymns at that. She could add this to the list of things she didn't know about him, but for the first time, a discovery pleased her. Slade couldn't be as cynical as he seemed. More importantly, he probably had nothing in his background to be afraid of. Any man who knew that many hymns, and willingly sang them in front of a lot of tough cowboys, had to have been brought up right.

He was coming this way. Pamela could hear his voice getting closer. Anxious to identify at least one of the hymns, Pamela stuck her head outside the wagon so she could hear better. But after listening just a few moments, she blushed to the tips of her toes and quickly withdrew her head.

Slade had changed over to the raunchiest song she had ever heard.

Pamela's whole body stiffened when Slade headed toward

her. For three days he hadn't approached her unless she was with someone else. For three days they hadn't discussed the roundup unless Dave sat next to her. *For three whole days* he hadn't spent a single moment alone with her.

Not once had he smiled at her or stopped by to ask how she got along. He didn't bring her morning coffee. Neither did his gaze wander in her direction. She knew because she watched him constantly. What else did she have to do while she remained in camp, her heart a lead weight in her chest, her soul eaten alive by the most terrible yearning she had ever experienced?

More than enough time had passed for her to regret her assumption that jealousy had motivated Slade's suspicion of Mongo. Compared to the feelings which tormented her now, her yearning to return to Baltimore seemed like a passing fancy.

Slade had called her a snob. Apparently he had forgotten conceited flirt. There were also a few remarks he could have made about her inability to see the nose in front of her face, but she was just as glad he hadn't. She'd said them all to herself many times over these last three days.

What conceit to think all she had to do was speak, and Slade, or any other man, would jump to do her bidding. What arrogance to believe her presence alone could make a man relinquish his every opinion. And what ignorance to assume she could parcel out her emotions while she expected the man to lay his heart at her feet. But most damning of all, what cynicism to suppose Slade's being a cowboy made him incapable of experiencing the same sensitivity or having the intellect of a man with a more sophisticated upbringing.

Pamela stopped berating herself abruptly. Slade approached her campfire. She summoned every bit of emotional steel she possessed to suffer through his cold, cynical discourse without falling on her knees and promising to do practically anything if he would just talk to her like he used to.

She had apologized, but that had made no difference. It might even have made him colder. Everybody knew things were strained between them, and they walked around her on eggshells. She wanted to yell at everybody, to tell them to stop pretending nothing had happened, but that wouldn't do any good either. Nothing would do any good until Slade forgave her.

And Pamela admitted she didn't know when, or if, that would happen. She felt a cold trail of tears run down her cheeks but made no effort to wipe them away. It would be futile. They would just be followed by more.

A few mornings later a decidedly bleary-eyed cook addressed Pamela over her breakfast.

"Ma'am, I'm afraid you're going to have to talk to Mr. Morgan about his singing."

"Why? He has a perfectly beautiful voice. I can't imagine why he hasn't told anybody about it before." Pamela hoped she didn't blush. She blushed every time she thought of the song she had heard. She hoped he hadn't sung it anymore. At least she hadn't waked up again, so she hadn't heard it if he had.

"Yes, ma'am, it is right purty, if you like that kind of singing. Personally, it's not my favorite, but that's not what I wanted to talk about."

"Surely the hymns aren't bothering the men?"

"No, ma'am, it ain't the hymns. Actually, they're right soothing. As long as he keeps off the ones about the coming of judgment day, it works pretty much like a lullaby for these fellas. They go right off to sleep thinking they're at their mama's knee once again."

"Then what is it?"

"It's about the songs he sings *after* he's done with the hymns."

Pamela just *knew* he would mention those songs. She

204

didn't know what to say, so she didn't say anything.

"Most of these boys is real innocents, ma'am. They ain't been away from home long enough, had money enough, or been around women enough to learn much about sinning. At least not the real important stuff. They shoot each other up now and then and do a little cheating at cards, but they're no more than innocent babies."

"Then Mr. Morgan started singing his *songs?*"

"Do you realize, ma'am, that Slade Morgan has taught them more in one of them songs about the weakness of the flesh than they're likely to learn in a month of Sunday's by themselves? Why, one of them boys from Mr. Shepherd's crew, and a real hard case he is too, he told me that he learned things in them songs he never heard tell about before. And he's been to New Orleans *and* San Francisco."

"What do you want me to do?"

"You got to talk to him, ma'am."

"You want me to stop him from singing those songs?"

"No. We want him to sing them first."

Pamela couldn't speak. She couldn't think of any adequate words.

"The boys know what's coming, and there's not one of them that'll go to sleep until Mr. Slade comes off duty. Ma'am, them boys are so tired from staying up to wait for them songs, they'd be liable to shoot themselves if they was to draw their guns. I don't know how half of them stays on a horse. You ain't never seen such a pitiful sight as them boys crawling out of their beds after a night of songs telling them about things that would make a Persian blush. Mr. Slade can spend the day catching up on his sleep if he likes, but them boys are so tired they're liable to try to put a saddle on a steer instead of their horse."

"I understand, Angus. I will speak to Mr. Morgan, but I can't guarantee the results."

205

Chapter 13

Pamela didn't want to talk to Slade about his songs. She'd almost rather have been forced to learn the words and sing them herself. Holding a service for the crew was one thing. Disapproving of guns wasn't very different. But she'd never done anything like this, and she wasn't happy about it.

She couldn't do what Angus wanted. It was unthinkable she should even mention those songs without asking him to stop singing them. It wouldn't have been so hard if things weren't strained between them right now. She didn't know how he would take it, and quite frankly she didn't want to find out. Slade Morgan was not a man to take kindly to having others judge his actions.

Pamela's father had taught her to always stand up to trouble. Right now she wished he'd taught her to be a coward. Then she could slink away with a clean conscience.

"I need to talk with you before you leave," she said as Slade finished his supper that evening. "It won't take long," she quickly added when he looked like he was going to refuse. She wasn't sure whether his look meant he didn't believe her or he thought it was an attempt to get him off alone. Right now she didn't have the courage to find out.

Slade rinsed out his plate with his cold coffee. "Shoot."

What an appropriate word Pamela thought. She felt like

somebody already had. At her. And they had hit her in the heart.

"It's about your singing." God, any other time she would have loved to talk about it. That beautiful sound seemed incongruous coming from Slade, so totally unexpected. But to say that now would only add insult to injury.

He didn't say anything, just waited for her to go on.

"Why didn't you tell me you had a voice like that. We could have used you to lead the singing. You couldn't help but hear how terrible it was." She sounded so stiff and formal. If he would just say something instead of standing there like a statue. God, she couldn't start thinking about Michelangelo again. She couldn't blush. Not now.

"When did you learn all those hymns?" That probably wasn't the right thing to say either, but he wasn't helping. It would be easier if he shouted at her.

"I told you I sang in the choir as a kid," Slade said at last. "The ladies said I looked like a cherub and sounded like an angel."

Something clicked in Pamela's brain.

"So that's why you grew a beard." She could tell that Slade hadn't meant to say so much.

"One more mystery solved. Soon I'll be an open book."

"Did you like singing?" she asked. He had unbent a little. Please, just a little more.

"It was about the only thing I did my mother approved of." Pamela could have bitten her tongue, but as Slade kept talking, he appeared to become less angry, more indifferent. "She used to give me a nickel every time I learned a new hymn. I think there was a time I could sing the book straight through." He looked searchingly at Pamela. "But you don't want to talk about hymns." Pamela shook her head. "I didn't think so."

The silence lengthened until Pamela couldn't stand it any longer. "Where did you learn those songs? The *other* ones," she asked, curiosity more evident than condemnation.

"You've been listening?" His eyes twinkled.

"Not after the first one," Pamela said. "But according to Angus, the entire camp lies awake every night. Apparently, they find the songs more entertaining than going to sleep."

Slade's lips twitched. "I gather you're working yourself up to some kind of statement."

"Not for myself," she hastened to assure him. "I've been asked to speak to you on behalf of the crew."

Slade's eyebrows rose. "And?"

"They want you to sing the songs first?"

"What?"

"Angus says the boys are losing too much sleep waiting for you to finish with the hymns. They want the songs first."

Slade's eyes positively danced with merriment, but his expression remained unchanged. "And you?"

"I want you to stop them of course."

"You disapprove?"

"Would you approve of songs like that if I were singing them about men?"

"It certainly would be a novelty."

Pamela could relax now. Slade was making fun of her. She was familiar with that.

"Slade, be serious. I wasn't going to say anything. I figured the best thing for me was to stay in my wagon and put the pillow over my head. But I can't have you keeping the men awake all night."

"And you can't have me singing the songs first." His eyes still danced.

"I can't ask you to." She grinned.

Slade grinned back.

That night Slade began with the songs. But he only sang two, and they were so polite he could have sung them at a boxed-lunch social. The crew was disappointed, but they soon settled down to sleep. Pamela didn't know whether to be relieved or disappointed. But she had never known her own mind when it came to Slade Morgan. Why should this time be any different?

Slade sat his horse on a rise about a mile from the camp. Green meadows and gently rolling hills dotted with ponderosa pine, alligator juniper, and several kinds of oaks gave the scene a feeling of pastoral calm. Distance stripped the cowboys' work of its urgency, and their search for cattle through the shade of the thickets and the depths of the draws looked more like a choreographed ballet than the harsh, brutal work it was.

But Slade was untouched by the beauty or the harshness. Using his field glasses, he could see just about everything that was happening, and he didn't like it. All day long he had ridden over the range, monitoring the work of all six crews, and he could find nothing wrong. That made him uneasy. He had always had a sixth sense about people, and from the very first he had known that Mongo Shepherd was as under-handed as he was rich and cocky. He intended to steal Pamela's range, by marrying her if possible, but Slade had no doubt he would use any method that came to hand.

At the same time, Mongo had very little patience. Balked for too long, he wouldn't wait until things were safe. He would press ahead. Slade had expected him to take advantage of the roundup, but ever since he shot the branding iron out of Peak Bolin's hands, even the most care-ful scrutiny had turned up no problems. Everything had gone so smoothly they were going to finish a few days ahead of schedule.

That would mean a return to the ranch, Dave's reinstate-ment as foreman, and Slade's departure for the trail to California. Slade didn't want that. Every time he thought about leaving Pamela, his resolve weakened. He kept telling himself that his love for her differed in no way from his infatuation with Trish, that it would burn itself out as quickly as it had sprung up, but he didn't believe it.

Because you don't want to believe it he told himself. You want to believe this girl is so deeply in love with you she'll give up everything she's ever wanted just for you. You're trying to convince yourself you've found a place where you can be yourself, where you can stop running from people and their guns.

You're wrong, and only a fool would hang around pining for a love that can't last. Don't kid yourself by thinking her defending you or letting you kiss her in the moonlight makes any difference. That's nothing but grasping at straws. You're not her type and you never will be. If you had any common sense, you'd know that.

You might as well ride out of here without going back to the ranch, his inner demon taunted him. Once her precious Frederick arrives, she won't be interested in you any more. And if Frederick doesn't settle your hash, Josh White surely will. No decent father would be willing to see his daughter marry a carnival has-been when she could choose a husband from the cream of eastern society.

Still, Slade knew he would go back.

You'd better pay some attention to what's going on here, or you might not get the chance he told himself. Someone *was* maneuvering them, he knew it now, but he couldn't figure out who or why. Somehow Mongo was the key to the whole thing.

He'd had no idea what he would be getting himself into when he fought Mongo that day on the ranch. Now after the turnup over that maverick, everybody expected some kind of showdown.

Why hadn't it come?

There could only be two reasons. Mongo was either a coward or he was waiting for something better. Since the first wasn't true, it must be the second. But what could he have in mind? He acted awfully cool, something Slade found

210

inconsistent with his character. Either he had his plans already laid and intended to wait quietly for the proper time to put them into action, something else Slade found inconsistent with his character, or he hadn't found quite what he wanted, preferably something that would raise him in Pamela's eyes while damaging Slade's reputation at the same time.

Slade tended to favor the latter. After all, Mongo was an easterner and they always seemed to favor verbal assassination. A western man was more likely to put a bullet in you and be done with it.

And why did he feel so certain he had been maneuvered into a confrontation with Mongo? Because one of the men he had seen talking under the tree was the man who roped the maverick. It would have been a simple thing to rope the wrong calf just about the time Slade rode into view. Nobody would have paid much attention. Everyone had their own work.

There would have been a confrontation and one of them would have been killed.

It could still happen, and after his shooting exhibition, no one would believe Mongo had a fair chance, not unless he had witnesses. So Mongo would be killed somewhere else and Slade blamed for it.

For that reason he had been extremely careful to remain in full view at all times. He sang whenever he rode the watch so no one could accuse him of slipping off in the dark. He slept in full view of the campfire and kept his guns with him at all times. He must have witnesses to his every move.

Of course he could be imagining everything. He had no concrete evidence, but no other explanation fitted all the facts. Nothing else explained why one of Mongo's own men would try to set him up.

Now if he could just convince Pamela his theory hadn't grown out of a jealous rage.

*　　　*　　　*

"I don't think I'd better," Pamela said to Mongo as Slade came up.

"But you've turned me down all week," Mongo complained.

"It's just not a good time," Pamela tried to explain. "You need to be with your men. I would be wanting to see what mine were doing. We'd only get in each other's way."

"I told you I would go anywhere you wanted."

"The lady has given you her answer," Slade said stepping forward. "Why don't you accept it like a big boy and go away. Didn't your fancy eastern education teach you it's bad manners to keep asking after you've been turned down."

"Damn you," Mongo cursed, his face flushed from anger and chagrin. "Go back to where you came from before I break your neck."

"I need to talk with Miss White, privately," Slade added when Mongo didn't move.

"Do it some other time, dammit. You've butted in every time I've tried to talk to Pamela these last three days."

"Maybe you should wait until the roundup's over. As Miss White said, this isn't a good time."

"I'll be damned if I will," Mongo said, starting toward him aggressively.

"Anytime," Slade said, and stepped away from Pamela, hands suspended above his guns. At this range neither man could miss.

"That's enough," Pamela said, stepping between them. "Your foreman is waiting for you, Mongo. You'd better go."

"Not until I fix this mangy cur so he won't bother you any more."

"He's not bothering me, Mongo, and I do need to talk to him. You seem to forget he's my foreman."

"I can't figure out why in hell you hired him. Your father never would."

"That's really none of your business. Now if you don't mind . . ."

"Aw hell, I'll go, but I'm telling you both. I'm coming back tonight, and I'm not leaving until I'm good and ready."

"I'll be here," Slade said. Mongo waited a moment, clearly strongly tempted to make his stand now. Then, with an oath that turned Pamela's ears pink, he turned and stalked away.

"Your boyfriend doesn't discourage easily."

"Not with you baiting him. You nearly started a fight."

"I'm not backing down from Mongo, with or without my guns."

"Has it ever occurred to you that every time you're around me, people start fighting or threatening to shoot each other?"

"I'm not doing the threatening."

"Mongo never behaved like this before you got here. He was a perfect gentleman."

"Maybe he's afraid of a little competition."

"Competition? Do you think I'm some cheap floozie to be fought over?" she demanded. "If so, you're badly mistaken."

"I just wanted to save you a little trouble," Slade said. "I didn't think you wanted him to keep pestering you."

"And when did you get to be such an expert on what I do or don't think?" Pamela demanded. Her temper, rubbed thin by several days of boredom and tension, came dangerously close to being out of control. "And while we're at it, you can also tell me when I gave you permission to decide what I will and won't do."

"As long as you're on this roundup, I'm responsible for you."

"That's nonsense. I was never your responsibility, not before this roundup, during, or afterwards. I don't want to talk to you any more. I'm so angry I don't even know what to say. We can't communicate, Slade. You were right when you said we were two people going in different directions. I just didn't want to believe you."

"You can't deny there's an attraction between us."

"I don't want to talk about that either. It looks like I

213

managed to miss the truth all the way around. But I won't any more. Now get out of my way. I'm going to take a ride. I need time to cool off."

"I've already explained why you can't."

Pamela spoke through clenched teeth, trying very hard not to loose her temper. "And I've already told you that you're imagining things. I don't know who shot Dave or Jody and I don't have any idea why, but there's no danger to me. Certainly not as long as I stay within sight of the men."

"You can't go, Pamela. It really is dangerous."

"I *am* going. Now get out of my way."

"No."

Pamela attempted to walk around Slade, but he stepped in front of her. No matter where she moved, he blocked her path. Her temper in shreds and ready to scream in fury, Pamela feinted to one side and then ran as fast as she could in the other direction.

She almost made it.

She felt Slade's vise-like grip tighten around her elbow. He reeled her in as effortlessly as a roped calf.

"Let me go," she hissed. "You're hurting me."

"Not until you promise to stay in camp."

"Never!"

"Then I guess I'll have to hold on to you until you change your mind," Slade said. Pamela could tell some of the anger in his voice had changed to hunger. "Of course I need to take a different hold. This one's too uncomfortable."

"Don't you dare, Slade Morgan," Pamela said in a fierce whisper as his arms started to slip around her waist. "The men are watching."

"I don't mind."

"I do."

"Then promise."

"Okay, blast you. I promise not to *try* to slip out of camp. Are you satisfied?"

Slade released her arm, still unconvinced. Pamela had

214

given up too easily, and that made him feel uncomfortable.

"You're a brute. No woman is ever going to be able to love you until you can trust her. You can't go around making people do what you want them to do, whether they want to or not, and expect them to like it."

"Not even when it's for their own good?"

"Not even then. Now if you'll excuse me, I need to go to my wagon." She spun on her heel, leaving Slade to wonder what she wanted so badly from her wagon.

He found out soon enough.

Pamela emerged seconds later carrying her rifle. "Now get out of my way. I intend to go for that ride."

"You just promised you wouldn't leave camp."

"I promised I wouldn't *try*. I said nothing about actually doing it."

"I'm not going to waste time playing word games with you. You might as well put your rifle up and settle down. You're not going anywhere."

Pamela raised the rifle. "Get out of my way."

"You'll have to shoot me."

"Don't tempt me. Right now I just might."

"I'm not moving, Pamela."

"The hell you won't," she said, so angry she didn't realize she had cursed. She put a bullet into the ground between Slade's feet.

"You missed."

"I didn't miss. That was just a warning."

"I'm still not moving."

Pamela fired off three rapid shots, but Slade's eyelids didn't so much as flicker. Neither did the eyes of the crowd which materialized virtually out of nowhere to watch the proceedings.

"You're going to have to be a little more careful. You might hit one of the spectators," Slade taunted her.

"Damn you," Pamela hissed. "You're no gentleman. You don't play fair." With a very unladylike growl of rage, she broke into a run and didn't stop until she reached her wagon and had closed the flaps behind her.

Then she broke into tears.

"What do you suppose the boss could have said to make Miss White so upset?" Clem asked Angus as the hands from the other outfits dispersed to their own campfires. "Never seen her move faster'n a slow walk before." He had been detailed to watch Pamela for the morning and had nothing to do but idle around camp.

"Whatever he did, she didn't appear to like it much."

"Naw, and it don't seem to be sitting too well on Morgan's stomach either."

"When two people start sparking, there's bound to be a little too much fire now and again."

"You mean Slade and Miss White?"

"Well it ain't you she's been taking long walks with, and it ain't you she's crying over?"

Clem whistled between his teeth. "I never would have figured them two."

"Neither did they. And the idea don't seem to be going down too well."

"What's her Pa going to say?"

"Don't know's it'll matter much. It's what Miss Pamela says that'll make the difference in the end."

Beans again! Pamela shoved her lunch away. She couldn't eat with her stomach so wrought up, and her stomach wouldn't calm down until she stopped being furious at Slade. And she couldn't stop being furious at Slade Morgan because he forbade her to ride. Not only did he do so in front of men from all six crews in the roundup, he had remained in camp all morning. Oh, he always *appeared* to be busy, but she knew he kept a watch on her wagon just in case she decided to try to sneak away.

And that had made her so furious her tears had ceased to

flow. Now she had another point to add to her growing list of grievances against him. No man had ever made Pamela cry, and she would never forgive him for being the first. She had washed her face, combed her hair, and climbed down from her wagon determined to show him she didn't care where he went or what he did.

But he had disappeared.

An hour passed with no sign of him. The men finished their lunch, and still he didn't reappear. Maybe he got bored and rode out.

But he had forced her to stay in camp.

"Clem, have you seen Mr. Morgan?" Pamela asked the boy as he handed in his empty plate.

"Not for a while. Did you want him for something?"

"Nothing that can't wait." Pamela replied.

"I'm riding out. If I see him, you want me to tell him you're looking for him?"

"No. I'll wait until this evening."

"You sure?"

"I'm sure."

"Well, you have a good afternoon, ma'am."

"You too. Be careful of those cows. I haven't seen one that looks the least friendly."

"Cows are naturally ornery when they don't get their own way," Clem explained. "It's their nature."

"I guess that's why I don't like them," Pamela muttered to herself as Clem walked off to saddle his horse. "They're too much like Slade Morgan. At least now I don't have to worry about running into him every time I turn around."

But as the afternoon wore on, she couldn't relax. Just the opposite. If she had been upset Slade would stand around watching her, her anger increased tenfold that he would go off while she had to remain in camp. He didn't even have to be present for her to do exactly what he wanted. Finally it got to be more than she could stand. She came to her feet and headed toward the rope corral where they kept the horses.

217

Every time she looked over her shoulder to make sure nobody followed her, she got madder and madder. Slade had reduced her to sneaking out of her own camp. It was intolerable. She would show him once and for all that she would not be bullied by him or anyone else. It only took a moment to saddle a horse.

She breathed a sigh of relief as she rode away and didn't hear the galloping hooves of Slade's hammerhead dun behind her. The success of her escape momentarily made her forget the humiliating circumstances surrounding her success. Okay, it was something less than scintillating victory, but at least she had shown Slade Morgan she wouldn't meekly obey his every command.

But she had hardly taken three calm breaths when a horseman emerged from the brush down the trail in front of her.

She first thought it must be Slade, but almost immediately she realized her mistake. She couldn't confuse anyone with Slade, not even at this distance.

When a second horseman emerged from the brush on the other side of the road and he, too, brought his horse to a standstill in the middle of the trail, Slade's warning sprang into her mind. A chill of fear ran through her body. Suppose these men did mean to hurt her. What could she do? She had left her rifle in camp, no one knew where she had gone, and she had gone too far from camp for anyone to hear her scream.

Should she run for it? She hadn't saddled her own horse, she hadn't wanted to attract attention, and she had no idea how much speed the little mare she had chosen possessed. Maybe the men could outrun her. They weren't far away.

Then she recognized them. They were her own men, Mercer Isbel and Pete Reilly.

"How are things going?" Pamela asked as she rode up to them.

"As well as can be expected, ma'am," Pete replied. The boys looked real nervous, but Pamela guessed they were

218

merely shy about being around her.

"You boys aren't helping with the herd?"

"Naw. Mr. Morgan told us to keep an eye out for strays."

"I don't see how there could be any strays here," Pamela said. "Surely you covered this area first."

"You never can tell," Pete said, looking even more uncomfortable than before.

"Well, I'll see you back at camp." But the men didn't move from her path.

"Wouldn't you like to go back now?" Pete asked anxiously.

"Yeah," Mercer chimed in. "It'll soon be supper time."

"It won't be time to eat again for nearly three hours," Pamela said, mystified. "Now move so I can get by."

"It would be a lot better if you went back, ma'am. Too hot out here and no shade."

"There's snakes, too. Sidewinders. Could spook your horse and leave you stranded."

"I appreciate your concern, but I'm in need of a good ride. Now let me by."

"Please, Miss White, won't you go back?"

"No."

"But you have to."

"May I remind you I'm the boss of the Bar Double-B, and I've just given you an order."

"Mr. Morgan made us promise not to let you leave camp, ma'am. He said if you tried to sneak out while he was gone, we was to take you back."

"Take me back!"

"Yes, ma'am. Mr. Morgan says it's too dangerous for you to be riding around by yourself."

"Mr. Morgan and I disagree on many things. This is just one of them. I have every intention of going for a long ride."

"Sorry, ma'am, but we can't let you go."

"You can't *let me?*" Pamela began to feel like an echo.

"Yes, ma'am."

"I'm your boss, and Mr. Morgan's employer. You don't have to worry about any repercussion. I shall see that he knows you relayed his message."

"He didn't say nothing about relaying no message."

"He said we was to keep you in camp or he'd notch our ears."

Pamela looked blank.

"It's the brand of a coward, ma'am. We'd be marked for life."

"Now you see why we can't let you go?"

"I can fire you both." Pamela didn't know why she said that. She would never fire them because of something Slade had done.

"It won't make no difference to Slade Morgan. He'll shoot our ears off anyhow."

"We might as well shoot ourselves."

"You'd take me by force if you had to?" She still couldn't believe Slade had turned her own hands against her.

"I'm sorry, ma'am, but yes we would."

Pamela considered digging her spurs into her horse and driving between them. She considered turning off the trail and making a dash for some brush-filled canyon. She considered screaming her rage loud enough for everyone in Arizona to hear, but she fell back on dignity. She would not allow them to usher her back to camp like a prisoner. She would ride with pride.

But Slade Morgan had better watch out. She now understood what people meant when they spoke of a murderous rage. When she got her hands on Slade Morgan's ears . . . well, never mind his ears. He'd be lucky if he had a head left.

Pamela jerked her horse around and headed back to camp.

She had barely arrived at her wagon when she heard several horses approaching at a gallop. She was still too angry over Slade's treachery to pay any attention, but even the red haze of her fury couldn't block out the shouts and the sudden commotion in the camps. She looked up in time to see them ride by her wagon. Somebody had been shot, and they were bringing in his body across the saddle.

It was Mongo Shepherd!

By the time she reached his campsite, his men had laid him on the ground.

"What happened?" she asked, though from the look of the wound she could guess.

"Somebody shot him in the back."

Pamela stared down at the body which had been so very vital only that morning. She didn't love Mongo, but any death made her sad. She felt even worse that he should have died by the gun. It only proved what she'd been trying to tell Slade all along.

She knelt down beside him. His arm lay under him at an awkward angle. Somehow it made her feel better to straighten it. But no sooner did she place his arm across his chest than she paused an instant to take his hand in hers once more. It felt warm and pliable. The sun might have kept the body from getting cold, but would it still be so flexible? Frantically Pamela searched for a pulse. Finally she slipped her fingers inside his collar until her fingertips moved over his jugular.

"He's still alive," she exclaimed coming to her feet in a swift movement. "Bring him to my wagon. We may be able to save him yet."

The next hour sorely tried her fortitude. After they moved Mongo to her wagon, she stripped him to the waist. Angus cut the bullet out—Pamela couldn't do that—she cleaned and bandaged his wound and did her best to make him comfortable. She couldn't tell if the bullet had touched any vital organ, but he had lost a lot of blood. His heart beat erratically.

Odd that the man who had seemed so impervious to danger, so much the master of his own destiny, the invader who had shattered the peace of their range, should lay helpless before her, his life hanging by a slender thread. This could happen to her, to her father, to Slade. She had told him she would fight, but Death hadn't come so close then. Was it worth it? Could any land be worth a man's life?

She tried to ignore the babble of angry voices, but the mention of Slade's name riveted her attention. Now she couldn't possibly ignore what they were saying.

"There ain't nobody else except Slade Morgan," a voice she didn't recognize shouted. "Everybody knows they argue every time they come near each other."

"Just this morning I heard him tell Morgan they were going to settle things this evening. Looks like Morgan didn't want to wait that long."

"Morgan doesn't have to shoot nobody in the back. He's too damned good with a gun." That was Pete Reilly. She wondered what had happened to Mercer. She hoped he had gone to warn Slade.

"Mr. Shepherd could kill him in a fist fight."

"Maybe, but in case you didn't notice, they didn't use no fists this time."

Pamela opened the flap and stepped down from the wagon just in time to stop the two opposing camps from starting a free-for-all.

"Slade couldn't possibly have shot Mongo," she said to the men she recognized from Mongo's crew, the ones who had brought him in. "Mongo was shot several hours ago, and Slade has been in camp all morning. Quite a few people saw him."

"Begging your pardon, ma'am, but nobody heard the shot. He could have been shot just before we found him."

"That's impossible. The blood on his clothes has dried."

"I don't say Slade did it himself," the man continued doggedly, "I'm just saying he's the only one who had any trouble getting along with the boss. He's the only one with a reason to do this."

There was a stir at the edge of the crowd. "And what might

222

that reason be?" Slade asked. It seemed only natural for the men to fall back so he could approach the center of the group.

"Slade." The name slipped involuntarily from Pamela's lips. "Where have you been?"

"Not far," he replied, but his eyes remained on Mongo's men. "I'm waiting."

Accusing a man of murder face to face is not a thing to take casually, especially when that man can hit six coins in the air at the same time. Pamela could almost see the steam go out of those boys.

"I didn't say you shot him, just that you and him had a lot of dustups."

"Sure, I didn't much like him, but that's not a reason to shoot a man."

"You and him almost came to blows this morning."

"Mongo couldn't seem to remember the location of his own campfire," Slade said. "I was just reminding him."

The men didn't say any more, but they looked like they would have liked to have said plenty. "How's he doing?" Slade asked Pamela.

"I don't know. He could die any minute."

"Keep him here where you can watch him."

"We'll take him back with us," Jud Noble said. He was Mongo's foreman.

Slade's gaze returned to the men, but this time it contained none of the sympathetic understanding of before. "If you move him now, you'll kill him. Besides, there's nobody in camp better able to nurse him than Miss White."

"But . . ."

"If you boys are so afraid I'll put a bullet in a sick man, one of you can stay with him. If he does die, I want you to be damned sure I had nothing to do with it."

"Now I've got to stay in camp," Pamela said. "It looks like you always get your way."

"If I had, Mongo wouldn't be shot. I'll be back. Pete, I

223

want to talk with you and Mercer," Slade said and walked off with the two men.

Pamela watched him go. All of her previous anger had disappeared. She would have given all she owned to run after him. For the first time in her life she was scared. Slade had been telling her all along there would be serious trouble, but she hadn't believed him. He had told her that he thought someone had set Mongo up, and she hadn't believed that either.

Now Mongo had been shot, nearly killed. If Slade was right, somebody would be trying to kill her, too.

The commotion was enough to rouse the Devil himself.

A horse whinnied in pain as the barbed wire cut into his chest; the sheets of tin buckled and boomed like thunder as iron-shod hooves danced upon the brittle surface; a dozen crystal bells jangled wildly in the night; two men cursed bitterly as they turned their horses and raced back through the canyon opening.

Gaddy came out of a sound sleep with a painful start. Grabbing up both guns, he fired wildly into the night. One bullet ricochetted off the canyon wall and smashed into a crystal bell. It shattered with a single shriek of shrill protest. The other clipped a delicate red flower off a tail cactus.

"It worked!" Gaddy exclaimed as his brain cleared sufficiently for him to understand what had just happened. "My barricade worked! Somebody tried to get in and it kept them out."

Jumping up in a burst of exuberant happiness, Gaddy danced across the protesting tin sheets, firing off shots into the air like a high-spirited cowboy riding into town after a long drive.

His horse, apparently deciding his situation had become unsafe, tore its reins loose from the tree limb where he had been tethered and returned to the barn at a gallop.

Chapter 14

For the next several days, Slade never left the sight of at least a half dozen people. He mixed with the men from all six crews, took his turn watching the herd at night, and slept in the middle of the Bar Double-B camp.

On one hand Pamela felt relieved she didn't have to worry about where he might have gone. After his challenge to the ranchers, she had been afraid he might ride out one morning and not come back. She didn't think anyone would drygulch him, but with the survival of their herds at stake, she didn't know how far these men might go.

On the other hand, his sticking so close made her uneasy. Why did he make such a point of being visible at all times? Avoiding trouble is easier than having to fix it, she told herself. Nothing prevents problems like seeing the boss on the job all the time. Her father had held the same philosophy for years, but still a tiny doubt nagged at her mind. She tried to drive it away, but it wouldn't go. She finally had to face it.

Could Slade be afraid of the ranchers? Pamela reproached herself for even thinking it. Hadn't he fought Mongo on her behalf? Yes, her perverse mind replied, but you had a rifle. Hadn't he laid down his challenge to the other ranchers in front of their crews? Yes, but he had them surrounded by his own men.

225

The more she thought about it, the more convinced she became that she had missed something important. Slade had never been afraid of Mongo. He just didn't think that way. There had to be something about this she didn't understand. But what she didn't understand, she couldn't help but doubt.

She'd ask Slade when he came in that evening. As long as he stayed her foreman, he was obliged to share his thoughts with her.

Why, a little voice asked? You've pooh-poohed everything he's told you so far. You didn't back him up when he sent Gaddy back to the ranch. You didn't support him when Dave said nothing would happen to the ranch, and you didn't believe him when he said it was unsafe for you to ride alone. That man would be crazy to tell you anything more. No point asking for trouble.

He already has a lapful of your trouble Pamela reminded herself. If he's willing to put his neck on the line, you ought to at least listen to the man. Nobody ever accused him of being crazy, and only a crazy man would stir up a nest of hornets without a very good reason.

My God! What if she had been wrong all along? Suppose there *was* someone they didn't know about pulling the strings.

How much more did she know about Mongo than she knew about Slade? For that matter, what did she know about the other ranchers? The answers didn't matter because the question that followed hard on the heels of the first two was much more important. Who's being right meant the most to her? Which did she want to believe?

There was no question. It was Slade.

As soon as she realized that, everything turned itself around, and she wondered how she could have doubted him for so long. Three times in one week he had put his life on the line for her without any promise of reward. She doubted he would have done differently even if she had been paying him. If Slade saw something as his duty, he didn't weigh costs or look for consequences. He just did it.

The more she thought about it, the more she wondered if the trouble they had earlier hadn't been a ruse to get her father to go to Santa Fe. He owned the largest ranch in the area. People listened to him. As long as he held firm, the other ranchers wouldn't be anxious to start trouble.

A shiver of fear knifed through Pamela. Could something have happened to her father? But almost immediately she dismissed the idea. Her father had survived the Civil War and more than twenty years of fighting Indians and rustlers. If they hadn't caught him by now, they never would.

But the notion that someone wanted her father out of the way had taken a strong hold on Pamela's imagination. When she combined this with Slade's suspicions, it made sense of several things she hadn't been able to understand before.

But who could be behind this and what did they want?

Pamela made up her mind to listen to Slade in the future, but right now they needed someone who knew more about the area, the ranchers and their crews than either of them did. Turning abruptly, she went in search of Dave.

His wagon had disappeared.

"He said he was going to take a nap," Angus said without looking up from his stew. "He got Sid to drive his wagon off into the trees so the noise wouldn't bother him. He's been doing it regular each day."

"I guess it's cooler, too," Pamela said. Poor Dave, she thought, he never needed naps before. It didn't surprise her he didn't want the men to know he had to rest during the day. It would make it all the harder to take over again after Slade left.

After Slade left!

He couldn't leave. She had to find some way to keep him at the Bar Double-B. She knew her father would give him a job, but could she convince him to take it?

"Tell me something, Angus." She had to know how the men felt. He would work with them, not her. "What do you think of Mr. Morgan?"

"I ain't paid to have opinions about the boss," Angus said, slicing potatoes into a heavy iron pot.

"Dave is your boss," Pamela said. "Mr. Morgan is just filling in until he's back on his feet again."

"It's the same thing."

"Not quite. You see, I thought I might offer Mr. Morgan a permanent job after the roundup, and I wanted to know what the men thought about him."

"That man ain't no ordinary cowboy," Angus said, his hands not moving now. "I've no doubt you can talk him into just about anything you want, but he don't belong in a bunkhouse. It ain't that the boys don't like him, they do, but he just ain't one of us. He's a natural born leader."

"You don't think he would agree to work for Dave?"

"He might and he might not, but I can tell you one thing. No foreman will ride comfortable in the saddle as long as he's around."

"Why? He's no trouble maker."

"No, ma'am. But people just naturally look to him to tell them what to do. The men fell to doing that without so much as a question. As long as he's around, it wouldn't make no difference who's got the top job. They'll still look to him."

"What about my father?"

"That's different. He owns the place, but then your father ain't hired him yet. I don't think he would either."

"Because you can't have your men looking to two different people for leadership?"

"Yes, ma'am."

Pamela strolled back to her wagon, her mind in a ferment.

"I need to talk with you," Pamela announced when Slade walked up to the campfire.

Slade poured himself a cup of coffee and squatted. "I'm listening."

She wondered why she'd never noticed the way his jeans glued themselves to his body when he squatted at the campfire. All the creases disappeared and his firm, muscled flesh was molded into one tight package.

"I need to speak to you privately," she said, tugging furiously at her thoughts to get them off his powerful loins. "Why don't we take a walk like we used to?"

Pamela hoped Slade couldn't hear the entreaty in her voice. Apparently he didn't. He didn't even look up.

"What do you have to tell me you can't say in front of Dave and Angus?" Both men acted like they were deaf, dumb, and blind.

"You won't know until I tell you, will you?" She tried to smile provocatively, but she'd never tried that before. She didn't know if she could. She probably just looked foolish.

"I don't have time to play games."

"Neither do I." At least she could speak provocatively. Her voice had always been seductive.

"Supposing I decide to stay right here?"

Pamela gave him an impish smile that almost brought him to his feet by itself. "I'll mount up and ride out of camp. Then you'll have to follow me."

Angus checked the contents of several pots and checked on his bread. Dave pretended to be dozing.

Slade sighed what he knew was the sigh of every man who has just given in to a woman for the umpteenth time. "I don't know who said a woman always finds a way to get what she wants, but he sure knew his stuff," he commented as he got to his feet.

Pamela didn't know why she'd been so struck by the fit of his jeans when he squatted. They were even more revealing now. They were loose enough to allow his body to assume its own contours but tight enough to accentuate them. Funny how she'd never paid much attention to the shape of a man's body before. If she had, she might not be so devastated by Slade's physical effect on her. Her mother thought all men

229

were obsessed with the female body, but she hadn't even hinted that a woman could be just as interested in a man's body.

Pamela wondered what her mother would have thought of Slade. Then she shuddered. She really didn't want to know.

"I didn't want to threaten you, but it seemed the only way to get you to come with me," Pamela said when they were out of earshot of Dave and Angus. She didn't look at him. She couldn't concentrate when she did.

"That wasn't why I came."

Pamela looked questioningly at Slade.

"Bob Sprevitt is watching you today. You wouldn't get a hundred feet."

Pamela struggled to control her spiraling temperature. "Then why did you come?"

"You obviously had something you wanted to say."

"And?" Pamela knew there was more. There always was with this cowboy.

"I wanted to," Slade said, letting the words out like a big gush of pent-up air. But once free of restraint, the words tumbled out like pecans out of a broken sack. "I was tired of practically sitting on my hands for fear I'd touch you or biting my tongue so I wouldn't say the things I was dying to say. Hell, I'm practically blind from staring into that fire."

"Why would you do that?"

"You know."

Pamela hoped she did, but she said, "I won't make any more assumptions. You still haven't forgiven me for the last one. Or accepted my apology."

Slade was disgusted with himself. Now that he had let down and allowed himself to say what he had been wanting to say for three days, he was right back where he started. Still panting after a woman who wanted someone else.

"It doesn't matter," he said. He didn't want to go into it. He just wanted to get this over with.

"Yes it does. I know I was wrong—I had plenty of proof to

the contrary—but I let my temper cause me to say things I didn't mean. I told you once before I had never been a good judge of people."

"Okay, apology accepted," Slade said with a crooked smile he didn't feel. "Now what was so important that you had to go to all this trouble to get me out here?" He held her at a distance, marking time until she would leave.

Pamela wanted to convince him of her sincerity, but instinct told her to wait. She had fallen into a pattern of wanting his attentions and then rejecting *him* when she got them. It would take more than words to convince him that anything had really changed.

"I wanted to tell you that I agree with you. I mean I believe you. About Mongo and all the rest," she added when his expression remained blank. God, he was handsome, even when he looked like he'd been hit between the eyes with a brick.

Slade hadn't misunderstood. He just couldn't believe his ears. But he restrained his enthusiasm. There might be severe qualifications to Pamela's new-found faith in him. So far the only thing without limit was her disdain for drifters.

"It was Mongo's getting shot that did it, wasn't it?" Okay, so she believed in evidence rather than him. It was still a beginning.

Pamela nodded. "He didn't want Dad to go to Santa Fe. Dad used to like Mongo. He thought I ought to marry him. But somebody wanted Dad out of the way. They knew that as long as he owned the Bar Double-B, the other ranchers would listen to him."

Slade doubted her father carried quite that much influence, but it fitted with all the rest. "Do you have any idea who it could be?"

"No. Except for ours, all the ranches are pretty much the same size. We were all getting along fine until Mongo brought his herds in."

"There wasn't enough grass for his cows, so everything

revolves around Mongo."

"What do you think will happen next?"

"I don't know. I was sure something would happen during the roundup—I don't mean Mongo's being shot. I never suspected that—but we'll be done tomorrow, and there's no sign of trouble. In fact, I get the feeling the other ranchers even accepted my challenge about keeping their herds on the other side of the river."

"Dad will be pleased. He might not even need the new men. I miss him," Pamela said quite unexpectedly. "I know he's not back yet. He'd be out here in a flash if he were, but there's bound to be a letter explaining why he's taking so long. Dad always writes. He wrote me hundreds of letters when I was away at school."

With her father's return, Slade's reason for putting off his departure would be gone. He had been determined to live in a fool's paradise for as long as possible, but it would be over soon, and he might as well face it.

"Dave says his leg is just about healed," Slade commented. "The end of the roundup will be a natural time for him to take over again."

Slade didn't want to give up the job. He liked being responsible for the crew, being close to the land, making decisions. He also liked being close to Pamela.

"What will you do?" She didn't know how to ask without making him think she wanted him to leave, but she had to find out.

"Drift I suppose. I may hang around a bit though. I'd like to meet your father. And I'd like a peek at the precious Frederick of yours."

"You needn't say it like he's a specimen to be kept under glass," Pamela snapped.

"I guess his coming to Arizona means he's slipped his leash for a little while at least. I hope nothing big and bad gobbles him up before he gets here."

"Slade Morgan, you're the most stubborn, opinionated,

egotistical man I've ever met. Just because Frederick isn't like you is no reason to disparage him. There are thousands of truly remarkable men all over the world, probably hundreds of thousands, who aren't in the least like you."

Though I doubt any of them are as handsome, her heart cried. But Pamela turned deaf ears to her heart. Her heart had gotten her in trouble in the first place. And after her common sense had extricated her, her heart got her right back into trouble again. Never, in all her life, would she have believed she could be such a woolly-headed female. Never would she have believed that a handsome face could completely override her common sense.

In all honesty, Slade wasn't so terrible. But that didn't matter. She simply wanted a different kind of man for a husband.

"Maybe it would be a good idea for you to head on to California. With Dave taking over again, it could get a little awkward."

Strands of his blond hair escaping from beneath his hat caught Pamela's attention. Straight as a stick and just as unruly, it was darker now, but she found him even more attractive when he was a little mussed. Not dirty, just a little untidy.

And Slade was always a little untidy.

"You firing me?"

"No," she hastened to add. They might be unable to agree on anything, but she didn't want him to think she thought he had done a poor job. "I just think that, under the circumstances, you might want to leave now. I take it you wouldn't accept a permanent job?"

Now why did she have to go ask that question? Suppose he accepted? Suppose he decided he wanted to stay at the Bar Double-B for the rest of his life? She couldn't stand the thought of that. Having Slade around the ranch every day, seeing his handsome face and disturbing body, knowing she only had to call his name and he would appear. No! She

233

couldn't stand it. She hated to admit it, but she might as well face facts. Where this man was concerned, she was nearly a functional idiot.

"No, I wouldn't accept a permanent job. I don't think I was cut out to be a cowboy. Seems everywhere I go, trouble's not far behind. You don't need that. Nobody does."

Now he had her feeling sorry for him. Why couldn't he stay the same? Why did he have to keep changing all the time? It was like being around six people instead of one.

"When you stop depending on your guns to solve your problems, you might find they're all gone. You can sneer at Frederick and the other men you scorn as Easterners, but they know how to live without fighting, killing, or stealing. When I think of all that's been going on these last few days, I don't know how I've kept from heading straight back to Baltimore."

"Because however much you're like your mother, you're also your father's daughter. You're a fighter."

"You don't know me. You don't know anything about me. For two cents, I'd give the Bar Double-B and every foot of land to anybody who wanted it."

"You'd fight tooth and toenail if anybody threatened to take away a single inch of what you think is yours," Slade replied. "You talk about Baltimore and your friends all the time. Maybe you are like them, maybe you will be happy when you return, but you're also a daughter of the West. You could no more give up your land than you can admit you're wrong. Just what do you think you've been doing out here this last week?"

"Putting up with an incredible amount of insolence from you."

"Why?"

"Because my father's gone and Dave's down with a bad leg."

"You've put up with me for the same reason you'd have

234

put up with anybody else who took this job, because you were determined to hold onto everything you have. You can sell it, give it away, even destroy it, but you won't let anybody *take* it from you."

"What makes you think you know me so well?" Pamela demanded. Her eyes flashed a message of anger, but Slade saw something else in their depths.

"Because a wolf can always recognize its own kind, Pamela. And whether you believe it or not, you're a wolf."

"Don't you dare, Slade Morgan! Don't you dare presume we're alike."

"I presume more than that," he said pulling her toward him. "I presume you want me as much as I want you, even though you're too damned tied up in knots to know it, or admit it if you did."

"If I wasn't so furious, I'd laugh in your face," Pamela snarled. "I don't *want* anyone."

"Deny you're trembling because you're in my arms . . ."

"I'm trembling with anger."

". . . or that your heart is beating wildly . . ."

"With rage."

". . . or that your lips hunger for mine." Before Pamela could reply, Slade's mouth came down on hers, claiming her lips in a deep, searing kiss.

Oh God, Pamela groaned as she struggled to keep from throwing her arms around Slade's neck, why can't I make up my mind about this man? You have, her mind shrieked, you made it up almost the moment you set eyes on him. You want Slade. You want him more than you've ever wanted anything in your life, but you don't want what he stands for.

Pamela gave up. Right now she couldn't possibly think, not with Slade scrambling her wits with his kisses. They called forth a similar response from her, a response that seemed wonderfully natural for all its strangeness.

Slowly, as the heat of his body invaded hers, her resistance weakened, and she molded herself to his frame, her sensitive breasts pressed hard against his chest, her leg captured between his thighs, the swell of his manhood pressing against the heat of her abdomen. Her arms encircled his neck and she yielded to his kiss.

It felt so wonderful to be in his arms, to feel their strength surrounding her. She had never been held like this, no one she knew back East would have dared handle her so roughly, but she liked the way he touched her. His hands were strong and possessive, but they were gentle, too. She felt valued and protected. Her father had always made her feel that way, but Slade had found a much more appealing way of showing it.

Oblivious to the soft sound of rough fabric rubbing together as their bodies strained against each other, Slade kissed her ear and the side of her neck. Pamela let her head fall back so he could have uninhibited access to her throat. She didn't want to do anything to stop him. All her life she had tried to behave according to her mother's definition of a lady. Her behavior now could never qualify, but she didn't care. She had never felt better in her life. If only the roundup could go on forever.

She felt Slade stiffen. Turning startled eyes on his face, she started to speak, but he placed a finger over her parted lips. Then she saw the bush move. Someone was huddled in the brush about twenty yards away.

"When I reach for my gun, drop to the ground," Slade whispered in her ear as he continued kissing it.

"Suppose it's one of the boys?" Pamela could hardly believe that even danger didn't have the power to take her mind completely off Slade's kisses.

"After that first night, I told them never to follow you if you were with me. I can take care of you myself." Slade's hands moved from the small of her back to her sides, closer to his guns.

The bushes continued to move soundlessly. Whoever was

hiding there was being extremely careful to make no sound. Could it be the man who had shot Mongo or the one who shot Dave and Jody? Were they one in the same?

"Now!" Slade hissed imperatively. She dropped to the ground and rolled away to the cover of some low rocks which cut into the soft flesh of her side. At the same time, Slade sprang in the opposite direction, dropped to a crouch behind a tree, and drew his guns.

"Throw down your guns and come on out," Slade ordered.

Being careful to remain behind the rocks, Pamela rolled up on her elbow so she could see. They could hear the scurry of feet in the dry leaves, but no one called out or emerged from cover.

"You've got ten seconds," Slade said, "before I spray the whole area with lead."

Silence.

Slade put a bullet into the rocks behind the thicket. "Five seconds."

The bush gave one final, brisk shake and a white-faced maverick calf emerged from the dark green leaves. It looked at Slade with wide, frightened eyes before dashing between them and into another thicket down near the stream.

After a moment of shocked silence, Pamela exploded with a peal of laughter. She pulled herself into a sitting position on the rock, but she laughed so hard she nearly tumbled off again.

"It could have been a gunman," Slade said, but he grinned too.

They both heard the sound of running feet. Everyone in the camp was coming to investigate the gunfire.

"You'd better think of something better than that. Once they find out you've mistaken a defenseless calf for desperate murderer, your reputation will be ruined."

When the cowhands came up, they found Pamela holding to her rock and Slade leaning against a tree, both the helpless victims of uncontrollable laughter. Nobody could get a word out of either one of them that made sense.

Pamela couldn't imagine why the marshall should be this far from town. Not that he had much in Maravillas to keep him busy. Still, she couldn't remember seeing him at the ranch more than once or twice during the last year. She hurried over to where he stood talking to Walter Nilson, Hen McCafferty, and Thurston Peck.

"Well howdy, Miss White," Marshall Taylor Alcott said, turning quickly to greet Josh White's daughter. "I didn't expect to see you out here." He winked. "Bet you wouldn't be if your father weren't away."

Pamela flushed in spite of herself. Marshall Alcott always made her feel like she ought to be home sewing samplers or doing something else conventionally feminine. A heavy-set man of medium height with thinning white hair, no one mistook the muscle for fat or thought his white hair meant his powers were diminishing. Still in his early forties, Taylor Alcott held this section of the Arizona territory under tight control the only way it could be held, with gun and muscle.

"Daddy left me in charge," Pamela explained, her chin rising just a mite as she spoke. "The roundup is just another part of the job. But it's not part of yours. What are you doing out here? You're not having trouble in Maravillas, are you?"

"Naw, everything's real quiet. In fact, with all the men away on roundup, it's too quiet. I was just wondering when the boys would be coming back to town. Ain't practically nobody got out of bed since they left."

"You mean the Wagon Wheel Saloon can't find anybody foolish enough to buy their rotgut whiskey?"

"Something like that," the marshall said and winked at Pamela. "Sure does seem quiet though. My jail's been empty for going on three weeks. I'm so lonesome I've started talking to my horse."

"You didn't come out here just for company," Pamela said. "Seems to me I remember you saying you didn't like long rides through the desert."

"Can't say as I do. Much nicer to sit in my chair in the shade."

"And let Junie Sykes bring you cold beer from the saloon."

"I can't turn it down, Miss White, not after she's walked all that way."

Pamela laughed, but she wouldn't be put off. "Come on, Marshall, confess. What got you out of your chair and away from Junie Sykes?"

The marshall's expression remained relaxed and genial, but his eyes changed. They turned almost yellow, a color Pamela didn't like.

"I came because I heard Mongo Shepherd got shot. Didn't like the sound of that. We ain't had a rancher killed in some time." His yellow eyes scanned the faces of the small gathering around him. "Have any idea who did it?"

"No," Thurston Peck said after a slight pause. "Nobody even heard the shot. Some of his boys found him several hours later."

"You don't know that," Jud Noble said as he broke into the circle. "He could have been shot right before we got there."

"Now take it easy, Jud," Thurston said, looking uneasy. "You know Miss White said . . ."

"I know what she said, but the only man who had a reason to want Mr. Shepherd dead is the Bar Double-B foreman."

"You're crazy," the marshall said, gaping in Jud. "Dave Bagshot wouldn't kill anyone."

"I don't mean Dave. Somebody shot him, too, and Miss White got herself a new foreman. Only this Morgan fella is trying to spark his boss, and he can't stand the sight of Mr. Shepherd. They had another run-in a few mornings back. The boss promised they'd settle things that evening, but

239

somebody shot him first."

Pamela couldn't stop the flush that turned her crimson when Jud mentioned Slade's courtship. Having nearly every eye in the group turn in her direction didn't improve the situation either. It wouldn't do her any good to try to explain her own confusion about Slade. If anybody had seen them kissing, and she could only assume now that someone had, they wouldn't believe her. In fact, they'd think worse of her. Ladies didn't go about kissing men they didn't like a great deal. If they did, they weren't considered ladies.

"Pamela's foreman was in camp all morning," Walter Nilson said. "He didn't leave until past noon. There's plenty can vouch for that. We're pretty sure somebody shot Mongo well before that."

"You can't know that," Jud insisted.

"Slade wouldn't shoot anybody in the back," Pamela said, finding her voice. "He doesn't have to." The marshall's gaze swung around to Pamela, his eyes more intensely yellow than ever.

"You hire a gunslinger, Miss White?"

"No, he used to be a trick shot in a carnival," Pamela explained, fervently hoping she didn't blush again. "He did a trick with some coins."

"He shot the hell out of six twenty-dollar gold pieces before they hit the ground," Thurston Peck said. "Damnedest thing I ever saw."

"You say Dave was shot and this Morgan became your foreman?" the marshall asked Pamela, his mind obviously trying to digest this new information. "How did all this come about?"

"Slade walked into the ranch a few weeks ago. His horse had broken a leg. His feet were in pretty bad shape so I let him sleep in the bunkhouse. Someone tried to burn my barn that night and Slade stopped them."

"You didn't tell us anything about your barn," Thurston Peck said. "Who did it?"

240

"We don't know. They got away. Took all of us to put the fire out. We wouldn't have been able to do it if Slade hadn't been there. When they brought Dave in, he'd been shot in the leg, he remembered he had worked with Slade a time or two before he hired on with Dad. I hired Slade mostly on his recommendation."

"Wasn't another of your men shot?"

"Jody. That was after Dad left for Santa Fe."

"I heard about that," the marshall said, allowing his gaze to slowly travel from one rancher to another. "It would be a shame to have a range war break out, especially after all these years of getting along so peaceably. I wouldn't like that. I'd have to spend too damned much time in the saddle." The ranchers' gazes didn't falter before the marshall's warning, but Pamela knew none of them would willingly take on Taylor Alcott. There were too many gunhands buried in the graveyard at Maravillas to make it look like a bargain.

"You keeping this Slade Morgan on after the roundup?"

"I offered him a job, but he turned it down."

"Moving on?"

"He wants to see California."

"Might be a good idea. People with a gun reputation attract trouble. There's always some fool who wants to see just how good he is."

"It seems unfair to blame Slade for what other people do."

"You're right, it doesn't seem very Christian, but then lots of things ought to be different from how they are. But I don't try and change things. I just deal with them like they are." Nobody seemed to have anything else to say. "I think I'll mosey over and talk to Mongo before I leave."

"He's in my wagon," Pamela said. "Slade insisted I take care of him," she added when the marshall looked a little surprised. "He also insisted one of Mongo's men stay with him," she said, pointedly looking at Jud.

"Maybe I'd better see this Slade Morgan."

"He's out on the range somewhere. He ought to be back by dinner."

"You want one of us to go find him, marshall?"

Pamela thought Jud sounded too eager.

"No, I don't think it's necessary." He started to follow Jud, but he stopped and turned back. "By the way, I got some information about a week ago on a man they want in some Texas town called Brazos. Seems he killed three men, all brothers. There's a good bit of curiosity about how he did it."

"But that's hundreds of miles from here," Walter Nilson pointed out. "Why would they be sending you information?"

"He's disappeared and nobody knows where he's got to. There's always the chance he'll drift through sooner or later."

"I don't know," Nilson said doubtfully. "That's a pretty slim chance."

"What's he look like?"

"That's another problem. Seems this fella wears a beard. Had it since he was a kid. If he shaved it off, there ain't nobody that'd know what he looks like."

Pamela felt the earth move under her feet. Slade said he had worn a beard his whole life! He also said he was drifting in from Texas by way of Mexico. Surely he couldn't be the man they were looking for.

"Is it murder?"

This time Pamela *knew* Jud asked his question with too much eagerness.

"Don't know. There was a good bit of money involved, the man's own it seems, but there's bound to be questions when one man kills three people, especially when they're known to be right handy with a gun."

"Anything else?"

"Not much, just that he was about six feet tall, in his late twenties, and pretty damned good with a gun himself."

Pamela felt too sick at heart to follow the marshall over to see Mongo. He couldn't have given a better description of Slade the day he walked in off the desert if he'd seen him himself. But Slade couldn't have killed those men. Not for a reason as silly as money. Frantically, she shoved aside all the evidence that Slade could have been the very man to do just that. She *knew* Slade, and no matter how callous he pretended to be about guns and life in the West, he wouldn't just kill people. She knew he wouldn't.

She wandered up to the campfire and poured herself a cup of coffee. She had to think, to figure out what to do, but her mind wouldn't work. She couldn't think of anything except that Slade couldn't have killed those men.

"Might be a good idea if you gave a listen to what Mr. Shepherd's telling the marshall."

"What?" Angus's warning roused Pamela from her reverie. She had to ask him to repeat his remark.

"I said Mr. Shepherd's telling Marshall Alcott Mr. Morgan shot him. He's even hinting he might have something to do with your father's not being back yet."

Pamela jumped to her feet and headed toward the wagon so fast she didn't see Angus's smile of satisfaction or hear him mutter, "Old Mongo's done burnt his bridges for good this time."

Pamela burst into the center of the group like a windstorm. "What have you been saying behind my back, Mongo Shepherd?" she demanded so furiously the man's perpetual air of superiority almost deserted him.

"Just what ought to be obvious to anybody," he said after he'd recovered from the shock of her words. "I haven't passed a harsh word with any man in the whole territory until that Morgan fella arrived. From the time I met him at the ranch, he hasn't stopped crowding me." Mongo realized that lying in his bed, still dangerously weak from his wound and speaking in a harsh whisper, made the audience sympathetic to him. He unwisely decided to press his advantage. "He's been hiding behind those guns of his

243

thinking nobody will touch him. But I told him I was coming back. He did this to try and stop me."

Pamela saw Mongo with new eyes.

"Liar," she snarled. "Slade took off his guns to fight you that day at the ranch. And even though he was wounded, he might have beaten you if I hadn't stopped the fight."

"Slade's been shot, too?" the marshal asked. "There seems to have been one helluva lot of shooting going on out here."

"One of the men who tried to burn the barn did it," Pamela answered the marshall before turning her anger back on Mongo. "You saw what he did to those coins. If Slade had shot you, you'd be dead, not lying here telling lies."

"It's not a lie that Slade had a beard when he arrived at the ranch."

"A man would naturally have a beard after traveling two weeks in the desert. He shaved the minute he got a chance to clean up." Pamela didn't know why she said these things, but words just popped out of her mouth. "You can ask Gaddy or Belva. They both saw him."

"You don't know anything about this man except that he can use a gun," Mongo insisted. "You had no business hiring a stranger."

"Dave knows him. Besides, we're short-handed."

"I kept begging you to let me help. I'd have given you all the men you wanted."

"No, thank you," Pamela said, drawing herself up. "We can manage just fine. Dad will be home any day now."

"That's another thing."

"You say another word, Mongo Shepherd, and I'm liable to shoot you myself," Pamela exploded. Mongo's accusation touched on her growing concern over her father's absence and made her temper even more brittle. "Dad told me before he left he might not get back in time for the roundup. He said Dave and I could handle things just fine ourselves."

244

"He hadn't counted on Dave's getting shot just about the time Morgan got here."

"Slade never left the ranch the first week, not for a minute. Belva and Gaddy will tell you that, too."

"You seem mighty anxious to defend that man."

"I'm as anxious as anyone to put a stop to all this shooting," Pamela said, "but I refuse to listen while people are accused of things they didn't do. I didn't listen to Slade's accusations about you, and I won't listen to yours about him."

"What's Morgan been accusing me of?" demanded Mongo.

"Maybe accusation is the wrong word," Pamela said, "but he did wonder why you decided to stop here. You brought in too many cattle, and there's plenty of open range west of here."

"I stopped because I fell in love with you the minute I saw you," Mongo stated. "Otherwise I might have gone to California before I stopped."

"We won't get anywhere just talking," the marshall said getting to his feet. "Anyway, I can't hang around here waiting for this Morgan fella to ride in. I have to go over to Botalla and pick up a prisoner, but I'll be back in about a week. I want to talk with Slade Morgan."

"The roundup will be over in two days," Pamela said. "He may be in California by then."

"In that case, he won't be my problem."

But Pamela couldn't dismiss him that easily.

Chapter 15

Pamela tried to keep her eyes on the surrounding desert, to concentrate on the backlog of work awaiting her at the ranch—the longer her father was away, the more she had learned about running the ranch—but she couldn't see or think of anything for worrying about Slade. But why should that surprise her? She had been trying unsuccessfully to put him out of her mind for the last four days.

He had to be the man the marshall told them about. There couldn't be any real doubt. He fitted the description right down to the last detail. True, she hadn't asked Slade himself, but she didn't want to hear him admit he was a gunslinger and a killer.

Or was she afraid he would lie and deny it?

Unable to reach any decision, she had sidestepped the problem by avoiding Slade. She used the excuse of having to nurse Mongo, but that fooled nobody, not even Angus. She didn't know what upset her more, the fact that Slade had probably killed three people or the death of her hopes that somehow their special relationship wouldn't have to end.

They would be back at the ranch in a few hours. A letter would be waiting for her from her father explaining his absence and telling her when to expect him back. Already Dave had resumed his position as foreman of the Bar

Double-B. Slade had no job; he had no reason to stay. It would be best if he left for California tomorrow morning.

But Pamela wanted him to stay, and that appalled her. She was even more deeply shamed by her desire to say that none of this mattered, that *nothing* mattered except her feelings for Slade. But feeling the way she did about all the pain and suffering caused by guns, how could she ignore what he had done?

What else might he have done? What had he done to make Trish leave him?

Pamela's shoulders sagged at the thought of the endless crimes Slade could have committed. With his expertise with a gun, who could stop him? And he would continue to attract trouble. People like him usually did. It would be far better if he left the ranch as soon as possible.

But no sooner had Pamela argued herself into that position than her heart rebelled. Maybe Slade wasn't the man the marshall described. Maybe this was all a mistake or a coincidence. She never had asked him. Nobody had. There might be a perfectly good explanation for everything.

She had a sudden impulse to ride right up to him and ask. And she would have if he had been there. But Slade had ridden ahead. He said he was still worried about her safety. She decided he was tired of talking to her and getting only monosyllables or a shake of her head for an answer. But she didn't dare talk to him. Once she started, she might not be able to stop.

"Bet you'll be glad to be home again," Angus commented. He was bringing in the chuckwagon because the cowhands didn't need it anymore. They were scattered all over the range now, and each man would carry his own supplies.

"Yes. Even though I didn't get to see very much, I did enjoy it."

"Just as well you stayed in camp. There's been too much shooting lately."

Pamela didn't have to tell Angus that Slade hadn't

allowed her to leave camp. Everybody knew that. "Do you believe what Slade says," she demanded suddenly, "this stuff about someone maneuvering everybody into trouble?"

"I don't know that I'd put it like that exactly. I don't know that Mr. Morgan would either, but something's going on. The boys all know it."

"But what? Who's doing it?"

"Somebody wants your land. Maybe they want everybody's land, too. As for who, I couldn't say."

"Couldn't or wouldn't?"

"Can't say because I don't know. Most likely wouldn't because it could get me killed. I ain't no gunhand, ma'am, not like Mr. Morgan. They could shoot me dead before I could even find my rifle."

Angus had fought by her father's side through the War Between the States and twenty years in Arizona. Now over sixty, his figure bent from the hard life in the saddle, his grey hair but a thin stubble, Pamela never doubted that he considered the Bar Double-B his home, one he'd be willing to fight for.

"I wish my father were here," Pamela said, utterly aloud a thought which had been running through her mind since Mongo's shooting. "He would know what to do."

"That he would, Miss. He surely would, but you listen to Mr. Morgan. You two may not see eye to eye, but that man's got a long head on his shoulders. There's deep trouble here. I have a notion it's been festering out of sight for some while without nobody suspecting. But in one week he's come closer to figuring it out than anybody else. You do what he says. Any low-down skunk as would shoot Jody in the back, and Dave and Mr. Shepherd too, well, he might not stop at shooting a female either."

They followed the curving trail around the base of the ridge until the entrance to her valley came into view. Slade blocked the path before her, still astride his horse, staring at something in front of him. Apprehension stirred in Pamela and she spurred her horse forward. When she reached the canyon opening, however, she halted as well, completely mystified by the collection of junk strewn across the opening to her valley.

It was Gaddy's barricade.

"Very clever."

"What is it?" Pamela asked.

"Apparently it's Gaddy's insurance policy."

"I warned you not to depend on him for anything important."

"You underestimate that boy. What is this?" Slade asked and spurred his horse forward. Pamela followed, but she couldn't see what had caught his attention.

"Apparently someone did try to enter the canyon. The tin is scarred. At least two horses."

Pamela could see the abrasions on the smooth surface of the metal, but it didn't mean whoever made them had intended to do anything wrong. They could have been bringing a message from her father. Why was Slade so suspicious of everyone?

Slade slid from the saddle and stepped up to the rope stretched across the opening. He pulled on it. He broke out in delighted chuckles when eleven crystal bells started to ring all at once.

"My Christmas bells!" Pamela exclaimed as she jumped down and immediately removed one of her precious bells from the limb of a mesquite bush.

"I imagine your visitors got quite a scare. From the looks of the tracks, they didn't waste any time getting out of here."

"You can tell all that from the ground?" asked Pamela, bewildered. The looked like just a bunch of hoofprints to her. She sighed. It was one more thing she had to learn if she was going to superintend the ranch properly.

She almost yielded to the temptation to think Slade had made this up to support his accusations, but it only took a moment for her to cast that idea aside. It had been her experience that Slade didn't much give a damn whether anybody believed him or not. He had to be right.

"You can collect your bells later," Slade said as he removed the rope and pulled the sheet of tin off the trail.

"I'll collect them right now. Ornaments of this quality are impossible to find in Arizona."

"It won't matter since you're going back to Baltimore."

Pamela couldn't deny his logic, but it only made her more determined to collect her bells. By the time she reached the house, he had gotten the whole story from Gaddy.

"That boy stayed out in that canyon every night," Belva added, just as proud of Gaddy as if she'd been his own mother. "He couldn't be watchful day and night, nobody could, but his trap sure did make a fuss."

"When was that?"

"Four nights ago, but Gaddy was taking shots at them so quick they practically hurt themselves trying to get away."

Slade turned to Pamela with an I-told-you-so look, but she withheld her praise. It would be some time before she could forgive Gaddy for breaking one of her precious crystal bells. "Where's Dad's letter?" she asked. "I need to know when he's getting back."

"There's only one letter, and that's from your friend in Baltimore."

"But there's got to be a letter from him," Pamela protested, unbelieving. "He promised he'd write. And he always does."

"I'm sorry, Miss White, but no letter came from your Pa."

"No message either?"

"Not unless those men were bringing it."

"If they'd been honest, they'd have come back," Slade said.

But Pamela didn't hear anyone. She could no longer deny the prowling fear that something had happened to her father. She didn't know who could have wanted to harm him

250

or how or why, but her brain's inability to provide her with specific answers didn't lessen her anxiety.

"Exactly what did your father say when he left?" Slade asked.

Pamela jumped. Her worry over her father had made her forget Slade's presence for the first time in two weeks.

"He said he was going to Santa Fe to buy some barbed wire and hire some extra hands. He said he would be back before the roundup, but if he couldn't for any reason, he would write."

"And you think he would have written?"

"Dad didn't talk much, he and Mama didn't have much to say to each other, but he loved to write. He wrote me every week while I was at school. Without all those letters to tell me what he was really like, I wouldn't love him so much."

"What route was he taking?"

"I don't know. You'll have to ask Dave."

"I think someone ought to go to Santa Fe."

"Do you think . . . ?" For the moment, all her reservations about Slade were forgotten.

"I don't think anything," Slade said quickly. "It's just better to know."

"I can be ready to leave by noon. Will you go with me?"

Odd, his reputation didn't seem in the least objectionable now. In fact, it provided her with solid comfort. She felt a twinge of guilt. She couldn't condemn his use of guns one moment and then depend on it the next without being two-faced. She'd already done that with the roundup. She wouldn't do it again with her father.

She didn't have time to worry about the probity of her ethics just now. She'd worry about that after she found her father.

Then she read Amanda's letter.

"They've changed their plans," she said looking at Slade in consternation. "They're arriving earlier than they thought."

"When?"

251

"Today. I've got to be here. I can't go off and let them come into an empty house."

How could she ask Slade to go look for her father, especially after the things she had thought about him? Not to mention what she had actually said! But who else could she ask?

"I can go," Gaddy volunteered. He looked unsure of himself, even a little shocked at his own temerity, but he held to it. "After all, he is my uncle."

"You're the perfect choice," Slade said before Pamela could voice the rejection on the tip of her tongue. "What's more natural than a boy looking for an uncle he hasn't seen in years?"

Pamela started to protest, but abruptly changed her mind. "You think he ought to keep his purpose a secret?"

"If your father's all right, it won't matter what he says. If not, then we don't want to make anybody suspicious."

"You think he's in trouble?"

"Do you?"

"Yes." Pamela didn't have to think about it. She had felt in her heart for some time that something had happened. The minute Belva said her father hadn't written, she knew it. In all her years at school, his letters never came late. Why should he change a lifelong habit now?

"I'll get Gaddy on his way while you get ready for your friends," Slade offered.

"Will you come up to the house when you're done?"

Slade nodded his agreement, but Pamela thought the look in his gaze had grown more quizzical than usual.

Pamela tried to steady her nerves. She didn't know why she should feel so underhanded about asking Slade to move his things into the bunkhouse. This was her home and she had every right to decide who stayed in it. True, she didn't need the room, there were more than enough for a dozen

252

guests, but Slade would undoubtedly feel more comfortable in the bunkhouse until he left tomorrow.

She wasn't exactly throwing him out. He had already told her he was leaving. With Frederick arriving any minute now, he didn't need to postpone his plans any longer. Gaddy had gone for her father and Dave was back on the job. She had everything under control. He could be on his way to California.

But Pamela had to be honest with herself. She wasn't doing it for Slade's benefit. She had thought entirely of herself, and that didn't make her very proud.

She no longer tried to deny her helpless infatuation with Slade. She ought to be thankful that Amanda and Frederick had decided to come early. If she were left alone with him for just a few days, well, she didn't want to think of what might happen. The odd feeling of weakness that coursed its way through her abdomen underscored the strength of her attraction to this man. She had become obsessed to the point of ignoring her own values, plans, common sense for that matter. He was like an addictive drug. As long as he was around, she couldn't think of anything else. She would be miserable after he left, but having Frederick here ought to make it easier. He would be a living example of the kind of man she hoped to marry, an unspoken rebuttal to the kind of man Slade Morgan was.

Too, she would be mortified if Amanda so much as speculated about her attraction to Slade. And she knew Amanda wouldn't have to be in the room with them for more than five minutes before she would begin to suspect. Give her a full day and she would know everything. Trust Amanda for that.

And then there was Mongo's insinuation that somehow Slade had something to do with her father's failure to return on time. She didn't believe that, there seemed no way the two could possibly have crossed paths, but the fact that it kept popping into her mind disturbed her. It had to be because of his reputation as a gunslinger.

253

Slade was a gunslinger, and gunslingers were not to be trusted. Her mind was clear on that part. Her confusion came from the fact that her body was saying something very different. She could feel her heartbeat. She was so much more aware of it when she was near Slade. It, the physical part of her, not her mind, was the driving force in her life now. Her belly felt hollow, hungry—and not for food. Her walk was different, too. She'd felt it, like there was some natural sway he triggered. Her hips felt looser. She wondered if he saw the difference. Did it show?

Her heartbeat was slow now, steady and clear, but her mind was still foggy, and Pamela continued to argue with herself until Slade entered the room. One look at him and she wondered how she could ever send him away. And if he did go, how could she keep from following?

Why didn't her father come home? She needed him to be strong for her. She needed him to tell her to do what she couldn't do on her own.

"Gaddy's on his way," Slade said as he came into the living room where he found Pamela. "We should know something in a few days. I've given him a route off the main trail."

"Why?"

"It's shorter and faster for one thing. If someone did harm your father, they may still be on the lookout for anybody leaving this ranch. I doubt there's anything in that," he added quickly when he saw fear come alive in Pamela's eyes, "but it's better to make sure."

"I really ought to thank you. You've handled everything so quickly."

"It's not necessary. That's a foreman's job."

"But you're not foreman any longer."

"Yes, well neither of us wanted it to last forever."

"I'd be much happier if you'd let me pay you," Pamela said. The words came out in a rush.

254

"You mean you wouldn't feel so beholden to me?"

"That's part of it. The work had to be done, it's a natural part of every ranch, and we expect to pay for it. I don't like having to be grateful to anybody for something I would have been perfectly willing to pay for."

"It would also make you feel so much better if you didn't have to be grateful to someone like me."

"I didn't say that," Pamela assured him quickly. "I know how I acted in the beginning, and I'm sorry for that, but I don't feel that way any more."

"But you still feel you couldn't marry a common cowboy."

"I was talking about a *job*," Pamela said, abruptly lowering her gaze. "Marriage is something entirely different. It has to be a voluntary relationship built on love, trust, and respect. Even that can't last if two people don't share some mutual interests and common values."

"And all we share is a lust for each other," Slade rasped crudely.

"I never said . . ."

Without warning, Slade swept her up in his powerful arms and pressed her so close to him she almost swooned. Her breasts swelled against the hard ribs of his chest; her fluttering abdomen caught against the swell of his groin.

"Tell me you don't want me," Slade challenged. His mouth descended on hers, his tongue inching its way into her mouth, probing, seeking, caressing until he almost swept her away by the power and sweetness of his kiss. His hands lifted her arms to encircle his neck and brushed her sensitive breasts in passing. The heat from his body turned her into an inferno of desire. "Tell me you don't want me," Slade said again.

"I want you," Pamela answered, her breath ragged with desire. "I want you more than I've ever wanted anything in my life." Her hands moved into his thick hair in a burning caress.

"Then why are you sending me away?"

"I'm not sending you away."

"You haven't said the words yet, but you will."

Pamela hid herself in Slade's embrace, hid from his words. "We don't have any future," she whispered into his shoulder. "You said so yourself many times," she added quickly before Slade could protest. "I may want you,"—Pamela paused to look up at Slade's face—"I *do* want you so badly I sometimes lie awake in my bed shaking with desire. But I want more than a relationship based on desire, no matter how tempting that might be. Marriage requires so much more." She looked at him, hard. "And I do mean to be married before I give myself to a man."

He stared back, his eyes growing sea-grey. "You once said that if you loved a man, you wouldn't need anything else."

"I don't remember. . . ." Pamela temporized.

"Do you love me?"

His stark question shook Pamela down to her foundations. She just might love Slade. She hardly knew what she felt, but she did know she had never felt about anybody like she felt about him.

"How can I love you when I don't know anything about you? Not any of the important things." To her shock and surprise, her heart already had the answer. If that man was Slade, it wouldn't matter.

"So we're back to my past, my *family,* are we? Do you think I'm a monster with some dark past that haunts me?"

"I'm not talking about your past now. I'm talking about *you!* I don't know who *you* are. I don't know anything about you. For all I know, you could be twice as rich as Mongo or the murderer the marshall is looking for." Oh God, she hadn't meant to say that. But it had preyed on her mind so much it slipped out before she could catch it.

"Do you think I'm a murderer?" Slade asked.

"I don't know what to think! You wander in from the desert and refuse to say anything about yourself. Two weeks later Marshall Alcott comes asking about a man whose description fits you tighter than your boots. What am I supposed to think?"

"If you had asked me, I'd have told you what you wanted to know."

But Pamela couldn't ask. As much as she wanted to know, she couldn't summon the words to frame the question. She was petrified of the answer he might give. She only had enough courage for half measures, and half questions.

"Let's say you didn't kill those men, that you never heard of them. Can you swear you never killed anybody else? Or that you won't kill anybody in the future?"

"No."

"No to which question?"

"Both."

Pamela staggered, and something inside her died. Hope, probably, but she couldn't summon the energy to care.

She slipped free of his arms.

So he had killed; whether these men or some other, he had killed. Could she even consider loving such a man? No. It was impossible.

"I was wrong about what I said earlier," she said. "Love isn't enough. There has to be more. And it's not money," she added quickly. "I could love a poor man if I believed in him, if I admired and respected him."

"And you don't admire and respect me?"

She was silent. She hardly knew which words to choose.

"I thought I'd done a right fair job around here in the last couple of weeks. Doesn't that earn me some kind of respect?"

"I do respect your work," Pamela quickly assured him. "And I trust you. It's just that . . ."—she paused, unable to decide which words to choose—". . . I can't accept a man who believes in killing."

"I don't believe in killing, Pamela. I believe in survival. If I hadn't killed those men, they'd have killed me."

"I'm sorry," Pamela said, making sure she didn't look into

Slade's eyes, "my brain may be able to accept that, but my heart can't."

"Doesn't look like I stack up very well next to your precious Frederick, does it?"

"I'm not comparing you to Frederick."

"Yes, you do, every time you look at me."

"I don't mean to."

"Is he the kind of man you want to marry?"

"Yes."

"Would you have married him if he had asked?"

"Once." That answer startled Pamela into realizing she no longer wanted to marry Frederick. Two years ago, before he married Amanda, she would have jumped at the chance to become his wife. Now, oddly enough, even though her admiration and respect were unchanged, she had no desire to marry him.

"Once?"

"Yes. Ages ago, perhaps, but not now. And don't you dare ask me why."

"What can I ask you?"

"Nothing," Pamela snapped. "And don't you dare tell me about *all the things I've done for you.* On more than one occasion I specifically asked you not to. And you refused any pay or reward."

"I didn't do anything because it was a *job,* and I refuse to let your money turn it into something it isn't."

"Why are we talking like this?" Pamela suddenly felt empty, drained of all energy. It couldn't change anything. It was pointless to keep going over the same territory. She just wanted it over. "I don't want you to leave with bad feelings."

"I didn't know I was leaving."

"Aren't you going to California? You said you'd leave when the roundup was over."

"It'll take a day or two to get a rig together and buy some supplies."

"I can let you have anything you need."

258

"Just as long as I leave today?"

"You can use the bunkhouse as long as you need."

Slade had been on the verge of giving up. He never doubted that Pamela kept him at a distance because of the marshall's mention of the man wanted in Texas. He'd even given up trying to prove to her that anybody could equal her wonderful Frederick. He had figured to remove his things from the house and disappear quietly while she and her friends were busy. But her effort to hurry him off made him dig in his heels.

In a way it was even worse than the night Trish told him to never come back. Trish had never made any bones about wanting money and social position. She would never have said she'd stay in Arizona for love, not if she could have gone to Baltimore instead.

But Pamela had said that and more. Only a fool would believe her, but he *had* believed and let himself hope that at last he had found a woman who was different, one who could love him without demanding anything more than his love in return.

The more he thought about it, the angrier he got. Dammit, he wouldn't leave, at least not yet. Maybe she couldn't make up her mind, maybe her principles were in a fierce battle with her desires, but he was in just as fierce a battle. He was fighting for a chance at a future he thought he had lost ten years ago, and he wouldn't give up this easily. He'd show her she couldn't give up either. He'd prove he had just as strong a hold on her as she did on him.

"If you're running me off, I guess I'd better take my good-bye kiss now."

At that moment, Pamela wanted him to kiss her more than anything else in the world, but she didn't know if she could and not call him back the instant he reached the door.

"I don't think it's a good idea."

"I'll take one anyway," Slade said, pulling her not unwilling body into his arms. "It'll give you something to remember me by."

You'll haunt my dreams for the rest of my life Pamela thought as she eagerly met his lips. The kiss came hard; his tongue demanded entrance to her mouth. Slade's body grew rigid against her, his hold became unbreakable, but Pamela didn't care. She didn't care about anything as long as she could cling to Slade this one last time, share in one last kiss.

But Slade didn't stop at a kiss. His lips found her eyelids, her forehead, her ears; he lit up any part of her he could reach with a trail of blazing desire. He pressed her painfully close to his body; he crushed her breasts against his chest; his inflamed groin ground against her abdomen. Pamela's whole body, now flooded with desire, begged to stay in his embrace until they merged into one.

She fought for release and lost. But if she didn't get away now, she might never be able to let him leave.

Slade refused to let her go. He covered her averted face with kisses, not tender but fiery hard and demanding.

"Let me go," Pamela whispered.

"Not yet," Slade said. His voice rasped from the physical hunger which had him in its coils. "I want you to remember me for a long time."

His hand trailed down the small of her back to cup her buttock. Slade pressed her more firmly against his engorged manhood.

"Don't . . ." she moaned, her protest swallowed by a kiss so all-consuming Pamela didn't have the strength to object. Nor did she want to. When Slade's other hand slipped inside her blouse and covered her breast, Pamela's nipples hardened against his fingers. She no longer tried to pull away. Slade captured her leg between his forcing intimate contact along the whole length of his inflamed body.

"Please," she murmured, not knowing whether she was asking for more or begging him to stop. His kiss deepened, his tongue probed more fiercely, his left hand rubbed her breasts until they swelled with an almost painful desire; his right hand, pressed into the small of her back, forced her body into contact with him from ankle to lips.

"You've tormented me for weeks," Slade rasped in her ear before he nibbled her throat. "Always just out of reach" . . . his mouth kissed the base of her neck . . . "hiding behind your facade of eastern manners" . . . his mouth went lower . . . "but your desires are no different from mine" . . . his mouth followed his hand as he lifted away the edge of her blouse . . . "You want me just as much as I want you."

She trembled. "No," Pamela insisted, but her body screamed another message.

Slade edged her against a wall and hurriedly unbuttoned her dress down to the waist. He paused to look at her as he pulled her bodice open. "You're so very beautiful, Pamela." He lowered his head slowly until he took her firm nipple between his teeth and tugged gently. Pamela almost screamed with the sweet agony that ripped through her body.

"Slade," she murmured, arching her back to meet him.

Her legs threatened to buckle, and Slade gradually allowed her to slip to the floor. But he did not release her nipple. His fingertip gently massaged the other aching nipple until Pamela's frenzy increased beyond the limits of her control.

Now it didn't matter that Slade was not like Frederick. It only mattered that he was driving her out of her mind.

"I want you to remember me," Slade whispered as his lips deserted one tortured breast to nibble on the other. "I want you to know what it's been like for me to be around you and be held at a distance. I want you to feel the agony you made me feel."

Pamela waited only a minute before she understood what he meant. Slade's hand burrowed under her skirt and his hand began to gently explore the burning, secret place between her thighs.

"Dear God!" she shrieked. No one had ever touched her so

intimately. Her body bucked against him, but that only brought her into closer contact with his engorged manhood. Such a small matter compared to the fact that he had stripped off her panties. Her innermost self was bared to his invasion.

"Slade, please, if you ever felt anything for me . . ."

"Why should I care about your feelings? You've used me and now you're throwing me out."

"I never did that. I'm sorry . . . ooohhhhh."

The palm of his hand found her, began to gently massage between her thighs. Spirals of desire coursed through her body, weakening her resistance, arousing even more need than she had ever expected.

"Slade," she protested again, but the tone in her voice had changed to one of wonder and surprise.

"This is what you do to me," Slade growled as he gently teased the threshold of her body. "Every time. This is what I suffered when you let me come close then pushed me away."

"I didn't . . ." Pamela said, but at that moment his finger slipped inside to touch a part of her she didn't know existed . . . "know," she gasped. A shudder racked her whole body. One explosion after another went off inside her until she was certain it would tear her to shreds.

"Do you like the way I touch you? Do you enjoy the need I give you? The need that grips you in your guts and turns you inside out?"

Pamela could only nod. She was beyond any kind of speech.

"Good. I want you to enjoy what I do to you. I want you to crave my hands on you."

His tongue circled her nipple at the same time his hand continued to turn her core into a caldron of desire. She seethed with an agony of need; she had no thought but to satisfy that need before it drove her mad. Instinctively her body bucked against this hand, driving his finger deeper inside. Gasping in response to that invasion, Pamela grabbed the back of Slade's head and pressed his hot mouth against her breasts.

"Do you want me, Pamela?" His voice was so ragged from the urgency of his unfulfilled hunger Pamela could hardly understand the words.

"Yes."

"More than you've ever wanted anything in your life?"

"Oh God, yes," she whimpered as she pushed against him, trying to reach the want buried deep inside her. "Please don't torture me any longer."

Slade's whole body shuddered with desire. Pamela wanted him! *Him!* She was *begging* him to do what he had dreamed of doing for weeks. She wouldn't hold him off any longer. She wanted only sweet harmony, oneness with him.

But he couldn't.

He felt only self-loathing. She didn't want *him*. She didn't beg for the satisfaction only he could give her. She was innocent, at least she *had* been, of what her physical appetite could do to her mind and self-control. He had used this knowledge to humble her because she had rejected him. Well, he'd done that—that was bad enough—but there was no reason to shame her. That would be unforgivable.

Abruptly Slade rolled away.

The shock of his sudden withdrawal was pure agony. Pamela felt like a red-hot coal dropped into a glacial lake. Her body still burned with agonizing need, but her muscles slowly relaxed as if all by themselves they knew her need would not be satisfied today.

For several minutes they lay still as their breathing gradually returned to normal, as her heart stopped beating so hard it hurt. But as the fire of desire began to cool within her, the searing heat of shame flowed over her like lava.

She wasn't safe from Slade. Despite her eastern education, her eastern friends, her eastern house, she was a wild lusty animal just like him. Moments ago she would have let him take her right here on the floor, would have welcomed it.

She had begged him to! All her training and manners and codes of behavior didn't matter. Underneath, she was just as hungry for his body as he was for hers.

She sat up and, dazed, began to button her dress. Her shaking hands tried to rearrange her hair, reposition her clothes, but her face was as white as a ghost. "I don't think I deserved that. I never realized the enormous power of one's physical nature. If I caused you to suffer only half what I have endured in these last minutes, I'm truly sorry."

She stood up.

"I didn't suffer any pain," Slade said, standing up, too, lest she run away. He grabbed her shoulders so she would have to look at him. "I suffered need, Pamela. Want. Longing. Desire. All hard to bear but all still delicious and wonderful."

But Pamela showed no emotion except in those beautiful eyes which now looked dull and lifeless. Everything had already drained away.

"This doesn't change anything," she said. "It's no good between us. You know that. It only makes it harder to part."

"So you're still determined to go back to Baltimore?"

"I've always meant to go back to Baltimore. You tempted me to change my mind. I almost did, too."

Slade towered over her. "I'll leave tomorrow."

"Considering what just happened, I think you should sleep in the bunkhouse tonight."

"Are you sure that's the only reason, or is it because of Frederick?"

"I don't think you two would get along, but that's not the reason any more."

"And what is?"

"I couldn't get a wink of sleep as long as I knew you were in this house." She looked him full in the face. "I'm not even sure if the bunkhouse is far enough away."

Slade pulled her into his arms. Their kiss was long and deep.

"You don't have to do this."

Pamela held firm. "Yes, I do."

"How do I know you'll be safe?"

"Frederick will be here. He can . . ."

"I should have known," Slade said, the inside of him freezing at her words. "You don't need anybody now that you've got Frederick."

"Don't. . . ."

"I'll get my clothes and be gone this afternoon. I don't want to do anything to keep you from giving your full attention to Frederick."

Pamela watched him stalk out of the room. There were only a few things in his bedroom. It wouldn't take him long to gather them up.

She fought down a desperate desire to call him back, to tell him that Frederick wasn't that important to her, that she liked him a whole lot more, and that telling him to go was the hardest thing she had ever had to do in her life, but she didn't dare. Her heart was too full. She would collapse into Slade's arms, and then she'd have to start all over again. She couldn't do that. She simply didn't have the strength.

The sudden thought that she would probably never see him again almost undid her resolve. It seemed inconceivable that he wouldn't always be part of her days, that she wouldn't hear the sound of his voice, feel the excitement of his presence, be able to see the smile slowly spread to his whole face. How could anyone have become so much a part of her in such a short time?

She couldn't be making a mistake, could she? Could she have changed so much she could live happily as Slade's wife? No, she hadn't changed that much.

But could she live happily without him?

She still hadn't answered that question when she heard Slade's footsteps returning. She would have to face him with courage alone.

But he didn't come back into the living room. He went

265

right on out the door. In a few seconds he descended the steps and started across the yard to the bunkhouse. He was leaving her without a glance, without a word. All at once she couldn't stand it. "Wait!" she cried and ran after him.

"Why?" Slade asked spinning on his heel. "Have you changed your mind?"

"N-no, but . . ."

Chapter 16

The sound of a rifle shot stopped Pamela in mid-sentence. A short burst of five or six shots followed before either of them could speak.

"It's coming from beyond the mouth of the canyon," Slade said as he spun on his heel. He couldn't run quickly in his boots, but he had the corral gate open before Pamela had recovered from her shock. Astride his hammerhead dun seconds later, he rode bareback down the canyon at a gallop.

Pamela ran inside to get her rifle. Unfortunately, Angus had already unhitched the chuckwagon, and she didn't even consider the possibility of riding bareback in her long skirts. Muttering in frustration that a lady should be forbidden to wear pants, Pamela started toward the canyon mouth, her rifle under her arm. But she hadn't covered half the distance when a buggy came careening around the corner. At first the driver, a man she had never seen before, seemed to be the only passenger. He lost control of the vehicle and its wheel hit one of the small boulders which littered the ground close to the canyon walls. The axle broke and two people came spilling out of the back. Instinctively Pamela knew they were Amanda and Frederick, and she broke into a run.

By the time she reached them, Frederick had gotten to his feet, but Amanda had not moved. The driver seemed to be out cold.

Her first good look at Frederick affected Pamela like a bucket of cold water in the face. *He looked ordinary!* Frederick Marchbanks Olmstead III, the wealthy scion of an old family and the darling of the most exclusive social circles in America, looked ordinary.

The long sideburns and coal-black hair parted in the middle, the tiny mustache, the tall, slim body lacking Slade's muscles were all familiar yet they seemed to belong to a stranger. Once he had put himself together and regained his composure, he would be his old, polished self again. But he would never be the man Pamela remembered.

And it was because of Slade.

"Are you hurt?" she asked between gasps for breath, wrenching her gaze from Frederick to Amanda. Her friend moaned loudly.

"What in God's name is going on around here?" Frederick demanded wildly, none of his well-practiced self-control in evidence. "We were riding along and some fool started shooting at us."

"Don't stand there jabbering, Frederick," Amanda commanded sharply when her moan didn't get the desired results. "Get me out of this tangle. I think my ankle is broken."

"Don't move," Pamela said setting down her rifle and kneeling next to her friend. "Let me check it."

"Good God," Amanda cried, in genuine pain this time, "you're killing me!"

"It's not broken. It's most likely no more than a mild sprain."

"It may be your idea of a *mild* sprain," Amanda replied, incensed, "but the pain is excruciating."

Just then a sidewinder slithered to the ground a few yards from Amanda. It had been driven from its warm rock by the commotion and it shook its rattle furiously.

"Don't move," Pamela hissed as she grabbed up her rifle

268

and blasted the venomous reptile into a bloody mass.

Amanda uttered a feeble groan and fainted.

"Jesus," exclaimed Frederick, his face drawn and white. "Is it always like this out here?"

"No. It's usually extremely quiet." Pamela looked down at Amanda, her hopes for providing her friend with an impressive show of hospitality dashed beyond repair. "We've got to get her to the house, but she can't walk on that ankle. You'll have to go up to the house and hitch one of the horses to the buggy. It's in the barn across from the bunk-house. The horses are in the corral. You'll have to catch one."

"I can't lasso a horse," Frederick told her. "And I doubt I could harness it to a rig."

Pamela realized the foolishness of her statement almost as soon as the words were out of her mouth. Frederick had always had servants to do that for him, but somehow she thought less of him for not making the attempt.

"I'll go. The driver obviously can't do it." Pamela checked to make sure he was alive.

"Do you think they'll come back?"

"No. Slade's gone after them, but I'll leave my rifle just in case." She knew Frederick was a superior marksman with a rifle. But she had only gone a few steps when the sound of hoofbeats caused her to turn. Slade had returned.

"Did you find anybody?" she asked, hurrying back.

"No, they fired from one of the ridges more than a thousand yards away. Too far to hit anything. Obviously they were just trying to scare your friends. Probably some-one's idea of an Arizona welcome for a pair of Eastern tenderfoots."

"That ought not be allowed," Frederick said, incensed. "I insist that you report this to the authorities."

"We're the only *authorities* out here," Pamela told him. "The nearest law officer is fifteen miles away." Amanda moaned, and all three of them turned their attention to the stricken young woman.

Amanda was nearly Pamela's opposite. She was petite, almost tiny in statue, but the energy sparking from her eyes, the vitality which radiated from her body, made an indelible impression on everyone in her presence. Her red hair, brilliant green eyes, and fair skin never failed to capture the undivided attention of most males within her vicinity. Her slightly plump figure gave her an opulent look which guaranteed that even the most hardened case could not long withstand her charms.

"Do something to get me off this ground, Frederick. I must look terrible." She looked up at Slade, shading her eyes to see him. Almost immediately her feminine instincts were on full alert. Pamela could sense it in every line of her friend's body, hear it in her voice, see it in the curve of her smiling lips. "Are you the man who thundered by us on that wild stallion?"

Slade smiled in response. "I was hoping to catch up with the prankster, ma'am," he replied.

"You won't leave me lying here while someone goes for a wagon, will you? I've already been attacked by a deranged person and a venomous snake. There's no telling what other dangerous creatures are skulking about in your terrible desert." She looked up coyly at Slade. "I just know you're strong enough to carry me."

"Really, Amanda, that's too much," Frederick protested, but Amanda paid her husband no attention.

"Could you?"

"Of course, ma'am," Slade said. He picked her up like she was a feather.

"I'll get the wagon," Pamela said between gritted teeth.

"We don't need a wagon, Pamela," Amanda cooed without taking her eyes off Slade. "This cowboy of yours will have me at the house before you reach the barn. Besides, the ride would undoubtedly jar my ankle."

Pamela struggled with an overmastering desire to see

Slade drop Amanda flat on her posterior. She also had a strong desire to slap that silly, virginal look off her face. Amanda was about as demure and shy as a jungle cat. Her poised approach to the world had been one of the attributes which first drew Pamela to her. Pamela had always been shy and unsure of herself at school. Nothing unsettled Amanda. Not even men.

But a deeper, hidden part of Pamela was shocked by the jealousy and animosity which overwhelmed her. Amanda was her friend and she had been hurt. She ought to feel sympathy and concern. Instead she felt jealous Slade had never found a reason to cradle her in his arms.

She didn't believe Slade's story about an Arizona welcome. He had said that for Amanda and Frederick's benefit. No, her friends had been shot at by her enemies, and she ought to feel responsible.

But all she felt was angry.

"The man may not be able to carry you as far as the house, Amanda," Frederick pointed out, earning Pamela's unspoken thanks. "It's a long way."

"You can carry me, can't you?" she asked in a voice Pamela used to think amusing when Amanda used it on other men.

Pamela didn't find it amusing now.

"Sure, ma'am," Slade said. He looked to Pamela as though he were asking her permission. He had never asked her permission to do anything before, and it infuriated Pamela that he should start now when she couldn't possibly refuse. She nodded her head in consent.

Slade headed toward the house as though he were carrying a featherweight. Pamela angrily pointed Slade's hammerhead dun toward the house and gave it a resounding slap on the rump. It broke into a gallop.

"I always did admire Amanda's ability to make an entrance, but she's outdone herself this time," Frederick said peevishly.

"You sure she didn't hire those men on purpose?" Pamela demanded.

Frederick looked startled, then broke out in a chuckle as he got Pamela's meaning. "No, the attack was in earnest. The rest you can put down to her ability to make the best of any situation. Aren't you going to do anything about that man?" He indicated the driver.

"He can come up to the house when he wakes up," Pamela said uncharitably. "Anyone who drives that badly deserves to be left in the road."

"You've become a little unfeeling since you came home," Frederick observed looking at Pamela closely for the first time.

"I'm sorry, but things are in a muddle right now. Then to have this happen, well, it's spoiled your visit."

"Oh, I don't know," Frederick said looking ahead to where Amanda snuggled happily in Slade's arms. "I fancy Amanda is about to enjoy a little flirtation with your cowboy. I don't imagine there's anything you could have provided to make her happier."

"He's not *my* cowboy and I didn't *provide* him so Amanda could practice her predatory skills. In fact, he was just about to leave for California when we heard the shots."

"He won't go now, not if Amanda sinks her hooks into him."

"Slade doesn't like women of Amanda's type," Pamela said. Frederick gave her a look comprised mainly of raised eyebrows. "He told me so."

"Then I know he's sunk. Amanda doesn't like anything so much as a challenge."

Pamela started to say that Slade was different, that he wouldn't be taken in by Amanda's tricks, but it was a good thing she saved her breath. Starting with the moment they reached the house, Slade spent every minute of his time at Amanda's beck and call, carrying her from one place to another until she was finally satisfied she was the center of

272

everyone's attention. He arranged cushions for comfort and shawls for warmth now that they were inside the coolness of the house and provided an appreciative audience for her charm and beauty.

Pamela would have given half her ranch to be able to throw them both into the hottest part of the desert.

At least she didn't expect him to help her dress for dinner! Somehow Amanda managed to do that on her own. But the effort so exhausted her she was unable to walk to the table under her own power, and Slade, the simpering idiot, couldn't wait to carry her.

Pamela ground her teeth and muttered some very unlady-like curses.

Amanda dominated the conversation at dinner.

"Of course the Worthingtons wanted us to visit them again, but I refuse to spend another summer in one of those drafty English country houses. Even if there is a Duke living practically at her front door. English stiffness is not confined to the upper lip. I find them insufferably proud, especially when Frederick can buy up at least half a dozen of them and still be a rich man."

"Isn't California a bit of an adventure, even for you?" Pamela asked, hoping to change the subject from English Dukes or their houses.

"Yes, but I've heard so much about San Francisco I couldn't wait any longer to see it."

"It would have been much easier to have taken a ship and crossed Panama."

"But so much less exciting." Amanda looked up at Slade. *"Much* less exciting. Besides, I wanted to see you again," she said turning back to Pamela. "You've taken so long about getting back to Baltimore." She reached over to give Pamela's hand a squeeze. "I had begun to despair of your ever coming back. We miss you very much."

Pamela was appalled that her first impulse was to snatch her hand away. Had jealousy made her that petty? And it was jealousy. There could be no doubt about it. She couldn't deny it no matter how ashamed she might be.

She never doubted Amanda's sincerity. Amanda *did* want her back. But she was thinking of the shy, admiring companion Pamela had been all through her teens. Amanda could have no idea how much Pamela had changed.

Until now even Pamela hadn't realized it.

Three years of managing her father's household, sharing in his decisions about the ranch, and living in the harsh, demanding Arizona territory had changed her from a starry-eyed, impressionable girl only too ready to follow the lead of her sophisticated friend into a woman who demanded that life come to her on her own terms.

And then there was Slade. Two weeks of being forced to question everything she had ever believed, of having her failings held up to the strong light of his scrutiny, had turned her into a woman even her father might not recognize.

"I'm sorry about the shooting prank. I'm afraid it has ruined your visit."

"Not in the least."

"But you can't ride or see anything, not with that ankle."

"But I can," Amanda announced happily, just as though she were giving Pamela a wonderful surprise. "Mr. Morgan has agreed to be my prop and stay for the next few days. He has promised to see I get wherever I wish to go."

Pamela turned to Slade, her jaw threatening to go slack in a very unsophisticated manner.

Frederick was more direct. "Damn it, Amanda, the poor man doesn't want to be at your beck and call for days on end."

"Slade can't resist a damsel in distress," Pamela said, determined to appear just as blasé as Slade. "Of course he's not very dependable. Gunslingers sometimes have to leave on a moment's notice." The openly sarcastic tone of her voice surprised even herself. Frederick looked at her in some disbelief.

"Are you a good shot?" Amanda asked Slade, her eyes sparkling with excitement. "Frederick is a perfect whiz with a rifle, but I don't really count that, not compared to a pistol."

"A rifle bullet can kill you just as quickly as any other," Slade said.

"True, but it doesn't require nearly so much skill. You are skillful, aren't you?" she asked suggestively. When Slade showed no response, Amanda shrugged slightly and continued. "Anyway, you're not as close to the target with a rifle. You have plenty of time to aim. There's no real danger, is there?"

"Only if the rifleman doesn't intend to hit you, like this afternoon. I know a dozen men who can hit a target at more than a thousand yards."

"But surely only the most lawless element would hide behind a rock and shoot at people," Frederick said. "I had been led to believe your western criminals were too busy robbing trains and banks to be interested in ordinary travelers."

"The biggest treasure in the West is land, Mr. Olmstead. For that even respectable men will do just about anything, even people from the East."

"Speaking of that," Amanda said, changing the subject, "I heard that Mongo Shepherd is somewhere in Arizona. He's the son of one of Daddy's classmates from Yale."

"Mongo's here," Pamela told her. "I see him fairly often. Would you like me to invite him over for dinner?"

"Not on my account," Amanda said. "I never met him. Daddy considered him too wild. He just happened to mention him when we were getting ready to leave. Now, if you don't mind, I think I shall go to bed. I'm completely exhausted from the trip, and Mr. Morgan is showing me the ranch tomorrow. I want to be all rested up for that."

"How are you going to manage?" Frederick asked.

"In a carriage of some sort," Amanda said majestically.

"Now, Mr. Morgan, if you are ready, I'd like to go to my room."

"Really, Amanda, you ask too much."

"Oh be quiet, Frederick, unless you propose to carry me yourself."

"It would be more suitable."

"But not nearly so exhilarating. Oh, Pamela, dear, I do hope you've placed Mr. Morgan in the room next to mine, in case I need something during the night."

"You are my guest, Amanda. *I* will see to you if you need anything."

"But you might not be able to provide everything I need."

"Then you'll just have to do without it," Pamela snapped.

If Pamela thought she had had trouble holding her temper through dinner, the next half hour severely tested her limits. Before Amanda could be settled in her room, she had to be lifted by Slade six different times. It wasn't the flimsiness of Amanda's excuses for these constant requests that irritated Pamela as much as Slade's willing compliance. He argued with her over nearly everything she did, but with Amanda he didn't seem to have a mind of his own. Whatever Amanda wanted, he did immediately and willingly. Even Frederick found it difficult to hold his tongue.

"I'm surprised you keep that man around, Pamela. He doesn't seem like the type to make a good hired hand."

"He's not really a hired hand. He wandered in here looking for a horse and stayed on to help us with the roundup. I told you he was just leaving when you arrived."

"From the look of it, he means to stay a while."

"We'll see about that. I am still the owner of this ranch."

"I didn't mean to upset you. Forget it. I was just curious."

"Don't worry. He won't run off with Amanda."

Frederick looked at her in utter bewilderment then virtually roared with laughter. Pamela didn't know why he found that so funny and decided Frederick was laughing at her.

She didn't like the feeling.

"After all these years, dearest Pamela, you still don't understand Amanda. She only wants two things from a marriage, money and position. Your cowboy is perfectly safe. He could own half of Arizona, but he's not related to the old monied families of New England. Too, I doubt your cowboy would tolerate the kind of flirtations Amanda enjoys so much."

"Why do you?" Pamela demanded. She couldn't decide which man made her angrier, but Frederick would do until she could get her hands on Slade.

"It doesn't mean anything. And we get along tolerably enough."

"But don't you love her?"

"Sure I do, but it's not something I want to make a fuss about. Good God, nothing would appall Amanda more than for me to come reciting poetry and poking flowers under her nose."

"But you've just gotten married. Surely you . . . I mean, you could almost be on your honeymoon." Pamela didn't know quite how to say it.

"That doesn't really come into it. We don't plan to start a family for a few years yet. In the meantime Amanda has her flirtations, and a man has . . . well you know what I mean."

Pamela couldn't imagine being married to Slade and being content with flirtations until time to start a family. She couldn't imagine Slade being willing to wait until the wedding night unless he had to. And though every man in the universe might think it perfectly acceptable to satisfy himself with another female, she'd kill her husband if he ever did that to her.

"If Amanda plans to drag us all over this ranch tomorrow, I'd best get to bed," Frederick said. "I'm not ashamed to admit the last few hundred yards of that trip took a little of the starch out of me."

"I'm sorry. If I had known . . ."

277

"It's not the kind of welcome I expected, but there's no harm done. Don't come down too hard on your boys. Good night."

She wouldn't say a word to the *boys,* but she would break Slade's head if she managed to get him alone. He had made a disgusting spectacle of himself, fawning over Amanda, picking her up at the slightest excuse, not moving away when she left her arms draped around his neck, not becoming sick to his stomach at the drivel she talked.

If he wanted to make a fool of himself, why couldn't he be a fool over her? She didn't have Amanda's family connections, sophistication, or wealth, but she was just as pretty. And she wouldn't sicken him with enough mindless, cloying, revolting prattle to make a normal person throw up.

That man had no loyalty. After all his talk about not leaving her while any danger remained, of pretending he loved her, he was ready to throw her over for the first female who flirted with him. That's just like a gunslinger, she thought to herself. People like that have no proper sense of values. They just use people and get rid of them when they're done.

"There you are," Slade said as he stuck his head into the living room. "I've been waiting for you in the kitchen."

"Have you come to find out what Amanda wants for breakfast so you can take it to her on a tray? Maybe you could offer to bring her a blanket during the night in case she gets cold."

Slade's eyes glittered brightly with a gleam that Pamela didn't trust and his mouth curved into the all-too-familiar smile that always demolished her resistance.

"Don't you start smiling at me, Slade Morgan. You know I can't stay mad at you then." She turned away but Slade turned her back around and forced her to look at him.

"So you *can* be jealous. I wondered. After the way you wanted to throw me out, I couldn't help but try to turn the

278

knife in your direction. I told you there was something between us that wouldn't let us go. I told you I was in love with you. I'm not interested in Amanda." He grinned again. "I have to admit to a few moments of pleasure watching you squirm. After the way you've been lumping me with the riffraff of the West for the last several days, that was balm to my soul."

"I never said you were riffraff."

"Yes, you did. You said I was a drifter, a saddle bum, a penniless loafer, and a whole lot more. That was before I became a presumptuous cowboy who had the bad judgment to fall in love with a woman far above his station."

"Slade, I . . ."

"But that's not why I waited for you. I wanted to tell you I almost left today. I was mad, madder than I've been in a long time, but I was also ashamed of the way I treated you. I would have saddled up and been gone if it hadn't been for your friends."

If he told her he was staying to protect Amanda from unknown assailants, she would hit him.

"But I would have come back. I won't leave until you can swear you don't love me and never will. Probably not until you tell me you love someone else."

Every bit of Pamela's anger evaporated. But then it always did when Slade turned on the charm. Only when he acted like the lord-of-the-manor or told her that her views about Arizona and Baltimore were all cockeyed could she look at him with any degree of objectivity. When he told her that he loved her, she was virtually putty in his hands.

"You didn't have to hover by her side like her personal slave," Pamela said. She hated to sound like a jealous cat, but she wouldn't allow Slade to use the mantel of chivalry as an excuse for fawning attention to Amanda.

But Slade had no thoughts to spare for Amanda. "I told you I wouldn't leave as long as you were in danger. After today, it's even more important that you not be left alone."

"You think they were trying to kill Frederick and Amanda?"

"No. I think they were trying to scare them away, at least make them shorten their visit."

"Slade, what's going to happen?"

She hated it when he talked like this. Not knowing what was going on made her feel helpless. She'd never paid much attention to the politics of open range grazing because she'd always intended to go back to Baltimore, but now her ignorance chafed her. She didn't want to be dependent on Slade to tell her what to do, but she had no other choice.

"I'm frightened," she said.

"You should be. I don't know how or when, but Mongo will make a push to get his cattle on your land."

"Mongo can't be behind this. Somebody almost killed him."

"Maybe, but he still wants your land. I think his men were the ones who came here while we were on roundup. And if it's not Mongo," Slade continued when Pamela started to protest, "then somebody's using his greed to further their own ends. Either way, you're the only thing standing in the way."

Pamela still found it difficult to put any credence in Slade's theories. She simply couldn't imagine people she had known all her life doing such things. There had to be some other explanation for the things that were happening. But she didn't have one.

"Do you think it's a good idea for us to go riding tomorrow?"

"We're safe enough as long as we're all together." He pulled her into his arms. "I mean to see that no harm comes to you."

Then he kissed her.

She stiffened at first. They were right back where they were this morning. Nothing was solved and nothing could work out. She shouldn't give in, but he'd said he'd stay on. And right now she didn't want him to leave, not even a little bit, and she quickly relaxed into his arms.

"You realize you're taking advantage of my momentary weakness," she murmured as his lips teased her ear lobe.

"Yes." He nipped her ears with his teeth.

"I believe you tell me these horrible things just so you won't have to go away."

"This is why I won't go away," Slade said as he gathered her in his embrace.

Pamela didn't quibble. Those marvelous, tingly feelings were flowing throughout her body again. As long as he kissed her now, the future could take care of itself.

It wasn't a greedy kiss nor was it hot and passionate. Rather it was gentle and reassuring. Disappointed at first, Pamela quickly decided it was just as satisfying in its own way as Slade's rough, demanding embraces. There was a promise to it of permanence, of a fire that would burn for years with life-giving warmth rather than exhaust itself with life-consuming heat. It was a new side to Slade, one she hadn't expected, but one she decided she liked very much.

As he walked back to the bunkhouse, Slade's brain bombarded him with questions. He hadn't expected the attack on Pamela's friends. There seemed to be no reason for it unless . . . unless they, whoever *they* were, were determined to isolate Pamela and the Bar Double-B so there would be no witnesses and no questions asked if something happened.

But that gave rise to a second, more frightening conclusion. If they were willing to go to such lengths against Pamela, it meant something had already happened to her father. If any of this made sense at all, then Josh White had to already be dead. And if that were true, anything else done in this continuing war would be aimed at Pamela.

Slade experienced the chill of fear, but a deadly cold anger grew in him also. He would find this villain who wanted the Bar Double-B so badly he seemed prepared to do anything to get it. Twice someone had sneaked into the valley. He had no idea what they intended to do the second time, but the attack on Frederick and Amanda signified, at least in Slade's mind, that they had the ranch under surveillance at all times.

He wondered how he fit into the unknown killer's plan— for he would call the man that now—if the man depended on him leaving or if he had already formulated a plan to get rid of him. Did the killer know of his reputation? He might be allowed to go on to California, but Slade had an idea this fella meant to leave no witnesses. If so, he was marked for death.

Mongo was in this somewhere. Of that much he was certain, but how much had Mongo instigated and how much had been directed by someone else? Slade doubted Mongo would stoop to murder. Besides, he couldn't imagine Mongo arranging his own shooting. If it hadn't been for Pamela, he would have died. No, that had been intended to start a shooting war between the two camps. Mongo's survival hadn't been part of the plan.

Could it also have been an attempt to implicate Slade, have him blamed for the shooting? The marshall's arrival, just after the shooting, seemed too pat to have been chance. No, some very cool, clever man, or woman, was behind this whole thing, calmly pulling the strings that made them all dance. Whether Mongo was in league with them or just a pawn, Slade didn't know, but the man was such a cocky egotist he was almost more dangerous as a pawn. If Mongo had been acting alone, Slade could have anticipated his moves. Acting alone *and* being manipulated by this unseen force made him impossible to predict.

"So Mary told him not to set foot in her house again unless he wanted to be thrown into the goldfish pond."

"What did he say then?" Pamela asked.

"He said he didn't in the least mind going for a swim as

282

long as she went with him."

"And?"

"She did!" Both women whooped with glee. "Her mother had a fainting spell and her father nearly disinherited her, but Mary's Mrs. George Frederick Astor now and ten times richer than her parents will ever be."

Amanda had spent most of breakfast bringing Pamela up to date on the doings of some of their friends. Slade and Frederick had left the table some time ago.

"You should see Dolly Appleton. You wouldn't recognize her now. She gained so much weight she'd make two of herself. And speaking twos, Hattie Evans had twins. The poor girl was prostrate when they both turned out to be females. Her husband practically deserted her. But not so much she's not pregnant again. She has hopes of more success before the end of the summer."

"It's hard to believe little Dolly has children. It seems like only yesterday she was too scared of men to come out of her room unless we pushed her."

"Some women make the adjustment remarkably fast." Amanda's tone indicated that she would be such a one. "Oh, I almost forgot. Do you remember Mrs. Kellibeg?"

"She was the one who drowned off the coast of Maine, wasn't she? Poor Amy's mother."

"So everyone thought. Well, Mr. Kellibeg had no sooner consoled himself with a persuadable widow than she showed up again."

"What! Where had she been?"

"In Italy. With the boys' tutor. He returned a month later."

"Poor woman."

"Not at all. She met this fabulously rich Neapolitan prince who was so captivated by her charm and beauty he asked her to live with him. Amy says their palace is bigger than the Vanderbilt mansion."

"How's Amy taking it?"

"She's decided her health would greatly benefit by a pro-longed stay in Naples. Of course she decided that *after* she met the young count who owns a whole island off the coast."

"If you girls don't stop gossiping, you'll miss the cool of the morning," Frederick said bustling into the dining room. "Slade has your chariot ready, Amanda. I'm instructed to bring you outside at once."

"Do you think you can?" Amanda asked. "Slade can do it easily, but he's so very strong."

"I can do anything Slade can," Frederick insisted.

He conveyed Amanda to the buggy without mishap but without Slade's style. Fortunately for the harmony of the morning Amanda refrained from pointing that out.

Pamela thought their ride would never end. Never had she been so anxious to get off her horse. Never had the valley looked so barren and uninviting. Never had she been forced to defend Arizona and the ranch so frequently. Never had she been so little in sympathy with Amanda and Frederick. After weeks of looking forward to their visit, she could hardly wait for them to be gone. Fortunately, they had a firm date to be in San Francisco or Amanda might never have been able to tear herself away from Slade.

Pamela sometimes found it difficult to remember that Slade loved her and that he was only helping Amanda until she could walk. She found it just as difficult to believe Frederick and Amanda loved each other. They got along amicably enough, except when they were arguing over the things Amanda asked Slade to do, but they had no warmth, no passion in their relationship. Pamela could imagine they were still in school, still merely friends meeting at parties and weekend gatherings at their family homes.

"The first thing I would do would be to get a gardener down here," Amanda was saying as Slade picked her up and carried her toward the house. "There's not a blade of decent

284

grass in sight. And then there are all those unsightly bushes and rocks tumbled everywhere."

"This is the desert, for God's sake," Frederick exclaimed. "You'd have to irrigate the whole damned place."

"Why don't you run along with Slade and let him show you his rifle, or whatever it was you were talking about earlier," Amanda said impatiently. "Pamela and I have things to discuss."

"All right, as long as you don't keep telling her how you'd change everything out of all recognition. I didn't think I would, but I rather like the place as it is."

"Go talk guns," Amanda said. "It's about all you men are good for."

"And another thing," Amanda said even before the men were out of earshot, "I'd damn that stream and make a nice lake. Plant it all around with trees, and in a few years you will have a nice cool place to entertain your guests outdoors in summertime. At least you're not plagued with mosquitoes."

"Neither are we plagued with guests," said Pamela. "You're the first people to visit since mother died."

"Good God," Amanda exclaimed. "I had no idea."

"It's not that bad," Pamela protested, horrified to see that Amanda actually pitied her for being forced to live so far away from civilization. "The other ranchers visit."

"How many are there?"

"Five."

"How far away do they live?"

"Five to ten miles."

"Do you mean to tell me there are only five families out here and that the nearest one lives five miles away?" Amanda turned so quickly she almost twisted her ankle again. Pamela helped her to a chair on the porch. "This is incredible. How do you ever get to parties?"

"We don't have any parties to go to."

"You poor child. You must come back before you forget what it's like to live in civilization."

"There are lots of people around. There's my cousin and all the cowhands. And of course Dave and his wife."

"But they *work* for you," Amanda replied.

Like working for someone else was a malady for which there was no cure Pamela thought to herself.

"There is a great deal to do," Pamela said. "I'm rarely even aware of the lack of social activities."

Yet just a few weeks ago you were pining for Baltimore and the meanest entertainment. Why can't you admit things have changed because of Slade? Until now you have felt exactly the way Amanda does about Arizona and the ranch.

"That's not what your letters said," Amanda reminded her. "It seems to me at least once in every one of them you said you were hoping to be able to return to Baltimore soon."

"It did seem strange when I first came home and was very lonely," Pamela admitted, "but it grows on you."

"Not on me," Amanda said with a shudder. "The West is fine to visit. We have seen some spectacular scenery, but it's full of the oddest people. Your Mr. Morgan is about the first acceptable one I've met."

"Slade?" Pamela said in surprise before she could think better of it. "He's a drifter and a gunslinger."

"That doesn't seem to matter to you."

Pamela wasn't fool enough to try to deny the obvious, but she wished she could have managed not to blush. That made her look like she felt guilty. She *did,* but she didn't want Amanda to know that.

"I can see why he's turned your head," Amanda said. "I saw that the minute I set eyes on him. I don't know about this gun business, but he's the kind of man that sets a woman's teeth to chattering. He's big, strong, incredibly handsome, and looks like he can handle any situation. He's perfect for a flirtation, but you don't want to make the mistake of marrying him."

"But if he's so wonderful, why not?"

"Good Lord, Pamela, I thought you had some sense.

Compare him with Frederick and tell me you can't see an important difference."

Pamela did, but she didn't want to tell Amanda what she saw. The difference might surprise Amanda.

"Frederick has money and position. Some day he'll have power as well. He can move in any level of society in this country, financial and political. And I'll go with him wherever he goes." As though on cue, they both looked to where the two men stood talking. "I admit Slade's dreadfully handsome. Oh, my yes. Even more so than Frederick, which I never thought possible, but his looks won't last any more than Frederick's will. In a few years his stomach will start to protrude, his shoulders will start to stoop, and he'll start to drive a wagon instead of ride his horse. Then what will you have?"

Pamela was tempted to tell Amanda she would exchange all the money and privilege in the world for a few years in Slade's arms.

"No matter what happens to Frederick, I'll still be Mrs. Frederick Marchbanks Olmstead, III with the money and connections to go anywhere I like and do anything I like. With your cowboy, you'd be tied to this ranch, raising a whole flock of kids."

The notion of bearing Slade's children hadn't occurred to Pamela. Oddly enough, she realized she had never seriously thought about having children at all. She didn't know why. It just hadn't come up. Did that mean she didn't want children, that she wouldn't be a good mother? Pamela jerked her mind away from such thoughts. She didn't even know if she loved Slade that way, and he hadn't asked her to marry him. Under the circumstances, thinking about children was a bit premature.

Chapter 17

"Do you love Frederick?"

"Of course I do," Amanda responded, surprised by Pamela's question. "Why do you ask?"

"Well, I've never been in love myself. You don't have to look at me in that cat-and-mouse way. I'm not in love with Slade, though I admit I am terribly fascinated by him."

"Fascinated? So that's what you call it," Amanda said with an indulgent laugh. "I would have called it . . ."

"Never mind," Pamela interrupted quickly. "I just thought if you loved someone, you wouldn't be interested in even looking at another man."

"You mean you're jealous of my interest in Slade?"

"Stop trying to turn my words against me," Pamela said irritably. "You're not even listening to what I'm saying."

"I'm sorry," Amanda apologized. "Start again, and I promise not to interrupt."

"I feel like such a fool asking somebody else to tell me how I feel," Pamela said, quickly forgetting her irritation at Amanda in her desire to get at the thing which had been bothering her ever since she first saw Slade Morgan. "I thought I knew all the answers . . ."

"And Slade appeared on the scene and knocked everything cock-a-hoop?"

"I never let myself fall in love with Frederick," Pamela proceeded without acknowledging Amanda's remark. "I knew he would never marry me, so it wasn't too difficult to keep my feelings under control. I did like two other men quite a lot, but I never felt like this. Not even with Frederick."

"What is it like?" Amanda asked. This time there was nothing cynical or mocking in her voice or expression.

"I hardly know how to describe it. Half the time I don't even know what's going on."

"It sounds rather uncomfortable."

"It's awful," Pamela confided, relieved to at last be able to share her doubts. "Not only am I suddenly entirely brainless and doing the most absurd things, I don't have any strength of character. You know I've got pretty definite ideas about things."

Amanda laughed heartily. "Don't I. We used to call you our conscience at school. We could always depend upon you to behave sensibly and advise us to do the same, just like our mothers. Oh, don't look so dismayed," Amanda said when Pamela looked crestfallen. "We loved you for it. You were so *intense.*"

"Well every word I ever said must be coming back to haunt me. I've turned into the most spineless creature you can imagine. Slade has got me questioning just about every idea I have, all my plans for the future, everything I ever thought about the kind of man I would marry, even my feelings about Arizona."

"You're not thinking of staying here!" Amanda exclaimed, shocked out of her attitude of sympathetic complacency. "You would dry-rot in less than a year."

"It's been three years, and I'm still sufficiently pliant to have two men fighting over me."

"Do I detect a note of pride in that boast?"

"Probably. I've been guilty of just about every other form of vanity since he's been here."

"You haven't given yourself to him, have you?" Amanda demanded, sitting bolt upright in her seat.

"Of course not," Pamela replied indignantly. "I said I was confused. I didn't say I had abandoned my wits altogether." Pamela stopped, conscience-stricken. She couldn't tell Amanda about those terrifying moments before they arrived. She couldn't share that with anyone, but she felt compelled to defend Slade's honor. "He wouldn't do that, even though I feel certain he would like to."

"Don't let him fool you with any gentlemanly-code-of-honor nonsense," Amanda said stringently. "That's all any man thinks about."

"Possibly, but Slade wouldn't take advantage of me like that."

Amanda started to make a sharp reply, but the rapt look in her friend's face stopped her.

"He's the most amazing man. He came in here looking like a worthless saddle bum, but he gave me a thumbnail evaluation of Jane Austen's books. He says he has an aversion to women, especially beautiful women, but every time I turn around he's doing something else for me. Can you imagine anyone with that face not having to fight women off? Yet he believes ladies don't like his type."

"I have to admit it was his looks that first attracted my attention," Amanda said with a gurgling laugh.

A slow smile of happiness began to spread over Pamela's face. "You ought to see him when he's hurt. That man would rather die than admit to feeling any pain. He insists he doesn't need anyone to take care of him, but I think he likes it when I do."

"Of course he likes it," Amanda said. "And if you give him half a chance, you'll have him on your hands for the rest of your life."

"He was leaving for California when you arrived. If somebody hadn't started shooting at you, he would have been gone before you arrived."

Amanda looked like she wasn't sure she believed that, but she let it pass with only an "if you say so" smile.

"He wouldn't let me pay him for working the roundup. He even paid for a horse nobody else can ride. The men took to him immediately, and there's not a rancher in the area who doesn't listen when he talks."

"Then you should marry this paragon as soon as you can get him to the altar," Amanda said getting to her feet. "Surely you're rich enough for both of you."

"He's wanted for murder in Texas. He killed three men."

Amanda sat back down with a plop. "Merciful God, and I've had him carrying me around for days. You even let him sleep in the room next to mine."

"He'd never hurt you."

"How do you know? He might kill us for Frederick's money. He could kidnap me for ransom."

Pamela couldn't help but laugh at her friend's lack of understanding of the West. "He wouldn't take Frederick's money if it were lying on the ground in front of him. And as for kidnapping, he'd defend us with his last drop of blood."

"Pamela, are you trying to tell me that this man has killed three people in Texas for some reason we don't know . . ."

"The marshall said he thought money was involved."

". . . but he would give his life to defend us, even return Frederick's money if he found it?"

Pamela nodded.

"Either you're crazy or I am," Amanda stated flatly. "I never heard anything more preposterous in my life. He sounds as quixotic as Robin Hood."

"More so," Pamela said, pleased with the imagery. "There are times when I'm afraid of him, or at least of what he'll do. He actually faced down the ranchers and their crews, *all at the same time,* with nobody but me anywhere near him. I was sure he'd get himself killed."

"What did those other people do?"

Pamela shrugged. "Nothing. Not after he shot the center

out of six coins and then showed them that our crew had them surrounded the whole time."

"Well, if you decide to stay out here, he sounds exactly like the kind of husband you'd need. But what would he be worth without his horse and guns and desert?"

"If you could just hear him talking about moonlight, you wouldn't have to ask."

"The man's clearly turned your head," Amanda said rather in the manner of a maiden aunt about to give a lecture to an erring niece. "But you can't let this fascination, as you call it, make you forget what you really want out of life."

"What's that?"

If Amanda had been more perceptive, she might have answered more carefully.

"What any sensible woman wants, a husband who can give her a comfortable life and a respectable position in this world. It's true we're called upon to provide them with children and put up with their attentions, but that doesn't last long."

"Do you think it's possible for a wife to enjoy her husband's attentions?"

"I don't know. Some of the women I know secretly profess to, but they're rather stupid, flighty creatures. I would hate to be thought similar to them in any way."

"But you and Frederick?"

For the first time, Amanda looked a little uncomfortable. "Frederick and I don't want a family yet."

"But what do you do at night?" Pamela was embarrassed to ask, but she had to know. "I mean, how do you lie in bed next to each other and do nothing?" She remembered the feeling that had overwhelmed her when Slade's burning skin touched her body, and she knew she couldn't sleep next to him night after night and not collapse into his arms. Even now, the memory of what she felt when he touched her intimately caused her to blush. Fortunately, Amanda thought she blushed because of the question she just asked.

"Frederick and I occupy separate bedrooms."

"I understand about now—it's because of your ankle— but what about when you're home?"

"We always shall."

"You don't want to be near him, in a physical way, I mean?" Pamela wanted to tell Amanda how she felt when Slade kissed her, about the ecstasy she experienced when he did more than that, but she feared her friend would categorize her as one of the stupid, flighty females who liked the same sort of vulgar pleasures men enjoy.

"No," Amanda said after a momentary pause. "I have thought about it—I think every woman does sooner or later—but I know what I want out of life. And from my experience, a woman who succumbs to the temptations of the flesh rarely achieves her ambitions. She certainly runs the risk of losing the respect and admiration of other women, as well as possibly her husband."

"But isn't it possible to love a man, physically I mean, and still be respectable?"

"I don't think so. I never knew anybody who did. It has such a coarsening effect on one's sensibilities. When it happens to be a man like Slade Morgan, I should imagine it would be an impossible task, even for the most remarkable female."

Pamela was unprepared for the rush of anger that washed over her. She had to bite her tongue to keep from making a reply which might have destroyed their friendship. What did Amanda know about Slade's code of honor, a set of principles far more rigid and inviolate than any social order in Boston or Philadelphia? How could she understand a man who would sacrifice what he wanted, deny his desires, endanger his life—and all for a woman who kept him at arm's length—when she was afraid to allow her husband even temporary ascendancy over her body? How could she know what it was like to be held safe in Slade's arms when she didn't want to share a bed with her own husband?

"You've misjudged Slade," Pamela said as unemotionally as she could. "He may look like a saddle bum, but I've never met anyone with better understanding or with more rigid principles." She remembered those night watches during the roundup and laughed. "Or who's been in church so often and knows so many hymns. He'd be more likely to reform my way of life than the other way around."

Amanda scowled at her friend impatiently. "If you don't get that man on his way to California soon, you'll be lost."

"What do you mean?"

"You could have married any of the men you met in Baltimore and grown quite fond of them in a few years. You would have had a quiet, comfortable life, probably taken pride in your children and been a prop to your husband, but you would have always been in control of your life."

"But if Slade stays?"

"You're practically in love with him, if you aren't already. I have the feeling that if you ever do fall in love with him, you'll never be able to bring yourself to marry another man, even if Slade should leave you."

"Is falling in love so bad?"

"I never intend to find out," Amanda stated. "Outside of the mortifying loss of command over yourself and your life, I imagine it would lead to a most unpleasant existence."

"But how, if you truly love the man . . ."

"There would undoubtedly be moments of great joy. And many women would envy you your happiness, would say they would give anything to be able to have a love like yours. But they wouldn't mean it. Your kind of love will also bring you great pain. I, for one, couldn't endure it."

"But Frederick?"

"I'm very fond of him, I expect I always shall be, but he'll never break my heart. I don't want anybody to have that much power over me. Why should I? What's it worth?"

"I think . . ."

"Don't tell me," Amanda said, putting a restraining finger

to Pamela's lips. "The day will come when you'll hate me for having heard the words. You've met a terribly handsome and exciting cowboy who looks like the man of your dreams. You're living a fantasy nearly every woman hopes for at least once in her lifetime. Enjoy it to the fullest. So few of us ever get the chance you've been given. I'm really a little bit jealous. But sooner or later you'll remember the not-so-insignificant matter of those three men he killed, and you'll realize you really have nothing in common with him. When that happens, come to me in Baltimore."

Amanda stood up and gave her friend a kiss. "Now I'd better see about my packing. I've enjoyed my visit even more than I expected, but we have to leave tomorrow if we're to be in San Francisco on time. I didn't bring my maid and I doubt your very pregnant cook could manage at all. It'll probably take me the better part of the evening."

"I'll help you."

"I wouldn't dream of it."

Pamela knew Amanda would give in if she insisted, but she wanted to be alone. She needed time to get over the shock of finding out that, after nearly ten years of considering Amanda her very best friend, they had virtually no thoughts in common. How could she have missed seeing what Frederick and Slade had already seen? And if she were so consistently wrong in her judgments of people, especially Amanda, how could she feel so sure she knew Slade?

But even that was unimportant compared to the realization that she loved Slade as she never thought she could love anyone. She wanted to be his wife, bear his children, take care of his wounds, lie in his arms at night, sit with him in the moonlight, ride by his side, face the world knowing he would always be with her.

She wanted it all, everything!

And she had no excuses to make, no beliefs to readjust, no feelings of shock or surprise to overcome. That had already been done. When she thought she was fighting Slade, she

295

was really fighting herself, convincing herself, demolishing the last of her resistance. Now there was no more reluctance, no more questioning. She knew she was doing the right thing, the only thing she could do.

Loving Slade was the most natural thing in the world. She only hoped he felt the same way about her.

Flashes of lightning, coming as rapidly as shots from a gun, turned the hallway as bright as day and rendered needless the candle in her hand. But as Pamela walked the distance from her room to Slade's, she was completely unaware of the deafening cracks of thunder that crashed back and forth between the mountain ridges or the drum of the rain as it pounded on the roof. The rain had been coming down in torrents for hours. There would be flash floods in the mountain canyons, but she didn't have a thought to spare for Amanda and Frederick who had left early that morning or for her men out on the range.

She must go to Slade. Nothing else mattered.

She raised her hand to knock on his door, but drew back before her knuckles could strike wood. Her knees shook badly. She desperately wanted to return to her room, but she didn't. She had been waiting for this moment for a day and a half. She knew if her nerve failed now, she would never be able to summon the courage again.

Even before she finished talking with Amanda, she knew she loved Slade. Her feelings didn't conform to anything she had expected to feel, and they obviously didn't follow the lines of Amanda's tepid affection for Frederick, but Pamela recognized them for what they were, total capitulation. She belonged to Slade, and she couldn't do anything about it.

It had been terribly difficult to ride next to him all morning, to sit across from him at dinner, to kiss him good night and not beg him to make love to her right then. But she knew he wouldn't. He had already refused her once when she begged him to quench the fires raging within her. She had to go to him during the night, when his resistance was at low ebb, when dreams had had time to stoke the flame of desire.

The door opened on silent hinges, and Pamela slipped into the room.

Slade came awake with a convulsive start that caused Pamela to clutch her throat in alarm. "What the hell are you doing here?" he demanded, shock and relief combining to deprive him of all ability to speak politely.

Looking at him now as he sat up in bed, confused and slightly alarmed, she forgot for a moment why she had come. Even now he looked impossibly handsome. His thick, dark blond hair was barely mussed, and sleep had softened the harshness of his expression. His bare torso caused Pamela's tongue to cleave to the roof of her mouth. She could follow the line of curly hair as it arrowed down his chest and disappeared under the sheet that barely left him decent. Slade was clearly naked in bed, and the realization caused a rod of white-heat to course through her body at break-neck speed.

"I wanted to talk to you."

"Now?" Slade exclaimed, incredulous. He, too, seemed to suddenly become aware of his nakedness, and he pulled the sheet higher over him. "Can't it wait until morning?"

"No."

"But I'm not dressed."

"I know."

Slade doubted the thin sheet was sufficient to conceal the state of his loins, but he had nothing else. He had left the blankets in the chest. Then, quite abruptly, the sight of Pamela's nipples, firm and erect, pushing against the fabric of her gown, told him that she was equally nude under her gown. "You aren't dressed either."

"It doesn't matter."

"Hell, woman, I'm not a eunuch. You can't just walk into a

man's bedroom in the middle of the night, looking like something out of his favorite fantasy, and expect to discuss Jane Austen."

"I don't want to discuss Jane Austen. I want to talk about us."

"That's even worse," Slade groaned. "Her heroines must have had their babies by immaculate conception. I don't think I could manage that."

"Stop joking, Slade. I'm serious."

"So am I. I'm just doing my best to keep from exploding. If you have any compassion for me, wrap yourself in one of those blankets."

"Does the sight of me bother you so much?"

"God, the woman *likes* to torture me," Slade moaned. "Yes, it's driving me crazy. Much more and I'm bound to do something desperate."

"Then you'd better put something over you too," Pamela said tossing a blanket in his direction. "The sight of your bare chest is causing me to feel quite warm."

Slade looked at her in startled surprise. Then a smile spread across his face until he was grinning broadly. "With both of us feeling too hot and bothered to act rationally, don't you think it'd be a good idea to hold off until tomorrow?"

"I know exactly what I think and what I mean to say," Pamela said as she draped a blanket around her shoulders. "That's part of what has got me so flustered."

"Still, I don't think . . ."

"Listen to me, Slade Morgan, and don't interrupt," Pamela ordered, a trifle desperately Slade thought. "I don't know if I'll manage to get started again if you stop me."

A particularly loud roll of thunder drowned out her words, but Slade said no more.

"I'd like to apologize for all the things I thought when you came here. Don't interrupt," Pamela said when Slade started to speak. "This is harder for me than it is for you. You were right, I was a snob, but I didn't know it. I wanted something different, better I thought, than life here in Arizona, and I rejected the people as well as the country. I have you to thank for showing me that there can be great beauty, even in Arizona."

"And the people?"

"People are the same everywhere. They aren't changed by the clothes they wear, the houses they live in, or the schools they go to. They might even act a little better for having a lot less."

"What makes you say that?"

"Amanda couldn't understand that a drifting cowboy, especially one without a penny to his name, would neither steal their money nor kidnap her for ransom."

"What have you been telling that woman?" demanded Slade. He reacted so abruptly his covers started to slide off. He recovered himself quickly.

"Actually I was asking her a question. She answered it, but not in the way either of us expected."

"What did you ask her?"

Pamela came a step closer to the bed. "How I would know when I fell in love."

"I see. And what did she answer?"

"She couldn't. She didn't know herself."

"But you know?"

"I knew the minute I saw Frederick. But you confused me with your ridiculous act of fawning compliance to Amanda's every wish. Why was it so important to make me feel jealous? No, don't answer that. I don't want to get sidetracked."

She came a step closer, and Slade felt the tension inside him build to an almost unbearable pressure. He drew one leg up to disguise the rapidly forming tent between his legs. Hard, he was, hard as steel. He didn't know how much longer he could keep his hands off her. The ferocity of the storm inside his body was about to destroy his reason and his control.

"I love you, Slade. I think I have from the moment I saw you enter the valley. Oh, I've fought hard against it, partly because of your arrogance, partly because I thought you represented everything I was running away from, and I guess some because I thought I was better than you. There were other stupid reasons, but I don't remember them anymore. I'm not even sure I care to. All I know is I love you, and I want you to make love to me."

A boulder-rattling clap of thunder caused the earth to move under them, but Slade had no question as to what Pamela had said. The words would probably remain engraved on his heart until he died.

"You don't know what you're saying." It hurt to say that, but he forced himself to remain in his bed. He couldn't honorably do anything else. If he took advantage of Pamela's weakness now, he would never forgive himself. She might come to hate him for it, and no evening of pleasure was worth a lifetime of remorse.

"I know very well. I've thought about it, and I don't expect you to marry me. I know I could never live in a cabin in the woods. I would want to, you don't know how much I'd want to, but I can't. I would grow to hate it and hate you for keeping me there." Close to the bed now, she put her fingers on Slade's lips to keep him from speaking. "But I can't let you leave without showing you how much I love you. Amanda said she thought I was the kind of woman to love only one man. I think so, too. I don't know if I can stand for you to leave, not if I don't have at least one night in your arms to remember."

Slade doubted hot tongs couldn't torture him any more than Pamela's words. His grip on the bedclothes was like iron. He knew if he dropped them so much as one inch, he would fling them off altogether. Didn't Pamela have any idea what she asked of him? To resist a direct request to make love to a beautiful woman, especially a beautiful woman he loved and who loved him in return, was agony much worse than blister-covered feet or a bullet in his shoulder.

"Slade, don't you want to make love to me?"

Slade took a grip on the side of the bed that would have dented a corral post. Desire shook him even more violently than the thunder outside shook the heavens. Making love to Pamela was the only thought in his head; it was the reason his body was rigid and inflamed.

"I've been thinking about making love to you for days," Slade confessed, "but I just can't love you tonight and ride off tomorrow and never see you again. Suppose you had a baby?"

Pamela couldn't suppress a feeling of disappointment. It would have been so much nicer if he had thought of her first, but she supposed men were always thinking about someone to carry on their name.

"If I loved you enough to make love to you tonight, and I do," Slade continued, "don't you think I would love you enough to want to stay and keep on making love to you?"

Pamela's heart was full once more. "I know you're not the kind of man to settle down, raise a family, and go to community picnics. I won't try to hold you. I only want to love you while I can."

"What would your father say?" asked Slade. "I can't imagine he would be pleased to come home and find his daughter sleeping with a vagabond cowboy."

A convulsive sob shook Pamela. "Dad's dead," she said before giving vent to a wail of deep anguish. "I know somebody has killed him."

Slade was out of the bed and enfolding her in his arms almost before Pamela could finish speaking. Somehow he managed to keep his grip on the bed clothes between them. As yet he was unaware of the draft on his backside.

"There could be lots of reasons why he hasn't returned yet," Slade said. He had hoped Pamela wouldn't come to the conclusion he had reached nearly a week ago.

"Why wouldn't he write?" she sobbed.

Slade didn't know what to say, so he held her more closely. Pamela held tightly to him, letting the fear and worry pour out of her. "Now you'll go away and leave me, too. I'll never see you again. I can't stand it."

Slade tried to soothe her. "You'll have Amanda and Frederick."

"That would have been enough before you got here," Pamela sobbed, "but you ruined them for me. You ruined everything for me except you, and you're going away."

Slade thought of the Texas sheriff headed this way determined to collect the price on his head. Pamela hadn't told him what Marshall Alcott said, but Gaddy had. How could he stay much longer when every day meant possible capture and return to Texas and certain death?

But he thought of the distraught woman in his arms and asked himself how he could leave. Surrounded by danger, her father probably dead, and the worst crisis yet to come. How could there be any question?

But more important, she was the woman he loved, the woman who loved him. From the moment he saw Pamela, from the moment he knew he loved her, hope had been growing inside him that he would find a way for them to be together. Even though everything around them seemed to be conspiring to destroy their happiness, he couldn't give up hope, not as long as he could be near her.

"I won't leave you," he murmured, dropping his head so his lips could kiss her ear, his breath tickle her hair. But unwilling to give her hope where he still couldn't see the way, he added, "Not until this is over. I make no promises after that."

"I don't ask for any," Pamela said as she pulled his head down for a hungry kiss. "All I want is for you to stay with me now, to make love to me while we are together."

"Pamela, I don't think . . ."

"Don't think. *Please,* don't think of anybody except me or

302

anytime except now."

Slade could resist no longer. He couldn't even think of the reasons why he should. All he knew was that Pamela was in his arms, and she wanted to make love to him as much as he wanted to make love to her.

She would have her night to remember. And so would he.

Slade's mouth captured hers in a hungry kiss, a kiss no longer constrained by limits. His tongue teased her lips until they slowly opened allowing him to gently slide his hot tongue into her moist heat. He wrapped his arms around her, his hands at the small of her back, pressing her to him, lifting her to meet his embrace. Pamela clung to him, her arms around his neck, her fingers buried in the soft hair at the nape of his neck, her sensitive breasts crushed against his hard chest. She felt this strange need to be as close to him as possible, to be absorbed by him.

Pamela encircled him with her arms, her soft fingertips brushing the rippling, corded muscles of his back. Hurriedly, roughly, Slade slipped the gown from her shoulders and exposed the soft skin of her neck. He loved the feel of her skin beneath his lips, his fingertips. It reminded him so much of the moonlight, pale white and utterly innocent. He traced circles with his fingertips—Pamela quivered when it tickled—and some knot inside him slowly unraveled. The kisses he placed on her shoulders were gently insistent, no longer harsh and demanding; the fierce need inside stopped driving him forward, as though for the first time in his life Slade knew he had the luxury of time.

"I dreamed of this from the first moment I saw you," Slade said as his hands moved restlessly across her back, unable to believe the feel of her, unable to believe that she was in his arms at all.

Pamela chuckled. "I know. Amanda said you men all want the same thing. But she didn't seem to understand that some women can want it just as much."

Slade looked deep into her eyes. There had to be no

303

question this was right. Being given a glimpse of a paradise he might never enter was hard enough. To know he had irreparably injured one of its most precious flowers would be more than his life was worth.

But there was no doubt in Pamela's eyes. Her gaze held his, steady and sure. A slow smile of happiness spread over her face. "I used to envy Amanda and Frederick. I don't any more." Once more Pamela's arms closed around him, pulling him close, and Slade willingly acquiesced. For many days and nights he had dreamed of the kisses he would lavish on her if he only could, of the hours he would spend cradling her in his embrace, of the utter bliss it would give his soul to be able to claim this woman as his own.

Oh God, why couldn't it go on forever?

He was afraid the few days and nights they would be allowed would cause more pain than total denial. He was afraid that after a small sip of the nectar of her love, he would be unable to turn his back on her. He was afraid his past would destroy the only woman he had ever really loved.

But now he was beyond his ability to stop. He loved Pamela body and soul, and for tonight at least he would think of nothing else.

The bed sheet remained between them, forgotten and unnoticed, still covering and separating their straining bodies. But when Slade's attention turned to Pamela's breasts, when his lips and teeth teased her nipples into swollen peaks of passion, it slipped to the floor. Slade's unrestrained manhood, stiff and impudent, its assault against Pamela's body already difficult to ignore, made it impossible to disguise the need which raged throughout both of them. With a grunt of animal need, Slade picked her up and carried her to the bed.

As he did her nightgown slipped from her body.

Pamela curled up next to Slade, content for the moment to let him shower kisses over her mouth, ears, neck, and shoulders, content to feel the nearness of his body, content to luxuriate in the comfort of his presence. Ever since he had torn down the barriers that afternoon Amanda and Frederick arrived, she had thought constantly about this moment, had dreamed of the culmination of the hard, physical hunger he had planted within her.

But now, even though his lips and hands were warming her body to a heat which would soon make it impossible for her to keep still, she derived her greatest pleasure from just being in his embrace. It seemed perfectly normal for her to be naked in his arms. She allowed her fingers to roam across his body, from the soft blond fur on his chest to the tense, corded muscles of his abdomen, to the still-red scar on his shoulder. Something inside her sang out *he's mine* and she felt a titillating thrill that it should be so. She allowed her hand to slide down over his side, across his hip, to caress his buttock and was ecstatic with the feeling. Not even the dimensions of his stiff, pulsating manhood, emerging from a tangle of hair only inches from her finger tips, or the knowledge that it must somehow enter her body, had the power to dent her euphoria.

This man is mine, her heart sang out. For as long as we live, no matter what happens, *he's mine.*

As though he was reading her mind, Slade warned, "If you touch me, I'll explode."

Her hand rested for a moment on his hip. "I want to touch all of you. I want to know everything there is to know about you."

"Then start by knowing that a man doesn't react the same as a woman. What may only cause you to quiver with pleasure can send me over the edge."

"You mean I can touch you everywhere except . . ." She stopped because she didn't know exactly what word to use.

"You can touch me anywhere," Slade told her. "Only not just yet."

"I don't understand."

"You will," he assured her as his hand made a rapid

journey over her ribs, feathered against the top of her hip, and dipped into the sensitive crescent between her thighs.

Pamela breathed quickly, the soft, whooshing intake of air betraying her shock at his rapid descent to the most sensitive part of her being.

"A man is more sensitive outside than a woman," he said, as his fingers gently rubbed against her. "You have something to guard you."

Pamela wasn't sure just how sensitive Slade was, but her body was suddenly unable to remain either calm or still. Every part of her felt as if it were alive and of a different mind from its neighbor.

Then he delved into her inner core and she thought she would self-destruct.

"Is this what you meant?" she asked, barely able to voice the words.

"Not yet," Slade replied, his own voice harsh and breathy. Pamela didn't know how the sensations attacking her could be any more sharp, any more breath-taking until Slade began to tenderly massage her nub of pleasure with the rough tip of his finger. Gasping for breath, her fingers dug into his arm as her whole body tensed and bucked against the waves of strength-draining pleasure that rocketed through her. The whole length of her body shivered with strength-sapping tension. She tried to relax, but Slade continued to torture her until she groaned in agony.

"Now?" she gasped, surprised she could still talk.

"Now," he replied, "but if you grip me like you're gripping my arm, you'll hear a scream of pain."

Only by concentrating very hard was Pamela able to keep her fingers from closing convulsively around the hard, hot object which throbbed under her palm. Slowly, tentatively, she allowed her hand to brush its velvet length and was rewarded with a growl of pure agony from Slade.

"I can't wait much longer," she said, as a shudder of

pleasure made her teeth chatter worse than an arctic blast.

"I may hurt you a little at first," Slade warned, barely able to articulate the syllables. Pamela's fingers had closed about him in gentle pressure and it was all he could do to retain his self-control.

"I don't care," Pamela answered as her body twisted beneath his touch. "You are driving me crazy."

"Relax and open yourself to me," Slade said.

Pamela was sure it was impossible for her to do either thing. Her body was rigid, beyond her control. But at Slade's gentle urging, she was finally able to open her body so he could enter. But even as he moved above her, his hand continued to torture her, continued to cause her body to writhe in sweet, seductive agony.

She felt a new pressure against her, nudging, pressing, stretching her uncomfortably, but all her concentration was on the finger which continued to inflame her senses.

Then suddenly it was gone. Her body collapsed in disappointment.

"I'm sorry," Slade said, and before she could ask why, he thrust into her.

A sharp pain caused her to cry out, but almost immediately she felt the same maddening sensation start all over again, only now it was being induced by the velvety-soft skin of Slade's thick, probing manhood.

"I won't hurt you anymore," he promised and sank his full length into her body.

Pamela was too overcome to answer. Waves of indescribable pleasure gripped her body from head to toe as she welcomed Slade's invasion of her body. She clung to him, hoping to drive him deeper, hoping he would reach the hunger that tortured her, hoping he could release the tension that gripped her like a vise.

As the waves of pleasure continued to wash over her with increasing force, her thoughts became more nebulous. Instinctively she moved with Slade, adjusted her rhythm to fit his, beame part of him until she felt she no longer existed separately.

Slade's body tensed, his rhythm became uneven, and his breath started to come in soft grunts. Pamela felt the muscles in her own body bunch and gather to welcome the last of his thrusts, to ride down the cresting wave with him. She felt herself being lifted higher and higher until, with breath-taking suddenness, securely held the entire way in Slade's warm, gentle arm, she catapulted down the other side into welcome oblivion.

Chapter 18

"Nobody's seen any sign of him," Gaddy said. "As far as they know, he's not been to Santa Fe this year."

They were in the kitchen. Slade sat at the table, Belva stood at the stove, and Pamela moved back and forth in between. She had stopped when Gaddy entered, certain of his news before he uttered the words. Now she groped for a chair and sank down.

It hurt Slade to see the bleak look on her face, the pain in her eyes.

"Did you talk to the marshall?" Slade asked.

"I talked to just about everybody in town," Gaddy replied. "I told them I had some important news he had to get in a hurry. Of course I also told them I didn't know for sure he had come to Santa Fe, just that somebody said they'd heard him mention going that way."

"He could have decided to stop somewhere this side of Santa Fe and order his wire," Slade said, turning to Pamela. "Anybody buying that much in one place is bound to start people asking questions he might not want to answer."

"Something has happened to him," Pamela said. Her face was haggard, her features forced into an expressionless mask. "He didn't go to Santa Fe because he couldn't."

"He could have gone somewhere else," Slade suggested.

"Where?" she asked, eager for the chance to hope once again.

"I don't know, but Santa Fe's not the only town that sells barbed wire or has gunmen hanging around. There're plenty here in Arizona. Probably more than Santa Fe."

"You think he went to Tucson?"

"That or maybe Tombstone. Maybe even Casa Grande. He could even have stopped at one of those new farming communities on the Gila River. They're bound to have lots of barbed wire."

"But no gunmen."

"Maybe not, but I bet they've got plenty of sons who'd rather spend their day on horseback than behind a plow."

"You really think Daddy's all right?" She wanted him to say her father was fine. She didn't know if she would believe him, but she wanted to hear it.

"I don't know, but your father must be a tough man to have taken this land from the Indians and held on to it for so many years. Such a man's not easy to kill. There's always a chance he went somewhere else. The mail isn't half so dependable here as it is back East. He could have sent you a letter weeks ago and it not be here yet."

"Nobody saw him along the way either," Gaddy told Slade later as they walked to the corral. "I stopped and asked several times. It's just like he disappeared."

Or somebody killed him before he got very far from his own land Slade thought to himself. He couldn't put his finger on it, but something about this whole arrangement didn't ring true. He agreed with Pamela that Mongo wouldn't have any reason to hurt her father. But if Mongo hadn't done it, who had?

"I've got something I want you to do," Slade said turning to Gaddy. "It might be dangerous, so think before you agree."

"What is it?" Slade could tell that Gaddy was excited about being able to do something important, but he could

310

also see the beginnings of caution, and that pleased him. He had handled the trip to Santa Fe well. He was growing up, maturing. It was time to give him something more difficult.

"I want you to visit every man riding the range," Slade said. "Talk to them, find out what's going on, what they've noticed. Ask them what they think. You can't tell them you're asking for me. Dave's foreman again, and they'll wonder what business I have nosing about. Just get them talking and then ask a few questions to steer the conversation in the right direction."

"That won't be any problem," Gaddy said with a sheepish grin. "They all think I'm pretty useless. They'll say just about anything in front of me."

"Play the fool all you like, but be careful," Slade cautioned. "If there is somebody else behind all this, he's ruthless. He's also very smart."

"You think he killed Uncle Josh?"

"Somebody must have at least tried. A man like him doesn't disappear without a trace."

"Well I don't understand it," Gaddy said. "Uncle Josh has ridden all over this territory for years. He knows every trick. He wouldn't be caught by a bushwacker."

"I don't think he was. The danger came from somebody he knew."

Gaddy stared, unbelieving.

"Somebody he knew very well."

"But who could it have been? You got any ideas?"

"No. One disadvantage to being a stranger is you don't know the people."

"I woulda said there was nobody to know."

"That could have been your uncle's mistake, too."

Slade lay contentedly, Pamela resting in the circle of his arms. He enjoyed the satin feel of her skin under his hand. They had shared a bed for only three nights, but already she

311

had become an integral part of him. He couldn't stand the thought of leaving.

Odd, for the last ten years he had thought that getting someone to love him would be the hard part. After what Trish and his mother had said, he'd assumed it was impossible. Now, at the worst possible time, when he was running for his life, it had happened without him doing a thing. And now his past threatened to destroy his happiness.

He was fooling himself to think the Briarcliffs wouldn't follow him. If they wired a description as far away as Maravillas, they meant to come. Maybe not yet, but soon. Sheriff Andy Briarcliff would never let up. He had always disliked Slade. Slade's having killed his three nephews insured he would hunt him as long as he lived. And he wouldn't care whether he took Slade back in a saddle or across it. He was a man who liked his reputation with a gun, and he used his position as sheriff to enhance it.

And what could Slade do? Kill him? That would bring the whole force of Texas law down on him in earnest. They'd probably call in the Texas rangers or the Army. There'd be no hope for him then. He'd simply have to give himself up to certain hanging or disappear into the wilds of Montana or Canada.

He'd never see Pamela again.

Even if she wanted to go with him, he wouldn't let her. It was not the kind of life he would ask the woman he loved to lead. He'd let them take him back to Texas before he'd do something as lowdown as that.

But that was assuming she would *want* to go with him, and Slade couldn't be sure she did. Pamela had some very strong ideas about guns and violence, she had told him so from the beginning. If she ever learned about his past, would she still love him? He doubted it, and he didn't think he was strong enough to stay and see her love for him die. Leaving would be better than that. At least he would have something to remember.

But could he leave? Could he give up this chance at happiness? Despite his past failures, there had to be a way if only he could find it. He wasn't guilty of any crimes. If he could only find a way to prove that. But how? Slade admitted he didn't know. But there had to be a way.

If he couldn't . . . well, there was plenty of time to think about that later. But one thing was certain. He wouldn't ask Pamela to become the bride of a hunted man. No matter what it cost him, he'd come to her with pride or not at all.

"A penny for your thoughts," Pamela said. She rolled up on her elbow so she could see Slade. "You've been awfully quiet."

"I've been thinking."

"I can tell it's not about something that makes you happy." Slade shook his head. "About the ranch or what happened to Dad?"

"Neither."

"You're thinking about leaving, aren't you?"

He nodded. "Ever since you said you loved me, things have been haunting me just about all the time. I lie awake for hours figuring, trying to come up with some other way, but there just isn't one."

"What are you running from, Slade?"

"My past, a man, a reputation, any one of which is more than enough to destroy any life we might be able to build together."

"Can't you go back and face it, get it over with? I'll go with you."

"If I go back, I'll be hanged."

So there it was, Pamela thought, despondent, the confirmation of her worst fears. Slade was a killer, a man who would be hanged, possibly shot on sight by a respectable citizen. But if this was so—and he had practically confessed it so it *must* be so—why didn't she feel sick to her stomach, filled with rage, or even coldly indifferent?

Because you love him, her heart whispered. And no matter

313

what he has done, you'll always love him.

But knowing the man she loved would soon leave her forever did threaten to make Pamela sick. Only the thought of Slade dead could make her feel worse. She didn't think she could endure that.

"How soon will you have to go?"

"I won't leave until you're out of danger."

"But if they'll hang you . . ."

"Only if they can take me back."

But as there would only be two ways Slade could avoid that, by his own death or by leaving Pamela, she couldn't see any advantage to either.

"If it's not safe, I think you ought to leave now," Pamela said. Those were the most difficult words she had ever said, but she knew she'd never forgive herself if he got caught because he stayed to help her. "Nobody has dared to put their cows on our range since the roundup."

"Maybe not the other ranchers, but Mongo is only waiting until . . ."

"I don't want to talk about the ranch and Mongo," Pamela said as she rolled off her elbow and pulled Slade over to her. "If you insist upon leaving me, I'm not going to waste time on cows. I never liked them, and I doubt I ever will. I have something more interesting to do. Can you guess what it is?"

Slade had no trouble at all guessing what Pamela had in mind, and though he would have liked to have had a thorough discussion of what she ought to be doing to protect her range, he gave in to the impulse to make love to her. They could always talk about cows in the morning.

Slade shifted his weight in the bed without waking. The steady rhythm of his breathing had remained unbroken for two hours. Pamela lay next to him, still in the circle of his arms. His eyes were closed, too, but the tears running down her cheeks, the damp places on her pillow, the occasional silent sob that shook her body told her she would get no sleep this night.

"It's Mongo Shepherd that's causing all the trouble," Dave Bagshot told Pamela between mouthfuls.

"What's he doing now?" Pamela wasn't eating. She had hardly touched anything since Gaddy returned from Santa Fe.

"Things it'll be hard to pin on him," Dave replied. "A couple of the boys have been shot at. But since they've been going around in pairs, especially since Slade taught them how to always keep one man under cover, nobody gets too close."

"Then how do you know it's Mongo?"

"I don't, not that I can prove, but there's plenty of hoof prints about that don't belong to any of our horses. And we're still finding cows of his we missed during roundup. The other day the boys found a couple dozen."

"What did you do?" Slade asked.

"Rounded them up and swam them back across."

"Why didn't you leave them? We've already told him we'll sell anything we find on our range in the fall." He was getting so angry he could hardly hold his tongue. He had been trying to talk Pamela into taking a firm stand, and now this had to happen.

"Pamela figured it was easier to take them back. People get mighty touchy when you start messing with their cows."

"I don't want any shooting," Pamela said.

"And what will you do when everybody realizes you don't mean to stand behind your words?"

"But we are. We're driving them back across the river."

"That's what you were doing before," Slade said. "Mongo's testing you. He's shooting at you, but you're not shooting back. I said you'd keep his cows and sell them, but

315

you're sending them back. What do you think he's going to do next?"

"I don't think he'll keep on."

"He still has hungry cows, doesn't he? You have the only range with enough grass, so nothing has changed."

"He's right, Pamela," Dave said, apparently considering a side of the problem he hadn't seen before. "If we don't do something to stand up to him, he's just going to keep pushing."

Pamela acted as though she hadn't heard either man. "Are you having any trouble with the other ranchers?"

"No. Slade seems to have scared them off, at least for now, but they're keeping a close watch on things. The minute they think we're losing, they'll rush in to get their share."

"Keep driving the cows back," Pamela said. "I know you don't think that's the smart thing to do, Slade, but I don't want a fight. I couldn't stand it if I caused any of our men to get killed."

"Can't you see it'll just cost you more men in the end?" Slade said, trying to hold his temper. "What makes you think Mongo has scruples just because you do? If you haven't learned one thing living out here for three years, and apparently you haven't, these last few weeks should have taught you that Mongo doesn't mean to give up. He's shot your men and attempted to burn your barn, brand your cattle, and drive his cows on your range. Are you going to wait until he kills somebody before you realize that while you're sitting here acting like a proper, well-bred lady, he's out there meaning to take what he can any way he can?"

Pamela was livid. She knew she and Slade disagreed totally when it came to handling trouble with the ranch, but she hadn't expected him to attack her position so savagely. Especially not in front of Dave.

"You know how I feel about violence."

"I know all that," Slade said, interrupting her before she could deliver her speech on the evils of guns and violence, "but we're not talking about what you believe any more. We're talking about what you're willing to *do* when you can no longer do what you would like to do."

"You surely can't want me to start a fight every time one of Mongo's cows strays onto our land."

Slade made an extremely rude noise when Pamela used the word *strays*. "We said we'd sell what we found here in the fall. Now, dammit, that won't work anymore. You stop sending those cows back and Mongo's going to think you've given in. If you'd never returned the first one, he'd be wondering if you meant to keep your word."

"That was my decision," Pamela said.

"It was a rotten decision," Slade stated bluntly.

"I supported it," Dave said.

"And that's rotten judgment on *your* part," Slade shot back instantly.

"So you would recommend that I do something that would force Mongo into a fight."

"You still don't understand," Slade said, his exasperation beyond hiding. *"Mongo is already fighting you.* No sane person decides to take something from another person without expecting a fight. Mongo knows that. He's just testing you to see how cheaply he can win."

"I don't believe land or cows are worth a human life," Pamela stated, but she had to admit her words didn't sound quite so lofty as they used to.

"Suppose, just *suppose* now, that your father has been laid up somewhere with a bullet in his side, a bullet put there by Mongo or one of his men, a bullet that could have killed him. What would you do about it? Stand around and wring your hands, moaning over the fact that Mongo hadn't played by the rules?"

"No. . . . I . . ."

"Because if that's what you'd do, you might as well pack up now and run after Amanda. Let Dave sell the ranch and the herd while you still have something left to sell. Believe

317

me, come fall, you won't have anything. You won't have anybody's respect either."

Dave mumbled his apologies and quickly left the table, but Pamela was so furious she hardly noticed his departure.

"I have no intention of going over the same ground again," she began, her eyes swimming with unshed tears, tears she wanted to shed because the cruelty of Slade's words were breaking her heart, "but I had thought you would have the courtesy, the *decency,* to allow me to express my opinions without ridiculing me." Suddenly her reserve cracked. She was no longer the boss of a ranch and its crew. She was simply a woman who was about to cry because the man she loved had hurt her. "How can you say you love me, how can you make love to me at night and treat me like this during the day?"

Slade jumped out of his chair and pulled her into his arms almost before the words were out of her mouth. "I love you more than I've ever loved anybody or anything," he said, "and I'll prove it to you as often as I have to, but I . . ."

"But you won't stop treating every opinion of mine that you dislike with scorn."

"I told you I don't know how to talk to women," Slade said.

"But you do. When you talk to me about anything except this damned ranch, I think you're the most wonderful man in the world. But just let us mention cows, ranches, or Easterners and you turn as mean as a sidewinder."

"I don't mean to be cruel, but I get plenty riled up when I see you acting like Arizona is some fancy country club and everybody is going to behave according to some gentlemanly code of behavior. Did you ever ask yourself why a rich man like Mongo Shepherd decided to leave the comforts of Boston? Did you ever ask anybody who knew him what he was like?"

"He said he wanted to see the West, that he didn't like living where it was so crowded."

318

"He probably left because he's the kind of person who can't get along in a society governed by rules, who can't stop himself from taking advantage of anybody weaker than himself. What will you do if he takes everything you have?"

"He isn't. I mean, he won't. Not as long as we keep driving him back. He'll know we mean to keep our land."

"No he won't. He'll take it as a sign you're soft. Then he'll make a big move, one you're not ready for."

"You think you know everything about everybody."

"No, I don't. I've acted the fool far too many times in my life to think that, but at least I can face the truth when I see it. No matter what I say, no matter what that man does, you're determined to go right on believing that somehow being born, reared, and educated in the East automatically makes a person better. I thought seeing Amanda again had taught you better."

"Amanda may not feel the same way I do about love, but both she and Frederick were appalled by the shooting."

She put her palms against Slade's chest and pushed him away, partly to see him better and partly because she was still furious with him, but he took her hands, put them around his neck, and drew her back into his arms. She didn't resist. She could feel the beat of his heart against her breast. It sent chills throughout her body.

"Listen to me closely because I mean every word I say. I love you. I will say it today, tomorrow, and every other day we have together. I will prove it to you every way I can. I would do anything for you I could, but I will not stand by and watch you throw away something your father gave twenty years of his life to build just because you've got a blind spot. You don't know it, but you're still a snob. You can't look at Mongo with the same eyes you use for the rest of the world."

"And you're still an egotistical male who thinks females are incapable of understanding the tough, brutal world of the western man." She ought to be thrilled by his loving words, not feel so cold and alone because of his critical ones.

"Not all women, just some. Ask Belva what she thinks. You might be surprised."

"What have you been doing? If you've been badgering that poor woman, and her practically ready to have that child any minute, I'll . . . I'll . . ." Pamela couldn't think of anything strong enough and left the sentence unfinished.

"I haven't spoken to Belva at all, but I've watched her eyes. Ever since that evening Dave was shot, she's been scared of something. Maybe you should ask her what it is. Now before you have a chance to become screaming mad at me again, I'm going away. I have an idea I want to work on a bit. I may be gone for a day or two—I'll stay in one of the line cabins—so don't worry. I don't write much, but I always come back."

"Slade, do you remember what you said about my father?"

The altered tone of her voice rivetted Slade's attention. He nodded.

"If he *is* lying somewhere with a bullet in him,"—her voice broke before she could say the next words—"or if he has been killed, I want the man responsible for it to pay. I know what I've said before, but if somebody killed my father, I want him dead."

"I can't find anything you can put your finger on," Gaddy reported, "but there's something going on. And I don't mean this business with Mongo's cows. The boys keep looking over their shoulders like they don't trust their best friend."

Slade and Gaddy were relaxing in the shade of a huge old pine. Gaddy leaned sleepily against the trunk which was about six feet in diameter. Slade stood with his foot resting on a small boulder as he looked out over the valley that stretched before him. It looked like an oasis of green in an ocean of brown. The air was cool and incredibly clear. The ridges rising up to the mountains on the horizon seemed only a short distance away. They were high up on the crest of the ridge which separated the valley from the open desert. Gaddy had come in the back way so no one would see him.

"I heard one of the boys say that Hen McCafferty and Thurston Peck have had some trouble, too."

"What kind?" Slade asked. This surprised him. Why would they be having trouble when they were only waiting to cause trouble for Pamela?

"Seems some of their boys have been shot at. Maybe one of McCafferty's got killed. I don't know, but they seem to think we did it. The only time one of our boys set foot on McCafferty range, he just about didn't get out with a whole skin. Must have been three or four McCafferty hands pouring lead in his direction."

"It's a good thing cowboys don't shoot too well," Slade muttered, but his brain was feverishly trying to fit this new piece of information into the puzzle. "Are we the only ones they suspect?"

"No. They ain't trusting Mongo's crew neither. Some of their hands had a terrible fight in town last week. At least two boys are laid up with busted ribs. One nearabout got his eyes poked out."

"You go back and see what else you can pick up. Somebody's trying to set the ranchers against each other. Though for the life of me I can't figure out who would benefit if there was a range war."

"Seems to me like the last man to survive would pick up all the marbles," Gaddy suggested.

"I know, but who will be the last man? And how's he going to make sure he *is* the last man?"

"Maybe he'll stay out of the fight."

"None of the men I met at the roundup will stand back from a fight. They got their land by fighting. That's all they know. That's one of the reasons Pamela's father was killed. He had enough sense to know the day of the gun was over."

"You think he's dead?"

"He's got to be. From everything I've heard about Josh

321

White, nothing would have kept him from returning or sending someone to tell his daughter where he was. No, if Josh White were still alive, he would be here and we wouldn't be having to deal with this problem."

"Pamela thinks he's still alive. *You* made her believe that."

"For weeks now she's been afraid he was dead. Haven't you noticed how strained she looks when a stranger rides up? I only wanted to give her hope, anything to ease the blow when it comes."

"Why?"

"Pamela doesn't have anybody now except you. It's a terrible thing to be alone, especially at a time like this."

"But you're here."

Slade's expression was bitter. "Maybe I won't be able to stay. Sometimes a man can't do what he wants, even when he wants it real bad."

"You got to," Gaddy protested. "You promised. Worse than that, you made her fall in love with you."

"Son, you'll soon learn that nobody can predict when they're going to fall in love. And when they do, there's not much anybody can do to stop it."

"I don't believe that," Gaddy said angrily. "Anybody could see Pamela had gone nutty on you. If anybody else had come in here looking like you did, she'd have thrown them out."

"I never intended to stay. . . ."

"Then there was all those times during the roundup when you had her off somewhere to yourself, sweet-talking her, making her think you were the only one who could save her bacon."

"Gaddy. . . ." But the boy was too full of his disappointment to stop for something as fragile as a soft word or a look of understanding.

"What did you do it for? Just so you could get her in bed?"

Slade's eyes narrowed in surprise. He didn't realize anybody knew their secret.

"I know she's been sneaking into your room since the night of the storm. I went up to the house to see if she was all right. She wasn't in her room, but I heard these . . . sounds coming from your room."

"If you'll just let me . . ."

"I couldn't believe it at first," he said, and Slade could see the bewilderment in his eyes, "not of Pamela. But then I figured that you'd stay and take care of her."

Slade wanted to say something that would ease the boy's hurt, but nothing would help but getting it out.

"But now you got what you wanted and you're running out. Must make you feel like quite a man, you coming in here a two-bit saddle bum and seducing the beautiful daughter of a rich man. It'll make a good story when you tell it in the saloon or around the campfire. *Yes sir, this girl was so hot to get into my bed I had to get myself wounded to keep her from climbing my frame right from the start. I had to get away before she wore me down to a nubbin.*"

"You don't think I would . . ."

"Well you ain't never going to tell such a story about Pamela, not if I die for it."

Gaddy drew his gun faster than either of them thought he could. But the shock of seeing his gun pointed at a man who, until a few moments ago, he believed to be the epitome of what he wanted to become, effectively dried up Gaddy's torrent of words.

"Go ahead and use it if you think that's what I deserve."

"I do," Gaddy said, his nerve badly shaken but his purpose still unchanged.

"Only let me give you a warning first. Once you pick up a gun, it's hard to put it down again. You kill me, and they won't let you put it down."

"W-what do you mean?" Gaddy asked, suspicious but interested.

"You shoot somebody and you make yourself a name as a tough man. You kill him, and you're a bad man. You shoot

323

someone with a reputation, and every cheap crook will be out after you."

"But I'm no gun hand," Gaddy protested.

"It won't matter. You'll be the man who killed Slade Morgan. You'll be famous. If they kill you, *they'll* be famous."

"You kill somebody?" Gaddy's anger was almost completely forgotten now.

"Yeah, and I've been running from it ever since. Do you want that, boy? What good will it do Pamela if you shoot me? That'll just mean she won't have anybody to stand beside her. Kill me and *you'll* be the one heading to California or Montana."

Gaddy's gun wavered and then dropped. "I didn't want to kill you."

"I know that."

"I was just so mad you would make Pamela love you and then leave her."

"I want to stay worse than anything else in the world. But if I don't find a way around the trouble that's on my trail, staying is only going to cause her more trouble than leaving. I don't want her to be the widow of a gunman. I won't have my kids growing up thinking their father was a common killer."

"I bet she would go with you if you asked her."

"And live the rest of her life on the run? Would you want that for your cousin?"

Gaddy shook his head.

"I'll stay if I can ask her to be the wife of a man she can love and respect, one with a name she can be proud to give her sons. I'll move heaven and earth to make that happen, but if I can't . . ."

Gaddy dropped his gun in its holster. He seemed to have gotten over his emotional outburst. In fact, he seemed remarkably like an adult. "But you'll stay until this trouble is over, no matter what?"

Slade nodded. "No matter what."

"Then I'd better get back. A new man rode in last night. He might know something about the other ranches. I'll be here tomorrow at the same time."

He's growing up Slade thought as he watched the boy ride off. But not fast enough. If only they had another year. Then Gaddy would be able to give Pamela the help she needed.

But they didn't have another year. He doubted they had another week.

The afternoon was so still Pamela could hear the horse even before it entered the canyon. "Come on in, Marshall, and sit for a while," she said as soon as Taylor Alcott pulled up. "You must have had a long ride."

Pamela really did want the marshall to visit for a little while, but she hadn't expected him to climb down from the saddle without more encouragement. He rarely stopped anywhere when he was on the trail, and he never took the trail unless it was business. Pamela could surmise from the grim expression on his face that it had taken some very unpleasant doings to drive him from his comfortable office in town this time.

"The ride in wasn't so bad," the marshall said as he settled into one of the deep, leather-covered chairs in Josh White's office. "Right pleasant when you consider what the desert can be like during the summer."

"Do you want a drink?" Pamela asked. She'd never entertained the marshall before. She didn't know what to offer.

"You can give me a shot of your father's whiskey," he said, then grinned. "You can't beat a Virginia man when it comes to knowing good whiskey."

"I understand Tennessee and Kentucky might want to dispute that with you."

"No problem," the marshall replied with a grin that belied the sternness in his eyes. "You tell them to bring along several bottles of each. I'll let them know what I think when I'm done."

"Sure you don't want more?" Pamela asked as she handed the glass to the marshall. The ounce and a half didn't look like much in the bottom of the deep glass.

Taylor downed the whiskey in one gulp. "Don't mind if I do, but just one more. I got to get back to town before nightfall."

After she refilled his glass, Pamela took a seat directly across from the sheriff. "Now that we've finished with the amenities, can we get down to why you came out here?"

"Can't it be just to look at a beautiful girl?" the marshall replied, but his eyes didn't reflect the smile on his lips.

"Not as long as Junie Sykes hasn't forgotten the way from the Wagon Wheel to your office," she teased.

The marshall's smile was genuine this time. "And to think you could hear about that way out here. There just don't seem to be much a woman can't find out."

"I must not be as good as the other women you know. I'm having a lot of trouble finding out why you came out here." Suddenly a cold chill ran through Pamela. "It's Dad. You know what happened to him, don't you?"

Taylor Alcott nodded.

"He's dead, isn't he?"

Taylor nodded again. "My heart goes out to you. This has to be a terrible blow."

Pamela struggled valiantly not to break down in front of him. Her rigid body sat forward in her chair; her eyes stared steadily at him. But not even holding her lips between her teeth could hide the telltale quiver. She tried to speak, but no words came out. She had thought she was prepared, but now she realized nothing can prepare you for the death of someone you love.

She had expected it, had prepared herself for it. In spite of Slade's reassurances, she had somehow known her father was dead. But the words hurt her more cruelly than she had

326

ever imagined. Now, more than anything else in the world, she needed the comfort of Slade's arms.

Taylor watched Pamela swallow convulsively several times to fight down the wracking sobs that threatened to overwhelm her. With a muttered oath, he got up from his chair, went to the liquor cabinet, poured himself out half a glass, and gulped it down. The huge swallow threatened to take off the top of his head, but he felt better.

Seeing his anxiety seemed to steady Pamela, and she got herself under control. "I think I have known for some time now," she said finally, "ever since I got back from the roundup, really. Tell me what happened."

"He was killed about a half day's ride from here. He'd barely gotten off his own land. Whoever did it got up close. He was shot twice, once in the chest and once in the head. Dead center both times."

"Why didn't anybody find his body before now? Surely during the roundup . . ."

"They killed his horse and caved a bank in over them. We might not have found him for a very long time, if ever, but that storm a few nights ago caused flash floods all up that way. It washed both of them a good ways downstream."

"And his body?"

"We buried him where he was."

"I want my father buried in a proper grave," Pamela cried. "Tell me exactly where he is. I'll take the buckboard out there first thing tomorrow."

"He wasn't fit to be moved," the marshall said as kindly as possible. "Maybe you might go after him sometime this fall."

Pamela stared at the marshall in horror. She had imagined that her father would always look just as he had in life. That he could have changed so much the marshall didn't want her to see him stunned her.

"We covered him real good with stones," the marshall said. "Wesley carved a real nice marker."

"I'll tell Slade," Pamela said. She couldn't think of any-

327

thing else to say. "He'll know what to do."

"Where is Mr. Morgan? I need to talk to him."

"He's not here."

"Where'd he go this time?"

"I don't know. Out on the range somewhere."

"What's he doing out there?"

Pamela forced her mind out of the vacuum into which it had retreated to avoid the horror of reality. She *had* to keep going until Slade got back.

"We're still having trouble with stray cows on our grass. He's trying to put a stop to it."

"When is he coming in?"

"I don't know. He went out this morning. He said he might not be back for a few days. Why?"

"I need to talk to him. I'll ride back this way in a day or two." The marshall had Pamela's full attention now.

"You wouldn't ride this far out of town unless something was wrong. What is it, marshall? Slade works for me. I insist that you tell me." Slade didn't work for anybody, but she felt justified in glossing over that fact just now.

"Just some talk, probably nothing more than idle rumor."

"You wouldn't walk as far as the Wagon Wheel for a rumor. *Tell me what it is!*"

"You'll find out soon enough. Damn, I hate doing this behind a fella's back. But Jud Noble has accused Morgan of killing your father. Said he saw him over that way about the time Josh must have left for Santa Fe."

"He's lying." The words were out of Pamela's mouth before she knew it. "He came off the desert from the south, toward Mexico. You can ask Gaddy and Belva. They were here when he arrived."

"I'm not accusing him. I just want to talk to him."

"He was on foot. His horse had broken a leg. He wouldn't have killed Dad's horse. He loves animals. You ought to see him with that old hammerhead. Besides, what reason would he have to kill a man he'd never seen before?"

328

"Take it easy," the marshall said as soothingly as he knew how. "I told you I wasn't accusing Slade. But I have to talk to him. There has to be a reason Jud Noble said what he did."

"He did it for Mongo," Pamela said without hesitation. "He's mad that Slade backed him down. And he's jealous, too. Mongo wanted to marry me, but I refused."

"You going to marry Slade?"

Pamela stared at him like she didn't understand what he had asked. Then she answered in a hollow voice. "No. He said he'd stay until Dad got back and this trouble was over, but he's leaving for California first chance he gets."

"Won't he stay now that your father's dead?"

"That won't make any difference."

"What will you do?"

"Me?" Pamela asked, almost as though she was surprised anyone would be interested in her. "I'll probably sell the ranch and move back to Baltimore."

Chapter 19

Marshall Alcott had anticipated several reactions, but not that one. "You can't sell the ranch."

"Why not? My mother hated it. I sometimes think the loneliness and bleakness of this country killed her as much as the overturned wagon. Of course Dad loved this place. He enjoyed the struggle and the success. He loved looking out on this valley knowing it belonged to him, but someone killed him because of it. I hate Arizona, and I don't want to live here!" A spasm shook her body, but no tears came into her eyes.

The marshall had never felt terribly comfortable around women. It was one of the reasons he hadn't married. But he felt particularly ineffective in times of crisis, the exact situation he found himself in now. He usually turned tail and ran when things got difficult. And that's what he did.

"I have to be getting back to town," he said. He gave Pamela a perfunctory pat on the shoulder, told her she'd feel better for a good cry, and left as quickly as he could.

Shock kept Pamela from collapsing.

She watched the marshall leave, taking her shattered hopes with him. Her hand flew to her mouth to stop a choking sob that never came. She staggered back into the house, running into walls and doorways, blindly searching for the comfort of her room. But it was Slade's door she opened and Slade's bed she collapsed on.

But she didn't cry. She couldn't. Everything inside her seemed all dried up. Her father was dead; Slade was leaving; she would be alone. She had been telling herself something must have happened to her father, but she hadn't realized until now how heavily she had depended on the hope he would come back.

Why wasn't Slade here? Why did he have to choose this morning to leave? How could she stand it until he came back? She didn't even know where he had gone. She couldn't have sent Gaddy after him even if he had been at the ranch.

The pain in her chest was excruciating, but she couldn't do anything to relieve it; she couldn't cry.

She couldn't lie still any longer, but getting up didn't help. She paced the room, but that only seemed to cause the pressure to build. It was almost impossible to breathe.

With sudden decision, she hurried into her father's office. She never drank whiskey, she didn't like the smell of it, but she knew it helped people endure pain. She was hurt, and she was suffering. She would do almost anything if she could get the pain to go away, to numb the crushing weight on her chest, to block out the reality of her father's death.

Pamela poured a small amount of amber liquid into the glass. She stared at it. The familiar smell, that hateful smell she could remember on the breath of men on several occasions, was strong. Her stomach threatened to rebel. She cast about in her mind seeking for some other way to relieve the pressure of the pain, but she had no other choice.

It didn't look like much whiskey. It was the same amount she had seen her father use, but then her father never got drunk. She poured until the glass was half full, but that was still only twice as much as she had in the first place. She wanted to be completely numb.

She filled the glass. Then not wanting to give herself time to change her mind, Pamela picked it up and drank deeply.

Before the first swallow could slide down her throat, her entire body went into a spasm of rejection. The glass slid from her hands and shattered on the stone floor as the fiery liquid violently exploded from her mouth. Pamela sank helplessly to her knees, her body heaving in furious rejection of the few drops of whiskey that had managed to slide down her throat.

Finally, exhausted by the endless retching that still gripped her body, Pamela managed to crawl over to a chair and pull herself into it. She lay there, gasping for breath, waiting for the last of the spasms to leave her.

But once she no longer felt sick, the weight of her grief descended upon her again, and Pamela groaned aloud in her agony. Staggering to her feet, she rushed outside.

The fresh air helped to calm her stomach, but it did nothing for the misery in her soul. And everything around her only made it worse. The house, the corrals, the bunkhouse, even the valley itself, everything bore her father's stamp. It was his triumph, it carried the imprint of his personality, and it was all around her. With a cry of torment, Pamela ran toward the corral.

She had to find Slade. She needed him.

She didn't remember saddling her horse. She only remembered riding for what seemed like hours and hours. Where would Slade be? What was he doing? She didn't know, but there were no line cabins in the valley. He had to have crossed the ridge and ridden into the desert.

She rode on and on. Unconscious of time or distance, she drove her horse forward until the heaving of the animal's sides as it climbed the steep ridge warned her to slow down, or the horse would give out before she found Slade. Pamela topped out on the ridge, and the glorious panorama of the desert lay before her.

She dropped from the saddle to give her horse a breather. Any other time she would have been in awe of the sight before her.

The ridge fell away before her giving her an uninterrupted view from the mountains in the north down to the river which divided her land from the other ranchers. Purple lupine, owl clover, and brilliant red Mexican poppies created a colorful mosaic in the desert below. From this carpet emerged the towering green spines of cactus or the gnarled brown-and-black branches of mesquite and iron-wood trees. Nourished by rich, volcanic soil and plentiful winter rains, the desert was alive with bloom.

But Pamela stared straight ahead out of sightless eyes, her only thought to reach the comfort of Slade's arms. She racked her brain trying to remember the location of the line cabins. There were several, maybe as many as a dozen, but she could only remember two. No matter. If Slade hadn't stopped at the first one, somebody else would be there and he would take her to Slade.

If she could just find the first cabin.

Pamela didn't know how long it had been since she left the house, but by now it must have been at least midafternoon. She knew very little about this part of the ranch. It lay a long way from the house. Only once did she have any reason to ride this far. A couple of years ago she had accompanied her father to take care of one of the men who lay seriously ill in the closest cabin. Pamela thought she could remember how to get there.

But everything looked different. Now that she didn't have her father to guide her, she was uncertain of every turn; she questioned every landmark. She forced herself to keep calm, to consider each turn in the trail, each canyon or butte meticulously. She had her reward when the cabin finally came into view.

But there was no one there. And no one had used the cabin for some time. It appeared to have been empty for months. Pamela climbed down from her horse. She had to think.

She hesitated to go back, to face the prospect of a night alone in the ranch house with all its painful memories. She would far rather spend the night in the cabin.

But she hadn't brought any food.

She had been in such a hurry to leave she hadn't done any planning. She hadn't brought any blankets or a change of clothes. She didn't even have a canteen for water. She could quench her thirst at a stream, but she had eaten very little for some time, nothing at all that day. She didn't feel hungry— she guessed she was still too upset—but she could hear her stomach growl.

She couldn't stay here, and even if she had wanted to go back, she would never reach home before dark overtook her. She had to go on. But she didn't know where to look for the next cabin. She remembered her father saying it was over the next ridge, along the spine of the ridge that ran down to the river, but she had never crossed the ridge.

Pamela caught her horse and mounted. If she had to go, she had to start now. She prayed there would be someone at the second cabin.

Two hours later the sun had begun to sink in the sky, and Pamela had still not found the ridge that ran down to the river. Twice she rounded the tumbled rocks at the edge of the fingers of the mountains that ran down into the desert, and twice she had seen the river disappear beyond yet another ridge that stopped far short of its sandy banks.

She had to face it. She would have to spend the night in the desert. Alone. She had nothing to build a fire and nothing to keep her warm. Even now the temperature was falling rapidly. She knew it would be very cold before long. She had to find shelter.

She turned inward, toward the gentle incline between the two ridges. Surely up there she would be able to find some place safe. If not a cave, maybe a sheltered spot behind a rock or under a ledge. At least she didn't have to fear rain. There were no clouds in the sky. She could already see the morning star.

Her horse walked slowly, its strength nearly gone after

hours of following steep paths and scrambling down precipitous trails.

Tree growth increased abruptly as she left the desert floor. Where before Pamela had been surrounded by creosote bush and mesquite, she now traveled under the spreading limbs of oaks and tall pines that blocked out the waning sunlight.

Pamela allowed her horse to travel at its own pace. It was impossible to venture off the trail, and she needed all her concentration to find a place that looked safe enough to spend the night.

Pamela pulled her horse to a stop between two huge pines. She looked around on all sides, but she saw nothing which could be used for shelter. Everywhere she looked she saw huge boulders and shelves of hard rock or hard-packed soil only very thinly covered with a carpet of needles. She didn't even see an indentation in the canyon walls deep enough to cover her if it should rain. She didn't want to continue. The fading light no longer reached under the trees. She would have felt safer if she could have returned to the desert floor, but she knew it was impossible. She would ride on a little farther, but she would have to stop soon, even if she had to sleep in the middle of the trail.

She started her horse moving once again, silently praying she would find shelter soon. As she passed under a thick limb of the second of the two pines, the blood-curdling cry of a mountain lion shattered the night. Her horse screamed in panic and reared against the restraint of the reins. Pamela looked up at the limb and into the glowing red eyes of a huge male cougar, crouched and ready to spring.

Pamela didn't remember attaching the scabbard to the saddle, but instinctively she reached for her rifle, found it, and aimed as the cat sprang from the tree limb. The last thing she saw was the huge, gaping jaws as the cat sprang at her from above.

*   *   *

Slade was reaching out to take the coffee pot from the fire when he heard the mountain lion scream. It didn't bother him, lions always avoided people whenever possible, but still he glanced over at his horse. The dun jerked up his head, pricked his ears, and sniffed the trail leading down out of the mountains. But he remained calm. The lion couldn't be close by. Slade had reached for his coffee pot once more when the rifle shot reverberated through the hills.

Moments later he heard the muffled sound of a galloping horse.

Slade dropped his cup and threw the saddle on the dun. The horse sounded like it was galloping out of control, and that could either mean the man was injured or, more likely, down on the ground. Moments later Slade galloped down the trail as fast as he dared in the darkness, afraid of what he would find.

He came upon the loose horse less than five minutes later. The blood on the saddle so preoccupied him he almost missed the brand. The Bar Double-B. It was Pamela's horse.

Slade had never known such fear. Even when he faced all three Briarcliffs, knowing there was virtually no way he could come out alive, it had been his cavalier disdain of danger that brought him through the gun battle without a scratch.

But now he felt the icy cold fingers of sheer terror encircle his heart. Pamela was somewhere back on that trail. And so was the mountain lion.

Heedless of the dark and the dangerous trail, Slade drove his heels into the flanks of the hammerhead dun, and the beast leapt away at a hard gallop. Pamela's horse followed behind.

Afterwards Slade couldn't remember that wild ride down the mountain side, the agonizingly slow minutes of sickening fear, the horror that he would round a bend and see the lion standing over Pamela's torn body. He was only aware of the need to find her no matter what the danger.

The scream almost unmanned him.

It was a woman's scream, the terror in her voice almost tangible. He descended into the enveloping shadows of the pine forest without slackening his speed. Only a stray beam of moonlight filtering through the trees kept him from galloping over Pamela and the lion. She lay on the ground, the lion on top of her.

Slade threw himself from his horse and drew his knife at the same time. Landing on the ground, he ignored the blood that covered Pamela's clothes, ignored her frantic efforts to escape the lion. He attacked the beast, driving his knife deep into his heart time after time.

Only when the lion failed to respond to his lethal attack did Slade realize it was already dead.

Flinging the carcass aside, he knelt down and swept Pamela into his arms.

"Dad's dead," she told him.

And then, held securely in the arms she had been searching for all afternoon, she cried.

Pamela lay near the fire, a cup of hot coffee in her hands. She had exchanged her blood-stained clothes for some of Slade's. The blanket covering her hid the fact that they didn't come anywhere near fitting.

"I don't understand why you didn't stay in one of the cabins," she said. "Why would you want to sleep on the ground when you could be sleeping in a bed?"

"For the same reason you set out not knowing where you were going instead of waiting until I got back. Blind, dumb, obstinate hardheadedness."

"I had to find you. I couldn't stay in that house, not alone."

"Why didn't you ask Belva to stay with you? Or you could

337

have gone looking for Dave and the boys. Anything except take out across unknown desert and mountains. You could have died out there."

"I don't need any more reminders," Pamela said. Shivers of fright still racked her body. "I just had to find you. That's all."

Slade set his cup of coffee on the ground and settled down next to her. "I'm glad, now that you're here. But if you ever pull a crazy stunt like that again, I'll . . ." Slade decided it would be better if he didn't say what he would be tempted to do.

"Did the marshall tell you how your father died?"

"Just that it must have been some time ago."

"Somebody knew what he meant to do in Santa Fe, and they waited to kill him."

"He said they shot Dad from close range. Slade, who would do a thing like that? Dad must have known the man. He must have pulled up on the trail and waited for Dad to ride up, never guessing he meant to kill him."

The tears threatened to overwhelm her again, but she doggedly held them back. She had done little more than cry in the two hours since Slade had pulled her from under the mountain lion. She had even continued to weep uncontrollably while he changed her clothes. She couldn't start again now. She needed to talk.

"Who could have done it, Slade? How could anybody who knew Dad shoot him and hide his body in a ravine?"

"The same man who's been manipulating Mongo. He's wanted your ranch all along, but he couldn't find a convenient way to start trouble before Mongo's herds arrived, at least not one which would also cover his tracks. Everyone had enough land for their needs. Then Mongo arrived and conflict became inevitable. When you decided not to marry Mongo, you gave the killer his opening. If he could eliminate your father and somehow prod Mongo into starting a

338

general range war, several of the ranchers might be killed, and all of this would be here for the taking. My being here just happened to be a lucky break. He figured I'd kill Mongo in that fight over the maverick. Failing that, and it did fail because of you, Mongo would be shot and I would be blamed for it."

"But you never went anywhere alone, so no one could blame you when Mongo was shot."

"Jud Noble tried hard enough. That's why I insisted you stay in camp. I already thought your father was dead. If anything happened to you—well, after that, it wouldn't have mattered to me what happened to the ranch."

Slade put his arm around Pamela and drew her close. He kissed the top of her head. When Pamela tried nervously to pull her hair back from her face, Slade captured her hand in his. She had lost her hair pins in the confrontation with the lion, and she wanted to put it back up.

Slade thought she'd never look more lovely, more approachable.

"When did you start to care for me?" she asked. "I mean *really* care?"

"When you took care of my blisters."

Pamela giggled. "That's silly. If you could have seen your face." She became serious. "You must have been in terrible pain all the time. Besides, I wasn't very nice to you."

"But you were. I didn't hear your words. I only saw that you were concerned for my feet. They were an ugly, bloody mess, yet you got down on your knees to help me."

"Will you forget about that," Pamela said impatiently. "I couldn't very well do anything standing up."

"You remember it your way, I'll remember it mine," Slade said, settling Pamela more firmly into his embrace. "When did you start to love me?"

Pamela didn't hesitate. "When I poured whiskey all over your feet and you didn't utter a sound. No, that's when it started. I think I fell in love on the front porch, when you talked all that nonsense about the moon and then bamboozled me into teaching you how to kiss."

"I still haven't completely mastered the technique. You got time for a lesson now?"

"As I remember, you were a quick learner."

"I'm a quick forgetter, too."

Pamela laughed in spite of herself. "I don't suppose it would do any harm," she said, "but make it snappy. I want to talk to you."

Slade pounced on her with a deep-throated growl, and Pamela happily surrendered herself to his assault.

Slade kissed her quite thoroughly. Then deciding he needed a bit more practice, he settled down to some serious work. Pamela found no fault with his efforts, but she was so afraid for him she couldn't be still. No matter how seductive his lips, how comforting his arms, or how fulfilling his love, her fear for his safety remained uppermost in her mind.

Pamela pushed his hand away when he attempted to unbutton her shirt. "There's something we've got to talk about," she said. She ducked her head when Slade tried to resume his attentions. "Come on, Slade. I need to talk to you, and I can't concentrate when you're kissing me."

"Wouldn't I be a failure if you could?"

"I guess so," Pamela admitted, "but try to be serious for just one moment."

"I was never more serious about anything in my life. I adore you, and I can't wait to make love to you."

"We can't right now."

"Why?"

"Jud Noble has accused you of killing my father. He said he saw you on the trail to Santa Fe the same day my father left."

Slade froze. It was as though his whole body had turned to cold stone. "Do you believe him?"

"Of course not, but there are too many things about your life you haven't told me about."

"Like what?"

"Like Texas."

"What about it?"

"You're the man Marshall Alcott was talking about, aren't you?"

Abruptly Slade got up and walked over to the fire. He told himself he had to control his anger, that Pamela wouldn't react like his mother or Trish, but he couldn't keep the familiar feeling of helplessness from worming its way into his soul. He couldn't ignore the fear that Pamela was going to reject him like everyone else.

"As long as I don't know anything about you, I can't help you prove your innocence," Pamela said when he didn't speak. "I tried to think of a way after the marshall left, but I couldn't. That's part of the reason I came after you."

"So now you want to know where I was born, who my parents were related to, and whether or not I can trace my ancestors back to a signer of the Declaration of Independence? Or would you prefer the Mayflower." He was angry and bitter, and it showed. Didn't his helping her count for anything? Must people always insist upon knowing everything about him no matter how meaningless it might be to the man he had become? He had thought at least Pamela had finally understood, but now it seemed she was no more capable of accepting him on faith than anyone else.

Pamela's heart went out to Slade. His face was a handsome mask of indifference, but by now she knew him well enough to know when he was suffering. How could she explain she didn't doubt him no matter what he had done when she didn't understand it herself? She wanted to know so she could convince everybody else of his innocence, that he was the most wonderful person in all of Arizona. He had to tell her everything.

341

"I don't want to know anything like that, not anymore. I just want to know about you. Why did you kill those men? Why were they after you? The marshall said he thought they were after your money. Was that it?"

"You don't think I killed them just because I wanted to?"

"I would never have thought that, not even the afternoon you walked in off the desert."

Slade felt some of the tension leave him. The fear that she would ultimately turn her back on him still lurked there, but he also began to hope that at last someone could see past his gun and the reputation that seemed to cling to him like an evil shadow.

Slade squatted down next to the fire. "They wanted my money and didn't care what they had to do to get it. I'd received an offer for my share of the carnival. I didn't want to go to St. Louis, so I offered Joe Swift—he was a friend—a cut if he'd bring me the money. Their sister worked for the carnival, I'd gotten her the job. She told them about the money. They were supposed to bushwack Joe on the trail, but he was a smart kid. They didn't catch up with him until he was almost home. They didn't kill him, but he was badly wounded. He made it back to me. He died in my arms."

"Those bastards told me they only wanted the money, but from the start they intended to kill me. They shot our horses and tried to set fire to the cabin. Only it was a soddy. So they used dynamite. Only reason I'm alive is I hid in a kind of cellar. I left Joe buried there. I figured it was a fitting tomb."

"Who were those men?"

"The Briarcliff boys, all three of them. They had me down a draw, and the only way to get out was past them. But they knew me and stayed out of sight. If they had to, they meant to starve me out. It took me four days to get the three shots I needed."

"But if you killed them in self-defense, why is anyone after you?"

"The Briarcliffs are a powerful family. Their father's a judge deep into politics and their uncle's the sheriff. Between them, they can keep the law after me for years. They want me back in Texas, and they don't care if I'm dead or alive. Either way they plan for me to end up six feet under."

"Why did you leave the carnival?"

"You want answers to everything, don't you?" He tried not to sound cynical, but it was hard. Explaining himself never provided any answers, only more questions.

"I've always wanted to know everything about you," Pamela answered simply.

"Did anybody ever tell you if you keep nosing around a person, you're bound to find out something you don't like?"

"My father."

"But you didn't listen."

"What do you think?" She smiled, and Slade couldn't help but smile back.

"I didn't leave, not completely. But after Trish threw me out, the carnival sort of lost its glamor. Trish turned me sour on people. I started hiring out to cattle outfits, but I kept going back during the carnival season. I was a popular attraction. Besides, I owned a part of it. I wanted it to do well."

"Will you ever want to go back?"

"No. When I agreed to sell out, I knew I'd entered that ring for the last time."

"What were you going to do?"

"I'd always wanted to go to California."

"Do you think you could consider stopping here?"

"I don't think I could work for Dave."

"What if I made you the boss?"

"You can't fire him. There's no cause."

"I don't mean to. There is one position above foreman."

"What?"

"My husband."

343

It took a moment for Slade's breathing to become regular once more. Pamela couldn't know it, but what she was doing was worse torture than the smell of food to a starving man. It was the one thing he wanted most in the whole world.

"Do you know what it means to be a hunted man?"

"But you're not guilty of anything except protecting yourself. You might even be able to convince them if you go back."

"As long as Andy Briarcliff is sheriff and his brother Jim is the judge, I don't have a snowball's chance in hell."

"We'll hire a lawyer."

"You don't understand, Pamela. Brazos is a closed town. I had been away for many years. I was a fool to go back."

"Slade Morgan, I'm not going to let you take a defeatist attitude. There has to be a way to prove your innocence, and we'll find it."

"If you're after all the truth, you might as well know my name's not Slade Morgan. It's Billy Wilson."

Pamela didn't know how she managed to keep from showing the shock she felt at learning the man she loved, the man she hoped would become her husband, was not only an outlaw but was using an alias. "I prefer Slade to Billy. I don't see much difference between Morgan and Wilson, but I don't see any point in practically telling them where you are."

"Do you really mean that," Slade asked, "that none of this matters?"

"Of course it matters. I wish it hadn't happened, but wishing's not going to change anything. And I don't care what you call yourself as long as I can be your wife," Pamela said. "I'll sell the ranch and move to California with you. We can even go to Montana if necessary."

"You don't have to sell anything, my darling. I have enough money for both of us."

"You can't know how expensive it is to live, even in Montana."

"I told you I sold my share on the carnival."

"But it couldn't have been enough to live on."

"My dear, sweet, practical darling, we sold the carnival to P. T. Barnum because we created too much competition for him. My share came to something over one hundred thousand dollars."

Pamela gulped. "I guess you *could* afford to pay for a horse and saddle," she said, breathless with the realization that not even Amanda could accuse Slade of marrying her for money.

"That and a lot more," Slade said sweeping Pamela up and swinging her around so hard she begged him to stop. "Where do you want to go? Between us, anything is possible."

Pamela tried to gather her wits. Her head was still spinning and she had to lean on Slade just to stand up, but she knew that the next few minutes were some of the most important in their lives. Slade was not a man to run, even when he was running from being forced to kill again. He would despise himself, and before long he would stop and face whatever was following him.

But for her sake, and the sake of the children she hoped to have, he would try to keep going on no matter what the cost to him inside. But Pamela couldn't ask Slade—and he would always be Slade. She couldn't think of him as Billy Wilson— to be anything less than he was for her sake. She couldn't tie him to a marriage that would force him to trade his honor for the safety of his family.

"Where would you like to live? If you could choose any place in the world, where would you *really* want to live?"

"I gather the mountain cabin is still out?"

"I'm serious, Slade."

"I'd rather live at the Bar Double-B."

"So would I."

"There's still the range war. And there's still the problem of who murdered your father."

"That's part of the reason." Pamela avoided his eyes. "I

345

want to find out who killed Dad. I want to see him dead."

"Are you sure?"

"Just as sure as I am that I want to marry you. The Bar Double-B is my ranch now. Dad poured his whole life into it, and nobody is going to take it away." Suddenly a horrible thought occurred to her. "I don't want you to think my wanting to marry you has anything to do with finding Dad's killer. I would marry you even if you couldn't hit the broad side of a barn."

"I know," Slade said, pulling her close. "You're going to marry me because you can't help yourself. You tried everything you knew to keep from falling in love with me, but you failed, madame. At least you have the sense to give in gracefully."

"You're no better. I don't think you changed your mind about California until you thought that lion had eaten me up."

"I never wanted to go to California half as much as I wanted to stay with you. I knew that from the first. I just couldn't believe you could love someone like me."

Pamela laughed. *"Someone like you* is exactly the kind of man I admire, the kind of man my father was. It just took me a while to discover it."

"And now you're content to marry a cowboy?"

"Perfectly, and not the least bit anxious to show him off to all my Eastern friends. If they all react the way Amanda did, I'd be lucky to get you back to Arizona in one piece. It seems your kind of physical appeal has no geographical limitations."

"Now you're making fun of me," he said, but humor danced in his eyes. "Are you done with your questions? We have some unfinished business, and I don't want to be interrupted for a while."

Pamela sighed happily. "My mother warned me about men like you. Amanda, too. She said you all want the same thing."

346

"I want *everything*," Slade said. "I'll never be satisfied with anything less."

"I promise I'll never offer you anything less," Pamela replied.

If anyone had ever told Pamela that someday she would make love next to a campfire in the Mazatzal foothills she would have been aghast. But tonight it seemed the most natural thing in the world. Everything was right and natural when she was with Slade. Just being with him made it that way.

Chapter 20

Dave and Marshall Alcott were waiting for them when they returned to the ranch. Slade's first impulse was to turn around and head right back into the hills. After what Pamela had said, there could only be one reason for the marshall to come back out to the ranch. But even if Slade's hammerhead dun hadn't been too tired to outrun a new-born calf, he wouldn't have turned back. He had decided to stay and marry Pamela. When he did that, he also made up his mind to stop running. No more accepting the whimsical twists and turns of Fate. No more "If I can't . . ."

"You had everybody worried sick," Dave said to Pamela. "Nobody knew where you'd gone." He came toward them before they could dismount. "Why didn't you tell Belva where you were going?"

"I'm sorry," Pamela said as she dismounted. "I was too upset to think. I couldn't stand it here knowing Dad was dead. I went to find Slade."

"At least you're back safe and sound," Dave continued. "You must be starved. Come inside and let Belva fix you something to eat. There can't be much food in those line cabins." It wasn't a statement. It was a question. Dave wanted to know where she'd been and what she'd been doing.

"I'm all right," Pamela said. Slade winked at her and she quickly dropped her head so Dave couldn't see her answering smile. "Slade found me before I starved. And you're right, there isn't enough in those cabins to feed a mouse. I'll have to see that something is done about that."

Her answers seemed to satisfy the marshall's curiosity, but Dave's eyes still darted questioning glances in Slade's direction. After all their private conversations during the roundup and the days they had spent at the ranch together, Pamela decided it was only natural for Dave to wonder what might be between them. But her private life was not his concern, and she didn't mean to satisfy his curiosity.

"Won't you come inside, Marshall?" Pamela said. "There must be some momentous reason for you to ride out this way twice in one week. I can't wait to find out what it is."

"You're not going to like it much. I have to take Mr. Morgan in for questioning."

"What for?" Pamela had already turned toward the house, but at the marshall's words, she spun around to face the three men. Her gaze went from one to the other. All three were hard and sober. Dave knew what the marshall wanted. Slade could guess.

"I'd like to know a little more about how Mr. Morgan came to be here just when he did. You see, after Jud said he saw Slade on the same trail as your father, I talked to Dave here. Josh was carrying quite a bit of cash on him, but we didn't find any money on the body."

"And since Slade walked in here with enough money to buy a second-hand saddle and a horse nobody would ride, you figured he must have killed my father and robbed him. Is that it, Marshall?"

"The thought did cross my mind, but lots of people could have that much money."

"Then what do you want?" Pamela looked at Slade, but he kept his face blank. He might as well have been wearing his beard again for all she could read his thoughts. But oddly enough, he wasn't looking at her or the marshall. Instead, he stared at Dave.

"A man rode into Maravillas two days ago," the marshall explained. "Says he's from Texas, a little town called Brazos. He's looking for that man I was telling you about, the one who killed those three brothers. Seems there's a right big reward for him. As a matter of fact, they're offering a thousand dollars. Now that's a fortune out here. Anyway, this man says he knows what this fella looks like. Known him since they were boys. Said he'd know him without his beard. Dammit, Pamela, I just can't ignore all the things piling up against Slade. First Mongo swears Morgan shot him, then Jud, and now this Ben Warren shows up describing a man that's got to be the spitting image of Slade if you put a beard on him."

"Ben Warren did you say?" Slade asked. "And he says he's known this man since childhood?"

"Swears he'd be able to recognize his skeleton," the marshall said. "I told him I'd bring you in so he could have a look see."

"He's not going," Pamela said, fighting down the panic which threatened to deprive her of her ability to think rationally. "All you have are unfounded accusations, circumstantial evidence."

"Why can't he come here?" Dave asked.

"He's got business in California," the marshall explained. "Can't stay past tomorrow. There wouldn't be time to go get him and bring him out here now."

"Then you'll just have to wait until he comes back through," Pamela said. "I see no reason for everybody to suit his convenience."

"Look, Pamela," the Marshall said, "I don't like this any more than you do, but there're some pretty serious charges being made against Slade."

"I'm not trying to stop you from asking him any questions," Pamela said, not backing down an inch. "Slade has

350

nothing to hide, but I don't see why you want to take him into town."

"I just told you."

"Well, I don't believe you. I think you mean to put Slade in jail and send him back to Texas whether he's the man they want or not. Besides, who's to say this Ben Warren isn't the man they're really looking for?"

"Because he doesn't fit the description any more than you do."

"And why should you believe a description from people you don't know?"

"I know Mongo Shepherd and Jud Noble."

"But Mongo is trying to get my land," Pamela said grasping at straws. "We told you at the time Slade couldn't have fired that shot. There were dozens of witnesses who saw him in camp all morning."

"But we don't know when Mongo was shot."

"He was shot hours before Slade left," Pamela said. "I've seen enough wounds to know when one is fresh."

"I still have to take him into Maravillas," the marshall said. "I only want to ask him a few questions and let this man get a look at him. As an officer of the law, I can't do any less. There's a warrant out for his arrest. I'll let him come right back if this man can't identify him."

"No!" Pamela cried. She whirled, grabbed the rifle from her saddle, and pointed it at the marshall. "Run, Slade," she cried. "I'll hold them both here until you get away."

"Now, Pamela, you . . ." the marshall began.

"Put the rifle down," Slade said. He no longer looked at Dave or the marshall. Just at Pamela. "I have to go with the marshall."

"But I don't trust this Ben Warren."

"To be frank, neither do I, but I can't run away from questions like these. Not if we ever hope to have a decent life together."

"What?" Dave demanded. Her disclosure had shattered

351

his usually unshakable composure.

"Slade and I are going to be married," Pamela said.

"And we plan to stay right here," Slade said to the marshall. "So I can't be running off to the hills every time you decide to drop by. Will you saddle me another horse, Dave? Mine's about done in."

"Sure," Dave said, and he led the hammerhead dun away. The horse bit him.

Pamela still held the rifle on Marshall Alcott. "I don't think he ought to go with you," she said, anger, and the marshall thought hatred as well, flashing from her eyes. "Trouble has plagued him from the moment he set foot on this place. He would have been gone long ago if I hadn't virtually forced him to stay."

"You told me someone shot at him when they tried to burn your barn."

"And Mongo picked a fight even though he knew Slade's shoulder was injured. He helped me through the roundup, he went after those people who shot at Amanda and Frederick . . ."

"You didn't tell me about that," the marshall said.

"Why should I? There's been no end to the things that have been happening. And you haven't done anything to stop it."

"This really isn't my jurisdiction, not this far from town."

"Then you've got no right to arrest Slade."

"I'm not arresting him."

"Aren't you requiring him to go with you?"

"More or less," the marshall admitted.

"Then there's no difference. Who's going to protect me and the ranch?"

"They won't bother you," Slade told her. "They're after me right now."

"What are you talking about?" the marshall demanded.

"I'll tell you later. We'll have plenty of time to talk." He turned to Pamela. "Put up your rifle. I can't kiss you with you pointing a barrel at my chest."

"Oh Slade," Pamela cried and threw herself into his arms. "Why didn't you run away when you had the chance?" The rifle clattered unheeded to the ground.

"When I decided to marry you, I decided to stop running. If I run now, you'll never see me again. Is that what you want?"

"No, but I don't want you at the mercy of some stranger. How do you know what he'll say?"

"I won't until I face him. Now listen to me for a moment. I don't want you to leave the ranch *for any reason*. Tell Dave to find Gaddy and send him back. And I want you to bring Belva up to the house. I don't want you here alone."

"I'm not afraid."

"But I am."

"Slade, what's going to happen?"

"I don't know, but I do know I'll be back. Nothing is going to keep me from you."

Marshall Alcott managed to busy himself readjusting the cinch on his saddle. He didn't like having to take Slade into town, but he preferred it to watching people kiss in public. He just didn't understand why respectable men and women couldn't save that sort of thing for the privacy of their bedroom. He hoped he wasn't too old-fashioned, but these modern morals were something he just couldn't get used to.

"I'm going to hold you personally responsible for Slade's safe return," Pamela said to the marshall. "If anything happens to him, I'll kill you."

"For a woman who doesn't believe in violence, you're sounding rather bloodthirsty."

"You're damned right, I am," Pamela said, surprising Slade and the marshall by the vehemence of her language. "Somebody killed my father, and now Slade's in danger. I never knew what it meant to lose someone you loved because of somebody else's greed, hatred, or carelessness. But I know now, and I guess I'm just not as much of a humanitarian as I thought. Someone killed my father. I mean to see that man

353

dead. The same thing holds for you if anything happens to Slade."

The marshall was silenced. Whatever he had expected when he came out to take Slade in, he hadn't expected to run into the flood-tide of hot emotion he had uncovered this afternoon. And he didn't like it. People could be dangerous when they got worked up, and a wronged woman could be more dangerous than a man. Partly because no one expected it of her. To look at Pamela, who would think she could be dangerous? But the marshall needed only one look to know she meant what she said.

Let anything happen to Slade and somebody was going to get hurt.

"While I'm gone you can decide where you want to spend your honeymoon," Slade said to Pamela, trying to ease the tension. "The marshall and I will deal with Ben Warren."

"Don't you patronize me, Slade Morgan. I've taken all the handling I'm going to take. For days you've been telling me that *a man has to do what a man has to do,* that there are things in this life worth fighting for, even worth killing for. Well, I finally agree with you, so don't you start backing down on me now just because you think it's more suitable for a man to do the killing. A woman can suffer just as much as a man, more probably, so I have just as much right to pull the trigger as you."

"Now Pamela . . ." the marshall began.

"Not another word out of you, you traitor," she spat, turning on the marshall. She stooped to retrieve her rifle and came even closer. "It's all your fault, you and your determination to believe any stranger that happens along, just because he's a man rather than me. You bring Slade back without a scratch on his hide, not even one do you hear me, or I'll make sure you leave here in the back of a wagon."

Tears hovered in her eyes. Slade started to step forward then changed his mind.

"Here's your horse," she said as Dave came up leading a

large-boned sorrel gelding. "Go if you have to, but if you're not back here before noon tomorrow, I'm coming into town after you." She grabbed Slade, gave him a quick, fierce kiss, and ran inside the house.

"I guess you get to unsaddle her horse," Slade said to Dave.

Alcott would have been disgusted if anyone had called him a romantic, but even he considered that a particularly prosaic response.

"Make sure she has Gaddy and Belva with her at all times. She's too upset just now to know what's best."

Dave nodded his agreement, and Slade swung into the saddle. "Let's be going if we must. I've been riding all morning and I'm anxious to have this done with."

They didn't talk for the first few minutes. Oh, Marshall Alcott spoke often enough, but Slade didn't answer him. The marshall studied Slade's face, but he couldn't decide what he thought of him. He was undeniably handsome. No wonder Pamela was crazy about him. If he was only half as good as she thought, he was surprised he didn't have dozens of females offering to give him their ranches and just about anything else as long as he married them.

He wondered if Josh White would have preferred him to Mongo as a son-in-law. And just as soon as he decided that he wouldn't, he realized that Slade was exactly the kind of man Josh had been himself. They might not have gotten along, but he would surely have respected him.

That is if he wasn't a killer.

And Marshall Alcott couldn't believe that either. He'd had occasion to be around a number of killers in his time, some of them female too, and Slade just didn't fit. There were some so good looking you couldn't believe they could be evil. Some acted so pious you'd think they passed up a calling in the church to go out and murder. Then there were some so quiet and mousey you'd swear they were scared of their own shadow.

But none of them rode tall in the saddle like Slade; none of them looked you square in the eye without flinching; none of them gave him the feeling that here was a man who would stand by you no matter what the odds; none of them was the kind of person for whom Pamela would have decided to stay in Arizona rather than go back to Baltimore. There was something missing here, and he didn't have any idea what it was.

"I can't let you take me into town," Slade said unexpectedly, breaking into the marshall's reverie. "If I do, I'll be killed."

"Now who'd want to do a thing like that?" the marshall asked. He knew Slade was up to something and he became very alert.

"If I told you, you wouldn't believe me."

"Try me."

"Let me try you with something else first. Would you like to know what's been going on these last few months?"

"Everybody would."

"Okay. Some time back, one man looked around him and saw two million acres of grazing land, the best of it owned by Josh White, and asked himself how he could get it for himself."

"And what did he decide?"

"Probably that it couldn't be done. So things remained real quiet until Mongo came in with his herds and gave him the opening he needed."

"I was wondering when you'd get to Mongo." His disgust showed how little credence he put in Slade's words.

"Oh, he's not the man, just the pawn."

"Mongo, a pawn?" The marshall became interested again.

"He didn't know it. In fact, if I hadn't known Mongo's type so well, I might never have realized there were two people at work here."

"Two?"

"Yes. The real villain was here long before Mongo arrived."

The marshall didn't know what to say, so he said, "Go on."

"Mongo's herds put pressure on everybody. All the ranchers had reason to want to be rid of him just as he had reason to want to be rid of them. When he started paying court to Pamela, they realized he didn't mean to leave. Everyone could also see his real objective was the Bar Double-B."

"But Mongo's not a killer."

"I agree with you. He's not above burning a barn or two, shooting at cowhands, branding mavericks, or swimming his herds across the river, but he's no murderer. The other man is. He knew why Josh White was going to Santa Fe. That was his chance. He followed him, and because Josh knew him, he got close enough to kill him. He buried the body and the horse because he didn't want them found until much later, if ever."

Slade paused. The marshall waited patiently.

"I imagine he planned to sit back and see what Mongo did. About that time I arrived on the scene and made things even easier. Mongo tried to burn the barn and brand mavericks. I got into a fight with him and dared anybody to put their cows on Bar Double-B land. Everything was all set for an explosion at the roundup."

"Why didn't it come off?"

"Me again. First day there, I saw six men, one from each crew, talking together under a tree. They were obviously meeting secretly, and that started me thinking there might be more to this than Mongo, that somebody was wanting to cause trouble for everybody. I made sure I was never out of sight of at least two people, and I made Pamela stay in camp. That way he couldn't do anything to us, or to somebody else and blame it on us."

"Then who shot Mongo?"

357

"He did. It was a desperate attempt to start trouble. My cinch is loose," Slade said and pulled up. "I need to tighten it."

"Don't be fool enough to try anything," the marshall said.

"What could I do on foot without cover?" Slade asked as he dismounted, his tone openly sarcastic.

"You never know."

Slade started to readjust his cinch and the marshall relaxed.

"What was your villain planning next?"

"To get rid of me. I was supposed to stay just long enough to start trouble. Either I was to be killed, blamed for a killing, or drift on. When Pamela and I fell in love, it changed everything."

"Is that why you said you'd be killed if you went with me?"

Slade stopped pulling on the cinch and rested both his hands on the saddle where the marshall could see them.

"There never was anybody in Brazos named Ben Warren. Somebody's set me up."

"Then you are the man they're looking for."

"What name did this fella give me?"

"Slade Morgan. What else?"

"My real name is Billy Wilson. That's what anybody who grew up with me would have called me. They might have told you I was calling myself something else now, but they would have asked for Billy Wilson."

"Did you kill those men?"

"They were trying to kill me. I had some money, quite a lot as it happens, and they seemed to think they'd enjoy spending it more than I would. They killed an innocent kid and dynamited the soddy where I was hiding."

"If you're so almighty good with a gun, how come you didn't kill them first thing?"

"They knew me and stayed out of sight. It took me four days to get the three of them. In the meantime, Joe died."

"If what you say is true, then why the warrant?"

"Their father is a judge. Their uncle is the sheriff. There were no witnesses. Their sister told them about the money. Now you see why you have to let me go."

"I see you're in a heap of trouble, son, but there are some serious charges to be answered. If what you say is true . . ."

"They'll hang me in Brazos. I probably won't even get a trial."

"Hurry up and finish with that cinch," the marshall said irritably. He wanted to believe Slade, but when you looked at everything he said in a critical light, it had to be the most preposterous farrago of lies he had ever heard.

"I'm done," Slade said, and suddenly the marshall noticed the gun in his hand. "I'm sorry you forced me to do this, but I can't go any farther with you."

"Shoot me, son, and you'll be in even worse trouble."

"I don't plan to shoot you, but if you force me, let me warn you I can disable your shooting hand and hardly break the skin. It's obvious you don't believe a thing I've said, so I'm going to have to prove it to you."

"Do you know who's responsible?"

"I didn't before, but I do now. It's the same man who hid this pistol under my saddle."

"Do you take me for a fool? That must have been Dave's doing, misguided though it was. He's the most loyal foreman any man ever had."

"That's probably what Josh White thought, and it got him killed."

"Then why should he help you? If Pamela's going to marry you, he'll lose the ranch in the end."

"This gun opens up all kinds of possibilities. You could kill me as I try to escape. That would end the trouble, but the way I shoot, I could kill you. That would also end the trouble because I would *really* be guilty of murder this time and I would have to leave Arizona. Not totally satisfactory because I'm bound to want to see Pamela again. I'd most certainly try to get back to the ranch, or at least convince her to meet me. I'd be a fugitive. They could shoot me with the law's blessing."

"She'd be a fool to meet her father's killer."

"But I didn't kill Josh White, and Pamela believes me."

"The more fool she."

"Don't ever call Pamela a fool. And if you want to be worthy of that badge, learn never to discount the intuition of a truly good woman. I imagine Dave's men are already on the lookout for me. It might not be too difficult to kill me, especially if my attention is on something else. For your information, I don't think Dave Bagshot's ambition is limited to Josh White's ranch. The other ranchers have been having their men shot at, their range overrun with strange cows. Start a range war where all the ranchers are somehow killed, and Dave could step in and take over. But there's no point in going on. You clearly don't believe me. . . ."

"I certainly don't."

". . . so I'm going to have to come up with the proof myself. I'm afraid I can't do that from inside your jail. I'd find it even more difficult from the inside of a pine box."

"Don't waste your breath telling me how anxious you are to find proof against Dave. You'll be in California before the week's out."

"You know, for a man who's been a successful marshall for close to twenty years, either you don't know much about people or you've drawn a complete miss on Pamela and me. I killed those men because they tried to kill me first, but I'm through running now. I love Pamela. I mean to marry her and raise a family. And I mean to do it right here."

"This is no way to begin, escaping from an officer of the law at the point of a gun."

"You give me no choice. It wouldn't do either Pamela or me any good for you to tell her you were wrong about me when you came out to tell her somebody shot me dead in my cell."

"I can protect you."

"Maybe, maybe not. Either way, I'd still have no proof of my innocence or Dave's guilt. And nobody knows everything I know. I didn't even tell Pamela because I wasn't sure until I found that gun."

"That's pretty slim evidence."

"It's as much as you've got on me, but I don't have time to give you the rest of it. He may be waiting for us along the trail. That's one man I don't trust. I have a feeling he shoots nearly as well as I do. Now I don't like to do this, but I'm going to have to ask you to step out of the saddle and give me your guns."

"What kind of man are you to take a man's horse and guns and leave him in the desert?"

"I need to make sure I get away, and I don't want you shooting at me from behind. I'm going to leave your horse a little ways down the trail, just far enough to make sure you don't follow me. I may leave your guns too. I haven't made up my mind about that yet."

"You realize that by doing this, you have made yourself an outlaw in the eyes of every law-abiding citizen in the territory," Marshall Alcott said. "They'll all be out to find you."

"By that time I hope to have enough evidence to show you that you were wrong."

"Look, young man, why don't you give me back my gun and go with me quietly? I'm right fond of Pamela, and I'd hate to see her in trouble. According to what you say, she's smack dab in the middle of a great bunch of it. I promise to look into these charges of yours."

"I can't take that chance. You'd probably let Dave sweet-talk you into thinking everything I've told you is a lie. Up until now, he's been too smart for me. If he hadn't left that gun under my saddle, I still wouldn't be sure he was the one. You'll be more likely to trust him than me. And if you decided to take me back to Texas . . . No, I think I'd rather have things in my own hands. Now give me your guns. And remember, in case you get any ideas, I can shoot your watch

361

off and never scratch your skin."

"You're making a big mistake."

"I made my mistake when I didn't turn away from the Bar Double-B. After that, everything else was in the hands of Fate."

"I'll get terrible blisters if I have to walk far," Marshall Alcott called out as Slade started his horses forward.

Slade laughed unexpectedly. "Next time you come out to the ranch, ask Pamela about my feet when I walked into her valley."

"Damned fool boy," Alcott muttered as he started walking. "And I liked him, too. How does he expect anybody to believe such a cock-and-bull story, especially with him running away like that? And without a shred of evidence either. Dave Bagshot's never done a suspicious thing in his whole life."

But the Marshall wasn't so sure of that when, a short time later, Dave came riding up unexpectedly. Instead of coming down the trail from the ranch, he emerged from the low hills. Alcott looked up at those boulder-strewn slopes and felt a deep scowl between his eyes. He knew that a few miles farther, those slopes closed in on the trail. He didn't like the idea that came to his mind, but in light of what Slade had said, it made sense. Anyone hidden up there would have a perfect shot at a passing rider.

"What happened, Marshall?" Dave asked. "Where's Slade?"

"Morgan had him an extra gun. Caught me by surprise."

"He take your horse, too?"

"Said he'd leave it up ahead. Didn't want me following him too soon."

"When did all this happen?" Dave scanned the horizon as though he hoped to catch a glimpse of Slade disappearing over a ridge.

"Barely half hour ago. Too late to go after him now. You mind giving me a ride? These boots are killing my feet."

Dave gave him a hand up. The marshall got the feeling Dave wanted to leave him on the trail, but he was soon settled behind the young man.

"What are you doing out this way?"

"I was on my way to meet Sid. When I saw you walking, I knew something was wrong."

Alcott didn't know why he didn't tell him that Slade said Dave had left him that gun. He hadn't done anything really suspicious, but Dave's showing up just as Slade had said he would was too pat. Maybe he was a fool for not trusting a man who in five years had given him no reason to distrust him, but Alcott decided to keep Slade's confidences to himself for the time being.

"You ought to leave here this minute and not stop until you reach Baltimore," Belva was telling Pamela. "With all this shooting and killing going on, there's no telling what'll happen next."

"I can't leave Slade," Pamela said, hardly aware of the young woman's words. Slade and the marshall had only been gone for thirty minutes, but she was crazy with worry. What were they going to do to him? She wasn't worried about Mongo and Jud's accusations, but suppose this Ben Warren identified him as the man from Brazos? Would Marshall Alcott insist upon sending him back to Texas?

"That man's been taking care of himself for a long time. And if I'm any judge, he'll get himself out of this scrape, too. It'll take more than your marshall to hold him in a jail. It's yourself you ought to be worried about."

"But I'm not in any danger. It's Slade the sheriff arrested."

"Why are you so stubborn?" Belva asked, her voice rising in frustration. "Didn't you hear what that man of yours said?"

"What do you mean?" Pamela demanded.

"Nobody cares about Slade, not really. They're after this

ranch. Your father's dead. There's only one thing keeping any man who wants this place from riding in here and claiming it. *You.* Nothing else. I heard Slade tell you that time and time again."

"What are you trying to say?"

"Somebody wants this place, and they mean to have it one way or the other. If they have to kill you to get it, they will."

"But I can't leave. This is all I have. I do know enough to realize that a poor woman is a forgotten woman, especially in the East."

"If you insist on trying to keep this place, go to Santa Fe and hire some gunfighters to hold it for you. But you stay away. There's going to be a fight soon, and a lot of people are going to be dead when it's over."

"How do you know all this?" Pamela demanded, aware that Belva knew more than she was telling. "If you know anything about what's happening to Slade, tell me."

"You don't ever listen, do you?" Belva said, completely out of patience. *"It's not Slade they're after. It's you!* It's your ranch."

"Who is *they?* Tell me if you know."

"I don't know nothing for sure," Belva replied.

At first Pamela thought she was merely sulking, but then she realized she saw fear in the girl's eyes. Suddenly she remembered Slade's words. "Who are you afraid of, Belva?"

"I don't know no names," the girl insisted, "but I do hear things. Dave and the other boys, they talk around me without watching what they say. There's going to be a fight soon. A big one."

"What do you mean? Is it Mongo?"

"It's everybody. When it's over, all the ranchers will be dead."

Pamela felt a chill of fear course through her. "And then?"

"One man will have everything. He'll have you, too."

"Who, Belva? Who is this man?"

"I don't know," she replied. She started to back away.

"You do know." Pamela grabbed her by the arm. "I'm not going to let you go until you tell me."

"I can't."

"Yes, you can. And you're going to tell me. Slade's life may depend on it. I don't really care about the rest of the ranchers, or the ranch if it comes to that. All I care about is Slade, and you're going to tell me if I have to beat it out of you."

"You won't hurt me because you're too soft. But *he* would. He'd beat me to death if I whispered one word. That's why I'm leaving."

"But what about the baby?"

"It's because of the baby I'm going. I don't care much for myself. I ain't never been worth much, but I want things to be different for my baby. I found me somebody who'll care for me and it. *He* doesn't. He only wants to use us."

"What are you talking about?"

A smile of affection momentarily banished Belva's haunted expression. "I like you, Miss White. You got spunk, but you're in too deep. Leave. Let your man handle it. He'll find you when it's over."

"I can't. I've got to be here when he comes back."

"Then you're a fool, and I can't do nothing for you."

And with that declaration, Belva marched out of the house.

Chapter 21

Slade stared down at his cup of coffee. Once again he found himself driven out into the wilderness, a fugitive from justice. It hardly mattered whether the charges were just. By now there probably wasn't anybody but Pamela who believed in his innocence. You can't be called a killer but so many times before people start to believe what they hear.

Escaping from the marshall was bad enough, but he could have gotten around that. The accusation that he shot Mongo was more difficult, but it was the warrant and the offer of a huge reward that could turn him into a permanent fugitive and destroy any chance he had of building a life with Pamela. With a thousand dollars riding on his head, it was only a matter of time before some sharp-shooting bounty hunter would come looking for him. Even the Bar Double-B crew might be tempted by that much money.

And then there were the people anxious to make a reputation by killing a famous gunman. That reward alone would make him famous. There couldn't be more than two or three outlaws in the entire West with that kind of price on their heads. This guy claiming to be Ben Warren might be an outlaw himself, one who was clever enough to have the marshall do his looking for him. It didn't seem there was any way he was going to escape being Billy Wilson.

And as Billy Wilson, he couldn't marry Pamela.

The thought of living without Pamela made Slade feel physically ill. It was no longer just the loss of a home, a wife, a community he could belong to. It meant losing the woman he couldn't live without. It might be easier just to go back to Brazos and let them hang him. Then it would all be over. There'd be no dreams turned into nightmares by the memories of what he'd lost. He wouldn't be reminded by every wife and child he met of the price he had had to pay. He wouldn't have to go on looking for happiness that was never going to come.

Hell! If he ever *did* go back to Texas, he'd kill every Briarcliff he could find.

Stop it, Slade told himself. He was falling into the old familiar pattern of despair, the same feelings of hopelessness which dogged him before he met Pamela. Things did look pretty grim, but he was still alive, he had his freedom, and Pamela loved and believed in him. He wasn't giving up, not when the reward was being able to live his life with Pamela at his side.

He would first concentrate on clearing up the accusations that he had shot Mongo and killed Josh White. He'd save Texas for later. There had to be a solution there, too. Maybe Pamela's idea about a lawyer was a good one. He'd have to think about that, but not at the moment. Right now he had to concentrate on proving to everybody, not just Pamela, that Dave Bagshot had shot Mongo Shepherd and killed Josh White.

And he had to make sure Pamela wasn't his third victim.

"All the boys say he's got to be guilty," Gaddy said, his mouth full of fried ham. "Otherwise, why would he have pulled a gun on the marshall?" He reached for another biscuit and covered it generously with gravy. "I never knew you could cook so good, Pamela. I thought I was going to starve now that Belva's run off."

"I like to cook. Besides, there's not much else for me to do with my time."

"Wait until you get married and have a passel of kids. You probably won't never want to see a kitchen again. My ma sure didn't." Gaddy stopped, his food half way to his mouth. Large tears ran down Pamela's cheeks. He'd never seen her cry before. In fact, he'd only seen one grown woman cry. He'd thought that was as miserable as he could ever be, but watching Pamela stand there, her eyes closed and the tears streaming down her face, was worse. She had scolded him and ordered him about, but she had also taken care of him. Now when he had a chance to help her, he didn't know what to do.

"I'm sorry if I said something wrong," he mumbled. "I can finish eating when you're feeling better."

"Go on, eat your dinner," Pamela said, as she angrily wiped the tears from her cheeks. "I'm just worried about Slade. It's been two days and nobody's heard a word from him."

"Ain't likely to either," Gaddy said, regaining some of his composure. "The boys ain't sure about Uncle Josh, but they're all-fired certain he shot Mongo. They ain't too anxious to meet up with him."

"He didn't do any such thing," Pamela stated, indignant that anyone wouldn't believe in Slade as blindly as she did. "He'd be right here with me this very minute if the sheriff hadn't come after him. He killed those men in Texas in self-defense, but he didn't do anything else they say he did."

"Well he ain't going to get anybody to believe that now, not with him taking Marshall Alcott's horse and guns and leaving him to walk."

"Dave said he left his horse down the trail."

"Don't make no difference. Taking a man's horse is a shooting matter."

"Men!" Pamela announced with disgust. "There's not two

in the whole territory with enough sense to see what's in front of their faces."

"I do, and I can tell you that if that Slade Morgan comes sneaking around here again, he's going to leave with a seat full of lead. He treated you shabby, and I mean to tell him so."

"Gaddy Pemberton, if you so much as aim your rifle at Slade, I'll shoot you myself. And then if there's anything left of you, I'll throw you out in the desert for the buzzards. If you think I'm going to house and feed a blockhead who hasn't any better sense than to shoot the man I love, then you're not as smart as I thought you were. And that never was very much."

"I ain't talking about those killings. I never believed Slade did that, but he promised he wouldn't run out. I ain't much on family feeling, Ma and Pa were too cussed mean for me to feel kindly toward 'em, but you treated me better'n your own brother. What kind of man would I be if I let Slade get away with smirching your name?"

Pamela horrified Gaddy by giving him a big hug and an even bigger kiss. Stammering and blushing fiercely, he didn't know which to rub off first, the kiss or the wet spots on his cheeks caused by her tears.

"If you really want to help me, you can continue to believe in Slade," Pamela said drying her eyes once more.

"I do, but nobody else does."

"I know, and that's partly my fault. Almost from the first Slade told me what was going to happen, but I wouldn't believe him. Then Belva told me the same thing before she disappeared."

"What would she know? She's just a . . ."

"Don't say it, Gaddy Pemberton. If you ever want to eat a decent meal again, you'd better get outside and make sure nobody comes near here without you knowing. Slade once told me we'd been underestimating you all these years. Well, now's your chance to prove it."

"Slade said that?" Gaddy stammered, scrambling to his feet in confusion, pleased by Slade's unexpected commendation, bewildered by Pamela's uncharacteristic pugnaciousness.

"Why do you think he left you to watch the ranch while we were on roundup? He knew somebody was going to try to get in here."

"And I stopped them," Gaddy said, pride making his slender chest swell.

"Yes, you stopped them. Now do it again. Only this time you'll do it without my crystal Christmas bells."

"You're never going to forgive me for that one I broke, are you?"

"I'd let you shoot the entire set to smithereens if I could just have Slade back."

The tears started again, and Pamela ran from the room. She didn't want to make Gaddy any more uncomfortable than he already was. Besides, there was nothing he could do. It seemed that Slade was the only male in the whole universe who knew what to do for her when she was miserable.

Pamela felt the hand over her mouth, and she started up out of her sleep in panic. Belva and Slade had warned her she was in danger. Why hadn't she moved to another room? Why hadn't she put Gaddy to guard the house at night?

"It's all right. It's me." Even whispered, Pamela recognized Slade's voice, and she threw herself into his arms.

"I've been so worried about you," she said between laughter, tears, hiccups and rough, greedy kisses.

"You needn't be. It's a lot easier to hide than it is to find somebody."

"Just hold me," Pamela begged. "I never feel so safe as

when you're with me."

"I've got all night," Slade assured her. "I won't leave until dawn."

Slade had told himself he wanted to go slowly, that he would savor every moment as if it were his last. But the intoxication of having Pamela in his arms once more destroyed all his desire for restraint. He wanted to consume her in one mighty gulp.

Her kisses, as hot and moist as his own, ignited the fire in his loins. It was all he could do to keep from ripping her gown off then and there. Only by concentrating on the taste of her lips and the softness of her skin was he able to channel the hot desire that flowed from every part of him. The discomfort caused by the tightness of his pants was only a momentary problem.

He stripped down to the skin.

The sheets felt smooth and cool, Pamela's body soft and warm, her lips sweet and hot. His tongue plunged into her mouth, seeking, probing, rousing Pamela to an equally passionate response.

Pamela thought he smelled different, and that intrigued her. No scent of soap or fresh, sun-dried clothes clung to him. Instead he smelled of a heavy, musky odor, a scent she found much more suggestive of the man she had come to love. He was unshaven, too, but she liked the roughness. It was hard and abrasive like the man she loved.

But his touch was as gentle as the kiss of the wind. His fingertips caressed her neck and shoulders, teased her ears, played with her hair, traced her eyelids, tickled her lashes.

"I dreamed about you every night," Slade murmured as his lips laid a trail of kisses down her neck, across one shoulder, and down her arm. "It was agony."

Pamela held him even closer. It was probably the nicest thing he had ever said to her.

But she forgot about everything when Slade's lips found

371

and sucked one firm, sensitive nipple and a fingertip systematically tortured the other. Her body arched against him as the fire in her belly spread to her whole body and made her shiver like a leaf in the wind.

Without waiting for him, she wriggled out of her silk nightgown, more anxious to feel his roughness next to her than the smoothness of the world's most priceless silk. It never failed to amaze her that his mere touch could kindle such fierce desire, but it was impossible for her to hold him close enough or tight enough. It was also impossible for her to remain still. Slade's assault of hands and lips roamed over her whole body. She was aflame with wanting him. His fingers gently rubbed against the little swollen nub of her passion. It sent flames swirling through her blood. He gently dipped a strong finger inside her silken lips.

Her own hand sought out his throbbing manhood. Gently she caressed its length. Slade clinched as though he had been struck.

"Oh, God," he groaned. She pressed him gently, and he lost all control.

He entered her hastily, but she didn't care. She was more than ready for him. She didn't want to wait any longer. She had dreamed of him as well, had lain awake for hours, her body stiff with unquenched desire. That was all at an end now, and she rushed to join him on a cresting tide of ecstasy.

"I didn't know what had happened to you," she told him much later. "I was so afraid someone would find you. They've all turned against you Slade, even our own men. You're not safe here."

"I know, but that's not important now."

"Yes, but . . ."

"Listen to me," Slade said and kissed her into silence. "As much as I hate to admit it, I didn't risk my neck sneaking into

372

your bedroom just for the pleasure of lying in your arms. I came to warn you that Mongo is massing his herd along the river. He means to stampede them onto your land tomorrow night."

"I'll tell Dave. He'll gather the boys, and we'll meet you about dusk."

"No. You'll have to do this yourself. They'll never follow me."

"When I explain that . . ."

"It won't work, Pamela. Dave Bagshot is the man behind this whole mess."

"Dave?" Pamela echoed, stunned.

"Yes, Dave."

"But he can't be. He's been the hardest-working foreman Dad ever had."

"Probably because he had decided this was going to be his ranch some day."

"How? I wouldn't marry Dave, even if he wasn't already married."

"I'm not sure he was going to ask you."

"But why?"

"I haven't got time to explain. Just listen carefully and make sure you do exactly as I tell you."

Pamela was still so shocked by Slade's disclosure, she found it very difficult to pay attention. But she had to. He had risked his life to see her tonight. He had to be right, and she had to believe him.

"You got all of that?" Slade asked when he was through.

"I think so."

"Just remember, no matter what objections Dave raises, you must do exactly as I said. I don't think he'll disagree, this raid serves his purpose too well, but don't let him change the smallest detail. You won't be alone," he added in a softer voice. "I'll be nearby."

"You will be careful, won't you?"

373

"Nobody has more reason to want to come out of this with a whole skin than I do. I'd take on every cattle-hungry crook in the whole territory if I had to. I intend to be sitting on the front porch twenty-five years from now, waiting for my sons to ride in for dinner, surrounded by a bevy of daughters sophisticated enough to satisfy even Jane Austen."

Pamela gouged him sharply in the side.

Slade let out a whoop loud enough to bring the boys in from the range. Fortunately he muffled the sound by burying his face in the pillow.

"I've got to be going before you get us both caught. I don't imagine the marshall took too kindly to my leaving him on the trail. He'd probably be mighty pleased to have a second chance at me even if his Ben Warren isn't around to identify me."

"He didn't go," Pamela said. "Seems his business in California wasn't so pressing after all."

"Now I wonder why I'm not surprised?"

"You think he was lying?"

"I know he was. There wasn't anybody in Brazos named Ben Warren when I grew up. There weren't any Warrens at all."

"Be careful, Slade. If they want you so bad they'll pay people to lie about you, they'll do anything."

"*They* is Dave. You've got to realize that. Can't you believe me?"

"I'm trying, but I've known Dave for so long. I just can't believe he would kill Dad."

"Greed does strange things to a man. I imagine he's been wanting this ranch ever since he got here. The idea of taking it just grew on him gradually. He probably wasn't aware of it until he'd figured out how to do it."

"I still can't . . ."

"Don't try. Just believe in me."

"I have no trouble doing that."

374

"Good. I've got to go. Remember, exactly at seven-thirty tomorrow."

"I should have posted Sid at the ranch instead of that worthless Gaddy," Dave was saying to Pamela. "Slade wouldn't have gotten by him." It was just past eight o'clock. The Bar Double-B men had been in position for almost an hour.

"It's okay, Dave. Slade loves me. He'd never do anything to hurt me."

"Maybe, but I still don't like the idea of that man being able to sneak into the house right under our noses. It makes us look stupid."

"Right now I need you to worry more about keeping Mongo's herd on the other side of the river. If they overrun our range, you won't have much of a reputation to worry about."

Dave hadn't put forth any objections. Considering the fact that from the minute he had heard about Slade's escape he hadn't stopped trying to turn Pamela against him, she was surprised he hadn't objected to her following the strategy of a man he now stigmatized as a liar and a killer.

But there was no questioning that Mongo's cows were being held near the river. Anybody could see that from miles away. Mongo had picked a good spot. There was no cover for Pamela's crew for at least half a mile and nothing to hold back the invading cows.

Pamela stared into the night, but Mongo had chosen his time well, too. The clouds obscured the slender new moon. Pamela couldn't see anything. Secretly she gave thanks for the dark night. Slade's whole plan depended on it.

Pamela listened intently. Ever so faintly she heard the muffled squeak of wagons. She hoped Mongo waited long enough for her men to prepare their bonfires along the river

375

bank. Slade said they should light them the minute the cows hit the water.

An hour passed, then two, and still the men hauled every bit of brush, deadfall timber, anything that would burn to the river. Slade said that Mongo's herd would hit the water along a wide front. The shock of a fire right in front of them ought to turn them. If not, the men were to shoot the leaders and block their path with dead cows.

"I'm going to see how things are going down at the river," Dave said finally. "I can't just sit here wondering."

"Hurry back and let me know."

"Sure," Dave said and disappeared into the night.

Pamela was unprepared for the sound of Slade's voice coming out of the dark.

"You still don't believe he's the one who killed your father, do you?"

"Slade!" Pamela exclaimed, her voice a suppressed hiss. "Where have you been?"

"I helped the boys for a while. They couldn't recognize me in the dark. But for the last half hour, I've been waiting for Dave to go down and have a look for himself." He kissed her. "I've been wanting to do that for hours. Knowing you were up here just made it that much harder."

"Should you be here? Isn't it too dangerous?"

"It's probably the safest place I could be. Everybody is fully occupied elsewhere. Now, let's see what we can find to entertain ourselves until Dave gets back."

"You're shameless, you know that don't you, but I love you anyway."

"That's only fair, after all the faults I overlooked in you. Don't you dare go after my ribs again," Slade hissed imperatively when Pamela tensed for the attack. "I don't have a pillow this time."

"Coward," Pamela cried and subsided into his arms, her own arms tightly encircling his waist. "You don't intend to

376

abuse me like this after we're married, do you?"

"I take a solemn oath to treat you like a Dresden doll."

"I don't think I'd like that. I'm sure this is a major tactical error, but I rather like your rough ways. At least when you make love to me, I figure you're doing it because you really want to."

Slade only managed by the barest good fortune to catch his crack of laughter before it exploded into the quiet of the night.

"I'll keep that in mind for the first time you accuse me of mistreating you."

"You do that all the time. What are we going to do about the people in Texas?"

Slade took a moment to realize that Pamela had changed subjects.

"We can't spend the rest of our lives hoping no one from Texas will wander through and recognize you as Billy Wilson."

"I could go back and try to convince them it was self defense."

"I won't let you go back there. I'll follow you all over the world before I'd take a chance on them hanging you."

"What kind of man would I be to ask you to live with a husband who's wanted for murder? Have you thought about what it would mean to our children to have their father hunted for the reward? Hell, I might as well be a criminal."

"*My* children would be much happier having a father who was alive than one who was found innocent after he had been hanged."

"They wouldn't leave us alone, Pamela, not for that much money. Anybody can come along and shoot me and be within their rights."

"You wouldn't have wanted to marry me if you'd known about that warrant and the reward, would you?" Pamela asked.

"I'd have wanted to marry you if the whole army of Hell was on my heels."

"But you wouldn't have agreed to, would you?"

"I don't know. I really don't."

"Are you going to change your mind now?"

"No, but don't ask me what I'm going to do," Slade said fighting for time. "Let's get through this problem first."

"I'll follow you no matter where you go, Slade Morgan. I don't care if you're wanted or if the posse is on your heels. I intend to be at your side for the rest of your life."

Fortunately for Slade, they could hear Dave returning, and Slade had to go.

"Remember everything I said, and don't believe anything you hear about me." Slade kissed her quickly and melted into the night just as suddenly as he had materialized from it minutes before.

The first shots were fired just before two o'clock. They were accompanied by a chorus of yells and hoots. A moment later, five thousand cows came to their feet and stampeded toward the river. The thunder of twenty thousand hooves supporting twenty-five million mounds of flesh, bone, and sinew caused the earth to shake under Pamela even though she stood a half mile away.

The bobbing mass of white faces was visible on even such a dark night as this, and Pamela tensed as they neared the river. Would Slade's plan work? Would the fires turn back the herd?

Then, just as the first of the cows reached the river, the night sky erupted into a wall of flames. A pile of brush a half-mile long fed by oil tar from a seep back in the hills illuminated the night like a blaze of orange-red sunlight.

Blinded by the conflagration and panicked by their instinctive fear of fire, the stampeding herd came to a shuddering halt. The followers tumbled over the leaders until they were all caught in one deadly, milling mass in the middle of the river. Now it was the Bar Double-B's turn to hoot and yell and fire shots into the air. Some threw flaming brands into the water above the heads of the terrified cows. In no time at all, the herd turned and thundered out of the river, headed back toward Mongo's camp. Mongo's crew fled before them in a desperate race to escape the churning hooves that could pound a man's body into an unrecognizable mass in seconds.

They abandoned their camp and their belongings. The herd raced through the campsite scattering bedrolls, cooking utensils, and overturning a sleeping wagon. Mongo Shepherd was inside. But no cloven hoof threatened his life. He had already been shot to death.

The night had grown quite cold. Since they didn't need to conceal their presence any longer, Pamela had Dave build a fire before she sent him down to evaluate their success. She put on a pot of coffee.

Pamela was expecting Slade when he materialized at her elbow. She had remained behind for this very reason.

"For a girl who's more used to the parlors and ballrooms of Baltimore, you make a pretty mean cowgirl," Slade said, coming to stand next to her, his arm instinctively going around her waist, drawing her to him. "That ought to make Mongo stop and think before he tries taking anything else of yours again."

"You don't think it's over?"

"No. Dave's still here."

"Are you sure he's the one behind it? Couldn't you be mistaken? Maybe it's one of the other ranchers."

"You still can't bring yourself to believe me, can you?"

"It's not a question of believing you. I know you honestly believe everything you say. It's just that Dave acts so normal, just like he would if he were innocent."

379

"I know. And that's why I have to stay in hiding a little longer."

"Slade, no!" Pamela protested. "I can't stand having you out there, not knowing if you're all right, worried sick that someone has shot you and you're dying all alone."

"I don't want to stay away from you any longer than I have to, but I've got to find some proof of Dave's guilt. The man has been amazingly careful. He's at a stand now, but I don't think he'll give up. He's come too far. He may do something soon, or he may decide to wait a few years. I have to force his hand. I can't live here knowing he's just waiting for the first good chance to shoot me in the back."

"We could fire him. Then he would have to go somewhere else."

"Then you'd always doubt me. I can't live with that either. And there's still the man who killed your father. Do you want him to escape?"

Pamela didn't understand why everything had to pull her in different directions. Why couldn't Slade stay with her *and* find out who killed her father? "No," she said, knowing she couldn't keep Dave on as foreman, wondering all the time if he really was the killer, "I don't want him to escape. Will that be the end of it? Will we ever be able to live like normal people then?"

"I hope so," Slade said, but the Texas warrant hanging over his head mocked his words.

"Are you going to be all right?" Pamela asked. "I worry about you having enough to eat and being warm at night."

"I'm more used to those hills than I am to your house," Slade replied. "It's going to take some time to domesticate me."

"I kind of like you a little wild," Pamela said. She was beginning to experience the familiar sensations she always felt when around Slade. "I never would have believed I'd say this, but I'm glad you're not like Frederick."

"I told you he'd be here. He never could stay away from that woman." It was Sid Badget's voice. Dave and Marshall Alcott accompanied him.

Slade had drawn both guns before Sid had finished his first sentence.

"It would be a lot better if you would come along without any trouble," the marshall said.

"I told you why I couldn't three days ago, marshall. The reasons are still the same."

"Can't you talk him into giving himself up, Pamela?" the marshall asked.

"And have him identified as a killer by a liar?" Pamela said indignantly. "Slade told me there never was any family in Brazos by the name of Warren."

"Maybe he changed his name," Sid said maliciously. "A lot of men do that to hide their past."

"Like you did, Sid?" Slade said. "Is there something in your past you're trying to run away from?"

"We're not talking about me," Badget replied. But even in the dim light of the fire, they could see his color fade perceptibly. His voice didn't seem to be so strong now either. "Why don't we go for him, marshall? There're three of us and only one of him."

"There are two of us," Pamela said. No one had noticed she had picked up her rifle from where it lay against the rock.

"And Slade could kill all three of us before even one of us could get our guns out of the holster," Dave volunteered.

There was a commotion of several horses approaching. Mercer Isbel and Pete Reilly emerged from the dark, Jud Noble between them.

"There he is," Jud shouted, starting forward and then coming to an abrupt halt when he saw the guns in Slade's hands. "He's the one I saw coming out of Mr. Shepherd's wagon. I'd swear it on a stack of Bibles."

"You don't have to swear anything," Slade said calmly. "I

went to see Mongo to try and talk him out of driving his herds across the river. I told him he was playing into the hands of the man who killed Josh White. But he wouldn't listen to me."

"You never told us you knew who killed Mr. White," Mercer said to Slade.

"I told the marshall here and Miss White. They weren't inclined to believe me. I didn't see any point in telling anybody else."

"Who is it?" Mercer demanded.

"Slade believes Dave Bagshot is behind all the trouble," Pamela announced. "He believes Dave killed my father."

"That's a lie," Dave said.

"I can't believe it," muttered Mercer. "Dave wouldn't do anything like that."

"Morgan killed Josh White," Sid shouted. "I saw him on the trail that same day."

"Why would he do that?" asked Pamela.

"For the same reason he killed Mongo Shepherd," Jud Noble announced.

Pamela's face went white. "Mongo's dead?" she asked.

"Shot through the chest and head, and Morgan here did it. I saw him."

Just like Dad, Pamela thought.

"I admit I went to see Mongo tonight, but he was alive when I left him." Outwardly Slade appeared calm, but Pamela knew him well enough to know this new killing shocked even Slade.

"I don't believe you," Sid said. "Arrest him, marshall."

"There seems to be a small problem," the marshall observed dryly. "Did you happen to notice he's holding a gun on us?"

"He can't get us all?"

"He can get enough, and quite frankly I'm not anxious to die just yet."

"But you just can't let him get away."

"I don't notice him trying to go anywhere."

"Aren't you even going to ask Slade for his side of the story?" Pamela asked. "Are you always going to take everybody's word except his?"

"I haven't accused him of anything, Pamela. All I want him to do is come into town for questioning. You have to admit there are a lot of questions that need answering."

"There's only one question I want answered," Pamela said turning to Dave, "and that's who killed my father."

"But I thought . . ." Mercer began, but no one paid him any attention.

"Slade told me from the very first what was going to happen," Pamela said turning to Dave. "But I can't believe you killed my father."

"I didn't, Pamela. There's no man in the world I thought more of than Josh White."

"But Slade didn't kill him either."

"Then let him come to town with me," the marshall said. "Once we clear up this Texas business . . ."

"No," Pamela interrupted. "Not as long as you're willing to accept the word of a perfect stranger over Slade. Slade, get your horse and go. I'll hold them so you get a good start."

"Don't let her do it, marshall," Jud said, his body tense and waiting for the signal to draw. "We can get them both."

"Are you willing to fire on a woman, Jud Noble?" Pamela demanded, swinging the rifle in his direction, "because that's what you'll have to do."

"Move so much as an eyebrow, and you'll be dead before you hit the ground," Slade said quietly. Jud relaxed visibly.

"Pamela . . ."

"Go, Slade. You know there's no other choice."

"But . . ."

"For God's sake, Slade, for once in your life can't you do something I ask without arguing?"

383

"I'm not leaving you here alone."

"Do you think any one of us would hurt her?" Marshall Alcott asked.

"I've thought so from the very first. Pamela, Jud and Sid were two of the men I saw under that tree. They're both Dave's men."

"Looks like a Mexican standoff," the marshall said.

"No, it ain't," Gaddy said, suddenly rising from his hiding place. He pointed his rifle at the center of Sid Badget's chest. "I don't know who killed Uncle Josh, but it dang sure weren't Slade. And I ain't letting anybody put his neck in a noose."

"I don't know nothing about these killings," Mercer said, "but I ride for the brand. If Miss White says Slade is to be let go, then I'm with her."

"Me, too," Pete Reilly echoed. Both men came to stand next to Pamela.

Only for the barest moment did Dave show surprise, anger, or any other emotion. When he spoke, his face was a calm and impassive mask. "The boys have spoken for all of us, marshall," he said, taking his place in the line. Sid immediately followed.

"Go," Pamela ordered harshly, and Slade vanished into the darkness.

"Do you mind if I sit?" Alcott asked. "A half hour is a long time to stand up in these boots."

"You're just going to sit down and do nothing?" Jud asked incredulously. "You're letting a killer get away."

"What do you propose to do with six guns aligned against us? You may think Pamela White won't shoot, but I assure you she will. There's an old saying I've kept in mind for years. *He who fights and runs away, lives to fight another day.* You might say it's part of the reason I've lived so long. And I intend to go on living. If you want to try to stop him, go ahead."

But Jud wasn't foolish enough to attempt to go up against

such a superior force. "You wait," he said as he prepared to remount. "I'm going to get our boys together. We'll comb those hills until we find him."

"These are my hills," Pamela said. "Set one foot in them and you'll be carried out in a pine box. Besides, after the way your herd stampeded through your camp, I doubt you'll find enough men to round them up."

"You realize I'm going to have to arrest you for aiding a suspect to escape, don't you?" the marshall said to Pamela as the sound of Jud's horse's hoofbeats began to die away.

"Nobody's arresting Pamela for anything."

"Shut up, Gaddy," Pamela said bluntly, but there was a good bit of affection in her voice. There was also a lot of fatigue. "I don't care what you do to me as long as Slade escapes."

"Just as long as we understand each other," the marshall said. "Now, can I pour myself a cup of coffee? It's mighty chilly out here. The cold gets in my bones a lot worse than it used to."

Chapter 22

Slade had been gone for an hour. Gaddy still mounted a personal guard over Pamela, but all the other men had disappeared except for the marshall.

The tension and hostility between them dissipated as they shared a cup of coffee next to the fire. The last of the blazes along the river died down to red coals, and the night once again became a blanket of black velvet. "Do you think Dave killed your father?" the marshall asked Pamela.

"I don't know. Everything Slade says makes sense, but I've known Dave for years. I just can't believe he would do anything like that."

"But you also believe Slade?" he asked.

"He's never lied to me, even when I wished he had. Besides, he has nothing to gain."

"He got you. I consider that quite a prize."

"I'd thank you for the compliment, marshall," Pamela said with a teasing smile, "if I didn't know you were referring to the ranch. Would it surprise you to know that Slade has more than a hundred thousand dollars in the bank? He got it from selling his share of a carnival."

The marshall whistled long and low. "So that's the money those men were after?"

Pamela stared hard at Taylor Alcott. The challenge in her

eyes was unmistakable. "I won't let you take him back to Texas, no matter how many warrants you have for his arrest. Those men tried to kill him. They did kill the boy who went to get that money."

"You really love him, don't you?"

"More than anything on earth."

"And you don't worry that he's after your money? He could be lying about that carnival, you know."

"You don't know Slade very well," Pamela said. She laughed softly. "He spent the first few days after he got here telling me I was a narrow-minded snob and swearing he couldn't wait to get back on the road to California. If Mongo hadn't been stupid enough to send those men to burn my barn and then try to force me to marry him, I wouldn't have been able to keep him here."

The marshall tossed the last of his coffee into the dust and stood up. "Well, I must say I hope things turn out for him. I rather liked him myself. But there's too much against him for my taste. I like a man to be more forthcoming."

"He always has been. It's just that neither of us believed him."

"Perhaps," the marshall admitted. "But if you don't believe him . . ."

"I said I can't believe Dave would kill my father, marshall. There is a distinction."

"So there is. Nevertheless, why do you hold to his innocence?"

"Besides the fact that I love him and would lie to you and every living person to protect him?"

"Besides that," the marshall said with an answering smile.

"I have always been a rotten judge of character. People I like from the beginning always turn out to be a lot less admirable than I believed them to be. I thought the very worst of Slade in the beginning. So he must be the best of the lot."

"A woman's instinct," the marshall said disgustedly.

"Never discount feminine instinct. It'll lead you straight to

387

the truth many times where facts won't."

"Maybe so—Slade gave me the same advice once—but quite frankly I'd rather depend on logic. I get nervous when I have to rely on hunches. Now we've chewed the fat long enough. Slade has had time enough to be halfway to Mexico."

"You believe that?"

"No. Strangely enough I don't, but it doesn't much matter what I believe. We'd better be going. I'd like to get to town before everybody wakes up. It'll cause less talk."

"You're not taking Pamela anywhere," Gaddy announced. He had set quietly for the last hour, said nothing to anyone, but he came to his feet now, between the marshall and his horse, his rifle in his right arm.

"Now look, son, you don't want to get into the same trouble as your cousin."

"You can't arrest me for protecting Pamela. She's no suspect."

"Thanks, Gaddy," Pamela said, "but there's no reason for you to get mixed up in this mess."

"Yes, there is. I believe what Slade says even if you don't. I think Dave killed Uncle Josh."

"He has no proof, son."

"He's got just as much proof against Dave as you got against him," Gaddy replied, "and you tried to take him to jail."

"That's not quite what happened."

"It sure looked that way to me."

"It doesn't really matter how things look to any of us," Pamela interrupted. "Nobody has enough facts to prove anything. I may never know who killed Dad."

"Dave did it, I tell you," Gaddy insisted. "Slade said so. He'll find the proof. He said he would, and Slade keeps every promise he makes."

"That's right," Pamela said. "he does."

"We need to be going," the marshall said. "I don't like the

idea of the drunks gaping at you when we ride in."

"I told you, she ain't going to nowhere."

"It's all right, Gaddy. I have to go with the marshall."

"Then I'm going with you."

"Did you ever stop to realize that if Dave is guilty, I'm going to need a new foreman. I rather had you in mind for the job."

Gaddy acted a lot like a wild bronco had just kicked him between the eyes.

"You'd have to be in charge of the whole ranch. You might as well start learning how to run it now. You tell Dave that while I'm gone, you're the boss."

Gaddy looked so stunned Pamela was quite satisfied with her gambit, and she rode off with the marshall. But her ability to judge character was at fault again. Gaddy did dwell enraptured on the vision of himself as the universally admired and respected foreman of the Bar Double-B, the prop of his cousin and her ineffectual husband, his advice sought by all, his very name enough to cause hardened criminals to seek sanctuary many hundreds of miles away. But no matter how wondrous the dream or how much he longed for it to be a reality, Gaddy knew that in truth Pamela thought he had Mesquite beans for brains. She was just trying to flatter him so he'd stay safely at the ranch.

"She won't listen to me, but I know who she will listen to," Gaddy said to himself as he set off for his horse at a run. "I know where he's hiding. And that's more than you know, Cousin Pamela."

"Why *are* you taking me into town?" Pamela asked the marshall.

"I already told you."

"It was a good story for the others, but not for me. You have no grounds to arrest me and you know it. No authority either. You think Slade's going to try to rescue me. You plan to catch him then."

The marshall had the courtesy to blush. "If that's what you think, then why are you going with me?"

"Slade doesn't want me left alone. He said I was the only thing standing between the killer and his getting the ranch. He's kept a constant watch over me from the beginning. Well, if I'm in town in your custody, I'll be safe. He won't have to worry about me. He will be free to find the evidence he needs. *Then* he will come after me. And he will come. You'll see."

"She wouldn't listen to me," Gaddy was telling Slade. "She insisted upon going with the marshall."

"Then at least she's safe," Slade answered.

"But what about Dave?"

"What about him?"

"He didn't go back with the boys."

"What?"

"I stopped by camp before I came here. They ain't seen Dave nor Sid since the dustup at the river. And Jody swears he heard them ride off. You think they've gone to stir up Mongo's men to come after you?"

"Those men are without a boss. I doubt there'll be a half dozen of them left come morning."

"Then what's Dave up to?"

"I don't know, but it's got to have something to do with Pamela. Mount up. We've got some riding to do."

The hammerhead tried to take a bite out of him, and Slade struck him sharply across the muzzle. "I don't have time to play. You keep your mind on business. You can pretend you're a mountain lion all day tomorrow."

Men closed in on them from all sides. Pamela knew a moment of fear, but when she recognized Dave Bagshot, she knew only confusion. She refused to leave the marshall, but a man she didn't know led the marshall's horse away, and she found herself alone with Dave.

"Why did you do that?"

"You didn't think we were going to let him arrest you, did you? The whole Bar Double-B outfit would have come with me if it had been necessary."

Pamela was irritated, but she was also pleased that her crew felt so strongly about her freedom. "I don't suppose there was any way for you to know, but I wanted to go with the marshall. Well, never mind. The harm's done now. Where's Gaddy?"

"Don't know. Last time I saw him, he was in camp." There was a pause. "Why?"

"I just thought he might be with you. He tried to stop us when I left. I thought maybe he had told you where I was."

"I don't need help from Gaddy," Dave replied, and the edge on his voice made Pamela glad Gaddy hadn't found her foreman. If he had told Dave he was the boss while Pamela was gone, there would certainly have been trouble. "Unlike Slade, I think he's nothing but a green kid. You're going to have to get rid of him."

"You know I can't send him away. He's my cousin. Where would he go? Besides, Slade seems to know just what to do with him."

"Well, Slade won't be here anymore, and I don't like the kid."

Pamela had been riding just a little in front of Dave. She jerked around to face him. "Slade is coming back. He's going to find out who murdered my father. We're going to be married."

"Pamela, I know how you feel about that man, but you've got to face the fact that he's a killer."

"He is not," Pamela denied hotly.

"He killed those men in Texas, he probably killed your father, and he killed Mongo Shepherd."

"No."

"He is rather handsome. I can see how a woman could fall

for him, but he's nothing but a smooth-talking gunslinger."

"He's not, and if you call him a killer one more time you can draw your pay immediately. He's going to be my husband, and I refuse to allow you to talk about him that way."

"If he isn't on his way to Montana before morning, and I'm sure he's halfway to the Colorado border by now, he's not going to come out of those hills alive."

"He wouldn't leave. . . ."

"Mongo's men are looking for him right now," Dave continued as if Pamela hadn't spoken. "And first thing in the morning, I'm going to set every man I can spare on his trail."

"I forbid you to . . ."

"And after I tell the other ranchers how he killed Mongo in cold blood, I'm sure they'll send us some of their men as well."

"Listen to me!" Pamela raged. She was so mad she could hardly control her voice. "Slade is not guilty of murdering anybody, and I forbid you to send any of my crew after him. And if you hear of any of the ranchers doing so, you come tell me immediately. In fact," she said, calming down enough so she wasn't shouting, "I think I'll visit each one of them myself. I have to go into town anyway to explain this rescue mission to Marshall Alcott."

"You haven't listened to a word I've said, have you?" Dave asked.

Pamela was startled. She had never heard Dave use that tone of voice to anyone, but certainly not to her.

"I listened, but I disagree."

"You still think he's innocent?"

"I know he is. You ought to know me well enough to know I wouldn't marry a man who would do any of the things Slade's accused of doing."

"I heard you tell the marshall you were a terrible judge of character. You're wrong about Slade, too, but you seem determined to marry him anyway. I can't let you do that. I wouldn't be worthy of the trust your father put in me if I did."

"You have nothing to say about whom I marry," Pamela said in imperious tones which did full justice to Slade's accusation of snobbery. "I don't know what my father said to make you think you had the right to approve or disapprove of my actions, *any* of my actions, but let me inform you right now that my choice of husband does not require anybody's approval. Good Lord, I wouldn't even allow my father to tell me who to marry. If I had, I'd have ended up married to Mongo."

"A woman should never be allowed her head when it comes to choosing a husband. She should always accept the judgment of the men of her family."

"Well I don't have any family, or any men in it except Gaddy, so it doesn't matter what they would have said. I'm going to marry Slade."

"I won't let you."

"What did you say?" Pamela demanded. She stopped and turned back to face Dave.

"I said I won't let you."

"You can't stop me."

"But I can." Dave took the bridle of her horse and started forward. Pamela pulled hard on the reins, but Dave's hold on the bridle was stronger.

"What do you think you're doing? Let go of my horse."

"I'm going to take you to one of the line cabins. We're going to stay there until they find Slade. After he's dead, we're going to be married."

Pamela was speechless.

"I'm not likely to be such an easy husband as Mongo would have been. I don't like my women to get to thinking they're more important than they are, but I won't beat you. Not unless you try to run away."

"You're out of your mind. You're already married."

"Belva's my half sister," Dave explained. "She needed

some place to stay while she waited for her baby. I knew Josh would never allow her to stay here if he knew the truth, so I told him she was my wife."

"The truth?"

"The father of that goddamned little bastard won't marry her."

"This is not happening to me. It can't be," Pamela muttered, hoping the sound of her voice would wake her from a bad dream.

"You'll have nothing to complain of," Dave assured her. "I'm not as good looking as Slade or Mongo, but I won't run around on you. And I'm a good cowman. I'll make this place into the biggest ranch in Arizona. I always told Josh he ought to get rid of those other ranchers, take the whole basin for himself, but he was too squeamish, said he had enough land to suit him. I don't. I won't rest until the Bar Double-B range covers every acre from here to Maravillas."

The weight of Dave's guilt hit Pamela like a physical blow. "You murdered my father," she said, her voice hoarse with shock. "Slade was right all along, and I was too stupid to see it."

"There's no way Slade Morgan or anybody else can prove I killed your father." But he didn't say it like a virtuous man protesting his innocence. He said it like a man who didn't care what she thought.

"And you killed Mongo or had him killed."

"Slade killed Mongo. Jud Noble told you he saw Slade leaving Mongo's wagon. But I don't have any sympathy for him. His kind doesn't belong here. We'll take his herd and sell it in the fall."

"You're lying, Dave Bagshot. You've been planning to steal Dad's ranch all along. You were smart enough to use Mongo's attempt to overrun the range as a cover. You killed Dad and you killed Mongo. Now you plan to marry me and eliminate the ranchers one by one until you control everything."

"What would be so terrible if that were true?" Dave asked, and suddenly the calmness of his pale blue eyes made Pamela shiver with apprehension. "You're going to be the richest woman in Arizona. I won't mind spending money on you. As long as I run the ranch, you can buy all the dresses and have all the servants you want."

"I'm not going to marry you," Pamela declared. "How could you think I would marry my Dad's killer?"

"I didn't kill your father."

But Pamela didn't believe him. She had never really *looked* at Dave. He had been around forever, and she had just taken him for granted. But now that she did, she could see in him the man who would plot for years, even a man who would shoot himself in the leg so everyone would think Mongo was responsible. Come to think of it, no one had ever seen that wound. Only Belva, and she'd been scared ever since that night. Dave probably hadn't been shot at all, just pretended to be wounded so he could cause trouble and blame it on Slade.

Now he was meticulously going over everything that had happened, explaining why Slade had to be responsible for killing her father and Mongo, why she would thank him someday for what he was doing now, why she would be so much better off married to him than to Slade.

"I'm not going to marry you," she said, suddenly, explosively. "And if you ever touch me, I'll kill you." Simultaneously, Pamela struck at Dave with her crop and drove her spurs into her horse's side. Dave had relaxed his grip on the bridle, and the unexpected lash of the crop across his cheek and shoulder caught him by surprise. A second blow across his mount's nose caused his horse to rear. While he was fighting to retain his seat in the saddle, Pamela's mount galloped across the desert.

Pamela's horse was faster than Dave's. It also had more stamina, but she had two disadvantages. She didn't know the terrain as well as he did, and the darkness obscured the few landmarks she did know.

In just a few moments Pamela was lost.

Taylor Alcott didn't know why he should feel so uncomfortable about riding with these men, but there was something about the atmosphere he didn't like. Serves you right for getting mixed up in something outside your jurisdiction, he told himself. You should have stayed in Maravillas and let Junie Sykes bring you your beer. You're too old, and supposedly too smart, to go looking for trouble. Enough of it turns up at your front door as it is.

"You boys don't have to accompany me any further," the marshall said to his companions. "I'm convinced I can't arrest Miss White. Never meant to do more than use her to draw Slade Morgan in."

"The boss said we wasn't to leave your side for nothing," Sid said.

The marshall didn't know the other man. He was grinning, and the marshall didn't like what he saw.

"Why don't you go ahead and tell him," the grinning man said to Sid. "It'll be fun to watch him squirm." The man laughed like he knew a joke the marshall didn't, but judging from his expression, it wasn't a nice joke.

"Shut up, Reese. You know Dave will kill anybody who breathes a word."

"Who's going to tell him? The marshall here?" He laughed again. "How's he going to talk with six feet of dirt in his face."

"You goddamned fool," Sid said angrily. He turned in his saddle, but Reese's gun was drawn before he had completed the half-circle.

"If you got anything else to say, you'd better think on it first," Reese said. Pure meanness gleamed in his eyes. "I don't mind an extra killing."

"What's the point of killing me?" the marshall asked. He

was careful to keep his hands on the reins.

"You know too much. And you might guess the rest."

"You mean I might guess that Dave murdered Josh White to get him out of the way, used Mongo Shepherd to start a range war so he could kill some of the other ranchers, and then killed Mongo and blamed it on Slade?"

"I told you he knew everything," Reese said.

"He didn't know shit before you opened your goddamned mouth," Sid shouted and went for his gun.

Reese shot him through the heart.

"Now, it's your turn, marshall."

"Not yet," a voice from the darkness called out.

Reese whirled to face his unseen adversary, but before he could determine the direction of the voice, the night exploded with a burst of gunfire.

Reese fell to the ground screaming in agony. Slade had put a bullet across the top of each wrist and notched his earlobes. Reese would go to the gallows wearing the sign of a coward.

"Sure am glad to see you," the marshall said as Slade and Gaddy emerged from the dark.

"Thought you might be," Slade said jumping down from the saddle. With quick, sure movements, he bound the groaning Reese securely.

"For God's sake, have mercy," Reese begged. "You can't tie my wrists after you shot them to ribbons."

"Watch him, Gaddy, and if he makes even one move, shoot him between the eyes," Slade said as he got back in the saddle. "Here," he said to the marshall as he tossed him the dead man's gun and rifle. "We've got to find Pamela."

"You trust me?"

"Do you think I killed anybody?"

"Not in Arizona."

"That's all I ask," Slade said and spurred his hammerhead sharply in the side. The marshall had to hurry to catch up with him. The dun was a businesslike horse when he put his mind to it.

"Look, kid," Reese said as soon as the sound of the galloping hooves died away. "I've got money. Lots of it in my saddle bags. You can have it all if you'll help me get away from here."

Gaddy glared at him for a moment. Then he knelt down and pulled off Reese's boots. Next he pulled off his socks.

"What the hell . . ."

"I'm going to ask you some questions. And if I don't like your answers, I'm going to shoot off your toes," Gaddy explained as he pointed the gun at Reese's big toe. "I figure it'll be a short conversation."

"Now you're going, then?" the doctors asked.

Reese wanted to... that or quickly retire, but before he could open his mouth at the words, she was explained with a touch of panic.

"Let's go to the gaol and go down from her. He didn't put the presses which are watched up her first," Reese said. Up to the gallows. Perhaps the age of doesn't..."

"Say, simple, it's serious," the marshal said at slack and...

Gaddy then just frowned a little.

"I wish you were much too." Gaddy said pointing down. First she said. "With words. Her movements, the bound the pressing Reese too tired.

"No? Don't take no hurry," Reese begged. "You asked a lot of us, after you shot them to pieces."

"Watch him," Gaddy said. "It'll be easier even now," the shooting between the eyes." She said she'd got near to the radio. "Here," he said in the marshal as he tossed him the dead man's gun and rifle. "We've got to find them."

"No what?"

"Do you think I killed anybody?"

"She in Arizona."

"Easy, still," Reese said and spurred his horse into the shadow the side. The marshal had to hurry to catch up with him. "He'd just as him if he'd hang when he put his mind to it . . ."

398

Chapter 23

Even though she was desperate to get away from Dave, Pamela knew it was too dangerous to gallop a horse in the dark. She slowed to a trot, but pursuing hoofbeats still sounded behind her and she spurred her mount forward again. But caution made her slow down just a few minutes later. Her horse would almost certainly go down if she didn't. A fall in the dark could kill both of them.

She heard no hoofbeats this time, and Pamela allowed her horse its head. It seemed to know where it was going, back to the ranch she hoped. She no longer felt safe anywhere, not without Slade nearby, but at least at the ranch she would have food, shelter, and ammunition. After the time she went looking for Slade without any of those things, she knew how important they were.

She looked about her apprehensively. Her horse followed a trail that led into the hills. In only a matter of minutes, the trees closed in on her and turned the night as black as ink. Pamela knew her horse would warn her of any danger, but fear gripped her nonetheless. She couldn't even see his ears to know if they were pricked, always a sign that something lurked nearby.

The night was so still the muffled sound of the hooves on the hard trail seemed inordinately loud. Every so often an iron shoe struck a slab of rock sending a metallic ring echoing through the night like a warning bell. Pamela prayed Dave was nowhere nearby. The sky was overcast and the air heavy, but sounds could carry for long distances in the night.

Two hours later Pamela's cold and tired body sagged in the saddle. She no longer listened for approaching hoofbeats. Her horse continued to walk steadily. Pamela didn't know how much farther they had to go, but even now the approaching dawn was beginning to turn the sky gray. She hoped the coming of daylight would reveal some landmarks she could recognize.

She didn't know what she was going to do when she got home. How was she going to contact Slade? He couldn't reach her if she went to Maravillas, but would she be safe at the ranch? Would she find Gaddy there? If not, she'd be alone now that Belva had run away.

And how did Slade plan to prove Dave instigated all the trouble? The other ranchers, the townspeople, even her own crew, wouldn't accept him without proof. She doubted Slade would stay any place where everyone distrusted him.

She had to help him, but how? No one had come forward as a witness to Mongo's or her father's deaths. Dave had no alibi for those times, but then neither did Slade. Worst of all, two lying witnesses put Slade in the vicinity of both crimes.

And then there was the gunfight in Texas. Instead of getting better, circumstantial evidence kept piling up until it seemed insurmountable. How could she help unravel the tangle? She was convinced there was a solution if only she could find it.

Engrossed in looking for answers, Pamela failed to notice her horse's pricked ears or tensed body. Only when he whinnied did she recognize the danger.

But it was too late then.

Dave Bagshot appeared out of the darkness to block her path, his hand firmly grabbing hold of her horse's bridle.

"I figured your horse would take you back to the ranch."

Pamela didn't waste time with words. She slipped from the saddle, hit the ground running, and lost herself in the trees.

"Come back here, you fool," Dave shouted. "You could get killed."

Dave was following—Pamela could hear his boots strike the rocks as he ran—but she slackened her pace just enough to look for a place to hide. The carpet of soft needles under the pine trees deadened her footsteps, but light from the rapidly approaching dawn made it very difficult to hide, even among the tree trunks.

"You might as well give up," Dave called out. "You can't possibly cross that ridge."

Instinctively, Pamela looked up and her heart sank. Trees covered most of the ridges running back to the mountains. On this ridge, however, bare rock made the last fifty feet a nearly vertical climb. If she could move along the side of the ridge, perhaps she would find a hiding place or be able to reach her horse before Dave could catch her.

On she ran. She climbed over rocks, crawled on her belly under lightning-shattered trees, and squirmed her way through thick underbrush. Her breath came in ragged gasps now, but she didn't dare stop. Dave was much stronger than she was. He might catch up with her any minute. He had to be right behind her.

But he wasn't.

Even though she listened intently, Pamela couldn't hear a single sound. But this time she didn't trust the silence. She *knew* Dave was out there somewhere, just waiting for her to stumble into his arms. But where?

She looked down at the horses. They had run a short distance, stopping almost directly below her. If she could reach them, she had a chance. Dave must know that too. He would be watching for her, but she had no choice. He would find her easily once the sun came up.

Pamela edged down the slope, moving with extra care. She wanted no accidentally dislodged stone to betray her location. She strained her ears to catch any sound of movement, but the morning was quiet. Not even the birds had begun to sing.

She was so close she could almost taste success when Dave stood up from behind one of the boulders along the trail.

"You're a very predictable woman," he said.

Instantly, Pamela whirled and started back up the slope, but Dave pounced on her before she had gone ten feet.

"Let me go!" she demanded. "You might as well kill me here. I'll never marry you." She fought to free her wrists from his grip, but he was too strong.

"Oh, come now. It won't be so bad. You might even get to like me after a while."

"I'm going to marry Slade."

"If Slade's not dead already, he will be before morning. I've got all my boys looking for him."

Pamela struggled to keep fear from taking control of her brain. They wouldn't catch Slade, he was safe she told herself. No one could shoot like Slade. They wouldn't touch him.

"All my men carry rifles. No fool would get close enough for Slade to use his guns."

She couldn't restrain her panic so easily this time, but Pamela determined to remain calm. What kind of wife would she make if she fell apart in the face of trouble?

"Even if Slade were dead, I wouldn't marry you. I'd go back East."

"You have no choice," Dave told her. The coldness in his voice indicated he had finished trying to cajole her into accepting him as husband. "You're going back to the ranch and you're going to stay there. By now Sid is already paid off the crew and replaced them with men loyal to me. Your cousin's gone, too."

"You can't just keep me here. The marshall . . ."

"Did you hear those shots a while back?"

Pamela nodded, suddenly too fearful to speak.

"That was the last of your marshall. Now there's nobody to stop me from doing anything I want."

"The other ranchers?"

"I've got men on their crews, too. Before long they'll be fighting each other. They'll all be dead before spring."

"Then Slade was right all along."

"I didn't kill your father," Dave insisted, "but I've always wanted his land."

Pamela didn't know why he continued to insist upon his innocence—maybe he thought she'd be a more willing wife if she didn't think he killed her father—but he apparently didn't realize it would be even more impossible for her to endure marriage to him if he killed Slade. If Fate forced her to become Dave's wife, she would also be his executioner.

He dragged her to the horses and unceremoniously tossed Pamela into her saddle. But before he could climb into his own, she hopped out of her saddle and escaped into the woods again.

"Damn you," he said when he finally caught up with and wrestled her to the ground. "Let's see if a rope can teach you to stay where you belong."

"You can't teach me anything," Pamela replied, furious. "I'll fight you for the rest of my life."

"You'll change your mind when you see how easy things will be if you cooperate. Like I said, I don't mind spending money on you."

He tied the ropes so tight they cut into the soft skin of her wrists, but she refused to let him know he was hurting her. She had to concentrate on getting away, on helping Slade.

Neither one of them was prepared for the sound of Slade's voice coming suddenly out of the grey dawn.

"Let her go, Dave," he called out. "This is between you and me."

Pamela's heart soared with happiness.

"Slade, he means to kill you," she called out. She caught a glimpse of Marshall Alcott and her heart swelled with hope. If Slade had somehow managed to rescue the marshall, then he would rescue her, too.

But as quickly as hope blossomed, it withered. In a single incredibly swift movement, Dave whirled and fired. She saw Slade's body jerk and then pitch from the saddle.

She started toward him with a scream of soul-wrenching agony, but Dave yanked on the rope. She fell hard on the ground. When she looked up, Slade was gone. He wasn't dead. He must be terribly hurt, but he wasn't dead. She kept telling herself that over and over again as Dave hauled her to her feet and dragged her behind the trunk of a pine that was six feet straight through. He held her in front of him, close to his body.

Slade had thrown himself from his horse and crawled to shelter behind a boulder, clutching a badly bleeding wound in his side, cursing the streak of common decency which made him call out Dave's name instead of shooting him in the back.

"You stay here," he said hoarsely to the marshall who crawled up next to him just a few moments later. "I'm going after her."

"You can't. You're wounded. If you don't get a doctor, you'll bleed to death."

"Not if you bind it up as tight as you can. It ought to hold long enough."

One look at the expression on Slade's face told Marshall Alcott there was no use arguing with him. "All right, but take off your shirt. I'll be damned if I'll ruin mine."

"Dave's going to use her for a shield," Slade explained as Alcott ripped his shirt into strips and began to bind up his side. "I'm the only one who can shoot well enough to get him before he kills her."

"He wouldn't hurt Pamela."

"If he had a crew of tough gunfighters, he could probably

hold the ranch without Pamela. I don't trust him not to reach the same conclusion." A grunt of pain escaped Slade as the marshall roughly pulled the bandage tight.

"I'm not very gentle," the marshall apologized.

"Just make sure it won't come undone." Slade had himself under control now. No sound escaped his lips nor did his expression change.

Dave's voice called out from behind the tree. "Morgan, come out or I kill the girl."

"Don't," Pamela screamed. "He means to kill you."

The sounds of scuffling behind the tree galvanized Slade into action. "Keep him busy so I can circle around and get a shot."

"Be careful. I don't put much past him."

"I will. He's holding my future in his arms."

Slade worked his way along the trail, trying to find a way to get across without Dave seeing him. He ignored the pain in his side. He couldn't think of anything else until Pamela was safe.

"I think he's dead," Slade heard the marshall call out. "Your bullet caught him in the side."

"No!" Pamela cried. She whirled on Dave in the full frenzy of her grief, and for a moment she almost broke free. When he finally subdued her with a fist to her jaw, his face was covered in scratches and his groin throbbed painfully where she had kicked him.

"Drag him out where I can see him," Dave called out, breathing heavily from his exertions.

"Hell no," replied the marshall. "You tried to kill me once tonight. I'm not giving you a second chance."

"I'll kill Pamela."

"Go ahead. She's not my woman."

Dave cursed viciously. "Look, all I want is Slade. Drag him where I can put a couple more bullets into him and I'll let you go."

"You know I can't do that."

The pain in Slade's side cut so deep he feared he might fall and not be able to get up again. He managed to cross the trail while Pamela fought with Dave, but the effort cost him a lot of blood. The bandages held, but the heat of his own blood soaked through and warmed his hand. Somehow he had to keep the creeping weakness from claiming him for just a few more minutes.

He dragged himself up an embankment, but every inch was harder for him than the last. Finally he found a place where he could steady himself against a boulder. He could see Dave's head and shoulder. He drew his gun, but a dizziness came over him and everything spun before his eyes. Sheer will-power enabled Slade to clear his vision. Pamela's life depended on his being able to remain conscious just a few seconds longer.

He focused as Dave shifted position. Now Pamela stood between the two of them. Slade steadied his hand against the boulder and took careful aim, but Pamela began struggling once again. Slade didn't dare risk a shot at the precious moving target. An engulfing blackness threatened to sweep over him. He couldn't dredge up the strength to fight it off any longer. If he was going to do anything to help Pamela, he had to do it now. He took careful aim and fired.

Then the blackness swallowed him.

The first thing Slade felt was the pain in the side. Then he realized he was being carried. He might as well have been a side of beef for all the care they took to keep from putting pressure on his wound.

"He didn't look to be this heavy," Gaddy complained to Pamela as he and Taylor Alcott dragged more then carried Slade from his horse and into the kitchen. "You should have gotten Pete and Mercer to help."

"I would have if I'd known you were going to maul him," Pamela said holding the door open and then pulling out a chair to prop him up in. "If the ride home didn't tear open his wound, your rough handling has."

"I don't know how he can bleed so much and not be dead," Gaddy said, totally impervious to his cousin's strictures. "Hell, now I've got the stuff all over me."

"You wait until you're bleeding like a stuck pig, Gaddy Pemberton, and see if I lift a finger to save your worthless hide," Pamela scolded as she threw open cupboards and pulled out drawers looking for the things she needed.

"If it hadn't been for me telling Slade what Dave meant to do, you wouldn't be here now," Gaddy replied, his youthful pride affronted. "Neither of you," he added, including the marshall in his glance. "You didn't know where to find Slade."

"Then you let him go off by himself while you watched a man too wounded to move."

"Slade only grazed his wrists. He could have been out of the territory before morning."

"If you two could postpone this argument until Pamela can plug up my side, I'd appreciate it."

"You're conscious," Pamela cried, and threw herself at Slade.

Slade wasn't quite sure how he managed to keep from giving vent to a howl of agony when the pain in his side suddenly magnified itself a hundred fold.

"Oh my God!" Pamela cried, throwing herself backwards almost immediately. "I didn't mean to do that. I was just so glad to see you awake. You don't know what it's like to have seen you looking like the dead for hours and hours."

"It's okay," Slade replied, pain turning his lips white. "It was only a twinge."

Pamela laughed in spite of her worry. "You wouldn't admit you hurt if your life depended on it. I'd give a lot to hear just one good moan of pain."

A twinkle appeared in Slade's eyes. "Ouch," he said softly.

"What?" demanded Pamela, her eyes swiftly moving from

her work to his face.

"Ouch."

A laugh threatened to erupt from Pamela. "Is that all?
You get this awful hole ripped in your side, bleed over fifty
yards of mountainside, travel three unconscious miles on
horseback, and all you can say is ouch?"

"Ooowwww?"

After the strain of the last twelve hours, Pamela was on the
edge of hysteria. Unable to contain her laughter, it bubbled
up and spilled over. She was so helpless she had to lean
against the table for support.

"You all right?" Gaddy asked, completely at a loss to
explain Pamela's mirth.

"I think it's a private joke," volunteered the marshall.

"Well I don't think it's fair for them to keep it to themselves," Gaddy said, aggrieved.

"You'd better get used to it. Married people do it all the
time."

"Damn," Gaddy said in disgust. "I wanted him to stay, but
I never thought he'd go and get married." He said it with
such disgust Slade sputtered with laughter.

"Maybe it's not so bad," Gaddy conceded. "I never heard
him laugh before."

But Slade's laugh had turned to a yelp of pain. "That's the
last time," he said, embarrassed at his show of weakness, "at
least until this thing heals."

Pamela sobered immediately and resumed cleaning the
wound. "What happened to Dave?" Slade asked the
marshall, hoping to keep his mind off the pain.

"He's dead," Gaddy answered first. "Shot right through
the heart."

Slade turned white.

"My bullet killed him," the marshall added quickly. "I
figured you didn't need any more to worry about."

Slade's color improved even though an agonizing pain
radiated from his side.

408

"Your bullet laid open a gash along his shoulder and the back of his neck. It was the prettiest shooting I was ever privileged to see."

"Then why . . ."

"I got away but tripped over the rope," Pamela explained. "He had a knife."

"Then we can't prove he killed Mongo or Pamela's father," Slade said.

"Yes, we can. Gaddy got a confession from Reese Jerigan. I'm not sure how, but Reese kept mumbling something about wanting to save his toes."

Gaddy flushed but didn't explain.

"Reese said Sid Badget lied about seeing Slade on the same trail as your Pa, so I guess that just about clears everything up."

"Except Texas," Slade said.

"I don't think I'd concern myself overly much with Texas. Out here in Arizona we like to do our own thinking."

"Still . . ."

"We can worry about that later," Pamela said, gently interrupting. "Right now all I'm worried about is getting you well again."

"I could use a drink," the marshall announced. "I didn't get my beer yesterday."

"Give him anything he wants," Pamela told Gaddy and dismissed them both from her mind. "It seems this is where we started," she said to Slade as she started to wrap the clean bandages around his chest.

"I never could seem to keep out of trouble."

"I can handle trouble, but do you always have to get in the way of a bullet?"

"It's the only way I can keep you kneeling at my feet."

"I'm not kneeling, Slade Morgan. And even if I were, I wouldn't be kneeling *to you*. This is going to hurt."

"I didn't expect it would feel good."

"I just wanted to warn you. If you were to show any sign of

409

pain, I doubt you could live with yourself."

"I'd howl like a baby if it was the only way I could keep you."

"Don't you dare," Pamela said, ducking her head to hide a smile of happiness. "I don't want Gaddy bounding in here asking if I've taken a knife to you. I can stand your great stone face a little longer."

"Can you stand watching me on trial for murder?"

Cold fear paralyzed Pamela. "What do you mean?"

"If I'm going to stay here, I have to go back to Brazos. I can't raise a family with that hanging over us all the time."

"I know." And she did. She had always known, deep down, that he would someday have to go back to Texas.

"You're not going to argue with me?"

"Would it do any good?"

He shook his head.

"That's what I thought. But I am going to make some conditions."

Slade's eyes narrowed.

"I'm going with you."

"No."

"I'm not asking you. I'm telling you. I want to go as your wife, but I'll go any way I have to."

"Pamela, this is absurd. There's no reason . . ."

"But first we're going to hire a couple of Pinkertons. If anyone in that town knows or saw anything, they'll find it out. They'll also protect you when we get there. Then I'm going to ask Frederick and Amanda to help me find the best lawyer on the east coast. I want them to realize they're not going to railroad you into anything."

"And if I don't agree?"

"I'll let you bleed a little more. Pretty soon you won't have enough strength to object to anything."

Slade stared at her, his eyes dark and unreadable.

"I mean it Slade. I won't be shut out of your life ever again. I want to know when you're hurt. I want to know when

410

you're afraid. I want to know when you need help. And I want you to *want* to tell me."

"Pamela, I can't . . . I'm not . . ."

"I know it won't come easily." She smiled fondly. "You'll probably have to write me notes in the beginning, but it'll come. All you need is practice. And we can start by going to Brazos together."

"You really mean that?"

"I mean to be by your side for the rest of your life, Slade Morgan. I certainly don't intend to make an exception for a rotten little town like Brazos, Texas."

"Come sit here," Slade said, patting the seat next to him. It was early evening. They had finished dinner and were sitting on the porch watching the stars come out.

"What about your side?"

"If you sit down real easy, I think I can manage to get an arm around you."

"No, you don't. I won't have you breaking your wound open again. Suppose I put my arms around you instead?"

But when Pamela's arms held him only feather-tight, Slade slipped his arms around her and pulled her close. There was an immediate stab of pain, but he figured it was worth it. He tried to bend forward to kiss her, but that proved too much. The pain was excruciating. He inhaled slowly and deeply and relaxed against the seat.

"Aren't you going to talk about the moon?" Pamela asked, a mischievous smile curving her lips. "There must be something we haven't covered yet."

"Do you dare jest about the moon, woman?" Slade said with mock severity. "The night has many offspring, and not all of them are as kind as the moon."

"Are you threatening me?"

"Of course. You did say you wanted to be treated roughly, didn't you?"

411

"I knew I'd regret that. Now I'll probably be forced to bear dozens of children, have no say in running the ranch, and beg on my knees before you'll allow me a new dress."

"Do you want lots of children?" Slade asked, suddenly serious.

"Not lots, but at least one or two. What about you?"

"I don't really care as long as I have you."

"You don't think I would ever leave, do you?"

"It all seems too perfect. How often does a man get everything he ever wanted? More than he ever dreamed of?" he added giving Pamela's shoulders a quick hug.

"I won't have you getting maudlin, Slade Morgan. Not when I don't have nearly everything I want."

"And what might that be, Miss White?"

"First, I want to change my name to Mrs. Morgan."

"I think I can manage that."

"Then I want at least two boys, and a daughter," she added.

"I thought you only wanted one or two."

"I changed my mind. I also need someone to help me cook, someone else for the cleaning—I can't take care of you and the babies if I have to do everything else—and I think we ought to look around for some girl for Gaddy."

Slade couldn't see the glint of mischief in her eye, but he could hear it in her voice.

"Of course I don't have nearly enough clothes, I want a vacation home in Newport, and I want to spend every winter in New Orleans. Dad never had enough money—for some reason those disgusting cows seem particularly hard to turn into cash—but you've got all that lovely money sitting in the bank."

"Something tells me I ought to use it to buy out the other ranchers while I still have something left," he answered.

"Then I want to redecorate the house. I saw this perfectly lovely place in Philadelphia one time. I want the ranch house to look just like it. After that I . . ."

412

Slade kissed her into silence. His side reminded him that it was far from well, but Slade persevered. Now was no time to start admitting to pain.

"I want your kiss more than anything else," Pamela said. "And just think," she murmured, "it won't cost a cent."

"It'll cost me everything I own," Slade answered, "but I'll willingly pay."

He then proceeded to make a substantial installment.

Epilogue

Marshall Alcott pushed open the door of the Wagon Wheel Saloon. Junie Sykes had been laid up with the influenza for two days and there was nobody to bring him his beer. He walked up to the bar, waited for his drink, and then looked around as he took his first sip. There was only one person in the saloon, a young cowboy digging into a plate of beef and beans.

"Mind if I join you?" the marshall asked.

"Be glad of the company," the young fella replied through a mouthful of food. "It gets mighty lonesome on the trail. A man needs somebody to talk to besides his horse."

The marshall walked over and sat down. "Been traveling long?" he asked after another swallow from his glass.

"All the way from Texas."

The marshall felt himself tense, but he waited until the boy had chewed his mouthful of steak and washed it down. "You ever heard of a town called Brazos?"

"Funny you should ask that," the cowboy said. "I just came from there. Been having themselves a mite of a fracas. Wouldn't have missed it for anything."

"What was it about?"

"Seems they had a crooked sheriff and a worse judge. Brothers. Used to terrorize the place right regular until some

414

guy planted the judge's boys six feet under. Seems they wanted the man's money, but he didn't much want to give it to them."

"Who told you that?"

"Hell, anybody coulda told me. Everybody in town was talking about it. Anyhow, this sheriff and his brother, the judge, apparently didn't see the handwriting on the wall. Either that or they can't read too good. The way I heard it, they were about to pull some legal shenanigans to take a rancher's herd away from him. Well, this judge and his brother, the sheriff, were in their office, fixing up the papers and such, and this man just walks in and shoots them. Didn't say a word. Just drilled them. Then he declared himself sheriff, had them arrested and their bodies hanged. The whole town turned out for the funeral. Seems it was quite a celebration."

"What about the warrants they issued?"

"The new sheriff appointed himself judge, too, and first thing he did was set about undoing everything those Briarcliffs had done in the last ten years. Them warrants went first."

"Then the man who killed those three boys isn't wanted anymore?"

"He's wanted all right. Everybody in the whole town is looking high and low for him."

"How's that?"

"They want to have a fiesta the likes of which you never seen, even in Texas. Without his getting rid of those nogood boys, they never would have gotten rid of that sheriff and judge. You wouldn't happen to know where he is, would you? I'd sure like to tell him there's a hero's welcome waiting for him back there."

"I might have seen him," said the marshall. "We had some fella drift in here last month. I kinda had me a notion he might be from Texas."

"Where is he now?"

"I wouldn't like to say for sure. He talked about going on to California."

"That's a shame. They sure would like to have him back in Brazos. After that rancher got everything cleared up, he went back to his cows. They'd probably make him sheriff."

"I don't think he would care for that. He struck me as pretty much of a loner."

"He's missing out on the best set-up a man could ever find."

"I don't know about that. If this fella I saw was your man from Brazos, I've a notion he's doing fine right where he is."

The marshall chuckled at some private thought. But the more he thought about it, the funnier it became. Pretty soon he was doubled up with laughter.

"What's so damned funny?" the cowboy asked, not entirely sure the marshall wasn't laughing at him.

"Nothing," the marshall said as he struggled to his feet. "Nothing at all." He left the saloon still chuckling.

The young cowboy looked puzzled and scratched his head. "Probably can't hold his liquor," he said and turned back to his food.